"PATSY!"

The Life and Times of
Lee Harvey Oswald

a nonfiction novel

DOUGLAS BRODE

"PATSY!"

For information about special discounts for bulk purchases, please contact Sunbury Press, Inc. Wholesale Dept. at (855) 338-8359 or orders@sunburypress.com.

To request one of our authors for speaking engagements or book signings, please contact Sunbury Press, Inc. Publicity Dept. at publicity@sunburypress.com.

FIRST SUNBURY PRESS EDITION
Printed in the United States of America
April 2013

Trade Paperback ISBN: 978-1-62006-190-9
Mobipocket format (Kindle) ISBN: 978-1- 62006-191-6
ePub format (Nook) ISBN: 978-1-62006-192-3

Published by:
Sunbury Press
Mechanicsburg, PA
www.sunburypress.com

Mechanicsburg, Pennsylvania   USA

Dedication

Once again
and
as always
for
Sue

INTRODUCTION
By Douglas Brode

So what precisely is a "non-fiction novel?" Obviously, the two elements included in this book's statement-of-genre are self-contradictory, at least at first glance. *Non-fiction* would imply this is a work of history, a representation of the facts as we know, or at least believe, them to have actually unfolded. *Novel* indicates a creative work of the imagination, ranging from pieces of pure imagination (science-fiction, epic fantasy) to more "realistic" (relatively, at least, as to the surface of events) novels set in the everyday world.

Let's note, though, the order of phrasing: 'novel' is the noun, emphasizing its primary importance; 'non-fiction' the adjective, implying a sub-genre of the form. And, as such, asserting that any historicity in the piece must be considered secondary, at least by the author, as to intent.

All of which might be boiled down to two basic concepts: 1) everything a receiver will experience while reading this book is absolutely true; and (2) none of this is real or should be taken as such. However artistically schizophrenic that may sound, this is the essence of a similar if not identical form of modern prose referred to as "creative non-fiction," if there the priorities are actually reversed. The two forms are related, though a work identified as a 'non-fiction novel' puts greater emphasis on the creative aspect.

These are contemporary and post-modernist off-shoots of what during the 20th century was referred to as 'historical fiction.' In that form, fictional characters were added to some actual situation, with the author allowed full rights to do pretty much whatever he or she wanted with the original aspects just so long as the factual backdrop was related authentically. That form of course still exists, though it seems less true to the spirit of how we see the world today.

One influential essay, "The Myth of History," effectively argued that we see things differently than did the previous generation. The revisionist impulse has a great deal to do with this. What for ages was considered indisputable fact all at once may be questioned as to its validity.

As a result, we are less certain about things—anything!—than any previous generation. But that cloud has a silver lining. For we are freed from a group-think that insists there is but one way to view events, thus all most conform to such an agreed upon 'truth.' There is much to be said for individual perception, even when employed to express an unpopular belief.

More often than not, such a singular vision replaces the long-standing one as the new final-word on the subject, only to be challenged again in due time. This can have to do with the interpretation of events, leading to books that reverse long-held attitudes about such significant presidents as Andrew Jackson and Abraham Lincoln. Heroes of one era can become posited as villains in the next, as the strange case of Gen. George Armstrong Custer vividly exemplifies. With a shift in values, the hero who tamed the wilderness can become the villain who tried to wipe out the Indians. At least in fictional and cinematic renderings. The best historical works, about these or other subjects, attempt a balance between the positive and negative traits of such figures, those rare historical people who in their own time achieve larger-than-life status (merited or not) and, after their passing, pop-culture immortality.

So goes the approach of level-headed intellectuals: Let's push beyond the simplistic Manichean extremism that would reduce everything and everyone to easily understandable clichés; let's rather go for the big picture, always far more complex if often at odds with itself. Nothing is as it seems to be. Perception is reality, though the tricky part is that our points-of-view continually alter, shift, emerge, evolve.

Shakespeare understood this better than anyone. Since he often drew from history of his own England for characters such as Henry IV or Richard III, included in such plays are many accepted 'facts' (some since dis-proven) as to their lives. But the Bard also felt free to exclude as well as include details, while changing the order of events, altering historical actions, and inventing whenever he wished. As to the latter, this occurs, notably, as to the motive of any one character.

Let's agree, for the moment, that Richard III killed those innocent princes in the Tower of London. (The murder may have taken place years after Richard's death, some historians now insist). But what was going through his mind at the moment? What might have been the emotions tearing through his frame? Basically, why did he do it, if he did it?

Historians, or at least those who believe he did commit the murder or at least ordered it, can never explain that. William Shakespeare did, because he was a dramatist. In the soliloquies and direct address to the audience, we learn why—or at least what Shakespeare believes may have been the reason why. So the

Richard III who slinks out on the stage is not the Richard of history but the Richard of Will Shakespeare's creative imagination, a fictional interpretation of a man who once lived and may have said some of the things and done some of the things that his flesh-and-blood precursor once said and did.

Knowledge of this discrepancy in no way detracts from the glories of the written (and performed) piece. Except, that is, for the narrow-minded who want all narrative works that draw from history to be presented as docu-drama; "Just the facts" as 'Sgt. Joe Friday' (Jack Webb) used to put it in TV's crime-busting classic *Dragnet*. However valid docu-drama may be, its own appeal should not, and does not, invalidate alternative genres, creative non-fiction included.

Four-hundred years ago, Shakespeare—like Sophocles some two-thousand years before that, though it's unlikely the Bard was familiar with that Greek author's work—freely interpreted people and events to his own needs. The Oedipus we encounter is not the king who presumably did rule Thebes at least a century before Sophocles wrote his play. While the drama contains some incidents which may have happened, they are presented through the prism of the author's own unique vision of life, offered up to illustrate his philosophical points rather than presented for their own sake. The same is true with Shakespeare, and any other fiction-writer who draws from history for his or her work.

The result is not a specific truth but a universal one. And if history has to be sacrificed to achieve that, so be it. The world would be a lesser place if we did not have Shakespeare's tragedies, or those by Sophocles. For they reveal inner rather than surface truths. From them, we learn less about events of the past than we do about ourselves in the present, as well as mankind yesterday, today, and tomorrow. We learn, from history transformed into fiction, what it means to be human.

In her appealingly titled "The Art of Fact," Barbara Lounsberry pointed out key characteristics of this still in-embryo approach: honing to what is known to have happened as closely as possible while inherently grasping that there are two versions (at the very least!) of every story; merging once separate conventions of "history" and "literature" in part because, before people became too sophisticated for their own good, long ago there was but one way of looking at the past, this best described as "mytho-poetic"; and that in approaching such stories, the writer must, whether he considers himself chiefly an historian or a writer of fiction, express his own self, balancing such self-consideration with a desire to communicate on some primary level with the public at large.

No subject matter more demands this sort of scrutiny than the events surrounding the assassination of Pres. John Kennedy. He was murdered by a single gunman; there were three people who fired guns that day. Debaters can argue until blue in the face, as they have done for fifty years, and never come to a conclusion as to what really went down and/or why. A novel, though, can provide the answer. Or, more correctly, *an* answer.

What follows is absolutely not intended to be the final word on this tragedy. Rather, the book is offered up as one more voice added to the generalized din, a way of seeing events that can and should be perceived through the broadest possible spectrum. This version is merely one more ray of color and light.

The Lee Harvey Oswald encountered here is the Lee Oswald of my own creative imagination, employing the man who once lived and died as a template upon which my own ideas and values are imposed. Mostly, the materials I have added have to do with his personal, inner life, particularly Lee's relationship with Marina, his wife. His thoughts and memories, all added by me, serve as the thread that is here passed through bead after bead of historical fact as to his deeds and actions. Most of them have been reported before; never have they been portrayed from the point of view that you will encounter here.

Like other Kennedy conspiracy enthusiasts, over the past half-century I've read most of the literature on the subject, as well as related subjects. These include the lives of all those participants (or possible/suspect participants), as well as any tome that might shed light on the manner in which the CIA, the FBI, the KGB, Castro's Cuba, the American anti-Castro Cubans, and of course The Mob that were possibly involved.

For my own book I drew freely from information and ideas in order to create a combination of collage and mosaic, rendered in words rather than visual images. Though no one theory completely convinced me, elements of each influenced the creation of the singular conclusion I reach. Again, though, I present that as nothing more than a possible 'take' on what occurred during those horrific moments that day when shots rang out in Dallas.

Of all the volumes (a selected bibliography appears at the end, though dozens of books, as well as hundreds of newspaper and magazine articles were devoured and digested), two in particular stood out. Edward J. Epstein's *Legend* struck me as the most objectively intelligent; Norman Mailer's *Oswald's Tale* the most appealingly outrageous and purposefully subjective.

Often, Mailer appears on the edge of slipping into a non-fiction novel approach. Perhaps that explains why his wrap-up seems so frustrating and disappointing. After coming close to creatively dramatizing what happened, he refuses to come down one way or another: Oswald did it alone; Oswald did it as part of a conspiracy; Oswald didn't do it. Achieving that, making a call based on all of his previous actions and public statements, was the incentive for my own volume.

Certain incidents involving Oswald appear in so many previous reports, even what supposedly was said, that I felt free to include them here. The majority of my lines of dialogue are invented. Yet even these have a certain sense of historicity: I did not allow my imagination to run free but attempted to guess at what they would most likely have said or done, considering the circumstances they found themselves in.

Mailer's book, like so many of the others, is akin to watching the movie classic *Citizen Kane* (1941) for the first time only to have someone snap off the projector a moment before the object that allows us to understand 'Rosebud' is revealed. Only by moving from non-fiction to the novel can this occur, even if that novel happens to be composed, by at least 97%, of facts. It's the three per-cent that makes all the difference and endows this version of those events with its reason to exist.

Douglas Brode
August 8, 2012

"Sometimes history can be so difficult to believe that we require fiction to make it seem plausible."

—an old Sicilian saying

5

BOOK ONE:

A FACE IN THE CROWD

"Hell is other people."

—Jean Paul Sartre

PROLOGUE: AS I LAY DYING
(PART ONE)

"I'm a patsy ... A patsy!"
—Lee Harvey Oswald, November 24, 1963;
11:21 A.M.

As he returned, albeit briefly, to a state of semi-consciousness, Lee Harvey Oswald, age 24 and with less than ten minutes left to live, vaguely recalled saying those words into a TV camera. He couldn't be certain as to when. Minutes ago? Perhaps. Years, maybe. A lifetime earlier or a split-second, if the concept called 'time' existed, something Lee had long since come to doubt.

Once those words were out, everything had suddenly gone dark, as if for a fade-out between a fifteen minute chapter on a television show and the commercials to follow. *Funny, isn't it?* Lee thought, if thinking correctly describes what the swiftly dying man's mind was capable of during those final moments. For now, thoughts and emotions could no longer be separated. The combination of the two tore through Lee's tight frame and his human consciousness, or what remained of it. With end-game right around the corner, Lee Oswald attempted to understand his own self—however racked with pain—as well as the nightmare-world that had come to enclose him during his less-than-a-quarter-century on earth. Meanwhile, everything around him came in and out of focus whenever Lee managed to flicker his eyes. Bizarre shapes and odd shadows registered, if little else.

At this moment, life—or what Lee could in his agony still perceive of everyday existence—resembled an old black-and-white movie. That made sense, for nothing had ever meant as much to Lee as The Picture Show, as his mother Marguerite long ago had so quaintly referred to it: the one and only place where he had ever been able to set aside the ugliness of his daily reality and discover a few treasured hours of respite in a finer world.

Funny, all the same. For Lee Harvey Oswald had always, ever since he could remember, desired to be famous. Adored by the masses, those very people he had over the years come to hold in contempt. Bizarre how he needed, hungered for their attention, even admiration, perhaps adulation. And, in the early stages of the second-half of the 20th century, that he inhabited for at least a little longer, fame had come to mean television. Appear on TV and your life is fulfilled. The whole world is watching, even as you always believed they ought to be doing.

I was about to tell all ... everything! ... but as I recall only the first words were out ... the prologue, so to speak ... "I'm a patsy!" ... then, before I could continue ... Wham! ... the noise, like thunder clapping ... or a pistol firing . . yes, that must have been it ... I do know the sound of a pistol ... rifles, too ... no, no, I can't let myself laugh. Hurts too much ... so let's try to remain calm, concentrate ... alright, I had spit those words out ... and repeated the last two, just so all would be sure to hear me, loud and clear ... and then I ... inflated ... like a little kid's balloon some mean man pops with his cigarette while passing by on the carnival midway ... no good reason to do so ... just to be mean ... oh, wait a minute, there was a reason ... they had to silence me ... of course! ... 'they' ... them! ... all of them working together.

*

An idea crossed Lee's mind, drawn up from some deep level of consciousness as if torn from the bowels of the brain by a mechanical claw. Like one of those games Lee had so loved to play at the sleazy entertainment palaces of his youth. When he'd grown uncomfortable with observing the freak shows, perhaps because those twisted, mis-shapen things—"not men, not beasts, things!" as Bela Lugosi had put it in an old film Lee watched on TV as a child and which simultaneously terrified and mesmerized him— reminded the insecure youth of his own self.

So off instead to games of chance. You slipped in a quarter, seized the handle, then controlled the claw, trying to grab hold of some stuffed toy or other object that momentarily appeared to have value if only because it seemed so far out of reach, near and yet tantalizingly distant on the other side of that glass and steel enclosure.

The process of winning your object of choice seemed easy, so very easy, until you tried and failed. Others could dump whatever the prize might be into the wide slot, at which point it rolled out and became yours, much to the amazement of all who stood about, eavesdropping at this moment of truth.

Lee had never won at such a game. People considered him with disappointed eyes, as they always had, in his earliest memories of life as hell right here on earth.

Someday, he had silently vowed, *it will all be different. I'll show 'em. Just wait and see. I'll dazzle you!*

But ... when? And how?

*

Unlike those ragged dolls, worthless except in context, now the idea he had furtively been grasping for rose to the surface. Something some artist had said—*Oh, I remember now. Warhol.* Andy Warhol. The guy who took Campbells soup cans, signed his name on the label, then sold them as "art," demanding large amounts of money from those who relished the privilege of being duped, at least as Lee Harvey Oswald saw it. One more aspect of the decadence that America, and the world, had fallen into during the first half of the 1960s. *The Sweet Life.* La Dolce Vita! The Sexual Revolution. All the rest of it. Old-fashioned values that had sustained the nation through the better part of two centuries suddenly abandoned now. Gone with the wind so to speak, their absence destroying the nation Lee so loved.

Not that he had any reason to. God, how America and Americans had kicked and spit on him, pretty much from day one. That didn't matter. Lee took solace from a line in a film, one of many he'd seen and never forgotten. Those great movie lines, experienced over and over again when he watched his favorite films on their later TV airings, branded into his memory buds as if with a hot iron. In this case, an exchange of dialogue that sustained him through the worst of times and inspired him during the best. Or, more accurately stated, the least of the bad.

A Frank Sinatra film, of course. Nothing meant more to Lee than Sinatra: the man, the music, and most of all The Movies.

It hadn't been Frank, the magnet that drew Lee to that picture for the first time at age thirteen, *From Here to Eternity,* who spoke the line. Montgomery Clift, playing Sinatra's best pal, 'Robert E. Lee Prewitt,' had been the one. Right there, in that character's very name, Lee felt entranced by his experience with the movie. His own father, who died shortly before Marguerite gave birth to Lee, had been named after that same glorious Southern general. Could this be a coincidence, or perhaps fate? Was that film, apparently meant for everybody, secretly speaking to Lee Harvey Oswald on some deep, secretive level? In case that were so, then he had better pay close attention to everything in it.

Monty was cast as a soldier at Pearl Harbor, right before the sneak attack. A great lightweight boxer, he resisted joining the Company team for deeply personal reasons. Once, while sparring in the ring with a pal, he'd accidentally blinded the man. Afterwards, 'Prew' took an oath to never box again. The Company Captain, a corrupt, cynical son of a bitch, wanted the championship trophy. Unofficially, he instructed his non-coms to put pressure on the kid. Making his life miserable, first with

9

extra latrine duty and endless drills up and down a mountain while carrying his M1. Later, when that didn't work, ordering men beat Prew mercilessly

"You must hate the army," Prew's girlfriend, a whore played by Donna Reed, sobbed after her lover explained to her what he's been put through; 'The Treatment.' as it was referred to in the military.

"No," Prew laughed in that wonderfully crazy kind of way only Monty Clift could manage. Not even Sinatra himself able to pull off *that* little acting trick. "I love the army." 'Alma' was stunned: "How could you?" she wanted to know, "after all it's done to you?" Prew thought that over before answering: "Just because you love something," he finally explained, "doesn't mean it has to love you back."

Lee had never forgotten those words. Whenever he watched *From Here to Eternity* again, first in run-down bijous that played old movies on their second or third go-around, later on TV after Marguerite decided they could finally afford one, Lee Harvey Oswald, son of Robert E. Lee Oswald, spoke them out loud simultaneous with Montgomery Clift as Robert E. Lee Prewitt. At such moments Lee felt that he, in his remote little corner of the world, and the hero up there onscreen were one and the same.

Lee loved America, as Prew had the army, though it had never yet loved him back. As to that dream figure in glorious black and white? That's the man he wanted to be. Or, if he could never be conventionally handsome like Clift, perhaps come to resemble Frank Sinatra as lovable little 'Angelo Maggio,' the scrawny, short guy everyone in the Company so adored.

Lee was short and scrawny. Why didn't people love him? He'd have to figure that out, transform from a caterpillar into a beautifully colored moth, to be accepted. Always, Lee tried to work on that. So far, it hadn't clicked. Someday, he'd figure out how to do it. Then, the moment of transcendence would occur.

*

Anyway! That artist on TV, speaking late at night on a small indie channel that carried *Open End* with host David Susskind. What was his name again? Warhol! That was it. He'd said something too, another of those phrases that greatly impacted on Lee's life. The gathered panel of experts—*how I so want to be interviewed on TV someday myself!*—had been speaking about the quickly changing fabric of life in our modern age.

"*Post*-modern," Warhol had called it, whatever that meant. How the new media, particularly television, altered everything. "In our time," Warhol announced, "everyone will be famous for fifteen minutes."

At the time, Lee scoffed at that statement. Marguerite, sitting on the couch beside him, said in that lilting voice of hers, with her *faux* Southern aristocrat-accent she'd picked up from watching Vivien Leigh as Scarlett O'Hara in *Gone With the Wind* as many times as Lee had *From Here to Eternity,* that she believed it to be true. Then again, Lee's mother always did accept everything she heard on television. "If it weren't true," she would insist, "they couldn't put it on TV."

Over time, Lee rolled that notion around and around again until it began to make sense. Everyone, after all, did include himself. Lee Harvey Oswald, the boy who so hungered for fame ever since he could recall: a lonely if almost beautiful baby, quickly turning into a homely boy before everyone's eyes. A child who grew up on the streets, without benefit of lasting friends or any sense of family. 'Everyone' included *him.* The lowest of the low, at least as other people apparently saw him.

Still, deep inside, L.H.O. held to a notably different vision of himself. The boy who'd been taunted by other kids until they tired of that, then ignored him. The invisible man, just like Claude Raines in the old movie, excepting that the character had willed invisibility on himself whereas he, Lee, had it imposed by others. Like the African-American character in that wonderful novel he had read by Ralph Ellison, all the while associating with the black man who went unseen in the eyes of whites passing by.

He, too, would be famous for at least fifteen minutes. Who knew? Maybe more. Perhaps his fame would have longevity.

Yes, Lee too would have his moment, though only if he pursued such a fruition endlessly, tirelessly, every day of his life. Fame and, with a little luck, immortality.

*

At 1:04 p.m. in the Parkland Memorial, Dallas, Texas, the same hospital where President John Fitzgerald Kennedy had passed away two days earlier, Lee Harvey Oswald stirred on his bed. The doctors and nurses observed the patient gasping desperately for breath even as they sensed that they were about to lose him. The medical people could not guess a final idea had passed through what was left of the 24-year-old's brain, still able to function as a terrible darkness closed in, tightening on the fast-fading cells that store memory and awareness.

A final thought and/or emotion Lee so wanted to share with somebody—them, anyone—while time remained to do so.

11

Something else I heard once. It too comes from a movie. I'm pretty sure. Most of what I know and believe does. There's an image in my mind and, in it, a great artist is interviewed by a pretty girl reporter. She asks him what he most wants to achieve in his lifetime. He responds: 'to become immortal, then die.' All the TV cameras on him. Just as, this morning, they were on me. As I always dreamed and hoped, the whole world was watching.

And, far more important, waiting to hear what I would say. I didn't get it all out—only the first part, 'I'm a patsy!'

That's alright. Seven days ago, I wrote everything down, the whole horrible business. What actually was going down as compared to what the public had been told by those in power and so believed. I handed my manuscript to a receptionist at FBI headquarters, right here in Dallas, a few blocks away from the book depository. With the inscription: "to be opened and made public in the case of my death."

Yes, yes, of course, so that means the truth will all come out. If the FBI can be trusted ...

Not that things turned out as I hoped, what with Kennedy gone. All the same, I achieved my life's goal. Became famous. And, as time may tell, immortal. I can stop struggling to hold on, despite all the pain. It's okay to let go—

*

Less than two minutes later, the doctors and nurses of Parkland Memorial gathered close as Lee Harvey Oswald departed this world. Afterwards, when questioned by the press about what they'd seen, each shook his or her head in confusion. What these medical experts couldn't grasp was how and why a man who must be going through such an unbearable ordeal had somehow managed to expire with a smile—a sneer, actually—on his face.

That secret, everyone decided, Lee Harvey Oswald had taken with him to the grave.

CHAPTER ONE:
DEATH WISH

"If surviving assassinations were an Olympic
event, I would win a gold medal."
—Fidel Castro, 1967

Eclectic, Frank Anthony Sturgis (CIA Codename: George) decided was the term to best describe the cityscape of *Habana.* At mid-morning, Sturgis had stepped out onto the sharp, jutting formation of craggy rocks by the harbor which tourists so loved to mount. Standing alone there, as if he were the most ordinary guy in the world, Sturgis had for the better part of an hour gazed out at the sharp, clean lines of El Morro lighthouse while the tide whipped white-tipped waves against its timeworn stucco surface, up onto the natural formation on which George stood. Droplets of salt water ricocheted onto his face. Later, after checking his watch to make certain he would be on time for his appointment, Sturgis strolled along the crowded *Malecon,* taking in the local color. This included diverse little shops where bright Cuban clothing and such enticing foodstuffs as cold pork sandwiches with thin-sliced-red-onion on a foot-long roll were hawked, in tandem with the charming array of happy, noisy people.

At noon Sturgis continued on to *Habana Vieja*, the historic old city. There, ghosts of conquistadores were rumored to peek out from every alley. Sturgis paused long enough to marvel at the diversity of architectural styles, each unique building reflecting some successive era from this city's 400-year history. *Yes,* he decided. *The correct term is eclectic.*

For now, during this sunny siesta hour, Sturgis (or more correctly the man who had gone by that name for the past eight years) had plenty of time to closely study the appealing if incongruous arrangement of structures. He sat uncomfortably in a wobbly metal-frame chair, hunched over a small matching table ever since arriving at Banana Royale, a humble café kitty-corner to the stately *Plaza de la Caterdral.* Impatiently, Frank Sturgis waited for his assigned rendezvous, commencing with the arrival of his contact. Little more than a hundred feet away, the vast baroque building that lent this plaza its identity stretched high into an unblemished turquoise sky, its solid frame flanked by crumbling palaces that had somehow survived the end of the Colonial period intact. Each offered its own striking contrast to the area's dominant centerpiece, the *Caterdral* itself, which in its grandeur commanded any visitor's attention: the history of Cuba, crystallized in the building's crumbling stones.

When will she show up ... ? The bitch, the bitch ...

Sturgis glanced at his watch: 2:35 P.M. already. Joe the Courier, his sea-green eyes glowing, had stopped by on time, handing George the anticipated packet at precisely 1:45. 'The Kraut,' as Sturgis mentally referred to the awaited young woman, apparently had decided to pull her 'how-late-can-I-make-my-grand-entrance-without-causing-you-to-throw-a-tantrum' routine. That was to be expected. Sturgis had never known a beautiful female who didn't believe her breathtaking appearance granted her special privilege to keep the whole world waiting. Desperate to contain his mounting frustration (how dare she be late on this all-important occasion?), George forced himself to focus his mind on the remarkable buildings and architectural *melange.*

The styles on view ranged from ancient Moors, Renaissance Spanish and Italian, to the art-nouveau style so trendy back in the U.S. during the 1920s. George appreciated each. Few people would have expected that from one in his profession. Thanks to a course he'd opted for at Virginia Poly-tech Institute while studying there on the G.I. Bill following his discharge from the Marines during WWII, he—Frank Angelo Fiorini then—grasped the background of each element in the wide spectrum as more casual tourists could not. Frank/George knew beauty when he saw it.

He had always respected and admired beauty, in art as in women ... this short, dark man whose complicated and varied life (Virginia policeman, night-club owner, gunrunner, agent) had led him here as a courier between the CIA and the Mafia, that powerful institution of organized crime with which his agency, known as The Company to members, had recently aligned.

If that freakin' bitch doesn't show, what will I ...

Then, all at once, there she was. A vision of loveliness as always, The Kraut floated toward George from around a corner, smiling brightly as if that solved everything. A triumph of her will would cause any man to forget all about being angry, even what he'd been upset about. She proceeded, in what appeared a ballet-like manner of moving, down an angular boulevard, not so much stepping across pavement like a normal human being, rather by some magic seeming to glide along on air itself. Approaching, she nodded and winked, basking in the confidence of beauty.

How did a corny song from some old Hollywood film put it? You stepped out of a dream ... Few women George had known and bedded were capable of the heat he'd experienced with The Kraut, that cool-as-an-iceberg surface (half-German, half English) dissolving the moment this beautiful little brat hit the sheets.

Not today, though. Not for me, at least. The Beard? Likely he'll have her. Then, of course, she'll 'have' him.

As George reached into a jacket pocket for the cellophane wrapped package of blue pills that Joe the Courier, aka Santo Trafficante, Jr., had instructed him to pass to her, the agent considered the sleek killing-machine he had, in only a year, created out of a pretty, giddy, oblivious teenager. Now, today, the still child-like beauty, assigned the Code Name 'Lolita,' looked like something out of an Ian Fleming novel: a deliciously duplicitous dame, elegant but deadly. A fictional female agent who enjoyed sex most when knowing the man in her arms was doomed to die there. First, *le petite morte*. Then, the Big Chill.

What pleasure such a woman took in slowly playing with her prey ... like a black widow spider, or some human tarantula.

God, if only there were time to fuck her again. I'd die for ... hey, that's funny. I didn't mean to make a joke but I did.

Yes, the CIA operative thought as he rose and seemingly shook hands with a friend who just happened to stroll by, one secret agent passing a packet to another, Lorita Morenz rated as a real-life Bond woman, if with a touch of an underage beach-bunny Swingin' Sixties dream-girl thrown in for good measure.

Truly, all men would agree, a woman to die for!

*

"Who is here?"

The moment that Fidel Castro stepped into his suite at the Havana Hilton on November 30, 1960, the communist dictator sensed someone had entered earlier, awaiting him in the dark. Instinctually, Castro's hand reached for the wall-switch so as to flip on the lights. Swift thinking prevented Castro from doing so. This hulking man grasped that so long as he and his unknown 'companion' remained in darkness, the intruder could not perceive him any more clearly than he could that hidden figure.

Castro maintained self-control, refusing to give in to a panic that urged him to turn and dart out through the still-partially open door, back toward the elevator. When silhouetted against the hallway light, he would offer an easy target.

Regaining his nerve with the speed of a man who has spent the past several years on the run, Castro kicked the door closed behind him. This decisive action plunged the living-room area of his suite into a pitch black, the window shades having earlier been drawn down. Who waited in the void? How anyone could slip past security struck Castro as beyond belief. Might one of his hand-selected bodyguards have proven susceptible to bribery?

"Calm down, Fidel. It's merely me."

Light footsteps in the dark, swiftly moving forward, all at once distinguishable. Every person has his or her own gait, this as much a signature as a finger-print. Simultaneously, Castro experienced déjà vu owing to the familiar pungent scent of deep, spicy mango, revealing the presence of a perfume he knew well. Then Castro felt the slender arms embrace him as had happened numerous times before, followed by a furtive kiss in the night.

"Lorita?"

"Yes, Fidel. Your own personal little 'Lolita'."

*

The female who occupied the room with Castro now glided to the wall switch, flipping on the lights. He marveled at the 19-year-old's body, displayed for his consideration in a skin-tight white sheath adorned with silver rhinestones. So she had come crawling back after all: the Bremen-born beauty who had made her way to Cuba, sought Castro out up in the hills during his exile, haughtily announcing to the stunned bearded-giant that she fully intended to become the divorced Castro's lover and confidant.

And, furthermore—*just look at me, Fidel*—there was not a damn thing he could do but succumb.

"I must share this great moment in world history which is about to occur. Be at the great man's side, when the hour of triumph arrives," Lorita had explained. He viewed her warily. Lorita might be an agent from right-wing dictator Fulgencia Batista. Or from the American Mob. Perhaps even the CIA.

A lethal Lolita, perhaps? I should send her away at once. Just in case. But of course she is far too lovely for that.

So Castro had taken Lorita for his mistress. Together, they would enter Havana atop a tank, several days following the New Year's Eve Revolution of December 31, 1958.

*

"How did you get in?"

"With this."

Lorita held high the key he had presented to her that first night together here, before the once-spectacular relationship soured. Castro recalled the incident that had precipitated her bitterness. Lorita yelped like a slapped puppy when he informed her that, having now been recognized as Cuba's supreme leader, perhaps it was time to reconcile with his estranged wife Mirta.

"*What*? You bearded bastard! After all I've—"

Whether a marital reconciliation could be managed, Castro explained, he absolutely must bring his son, young Fidel, here to live with him.

Listen to reason, will you? The legendary American newsman Edward R. Murrow had contacted him, requesting a "Person to Person" interview for CBS later that year. Imagine that!

"I want to sit beside you at that moment," Lorita said.

"Lorita, stop screaming. Be reasonable."

"Reasonable? If you truly loved me, you'd want the entire world to know of our great love."

"Even a communist must deal with appearances—"

"You're a phony. Everything I believed that you stood for was but a show. You're no better than the man you ousted."

At that moment, Castro's ego deflated. His mind knew that Lorita had spoken a truth he lived in daily denial of. The giant then lost control and slapped Lorita hard across her cheek. He knew this to be a great mistake even before the contact could be completed yet had not been able to halt the movement of his arm in mid-air. As his club-like hand whacked against the tiny female's face, Lorita emitted a shriek which resounded throughout the room, likely the entire hotel. Castro knew that momentarily guards would rush in to check on his well-being.

Before that could occur, Lorita leaped up off the couch and vaulted out the door. She tore past captain of guards Puto Valle and several others who, stunned by the sight, threw themselves up against the corridor walls, allowing this raging banshee to pass. However lacking in education, all knew one line of poetry by male instinct: Hell have no fury like a woman scorned!

*

"Why did you come back?" Castro asked as Lorita confidently marched to the living room's far end. From there, she jauntily proceeded to enter the adjoining bedroom the two had shared for a glorious period, their intense bouts of sex deeply missed by this prominent world leader. Castro had but two weaknesses: fine Cuban cigars and lovely women from anywhere. Young women in particular; Lorita had been seventeen when first they met.

Why do we men so desire the Lolitas of this world?

Castro could not phrase the answer to his unspoken question. He understood that, like all men, most of them less ambitious and accomplished than himself, her youthfulness appealed to him as much as her slender shape and Baby Doll face. Like every student able to get his hands on a copy of Vladimir Nabokov's forbidden tome, young Castro had read the era's most talked about novel while pursuing law at university ... dreaming about the forbidden pleasures described therein.

Might a touch of Humbert Humbert exist in every man?

"Guess," Lorita responded.

That is so like her. Flirtatious, enticing, always eager to play out her little-girl games.

Once, a year earlier, she'd insisted he dress up as a 1930s Chicago gangster while she costumed herself as his flapper girl in a short skirt of the type worn by women in Hollywood movies depicting that era. Had they reflected the truth about the jazz age? Who knows, who cares! The idealized world up there on the silver screen was so preferable to its real-life predecessor. On yet another occasion, Lorita had arrived with a box containing a pirate outfit for him, harem girl costume for herself. Their Arabian night had followed, lasting until dawn crept in through a thin crack between the drawn shade and the window's bottom.

That night, their bedroom transformed into a rediscovered Bagdhad. Not as that city had ever been but as recreated by Hollywood as a garish fantasy for mass consumption. The suite could be any alternative-world they chose to imagine. During technicolor nights, reality virtually disappeared, replaced by Tinseltown fantasies Lorita conjured up and Castro shared.

Often, Lorita had insisted that her Brute Man, as she half-jokingly referred to Fidel, play out with her some elaborate scenes from specific films she had watched as a child. Lorita, having long since memorized the dialogue, now committed it to paper, insisting that Fidel learn his lines and not deviate from them. Magic reigned supreme, at least until the morning when he would put on his fatigues and return to the office.

"What do you most want from life, Lorita?"

"You'd laugh if I told you."

"No, no. I promise not to."

"Alright, then. Everything I've ever seen in the movies. American movies, that is. Not those horrid 'realistic' ones the European filmmakers now choose to produce."

That was then. This, now. Things change. Loyalties are tested. Love dies. Or does it? She did *come back—*

"Again, Lorita. Why are you here? To forgive my rash act, which I've already apologized for, and return to me, or—"

"'Or' *what,* my 'brute'?"

Moving without realizing he was doing so, mesmerized by her presence in a manner he remained unaware of, Castro followed Lorita into the bedroom. If he had carefully thought through what could follow, Castro might have held back in doubt. His mind, though, was not at this moment the organ that controlled Castro. Dutifully, he trudged along as Lorita danced off ahead of him, a wood-sprite from some fairytale. Castro felt drawn as if by a magnet, his cumbersome feet helpless pieces of metal, pulled by some invisible force he could not control...

"So, Lorita. Now: Do you kiss me or kill me?"

Already, Lorita had slipped out of her silk sheath, this crumpled in a shimmering heap on the floor. She wore only her Midnight Black lingerie, presenting herself to Castro as he had most loved to gaze on her. By the time he finally stepped into the room, Lorita was curled up on the huge bed like some smug, self-serving Persian cat. She even purred with superiority.

"Tell me, Fidel: which do I appear about to do?"

"Perhaps first one, then—"

"Come," Lorita whispered, stretching her slender arms out invitingly. "Either way, accept your fate."

"Dust be my destiny, then?"

"You, and every man who ever lived."

*

"So," Lorita asked after they were, at least temporarily, finished, "are you alive or dead?"

"In a manner of speaking," Castro responded with a half-hearted laugh, "dead to the world."

"But your great worry has not materialized. There may not be much of you—or any man—left after I ravish my lover. Still, Fidel, your heart beats. You breathe."

Even in the darkness of the bedroom, just enough light from outside trickled in a window where the shade had been less than fully drawn that Lorita could make out his frown of concern.

"The night is still young. My guess is that your little drama is but partially played out."

"You know me too well," Lorita laughed. This was not one of her agreeable child-woman giggles. Lorita's tone struck Castro as provocative. "Yet you allowed me to join you here. Why—"

"I could not send you away." He ran his hands over her tight frame, enjoying each contour, every curve to her hard boned structure and the soft white flesh covering it. "You knew I would not be able to so."

"Yes," Lorita coldly answered. "I did know that."

"Yet it was important to you that I say so?"

"Of course. You men experience the world primarily through your eyes. Women? Our ears. Things must be articulated for us. We need to hear such words spoken, even if we already know."

"I don't—"

19

"Understand? Of course not. But how could you? No man ever understands how a woman thinks. Or feels."

She rose up in bed and, with a sudden and swift movement, swiveled about like some sleek jungle cat moving on all four paws, then perched herself above him, staring down arrogantly. Castro, his thick body weighing him on the bed like an anchor, gazed up at the elegant creature. Seemingly so vulnerable, all the same the true conqueror, at least for the moment, of a man who had conquered this sector of the globe.

Lorita considered Castro with eyes no longer sweet, as they had appeared minutes ago; now, suddenly hard, cruel, rapturous in the power she wielded over him. The Beard! Feared by many, adored by just as many others. Yet a slight female, little more than a hundred pounds in weight, reigned over one of the world's most important and powerful men.

Always, from the beginning of time, it had been this way.

Though Castro might have crushed her with his large hands, he could never do such a thing. His fate rested in her small hands and, he knew, equally small mind.

Men are such fools. Thank God for that! Or what would we women do? Even now I can feel his naive male anticipation. He waits to learn whether he will live or die. Well, you wait. Don't worry; it won't be long before Fidel learns his destiny.

"So," he sighed as she leaned down, certain in her movement to lightly brush her warm, light-brown hair across his face, "you would kill me after what we've just experienced?"

"Well, Fidel, I certainly wouldn't have killed you *before.*" With that, Lorita lowered herself further, kissing him.

A split second before she pulled her mouth up and away, Lorita bit Castro's lower lip. When he yelped like a puppy dog surprised by a sudden whelp, her lithe body experienced orgasm.

"That hurt," Castro whined.

"It was supposed to," she answered before, while tossing him a tantalizing glance, she slipped off. Standing upright now, Lorita seized her black-bikini-bottom and drew it up and over her legs with a finesse suggesting worldliness far beyond her years. It occurred to Castro that Lorita purposefully only half-dressed when she did not also restore her bra to the rich rack of flesh the shimmering velvet device earlier held firmly in place. This allowed Lorita's sweet breasts to swing provocatively as she moved. Castro watched spellbound, amazed at the infinite ways in which such a women could, with the simplest gesture, reduce a man, even a great man, to rubble.

"I'll be back," she cooed. Lorita reached for her purse and tip-toed toward the adjoining bathroom, where she had so often cleaned herself after the fact, to coin a phrase.

"To ... finish the job?"

"Oh, Fidel," she sighed, "stop, already. It was fun playing out our little scenario. That's over now. Both of us know that was nothing more than one more movie-game of choice."

"Was it?" he called after as Lorita closed the door. "Then why return to me? You still haven't explained—"

*

The bathroom light switched on, the door now locked behind her, Lorita reached into her purse and drew out an ovular-shaped bottle of cold cream. Here Lorita had hidden the botulin pills passed on to her by her CIA contact Frank Sturgis, he having received them from the Miami-based mobster Santo Trifficante; to 'George' from 'Joe the Courier,' according to their codenames.

The time had come. Lorita would in a moment employ the capsules to kill Castro. She knew the man referred to by his enemies as The Beard (a codename too) well enough to guess that on some level, however deep within his dark psyche, Castro longed for it. During their time together, he—supremely confident in khakis in public, what he brazenly referred to as 'the world of men'—had revealed his many insecurities and private fantasies to the woman beside him late at night, when sleep, desperately longed for, refused to descend and offer its healing powers.

No man, Lorita understood, ever sensed his mortality more than Castro. Intriguingly, he did not, like most people, fear death itself. For Castro, horror existed in the thought of a bullet or knife wielded by some male assassin. On the other hand, an obsession from youth haunted Castro's imagination: to 'pass' in the arms of some dark angel, a *belle dame sans merci*, as some poet put it. As a child, he had seen a vampire movie. In it, a beautiful woman wearing a black velvet cape approached a male victim, biting him on the neck with her fangs. The young Fidel wondered, in the clammy darkness of that theatre, whether others in the audience, like himself, did not so much fear this mysterious figure but longed to be her next victim.

To die for love ... Every man has his secrets. This, Lorita knew, was Castro's private fantasy. No one knew but she. Perhaps he had whispered this to her in some perverse hope that Lorita would make his dream come true.

Well, now: your fantasy is about to become real ...

Lorita opened the jar, sticking her right hand inside to remove the pills from their creamy ivory-white base. Such a wonderful inspiration this had been, hiding them here. Even the oh, so careful Valle, the most loyal of bodyguards, had not thought to search in this unlikely spot while inspecting Lorita some hours earlier. Never trusting of her, Valle had appeared eager to find some sort of weapon on Lorita's person. There had been none. So Valle allowed her to pass, gloating at the thought of white-hot passion which his beloved leader would soon enjoy.

In a moment Lorita would, pills in hand, exit the bathroom, rejoin her Fidel, slip the botulin into the glass of water her lover, always consumed by thirst, invariably kept handy on a stand beside his bed. She would hand him the glass, excitedly watching as he accepted the drink. Of course, he would again consider her closely, wondering if this were indeed his moment of truth. But he would drink. Of that, she had no doubt.

For Castro had to learn if Lorita's surrender had been only an elaborate ruse. There was but one way to discover that for certain. So Castro would drink. How had an ancient philosopher that her Brute Man once quoted, many months earlier, put it? *The end of man is to know.* Despite his undeniable greatness, Fidel Castro was in the end nothing but a man. So he would follow the way of all flesh ... and at the end ... 'know.'

"Oh!" Lorita gasped, realizing something had gone terribly wrong. The botulin pills, which she believed would remain solid in the cold-cream base, had decomposed. Mistakenly she'd assumed their coating was hard enough to maintain itself here. George had informed her that any extreme heat might render the pills unusable. He hadn't said a word about cold! Teary-eyed, Lorita stared down in disappointment. The odd blue color had leaked through the ivory cream, making it appear like semi-liquid marble. Castro could hardly be expected to swallow *that.*

Only a moment before, she had embodied the perfect female assassin: sleek, cool, determined. Like something out of one of the James Bond novels George, during her period of training, had given to her read. Now, Lorita felt like a loser: naïve, inept.

What to do? The answer to that would have been predictable to anyone who knew her. Lorita stomped her feet, furiously shook her head, then sat down on the toilet and wept like a baby.

*

Do I hear Lorita sobbing? Yes, I'm sure that's what the sound is. What's wrong now?

For a moment Castro considered hurrying across the room and joining her to comfort his Lolita. Lorita always succumbed to some sort of sentimentality women revel in and men cannot grasp.

Perhaps, his ego wondered, *she cries because she really did love me. And, having rediscovered the joys of sex with her Brute Man, understood that she would never be able to leave again.*

Castro's spirits rose as he considered the possibility that, from this day forward, she would agree to exist as his secret lover, even as he'd suggested a year ago. Finally, his infantile male fantasy would at last become a wonderful reality.

Then Castro's ever-dormant paranoia sprang to the surface. This might be something more cryptic, closer to the nightmarish fantasies that had consumed him while they sighed with joy in each other's arms. Fidel remained still for the better part of an hour while Lorita wept behind the closed and locked door.

Sooner or later, she must emerge. Then, I will know at once from her eyes what this latest temper-tantrum is all about.

*

"Oh, God," Lorita whined, all the faux style and performed-sophistication gone from her movements and manner. The skinny girl with the big boobs finally opened the bathroom door. She staggered across the floor to the bed, dropping down like a wet rag. Lorita cried uncontrollably, waving her thin arms in utter frustration like an eight-year-old who did not receive her gift of choice on Christmas morn, wallowing in self-pity.

"I could fuck up anything," she at last hissed.

"Except a fuck."

"Right! The one thing I'm *always* good at."

Castro roared. "What is it?" he asked, stroking her sugar-scented hair. Lorita managed to raise her now puffy face up to confront Castro, her bloodshot eyes locking with his.

"You tell me."

For a moment, Castro froze. "Hmmm?" Then he understood. "It's as I guessed. You came here tonight to kill me." She nodded. "For yourself, your false belief I betrayed you? Or as an agent for some outside—"

"Does it matter?"

"To me? Considerably."

"Well, that's one of those things you may never know, not for sure. I won't tell you, even if you said that you would spare my life in exchange." Lorita sobbed again. She was, he realized, fearful as to what she believed he would next do.

"Just one moment, my dear, darling girl."

Castro reached down and across to the bedside cabinet, yanking open a drawer. Wiping a wet residue of tears and make-up from her cheeks, Lorita arched herself around so as to see

23

what he had drawn from it. Her eyebrows rose at the sight of an automatic pistol.

"I knew it," she wailed. "You would—"

"Don't be silly," Castro reassured her. He repositioned Lorita up into a sitting position so that she again straddled his immense male girth. Now, though, as her breasts swung back and forth, like a pair of feminine pendulums, she struck him not as provocative, only pathetic.

Lorita's Brute Man handed her the gun. Her eyes revealed confusion. He smiled manically.

"Go ahead. Your assignment was to kill me? Do it."

Castro glided the gun toward his face, opened his mouth, lowering his lips around the cigar-shaped barrel. If Lorita did as instructed, the last thing on earth Castro would see before his brains exploded out the back of his head, onto the pillow, would be her breasts swinging like two exotic dancers at a Havana casino, performing in perfect tandem ...

Lorita shifted positions, squinting, trying to find a solid position, tightening her grip on the trigger.

"Wow," she exclaimed. "Just like in the movies!"

Spy thrillers, she meant. With the advent of the 1960s, such *Kiss! Kiss! Bang! Bang*! projects had been shot in Asia and Europe, becoming popular on the international market. In a radio report Lorita heard, owing to the new tolerance that overtook America following the election of young JFK as president, a James Bond book was being filmed by a Hollywood company, the American mainstream apparently ready for such kinky stuff.

She had read *Dr. No, Casino Royale* and all the others, at the suggestion of Frank. He had explained that Lorita must, in real life, emulate Fleming's lethal literary ladies. Become in actuality what they embodied in his fictions. Perhaps not so imaginary, though. George explained that Fleming, whom he knew, based those 'Bond girls' on daring women he, as an English operative during and after World War II, once worked with.

Perhaps there was no true, certain dividing line between fantasy and reality. Maybe each impacted on the other. At any rate, those novels provided her education. Lorita's job now was to live out what others read about, saw at the cinema, only dreamed of doing. For her, this constituted her ordinary life.

Well, perhaps not ordinary ... everyday yes, but—

"Oh," Lorita squealed as he entered her again, fighting his way past the weak barrier of her panties. "Just imagine: In only a moment you'll be coming and going at the same time!"

*

Castro had remained supremely calm through all this. That unnerved Lorita, though she readied herself to complete the assassination. Yet a minute went by, then another, she unable to consummate what she had arrived for. Those pills would have allowed Lorita to remain remote from the administration of death. To pull the trigger, witness her lover's head explode like a dropped melon, brains splattering everywhere?

Ugh!

It was, simply, too much. Hard as she tried Lorita found herself gradually relaxing her finger from the trigger. "I can't," she wailed, removing the barrel from Fidel's mouth.

"Of course you can't." With a firm movement he took the pistol from her hand, returning it to the open drawer.

"Now what?"

"Leave."

"Just like that?" She snapped her fingers. Castro nodded.

Wanefully, Lorita pulled herself up off the horizontal slab of male flesh and stood upright, a sad rather than glamorous figure in the now ripped strip of material partially covering her nakedness. Lorita glared back at the rough beast sprawled naked on the bed. Then, as if nothing untoward had occurred, she regained her composure, sniffed, and set about dressing, holding back tears. Once the silver sheaf again adorned her frame Lorita gathered up her purse and made ready to leave.

"Goodbye, brute man."

Cautiously, she stepped past Castro and out the door, back into the main room without a parting glance. Once there, Lorita stopped, pulling a small object out of her purse.

"Here," Lorita called, turning to toss the key back onto the bedroom floor.

"You won't be coming back, then?"

"Never."

"Will there be others?"

"That's not for me to say." She made ready to exit but halted again, glancing back over her shoulder. "When you said to me, 'no one can,' what did you mean?"

Castro gloatingly smiled from ear to ear. "I am Fidel. My destiny is to guide Cuba into its future. That was written in the stars a million years ago. No one can interfere with fate. Not even a woman as willful and wicked as you."

"Me, wicked? *You're* the one!"

"Have it your way, Lorita. You always do."

Lorita did not know how to respond to that, so she exited the room, the suite, the hotel, and the life of Fidel Castro.

It's the Mob, Castro thought, *remaining stock-still in the darkness. The Mafia has declared open war! Or, no. Maybe the CIA. Which one most wants me dead ...?*

My worst nightmare would be both ... working together.

*

Why is it that we always think of the perfect thing to say once it is too late? For years following her hurried departure, Lorita rolled over in her mind what she might have told Fidel. Never had she revealed to him that, when she left Germany at age fifteen— truly a Lolita then—Lorita had not gone directly to Cuba to seek him out. That had been her great lie during their first meeting up in the hills. Lorita journeyed to Venezuela. There she schemed to meet and seduce Pres. Marcos Perez Jimenez, the right-wing Junta dictator. Though married, Jimenez set her up in a suite at majestic Humboldt Hotel, overlooking Caracas.

The two spent many a pleasurable hour in the king-size bed until in 1958 the communists staged a coup. Then Jimenez hurried off to America. In the land of freedom and democracy this brutal former dictator received the Legion of Merit for distinguished resistance to The Red Menace.

Sadly, he took along his wife and family but not Lorita.

Guessing that the next great Third World leader would be a communist, this the coming thing in under-developed countries, Lorita determined to become mistress to such a man. Those in the know she spoke with insisted that Fidel Castro would likely emerge as that personage. So off little Lorita trekked to Cuba, proving once and for all that the power of female beauty over the male cuts across all existing political lines.

Damn! If only I'd have thought to mention to Fidel that he'd accepted the castoff mistress of a diehard fascist as the great love of his life, such a revelation might have killed him faster than botulism or a bullet.

Why didn't I think of it then?

*

For once, and to Frank Sturgis' amazement, The Kraut showed up not only on time but early! This would be the final meeting. Their designated place, once again, was Banana Royale, 24 hours after the previous encounter. The man called George had been listening to Radio Cuba all morning. *Nothing.* Concerned, he next poured through the papers. No major revelations. Life appeared to be normal in Cuba today. That could only mean one thing: The assassination attempt had failed. This was confirmed by Lorita's rare on-time appearance, in and of itself spelling disaster.

Approaching, she employed the last refuge of a female scoundrel. Weeping openly, Lorita collapsed into George's masculine arms, spitting out a semi-coherent rant.

The Bond Girl? Gone. In her place? This sad little loser.

In a cold Cream jar? You must be kidding ... !

As he sent her packing, George wondered whether she ought to be eliminated as a security risk. If so, he would do to her what she failed to achieve with Fidel. Enjoy Lorita's fine body a final time, then ...

No. Why kill such a total klutz? Let her talk to anyone she chooses. Nobody in his right mind would believe anything such a train wreck says. Go on your merry way. And good riddance!

Now, though, he would have to meet with Joe the Courier. Inform the man born Santos Trafficante, Jr. as to what had gone down ... or rather failed to go down. Discuss what they ought to do next.

No question Castro must die. Enough with pretty women. Deadlier than the male? That adage suddenly seemed a bad joke.

George already had something else in mind. Pick a man to do the job. Some obscure fellow, secretly dreaming of glory, greatness, immortality even, while plodding unnoticed through the world. No more take-your-breath-away bitches! Some face in the crowd, an invisible man. He had several candidates in mind.

George and Joe were due back in Florida tonight. The next week they were expected to arrive in New Orleans for a top-level meeting with mob boss Meyer Lansky, where this current problem would be discussed. The Big Easy! Sturgis' favorite city, other than what he had discovered in Havana, for daylight decisions and late-night debauchery. How he loved Bourbon Street.

In truth, the top candidate on George's list had often walked that street in his youth. Feeling worthless, powerless. Dreaming of greatness, with not a clue how it might be achieved. Eager to be found, fearful that he would forever remain obscure.

CHAPTER TWO:
THE LATE MATINEE

"I lost it at the movies."
—film critic Pauline Kael, 1966

One clammy afternoon in late April 1954, six years before Frank Sturgis returned from Cuba and, while in New Orleans, set about deciding on the right person to kill Castro, the nowhere man 'George' ultimately picked wandered aimlessly along Bourbon Street. Head bowed low, eyes on the concrete, Lee Oswald drifted past Po' Boy shops, Dixieland dens, and sleazy strip clubs.

Above the rickety door to each, neon lights blazed like electric-rainbows in the warm afternoon drizzle. The time: just before three p.m., after the lunch crowd abandoned such *declasse* havens from the real world; before the early evening clientele trickled in. At this awkward juncture in the daily pattern, few frequented the garbage-laden streets, where blues and jazz poured out of shabby, timeworn, ever-enticing buildings.

That explained why this particular visitor arrived now. Lee hated crowds, more than almost anything. Except perhaps being alone. That made no sense at all. Then again, little about Lee Harvey Oswald ever seemed 'right' to those whom he, in the privacy of his mind, dismissed as The Normals.

Others sensed this in the youth's personality on meeting him. For all of his fifteen years, strangers had made it a point to keep their distance. Here, other stragglers passing through the dreary weather, soft rain on neon transforming urban decay into a lurid phantasmagoria, drifted past without making eye contact. Lee turned up his jacket-collar and pushed on, if with no particular place to go. As was always the case.

In his vision—that bizarre, unique way in which L.H.O. always had and, for the remainder of his brief life, would perceive the world—he'd brought the lousy weather down on this part of The Big Easy simply by showing up. He was cursed, carrying an invisible mark of Cain wherever he went. This rain, that ruined a potentially pleasant day for others, had been summoned by Lee's immense capacity for negativity. Or so he believed.

A scrawny kid, oblivious now to the rich Creole culture and Cajun lifestyle surrounding him, Lee had only a single thought on this even grayer day than usual: why had he been born? In all truth, he wished that event never occurred. As Lee had done several times previous in in his miserable excuse for a life, the youth considered purchasing a pistol at one of those seedy pawn-shops located on side-streets, then pointing the barrel at his head, bringing the dark farce to an end.

Why not? All that awaited him on the morrow was more of the same. Lee despised his existence, perceiving himself one of nature's mistakes. Maybe there was, as his mother Marguerite insisted, a better place up there. If not, oblivion would likely prove preferable to more of *this*.

Lee had spent the morning seated in a cramped apartment he shared with his mother at 1454 Saint Mary Street, listening to an album of heartbreaking songs that touched him in a way current pop hits by performers such as Patti Page and Doris Day, popular with The Normals, did not. The selection of mournful saloon-ballads was performed by Frank Sinatra. The disc, "In the Wee Small Hours of the Morning," had been released by Capitol. After catching the title tune on the radio, Lee had hurried out to purchase his own copy. During the past week he'd listened to it, again and again, each day at precisely the same time.

Lee owned other Sinatra albums, but this one struck him as special. In the past, The Voice always presented diverse styles on his latest 33 1/3 L.P., ranging from slow, sultry romantic tunes to upbeat swing. A Concept Album was how the guy at the record store described this disc after congratulating Lee for not, like most other kids, purchasing "Rocket 88" by Ike Turner or "Rock Around the Clock" by Bill Haley and the Comets, both of which this salesman carried only out of economic necessity.

"I'm not like most kids my age," Lee replied. He despised the New Music which overnight became all the rage with typical teenagers. Lee considered rock 'n' roll emblematic of everything that had gone wrong with the world during these past few years. Besides, if others of his age group loved it, he—despising them for their normalcy—must go entirely in the other direction.

"I knew that the moment you walked in," the store owner said. Lee wasn't certain if that were intended as a compliment, an insult, or merely an observation. Carrying his purchase, Lee made his way back to his current living space which, if things proceeded as usual, would be relegated to a past address in three months. Marguerite would raise a finger on high, not unlike a Puritanical schoolmarm about to deliver a lecture, and announce, as she had many times before: "We must move!"

As if that, in and of itself, would solve all of this family's multitude of problems.

"A fresh start. New surroundings. This time it'll all be different, Lee. No, don't cry. And don't laugh. It scares me when you laugh like that, even more than when you cry."

But things didn't become better. Years later, while Lee served in the Marines, a smart top sergeant shared a phrase Lee never forgot: "There is nothing more stupid than doing the same thing time after time, always expecting a different result."

While home on leave from the service (another temporary home, as with all the others), Lee had tried to explain that to Marguerite. She didn't get it. Told him to stop bothering her with silly talk. Then left for hours, not the first time she'd done so. On more than one occasion, Marguerite disappeared for several days, eventually wandering back, blithely smiling.

"How's my boy? My baby boy? Lee? What's ... wrong?"

Lee spent that leave in New Orleans mostly alone. When she returned to their shabby apartment, Marguerite announced she had experienced an epiphany: They must move back to Fort Worth at once. Or maybe to New York? Hadn't they been happy there, living with Lee's half-brother John, Marguerite's son from her first marriage, and his wife? No, actually.

Bad as things had been everywhere, that struck Lee as the worst. Except for the Bronx Zoo. That, Lee adored. When no one else stood nearby he'd whisper to the animals. They loved him! Lee sensed that they waited patiently for his return, he the only visitor beyond those bars who felt as caged as they did.

Animals were wonderful. So sincere. Not like ... people.

Otherwise, New York had not been so good. In fact, awful.

*

What made this day different, somehow worse, than all the others? He'd woken with a start, as always, at seven. Marguerite was even then leaving for work. Wherever they lived, she always managed to find a job, more often than not on some managerial level. This required her to leave at dawn and return at dark.

Lee moped around the current house during daylight hours, then headed out in the evening, to whatever solace he found out there. Some dreary bar or greasy-spoon-diner, worthy to serve as model for yet another melancholy Edward Hopper painting. There, other nighthawks met to join in world-weary conversation.

Always, Lee sat alone, a stale beer or watery cup of coffee before him. Purchased not to consume, necessary if he were to be allowed to remain undisturbed. Always too there were The Movies.

Not first-run houses, frequented by couples and families. When Lee wanted to catch a flick, he'd head for some second-run theatre, likely in disrepair. Their forlorn appearances vividly reflected the way this patron felt about himself.

In such a run-down enclave Lee could drop into a torn seat for several hours of oblivion. The equivalent, in whatever town he happened to inhabit, of 42nd Street in Manhattan, where crowds of derelicts, hipsters, and kids who wanted to perform forbidden acts in the smoke and semi-darkness conjoined: where last week's wanna-be hits were now relegated to today's also-rans, and the 1948 Western epic *Red River* with John Wayne played forever.

At such downtrodden bijous Lee found himself swept off to dream worlds, more true for him in their drab-noir black-and-white or glossy Technicolor than unrewarding every-day life.

Even in such a sordid place, the clientele composed of out-of-mainstream types similar to if not as extreme as he, Lee would make it a point upon entering to check out the crowd, then locate a seat as geometrically far from all the others as possible. That way, he could be alone in the crowd.

True, he hated being by himself. Far worse though was being with other people. What Lee most hated was being alive. The central question of his life had always been: Why was I born?

Always, when in the south, he would veer to his left and sit in the section reserved for colored people. Though his skin might be white, Lee alone appreciated how alien they must feel as a minority group. He himself constituted a minority of one.

*

I could use a movie. Maybe there's a theatre around here. If I happen upon one, I'll go in. No matter what's playing. I'll catch a movie and I'll feel better. Or at least less bad.

When the going gets tough, businessman Joseph Kennedy once claimed, the tough get going. The weak? They head for the nearest movie. Hoping for oblivion. The smart ones on some level sense that what movies offer is less an escape from reality than a means of comprehending it. Filled with iconic visions that alter, perhaps without our realizing it, the way we see, act, and live once we've drifted back out of the theatre, onto the street; changed, if in ways we do not always comprehend.

Lee had always been one of 'the weak.' Today, his stress felt more impossible to bear than ever. The pain began with the arrival of the morning mail. Ordinarily, Lee did not bother to fetch it. Marguerite would do that when she returned. There was never anything for Lee, anyway. Who would write to him?

Suddenly, he felt an uncontrollable instinct to retrieve whatever had been dropped off in the rusty metal box out front.

Minutes later, as Lee dropped bills, form letters and a *Life* magazine down on the table, he recognized John's writing on an envelope. The letter was addressed to Marguerite. John so rarely wrote her. On some occasions, they might receive a note from Lee's older brother Robert Jr. Not John. Lee's half-brother hated to write, would go to the expense of calling long distance if he wanted or needed to confer with Marguerite.

Though Lee harbored the greatest respect for a person's privacy, he found himself giving in to temptation. First, Lee tried to ease the envelope open, sliding a knife under the seal, planning to re-seal it so Marguerite wouldn't know. Lee had bungled that, as he managed to do most everything, by tearing the paper. Frustrated, he ripped the envelope open, figuring that later on he'd lie and claim to have done so by mistake.

What Lee read devastated the fifteen-year-old:

Hello mother
Hope this finds you well. Lee too. I am truly sorry that you had to leave under such awful circumstances. My wife could stand no more. Nor could I. Enough on that. We will talk about it someday when the wounds heal. Perhaps. I need to tell you about a conversation I had with Dr. Hartogs. He called and sounded concerned as he told me about his last meeting with Lee. Dr. Hartogs is much upset for Lee. He believes that Lee needs help and as much as possible. He says that if you do not find a doctor down there he has no idea what might happen. I know how you dote on Lee and spoil him something awful. But even you must grasp that he is a strange boy. That doesn't mean bad. I don't mean that. Mother, in all truth I do not know quite what I mean. I don't have the words, not being educated. But Dr. Hartogs does. He is a wise man and a good one too. Clearly he cares about his patients. Other people, also. Dr. Hartogs says that if Lee is not looked over properly he could be a danger to himself. But beyond that he might prove a danger to others. I don't know quite what he meant by that. He would not speak any more on the subject. Mother, the man knows something! I can only hope that you realize the seriousness of this situation and take action. Lee needs help!

Your loving son,
John

Suddenly out of control, Lee tore the letter into bits, wildly tossing them in the air like makeshift confetti. His laughter rolled out of control as the shredded pieces fell. Afterwards, and for a long while, Lee stood in the kitchen, barely moving, wailing at the top of his lungs.

Then, hoarse, Lee grabbed his jacket and ran out onto the street. How dare his brother write such a later?

Spoiled and sick, that's how my brother, maybe the world, sees me. You know nothing about me! None of you. No idea who the person is, living under this skin I was cursed with ...

*

All at once, there it was: a theatre. Turning a corner, Lee bumped into the booth out front. Lee glanced up at the marquee and noticed the current film starred Sinatra. This must be preordained! He'd watch the guy he'd listened to through the wee small hours of the morning, when the whole wide world was fast asleep.

Incredibly, when Lee scanned the schedule of showings, he noticed that the Sinatra film would start in five minutes. How was that for timing? This, Lee decided, was meant to be. He would watch this film because it was so written that he would.

Lee purchased a ticket for one dollar and headed into the musty auditorium. The stale air reeked of yesterday's popcorn, cheap cigarettes, and urine on the floor back in the bathrooms. Lee scanned the area, found himself a soiled seat in the colored section, where he would feel most at home, and plopped down.

The titles rolled over a black-and-white background that depicted a small town somewhere in the southwest. The film's title turned out to be at one with this burg: *Suddenly*. Rugged Sterling Hayden played a local lawman who had little to do but provide directions for passers-by whenever they mistakenly pulled off the main road and needed help finding their way out of here.

Initially, Lee felt vaguely disappointed. The low-budget production values were bad enough. Where was *Frank?* Lee tried to concentrate as Hayden bird-dogged some middle-aged woman whose husband had been killed in Korea. The sheriff hoped to get her to marry him so he could take care of the lady and her kid.

Problem was, she couldn't deal with the thought of Hayden, as a law enforcement professional, carrying a gun. That's what had stolen her husband's life.

Lee did appreciate something Hayden tried to tell her: "Guns aren't necessarily bad. It depends on who uses them."

Amen to that! Lee had discovered the joys of gun-ownership at age eight, after Marguerite without warning up and decided to travel from Louisiana to Texas. Less than a week later, they'd relocated in downtown Fort Worth.

Lee soon learned that the boys in school all headed out onto the adjacent prairie whenever they had free time. There, they'd shoot at jackrabbits with .22 caliber rifles. Every boy owned one. Always the loner, Lee had not been invited to join in. Marguerite, like the woman in this film, expressed an intense dislike for fire-arms. Eventually Lee talked her into buying him one on his birthday, October 18.

Later that afternoon he headed out to practice. By himself, other kids having sensed something different—'queer' even—about this new arrival. No matter. He'd grown used to it.

Lee did not have much luck at first. He was not a natural shot. No matter. He'd fire round after round until he got the knack of it. One thing he did grasp: shooting would from this moment on forever be a part of his life. He enjoyed the kick of the butt against his arm, the jolt he experienced; that sudden, unique smell of powder as a small blue cloud rose in a swirl and passed across his face.

Maybe the reason he didn't score so well was that the last thing in the world he wanted to do was kill small animals.

That, the Normal Boys loved. Lee? He'd have to find something else. Something that deserved, maybe even needed, killing. Well, he was young. There'd be time a-plenty for *that.*

*

In the film, the woman's eight-year-old, nicknamed 'Pidge,' was kind of cocky, perhaps because he'd been raised without a father. Lee could relate to *that*. Pidge and his mother lived in a small house up on a hill above their town. Not so much a hill, really, as ... how to describe it? ... a grassy knoll.

Anyway, Pidge wasn't allowed to watch war movies because his mom felt it best to keep violent stuff from her boy.

Marguerite had tried that, though her insistence had the opposite effect. Such entertainments became Lee's forbidden fruit. He'd sneak off to watch war films whenever he could. Not only did Lee enjoy them, like most boys his age. Owing to her attempted censorship, he became obsessed with them. The more violent any movie was reputed to be, the more Mother wanted to keep Lee from catching it, the more desperate he was to see it.

Hey! I came to see Sinatra. Where the hell is he?

34

*

Everything up there on the big screen changed when a wire reached the sheriff that the president of these United States would arrive that afternoon for an unscheduled train stop. The great man would disembark in their village, where Government Men would be waiting with limousines to rush Mr. President away to a pre-arranged top-level secretive meeting nearby.

At last, Sinatra arrived on the scene, wearing that Ring-a-Ding hat he clearly adored, perched on his head in a wise-guy manner, precisely as on the cover of one of his record albums.

Dressed in a dark suit, flanked on each side by colleagues, Sinatra showed up at the house that lady shared with Pidge and her father-in-law. Frank, more correctly his character "Johnny Barrows," explained he was FBI. He and his men had been assigned to stake out this place to ascertain no suspicious strangers showed up. There had been rumors of a possible assassination attempt, and they were here to prevent it.

Yet something dark and ugly flickered in this man's eyes. What's going on? Lee wondered.

That became clear when Johnny Barrows shot and killed a Secret Service Man who stopped by on a routine check. He also wounded the sheriff. Johnny was actually the person that the government men were trying to capture. He'd arrived to kill the sitting-president.

All at once, Lee found himself drawn deeply into the film. If initially he had associated with Pidge, that changed as Lee instead began to feel at one with Johnny Barrows. This short, angry runt of a man up there on screen reflected the equally short, equally angry runt sitting in this obscure theatre.

"When I was in the army," Johnny explained to his captives, "I did a lot of chopping." Pidge called out that Barrows was a coward. "You're wrong about me," Sinatra said. "In the last war, I won a Silver Star. Killed 27 men, all by myself."

The smile on Barrow's face might best be described as a mean-spirited sneer. That hit Lee hard. Hadn't his psychiatrist back at Brooklyn's Youth House only a year earlier insisted that if Lee were ever to be accepted by society, he must first wipe that "mean-spirited sneer" off his face?

It's as if Sinatra is playing ... me!

Even now, Lee could recall the words his analyst, Renatas Hartogs, had read from the paper scheduled to be circulated as his official report on this 'bad boy' who'd been truant from P.S. 44 so often that Lee finally had to be removed from his mother's apartment and relocated in a home for wayward boys.

"Lee has to be described as personality-pattern disturbance with schizoid features and passive-aggressive tendencies."

How self-assured Hartogs sounded. Not that the man had dismissed Lee as worthless. Hartogs described Lee as a "13-year-old-boy with superior mental resources." Hartogs had discovered no evidence of "neurological impairment." If Lee would only apply himself, he might achieve success at some trade.

Then Hartogs had removed his large glasses, ran a sweaty hand through his thinning hair, and sighed as he explained his fears to the vulnerable boy before him. Something had gone awry in Lee's life's experiences, pretty much from day one.

Yes, there remained a glimmer of hope that Lee could yet be rehabilitated. Still, Hartogs's psychology held that the first five years in any person's life shape him forever. Lee's own early years were, in a word, horrific.

You enjoy total power over me, doctor. I realize that. Keep me here, send me home. How it must feel to exert such authority over another human being! Someday I hope to—

Power, even some small semblance of it, had not been a part of Lee's life until that day when he held his first gun tight. Aiming at a target, pulling the trigger, experiencing the kick, knowing that if he so chose some life would come to an end ... all of this offered a rush, release, a sense of satisfaction.

I am nobody. Yet I hold the power of life and death in my hands. Jackrabbits? Small potatoes! Johnny Barrows knew the score. You could see it right there in Sinatra's gleaming eyes.

The president? As a hunter might put it, big *game!*

*

Trying to discourage Sinatra, Hayden ran through all the assassination attempts in American history, emphatically pointing out that the shooter always got caught in the end.

"It's never been done," he noted in that sardonic voice that qualified this actor as the era's king of the tough guys.

"There's always a first time," Sinatra hissed in reply.

That's true, isn't it? Whether it's trying to build a plane that flies, inventing the atomic bomb, or shooting the president ... people try and fail ... so many fail that failure comes to seem inevitable ... until someone succeeds ... someday, I bet, people really will go to the moon ... and someday someone will shoot the president ... and get away with it.

"I hate crowds," Sinatra admitted, visibly shivering.

Me, too! Hate 'em. It's like that for Johnny? For Sinatra?

"You're an American citizen," Hayden countered.

"And at five minutes after five," Barrows/Sinatra leered, "I'm gonna be a very *rich* American citizen."

Of course! That's the ticket. Money meant power ... power meant ... everything. If you have money, you have power; you have power, it doesn't matter what you look like, where you've been, what you've done. Money bestows power; power brings women ... beautiful women ... and ... everything else we poor slobs sitting out here in run-down theatres across the country hunger for ... watching as someone else enjoys the goods.

How many people dare to say I'm gonna get me some of that? One in a million, maybe. Could one of those someday be me?

"Don't you have any feelings at all?" the housewife demanded of this nasty little man before her.

"No. They were taken out of me by experts."

Oh, I know that feeling. Experts like Dr. Hartogs.

But how can anyone not experience feelings? she asked.

"Feelings are a trap," Sinatra/Barrows explained. "Show me a guy with feelings, I'll show you a sucker." She stared at him, unable to comprehend much less speak. "A weakness. Makes you think of something besides yourself. If I had any feelings left, it'd be for *me. Just* me."

That's it. The key to ... I don't know ... Survival? Stop worrying about Marguerite and how whatever I do impacts on her ... from now on, I've got to be more like Johnny Barrows.

*

The parallel proved far from precise. "My mother wasn't married," Johnny Barrows confessed. "My old man was a dipso."

As for his own old man, Lee had never known him. Robert E. Lee Oswald died two months before Lee's birth. Maybe that was better than growing up with an alcoholic. Likely about the same.

Yes, Marguerite had been married, then in time remarried. Still, Lee's experiences and those of this onscreen character still seemed pretty much congruent.

"They left me in a house," Johnny wept. That, Lee knew all about. First there had been Bethlehem Children's House when he was three. Most people couldn't remember anything about what happened to them at such an early age. Lee did. Almost every night, he still experienced nightmares about being there. Dream of sleeping in that place; dream of dreaming there, too, wanting to be back with Marguerite. Sleeping beside her in one bed, as they would do, when together, until he reached the age of fourteen.

At the time, Marguerite claimed that she couldn't afford to support her boys. His older brother Robert and half-brother John were temporarily abandoned too. Lee would wake up in

Bethlehem ... what an ironic name for a hellish hovel! ... crying for her. Other kids heard, and tagged him a Momma's boy, then beat Lee whenever Robert or John weren't around to prevent such bullying.

He was out, now. Mentally, he'd never escaped that place.

Later, in New Orleans, or Fort Worth, or the Bronx. Youth House, wherever he happened to be, always it was the same thing over and over again ...

I wake up screaming! Having experienced yet another dream within a dream within a dream. There's no one there to comfort me; I'm alone in the dark. Always have been. Always will be?

Lee firmly believed that it couldn't get any worse than Bethlehem until he landed in the Youth House. Purgatory well described Bethlehem only after he'd experienced the daily horrors of his next home away from home. The beatings by other boys, those who, like him, had been scooped up by authorities and dropped down here; the last, worst place for those who did not, could not fit in. Supposedly for their benefit, to somehow try and make them 'better.' Or so everyone in authority claimed.

Actually, Lee came to believe, to isolate them all from everyone else. The Normals! Sacrifice the few to save the many.

Even here, in the land of the loners, Lee became the loner. An outsider among outsiders.

The lowest rung on the totem pole of life ...

*

"Who's behind it?" Sterling Hayden wanted to know.

"I haven't the slightest idea," Sinatra replied without emotion. What most fascinated Lee was that Johnny, all set to whack the president, considered himself a patriot.

"I won the Silver Star!"

That gave Lee an idea, or more correctly brought an earlier one back. He *must* join the service. The image of Robert in full-dress uniform, home on leave, had inspired Lee. Reading Robert's Marine Corps manual caused the impressionable child to choose that branch of the service as the only one for him.

If they'd take him. Lee had been shooting for pleasure for several years now. With training, he might become good. A sharpshooter, perhaps. Special. Superior at something. Finally.

Maybe he too could kill 27 men? There wasn't a war going on right now. Things quieted down after the Korean conflict came to its unsatisfying conclusion back in 1953. Chances were, another would start up somewhere.

Hadn't some senator stated on the news that America might have to make our stand against the Reds in Southeast Asia?

Why wait for it to begin? Join now. Be prepared, like one of those despicable Boy Scouts who refused to accept me into their troop for reasons best left unremembered.

"Louisiana white trash," they'd taunted him in Fort Worth.

That's alright. He'd show 'em, now that he had a sense of direction. That's what Lee had always needed. Well, here it was.

As soon as he exited the auditorium Lee would locate a recruiting office and sign up. The thought of doing so had been there for some time, if in a vague form.

Now, the idea of becoming a marine coalesced, defining him.

*

Precisely what had pushed Johnny Barrows over the edge? the sheriff wanted to know. With that, the snotty grin disappeared. Suddenly, he appeared vulnerable. "A man can stand for so much and no more," the little guy whined to the all-American giant. "Before the war, I drifted ... and drifted."

Like me! Seventeen homes, to use that term loosely, in fifteen years. Born on Alva Street, New Orleans. Over to 1242 Compass less than a year later. 1010 Bartholomew in another six months. Ninety or so days after settling in there, 83 Pauline Street, followed shortly by a rush to 111 Sherwood.

At that point, Marguerite temporarily threw up her hands in dismay. Off to a Bethlehem sorely lacking in Jesus. Two years later, God alone knowing where she's been, Marguerite shows up. "Lee? Pack your stuff. We're moving to Texas," she announces in her jaunty way. Three weeks later, 4801 Victor Street in Dallas.

No good! Two months after, Granbury Rd., Fort Worth. Wait! "Texas was a huge mistake." Back to Louisiana, 311 Vermont Street in Covington. "No!" Back to the Lone Star. 1505 Eighth Ave., Fort Worth; January '47, 3300 Willing Street; in four months time across town to San Saba Street. The following summer, 7408 Ewing.

"Lee? Pack up your stuff. We're moving to New York!"

Crumbling tenements. Filthy streets. Rats in the corridors. 325 East 92nd Street in August '52; 1455 Sheridan Ave. in the Bronx by September. Youth House next. Something out of Dickens, who captures the unfairness of society like no other writer.

An avid reader, Lee had already consumed *Oliver Twist, Hard Times*, and *Bleak House*. Despite the dyslexia that made reading difficult, even painful, Lee tore through book after book.

Hey, at least it can't get any worse. Right? Wrong.

"We made a huge mistake," Marguerite wails. "Gotta get back to our Southern roots!"

39

So it's 757 French Street, New Orleans, January '54. Right town, wrong location. 1454 Saint Mary Street. Maybe we can stay here a while? "I don't know. There's a nice apartment opening up over on Exchange Place. Lee? Why are you sobbing?"

"Drifted and ran," Johnny Barrows continued. Lee knew *that* feeling. Oh, how he loved watching Sinatra. Like Lee, Frankie was short. Lee spent hours staring into a mirror, wondering what Sinatra had that he lacked.

A Voice. That was it. His singing talent had provided a skinny kid from New Jersey with the key to moving up and out. Lee was not blessed with such a genius-level vocal instrument.

Maybe that's alright. All I gotta do now is figure out what I've got that no one else has. Some hidden gift, an undiscovered skill. Who, after all, is Johnny Barrows? Sinatra without the voice but with a gun. Johnny got his gun? Fine. Lee will, too!

"Always I felt lost in a great big crowd. All those faces scratching and fighting. Then the mist would clear and I'd see those faces. And those faces would be *me* ..."

At that moment Barrows did something Lee had never noticed before in a movie. Sinatra stopped talking to Hayden. Wandering around the room, he stepped up to the camera, speaking into it, as if aware that he was not only Johnny Barrows, a character in some film, but Sinatra, playing Johnny. Addressing his audience.

Or, maybe, only one person out there in just one theatre. A little man much like him, likewise trembling in the dark.

Whoah! Now, I get it. Last year, everyone thought they saw the real *Sinatra in* From Here to Eternity. *That lovable, goofy Italian kid you wanted to reach out and hug. They were wrong. That wasn't him. It* was *acting. That's why they gave him an Oscar. Huh!*

I bet all of you sitting in the dampness of this miserable excuse for a theatre think you're getting to see what a great actor this guy is? No, you idiots. This is him.

Why, Frankie's even wearing his signature hat to let us in on that. I know, because I read all about the daily terrors back in Hoboken. His mother, performing abortions on teenage girls with knitting needles, earning money to buy pasta and feed her family. Young Frankie, ridiculed as the son of a mass-murderer. The guy had it as bad as me. Worse, maybe, if that's possible.

Which explains why I've always been devoted to him perhaps. Someone who comes from no better beginnings than myself, only to rise from those ashes, Phoenix-like, and become a kind of God.

It can *be done. Sinatra achieved it with his God-given gift. Inside me, there must be one as well. Everyone receives something special at birth. The problem for most people is that they never discover it.*

Well, that won't happen here. I don't know what it is yet, but I'll keep searching until ...

*

"War changed everything. People began to notice me."

They'll notice me, too. Once I get into a war and kill 27 men. Only I'm a lousy shot. No problem. I'll practice. Once in the marines, they'll teach me to ...

Kill! Germans, Japanese, Koreans. Vietnamese? It doesn't matter. So long as I kill somebody. Enemies of America only, though. Like Johnny Barrows, I want more than anything to be a good American. Don't ask me why, considering the bum deal I got from day one. That's what I want. To be remembered as a patriot.

But ... again, now, I'm confused ... how can Johnny assassinate the president and still remain such?

"At five I will kill the president. At five after five, there'll be a new president. Nothing changes. Otherwise, I wouldn't have taken the job." Johnny came out of his forlorn reverie. "I'm no traitor," he insisted.

That's it! That explains everything. How you can kill the president and still remain a patriot.

When it's over, Johnny insisted, he'd return to being a face in the crowd. "After I do this this one last job."

Me too. I've got to get there. Wherever it is. Whatever it takes. Just tell me who to kill! And now, at last, I think maybe I know how to do it ... I've found my path in life ...

*

At 5:47, the show let out. Moviegoers drifted off, on to other things. Lee staggered away. He recalled an English teacher at Beauregard Jr. High who'd lectured her seventh graders about Greek tragedy. At the end of a play, a truly great play, you're not merely moved by what you've witnessed. Something beyond that. Your life is changed. Catharsis was the word she had used.

Maybe that's true about Greek plays. Have would I know? It was the same old lady, best teacher I ever had, told us about fate. How it rules over free will. You do in life what you must, not what you want, and the secret is discovering your destiny. Written in the stars eons ago, whatever it turns out to be.

I did sense right off that I didn't happen to wander into this theatre by accident. This is part of some master plan. My job is to figure out my role in that great invisible book.

"Don't play God," the sheriff had begged Sinatra.

41

"But that's the way it is," Johnny informed him. "When you got a gun, you are a kind of God." Lee had gulped hard, sitting in the semi-deserted, depressingly sordid auditorium, listening as Sinatra summed it all up: "Without the gun, I'm nobody."

Got you! Time to move on. Stop being Johnny Nobody. Become Johnny Barrows. I must get into the service, just like Sinatra up there. What had some director once said that I read in the newspaper? "It's only a movie ..."

No, it isn't. Not in some cases. This, for instance.

Only a movie? For everyone else, maybe. They can head home, have dinner and a beer, flip on the TV, fade into oblivion until tomorrow, early morning, then get up and do everything all over again. Next week they'll be another film to see. Color, perhaps.

Normalcy! Not for L.H.O. This movie defines me. And my future. All at once, everything feels as if it's set in cement.

*

For a while, Lee stepped aimlessly through the early evening mist. Then he found himself standing in front of a Marine recruiting center. Delighted, he hurried in.

"You're too young," a straight-as-a-ramrod lieutenant told him. "Come back in two years. Maybe then—"

Rejected. Again! Precisely what I most didn't need today. Two friggin' years? What'll I do to fill the hours? Alright, I'll find menial work. Bide my time. Practice shooting whenever possible. Read a lot. History, politics, bus station books.

Hours later, before falling asleep, Lee listened to the Sinatra album again. Mellow, morose. Capturing the loneliness, the emptiness, the abiding sense of isolation for life's losers.

He sings the way I feel.

Best of all, he whispered into my ear earlier today, via that film. Told me what I must someday do.

I must, in time, kill some sitting president of the U.S.

Thank you, Mr. Sinatra. Frank forever!

CHAPTER THREE:
THE MAIN EVENT

"Rumors that I pal around with known
criminals are nothing but dirty lies."
—Frank Sinatra, 1947

On February 14, 1947, thirteen years before Frank Sturgis visited Havana to oversee the proposed 'Operation: Lolita' assassination of Fidel Castro, seven years previous to Lee Harvey Oswald's stepping into a Big Easy grind-house to catch *Suddenly*, the star of that eventual film majestically positioned himself on a sprawling wood-panel stage before an adoring crowd composed of American Mafiosos, Cuban politicos, and Hollywood celebrities.

Frank Sinatra beamed at those arrayed before him in the cavernous banquet hall of Havana's Hotel Nacional. The then-32-year-old singing-sensation had flown into Jose Marti airport four days earlier, learning after arrival from his host, Charles Luciano, the supposed reason for this requested visit would be a full-scale gig by a man now known as The Voice.

That would easily be accepted by the authorities in both countries, as well as the media. The true motivation provided a more pressing excuse for this hastily arranged trip. A small suitcase which Sinatra had carried on board and clutched tight during the ninety-seven minute flight didn't transport his fresh underwear and socks but a special delivery for The Mob.

Now, this impromptu show for friends and family (in every sense of that term) drew down the curtain on Frank's whirlwind visit. All present oooohed! and aaaahed! as he casually crooned about the joys of "drinkin' rum and Coca-Cola." Performed to what would soon become known in the States as the lilting Mamba beat, that song encoded the about-to-be-realized dream of a financial union between Havana's longstanding if dormant raw materials and the heightened business acumen of an unsavory corner of America's financial communities.

This splendid concert served as a cover in case anyone should venture to ask why Sinatra slipped away from radio and recording gigs in the City of Angels, where he also danced and sang his way through gaudy musicals for Metro-Goldwyn-Mayer.

However happy Frank might appear now, in the limelight, basking in adulation and accolades, that was but a facade for the less than pleasant actuality of his life. Nor had it ever been easy for this fugitive from a rough section of New Jersey's poorest Italian enclave. The star's popular image, all smiles and sweetness, allowed him to mask deep, smoldering insecurities that tortured this famous, gifted, complex man all his life.

"Thank you," he beamed, standing center-stage. "Thank you!" Loud applause. A wide grin in return.

This happened to be a particularly troubling time. During the postwar years, a new form of country-western, pioneered by one Hank Williams, added steel guitars and a pounding rhythm to traditional rural music. One entertainment-observer referred to this emergent musical style as The Big Beat. Surprisingly, the warbly hard-edged sound spread to the Midwest, then up to the industrial north thanks to recently created super-stations, able to beam programming a quarter of the way across our nation. Now this New Music, as others called it, had coalesced with soulful black jazz from the ethnic south and blue-collar angst pouring out of crowded New York factories and Pennsylvania mine shafts to form an emergent, and important, musical idiom.

Several years hence it would be dubbed rock 'n' roll. Already, this blend of contemporary hillbilly and old-time folk, underscored by electric guitars, had knocked pop standards, Sinatra's specialty, off the charts. He could only hope, trust, and pray that this phenomenon would prove to be a passing fad.

As if that weren't enough, MGM's big-wigs, always keeping a close collective eye on box-office returns, had come to the conclusion that Frankie's reign as idol to the bobby-soxer set was over. As a result, and according to their ownership of his services via a long-term contract, MGM now featured him in less prestigious pictures. Sinatra ran scared, and for good reason. Though a huge star, Frank knew he could lose all that he, with mentor Charley, had achieved. He vowed not to let that happen.

Perhaps he'd need to ask Charley to speak directly to the Hollywood suits. It had been Charley who, a decade earlier, "persuaded" Tommy Dorsey to let Frank out of his long-term contract so that the youngster could emerge as a solo artist. Nobody's fool, Frankie knew the way things worked. You wanted a favor, you performed one for Charley first. Which explains, when Sinatra got the word as to this delivery, he didn't hesitate.

Nor did he ask any questions about the suitcase's contents when it arrived at his home with the word that he should deliver it to Charley. When the call came, Frank Sinatra answered.

*

Though the message had come to him from Meyer Lansky in Chicago, Frank's introduction to the Pearl of the Antilles had been arranged by Salvatore Luciana. Now Charles Luciano, older than Sinatra by 19 years, he had been born in Lecara Friddi, the same simple Sicilian village which those humble people Francis Albert claimed descent from had early in the century abandoned, hoping to find fame, fortune and their fates in America. The former two would be a long time in coming. As to Cuba, Charley, as his friends called him (the nickname 'Lucky' was created by enemies who had failed to eliminate him) first arrived on the lush island shortly after World War II wound down. 'Lucky' had again proven that his nickname fit like the proverbial glove.

He had been released from Great Meadow prison. Charley was sent there (after stints in Sing Sing and Clinton State) after his conviction on charges relating to prostitution. An ambitious Republican, Thomas Dewey, he an aspiring presidential candidate, put Charley away to forge a reputation as the next Eliot Ness. From behind bars, Charley continued to run things in the Mob. Initially, he passed orders on to his second-in-command, the Sotto-capo Vito Genovese, later to Vito's eventual replacement, Charley's old pal Frank Costello. Both tried to coordinate their activities with those of Lansky and the Jewish mob, these two organizations having merged into The Combination. Neither could manage a working relationship as casual and efficient as the one between Luciano and Lansky, based on a childhood friendship.

However unpleasant a prison cell may be, Charley never lost a sense of himself as a true American patriot. When the U.S. military determined that the invasion of Italy must begin with an upward strike on southern Sicily, Charley offered his full services. The only way in which such an attack could succeed would be if the local Mafiosi cooperated. That would not happen unless members of that Sicilian organization first received some sign from one of their American counterparts. So Luciano, by means known only to him, communicated a green light.

For a price, of course. Always, there is a price.

After victory was achieved, the U.S. had to find some way to say 'thank you'. Simply letting Lucky walk free? Out of the question. Instead, the unanimous decision was to deport him back to Italy, where Charley could live as a free man. Even Dewey, the G-man who sent Charley up the river, agreed that some sort of compensation had to be extended. The catch was, Luciano had to exit the U.S. at once. There was no schedule, however, as to when he must arrive back home. Charley took the brief flight down to Havana and for the next year ran Mob operations on America's mainland from there. Luciano communicated daily via phone with Lansky and their man in Miami, Santo Trafficante, Jr.

In Havana, Charley noticed strong business opportunities itching for proper exploitation. These included two casinos located in an area referred to as Oriental Park, a race-track currently in disrepair, once magnets for wealthy U.S. fun-seekers during the Roaring 1920s. During what had been tagged The Jazz Age, American horse-owners and jockeys cruised on down to compete. Along with them arrived rich tourists eager to squander stock market earnings in exotic destinations. While Prohibition remained the law of the land back home, here they could enjoy alcohol, gambling, music, food, and raw, open sex.

With an emphasis on the latter. Dark sex. Forbidden sex. The kind of sex that smart-suited business types in respectable places like St. Louis, Kansas City, even Dubuque IA secretly hungered for and could afford. Leaving their straight-laced public images at home, such people traveled to Cuba in droves.

All that came to a swift end with the stock market crash of October 29, 1929. After Black Tuesday, ever fewer people were in a position to pony up the dough. As a result of America's crisis, things quickly turned desperate in Havana. The casinos, at best half full during the early-to mid-1930s, lost their luster. By The Great Depression's end, the track opened each day mostly for locals, these not from the respectable social strata.

This might have continued until the dissipating buildings were eventually torn down for firewood had Charley not one fine day taken a mid-morning drive out to play the horses. After a close consideration of his surroundings, Luciano sensed that, as in time strength gradually returned to the U.S. economy, here was a perfect place to re-develop for those who would shortly enjoy affluence, able to as in the good old days spend and play.

*

"I told ya so," his pal Meyer laughed when Charley soon mentioned his discovery during a phone conversation. Lansky came to a similar conclusion way back in 1938, when he visited Cuba. Meyer fell in love at first sight with this rich green island, caressed by tropical breezes and gentle trade-winds. At least, that is, when some hurricane didn't coming roaring by.

As to the people, Lansky recalled enjoying them immensely. Most Cubans displayed a fundamentally gentle, open nature, their joyous celebration of life apparent in every graceful movement. They would stroll, almost dancing, along narrow boulevards. The women in particular caused him to marvel: Their bold femininity struck Meyer as provocative in a natural way, allowing these coffee-colored girls with big, bold eyes to appear innocent even when they rolled over at a moment's notice for American dollars.

So many were beautiful, their hue an appealing combination of Caribbean natives who had called this place home long before recorded history, and the Spanish, arriving in large numbers after Columbus claimed the nearly 2,000 mile main-island and its nearby archipelagos for that country in 1492. Spain ruled for the next four hundred years. That era came to a close when a controversial war with America caused Cuba to briefly fall under U.S. domination, in time emerging as an independent nation in the evolving modern world.

As to Lansky, he had arrived owing to a call for help from the then-current political leader, military dictator Fulgencia Batista. The fascist had forced his way into power five years earlier, ruling like a reincarnation of some medieval warrior-king. Though not the president per se, Batista commanded the country as the army's Chief of Staff. This allowed him to lord it over whoever supposedly ran things at any one moment.

Deeply concerned as to his country's stalled economy, Batista gazed northward. Smart, in an animal-cunning sort of way, he sensed that his huge capitalistic neighbor might well prove the perfect partner for bringing his dream of a wealthy Cuba to fruition. Various American corporations were contacted about mining the rich mineral resources, notably nickel. Batista also guessed that Oriental Park could be restored to its former glories, if people up in the U.S. in a position to finance such a considerable undertaking were willing to fly on down to oversee the make-over, as well as invest in this project.

Lou Smith, a soft-spoken, middle-aged entrepreneur who managed several tracks in New England, was contacted and did express interest. As often happens, one thing led to another. Lou was overwhelmed with various business deals and never got around to making things click. He hadn't forgotten about the offer, though, and in time passed the project along to a trusted friend from bootlegging days. That's when Meyer got the call.

"I'll have to check first with my partner," he informed Lou. Lansky and Luciano conferred the very next day.

Sure, Meyer. Go on down, take a look around. Who knows? Maybe it'll lead to something. If not, freakin' enjoy yourself. Jesus knows, you've more than earned a vacation.

*

"It's beyond belief." Lansky rhapsodically informed his friend and partner upon return. These two had been inseparable since early in the century. On New York's East Side and all through Little Italy's fabled mean streets, they wrestled control away from the older order. An earlier generation of immigrant mobsters, the well-heeled mustachios, had controlled the rackets pretty much unchallenged until the mid-1910s. The sudden arrival of these arrogant young turks altered everything. The word on the street: Meyer and his Jews provided the brains, Luciano's Sicilians adding the necessary muscle.

However much a simplification that may be, their ongoing cooperation created a formidable organization. From day one, this secretive power-structure—The Combination—was built on mutual trust and a genuine liking between the frail accountant and his cold-eyed partner. Opposites that not only attracted but clicked, Lansky and Luciano created and to a degree perfected organized crime as it would exist through 20h century America.

"Okay, already. I believe ya, Meyer."

"The Depression's gonna be over soon."

"I know."

"We gotta do this, Charley."

I told ya. I'm sold."

"When?"

"Right away."

"Honest?"

Grinning, Luciano spread out his arms. "Would I lie to you? My adopted kike brother?"

*

However sincere Charley may have been, the plans Meyer formulated were set on a back-burner when war broke out in 1941. By then, Charley had been imprisoned, requiring Meyer to zip back and forth between Chicago and New York, then on down to Miami and Tampa, where their coalition owned a considerable number of businesses. Lansky had to do the leg-work he and Charley previously shared. In due time, he also had to head west to Las Vegas after Bennie Siegel insisted on building what most mob members believed was one more of their volatile pal's nutty ideas, a financial fiasco in the making: the Flamingo.

Who in his right mind would want to travel to Nevada, for Christ's sake? If we didn't already suspect Bennie's got bugs in his brain, here's the proof. This according to Frank Costello.

Though Siegel hadn't lived to see it, whacked by his own gang-backers after the Flamingo's costs skyrocketed far beyond any acceptable level owing to his obsession with a two-timing whore, Vegas did turn out to be profitable. Still, the Flamingo sat there like a steel and concrete albatross on an arid stretch of uninviting desert. A fountain in no man's land. Cuba? Eden revisited! Cuba it was, then, for the time being.

As a result of such complex re-organizing, on December 26, 1946 a summit meeting was arranged in Manhattan. Batista arrived sporting his military uniform with enough medals to weigh down a full-grown bear, his presence topped off by a tan cap with black visor that dwarfed the man's head and caused this inherently cruel person to appear slightly comical. He had flown up for the occasion. Contracts were signed, hands shaken, toasts offered.

From that moment on, The Mob was in. Cuba would never be the same, for better or worse.

Better for some. Worse for others.

*

Six weeks following that summit meeting, on the morning of Sinatra's arrival, a gun-metal gray limo awaited the guest of honor's disembarkation from a state-of-the-art airliner. The sleek auto sped the star past a neat line of swaying palms to the city's upscale Vedado area. During the drive, Frank clung to the briefcase, held squarely on his lap. Inside, as he well knew, were two-million dollars the Mob in general, Charley specifically, needed to cover some unexpected costs.

Lansky had rung up Sinatra in Hollywood, suggesting he head south to cheer up their mutual pal. Do "a favor for a friend?" Sinatra understood what that meant. He would once more serve as courier. Other travelers might have to present carry-on baggage for a routine check. Frank *Sinatra?* Miami guards would request an autograph, then politely usher this lofty passenger on board.

Giddily, Sinatra agreed. Always, Frank experienced a rush when allowed to live out his secret fantasy of being a gangster. He'd grown up watching Humphrey Bogart play such characters and longed to do so himself, if only MGM could get beyond their limited friggin' vision of Sinatra as a light-comedy performer.

Oh, well ... maybe someday ...

Once ensconced in his seventh floor suite, Sinatra had rung up Luciano in his rooms on the eighth. Charley had temporarily abandoned his lush villa in Miramar. There, he neighbored with previous and now-again (if temporarily) president Ramon Grau San Martin. Charley wished to spend every possible moment with Frank.

"I'm here."

49

"Bring anything along?"

"Sure."

"Really? Mind telling me what?"

"It's a surprise."

Years earlier, Luciano had unofficially adopted the skinny aspiring singer from a seamy section of Hoboken as his kid-brother. Whatever Frankie's moral failings, disloyalty to those good to him did not rank among them. He like Luciano believed dedication to someone who did favors for you in the past served as a qualification for men worthy of respect. Men of honor.

When half an hour later they met in the brightly-lit bar for rum cocktails and Montecristo cigars, Charley immediately took possession of the all-important briefcase. Once that deal was done, he asked Frank what he thought of his accommodations. Though the singer tried his best to cover any disappointment, Charley saw through Frank's act. Yes, the Mafioso admitted, everything is a bit shabby still. Expect the same from the Oriental, which they would visit that afternoon.

Meyer had already focused his entrepreneurial talents on solving such problems, lining up top designers to transform *declasse* La Habana into a decadent Shangri-La. Once completed, they could attract the big rollers from back home. And, for that matter, from all around the globe.

"Sounds like Meyer's kind of job."

Charley nodded. "He loves all that kind-o' shit."

Frankie smirked. "And you, my friend?"

"Let Meyer do the grunt work. Me? I'll enjoy the results."

"*We'll* enjoy the results."

"Hey, you skinny friggin' wop. When did I ever do anything without you?"

Both laughed loudly, even harshly, at the raw truth of this statement.

*

Reclaiming Cuba's obviously ripe, too-long latent potential had been one subject of a series of top-level mob meetings held here a month and a half earlier. 24 major-league racketeers, including host Lansky and such flamboyantly nicknamed figures as Joey Adonis and Joe Bananas, arrived amid great fanfare and were welcomed as Herculean champions arriving in ancient Greece for the first Olympics. After some heated discussion, they agreed to name Charley the *copo di tutti capi*, "boss of all bosses." Luciano would be the first man to hold that position since he helped abolish it fifteen years earlier in favor of a board of directors known as The Commission. This had brought La Cosa Nostra's line of procedure more in line with that of so-called legitimate American business interests.

But these were rough times. A strong, no-nonsense leader was needed. "All agreed? Fine. You are the chosen one, Charley."

After deciding that once-beloved Bugsy Siegel had gone cock-crazy over his hottie Virginia Hill and could no longer be counted on to perform rationally for the organization, Charlie encountered no resistance when he announced that Ben had to be whacked. One of the Italians, probably Johnny Roselli, would be assigned to the hit. That's the way things worked: whenever one of the Jews warranted elimination, the Italians did it and vice versa. That way nobody had to rub out one of his own.

This unanimously decided on, then set aside, the mobsters moved on to such immediately pressing issues as Vito Genovese's intolerable moves into other gangsters' lucrative waterfront properties, as well as the controversial decision to create a French Connection, as all here had tagged it. This would allow raw heroin to be sneaked into the U.S. from that country as part of the Mob's swiftly expanding international narcotics trade.

Finally, the time came to talk about Cuba, their lovely host country, and the full development of a lavish offshore playground on these shores. For those who had accepted entrance into the drug trade with serious trepidation, Cuba appeared to be a cash cow all could delight in. After some discussion about operational procedures, the group picked Santo Trafficante, Jr., headquartered in Florida, to serve as their permanent contact person: a go-between who would pass the word, whatever the word happened to be, from stateside headquarters in the northeast, where Lansky continued to hold court, on down to this island.

Unless, that is, Luciano found it necessary to board a boat for Naples and run things from there. Meanwhile, word would go from Chicago through Tampa to Charley in Havana and back again.

As for Sinatra, an invitation had been extended. Come! Play, perform. Frankie would have loved to oblige. One problem stood in the way: his wife Nancy. The much-challenged woman had tolerated his flings throughout the year, even as he grew ever less sensitive as to her feelings by openly escorting his latest mistresses around Hollywood. Nonetheless, Nancy laid down the law when it came to being home with the kids for an elaborate charade every Christmas. The full Sinatra clan staged an annual holiday pageant, pretending to be the perfect all-Italian-American family. They did it for the kids, Frank and Nancy assured each other: young Nancy, now seven; Frank Jr., just two.

*

As to the former Miss Nancy Barbato, Frankie had married the lady at age nineteen for one reason: his mother Dolly told him to. Nancy, a nice Italian girl, hailed from a decent family in Jersey City. Solid middle-class at best, a wedding to someone so respectable qualified as a giant step up for the Sinatras.

"Ma, I don't wanna get married," Frankie whined.

"What?" Dolly demanded. "What are you hopin' for?"

"I've got a good voice, Momma. I wanna be a singer."

She slapped him hard across the cheek. "That's crazy."

"Why? Momma, this is America. Anyone—"

"Nothing but a dream."

"Dreams sometimes come true."

"Look around." Dolly pointed to one after another of their humble pieces of furniture in the crowded home. "Did my dreams come true? Did your father's?"

"Mine will. I know it."

Dolly shifted tactics. "Alright, then. Go out and be a singer. Give it a try. A nice wife can support you."

"No wife of mine will ever work."

Another slap, harder still. "Shut up. Listen."

"I'm listening, Momma."

"She's the kind of girl won't mind taking a job until you get success or come to your senses. Either way, you need a good, solid wife. Nancy's the one."

Frank hesitated. He didn't want to be hit again, but he had to say it. "Momma, she's not pretty."

"Pretty! Who cares about 'pretty'? Look at me! I was pretty once. How long did that last?"

"But I *love* pretty girls. Especially blondes—"

A third slap, this one absolutely nasty. "Stay away from them tramps. Italian girls—"

"There are Italian blondes."

"Not many. Look, you gonna marry Nancy. That's that. Search her face and you'll find something pretty there."

"I'd have to look hard."

"Her smile. She got a nice smile."

"People do call her Nancy with the laughing face."

So Sinatra married Nancy Barbato on February 4 1939. They moved into a small Jersey City apartment. He found work as a singing-waiter. She supported him throughout the lean years, shopping frugally for food, creating most of her own clothes from patches of left-over material, laboring at secretarial jobs. Frankie hit the big time thanks to a much-deserved First Place win on the

Major Bowes' Radio Show, this followed by a lucrative tour with the Harry James band, playing venues like the Rustic Cabin in Englewood.

There, the top bandleader in the business, Tommy Dorsey, caught his act. The bespectacled gent, knowing talent (perhaps genius) when he heard it, hired Frank away from his long-time competitor. That led to Hollywood, Frank's obvious charisma quickly catching on with American moviegoers.

But if Nancy figured now maybe they had it made, she had to reconsider when word of her husband's dalliances first leaked in from girlfriends who had seen and heard stuff. This in time poured over her like a massive flood. Because the most plentiful human species in Los Angeles, entertainment capital of the world, were Frank's favorites: Blondes. Big blondes. Little blondes. Natural blondes. Fake blondes. Blondes with big boobs and asses shaped like the caboose on the Orange Blossom special.

The wide, wonderful world of blondes. Not that brunettes were to be scoffed at. Take Ava Gardner, for instance ...

*

When the cigars had burned low, the final cups of choice espresso sipped, Sinatra humbly handed Charley a silver lighter. The words "To my dear pal Lucky from his 'kid brother', Frank" were emblazoned on its surface in an overly refined lettering style suggesting a touch of class to people who have no real knowledge of that elusive commodity. Charley nodded warmly as he accepted this peace-offering. He well knew how pussy-whipped Frank was, not only by Nancy but any other woman he became involved with. Realizing that Sinatra, as always insecure under his surface-show of cockiness, needed to hear the words spoken loud and clear, Charlie assured Frankie that there were no hard feelings as to the latter's failure to appear at Christmas.

"Next time? Bring Nancy along."

"Maybe I'll do just that."

"And the kids. They'd love the beaches."

Already, though, the singer's mind whirled off in a very different direction. Liking what he'd seen so far, Sinatra hoped a return engagement in the near-future would allow him to impress the starlet to end all starlets, more or less the sex symbol equivalent to *capo di tutti capi*: the blonde to beat all blondes. Frank had become enamored with one Norma Jean Baker.

This baby-doll had, like so many others who hung around the studios hoping for some hand-out role in exchange for anonymous blow-jobs with ranking executives, had like a loyal dog been thrown several bones: bit parts in big movies like *Scudda Hoo!*

53

Scudda Hay! Also, she'd been cast as the lead in an upcoming shoestring-budget item called *Ladies of the Chorus*. With a little luck that one could make her a star. If not, she could keep trying, like an endless string of well-built glamour-girls before her.

Maybe Norma Jean would prove to be that rare case—like Jean Harlow, Betty Grable, Lana Turner—who hit the big-time. That was rare, but it did on occasion happen. With her child's eyes and womanly torso, no question Norma Jean could become a silver-screen goddess. That ass, those curves? With Frankie's help. Which meant a little help from Charley as well.

"You're thinking about someone. And it ain't Nancy."

The signature sideways sneer, followed by: "Right!"

Then Sinatra and Luciano briefly parted, each heading back to his respective suite to shower, shave, dress. An hour later, Charley spirited his guest off to the Oriental Park in Marianao. They spent their first afternoon together there, accompanied by attractive local girls wearing garish outfits. They spoke only a smattering of English but well knew the score. Looking the racetrack over, Sinatra felt that the scene did appear listless. As they'd agreed, if anything could turn that around it was the mind of the man Charley referred to as The Accountant, Meyer.

After several hours, the sun became unbearably hot so they returned with the women for a light late-lunch of crab salad in Hotel Nacional's most exclusive dining room. Each man afterwards retired with his woman for a nap. Sinatra swept his lithe beauty up in his arms and under the sheets. Once there he promptly fell asleep, snoring loudly. Exhausted, as he would later convince himself, from the flight, the day's activities, the considerable amount of alcohol he'd consumed.

The lush woman lay beside his scrawny body, knowing Frankie was supposed to be the world's greatest lover. Considering the circumstances, this disappointed beauty could not grasp why.

Late in the evening the old buddies, having ditched their first set of women, caught a spectacular floor show at Sans Souci casino. Guzzling down one Cuba Libre after another, the drink Charley had personally concocted from rum, Coca-Cola and lime juice, they ogled the nearly-naked mulatto dancers. The girls' light-brown faces appeared radiant in the spot-lights; their bodies, strong and solid in a way most American women were not built. And how these beauties could move!

Smiling like happy idiots at the two Americans in expensive white suits seated in the front row, the girls' eyes mutely communicated they were more than willing to share their choice flesh after hours with such men of money and power. The barely-draped dyanmos performed frenetic dances that owed much to ancient voodoo rites. Their feather-adorned costumes, or what there were of them, had been cut from elegant silks and satins, sequined with tinsel. They sported brightly feathered masks, adding an aura of mystery. Here was the first thing Frankie had seen in Havana to convince him that once word spread, well-to-do Americans would fly down to the glitzy New Cuba that Meyer would design, Charley would build, and Frank headline.

*

Even as dawn approached, the two men, accompanied by the most attractive dancing girls, still in the ornate costumes and (at Frank and Charlie's request) wearing those feathered masks, crawled into the limo. The party roared off to visit the worst slum Frankie had ever observed, the bottom rung of Hoboken included. Frank's family home back on 415 Monroe Street had been the Waldorf Astoria compared to this! Narrow, winding, unlit and unpaved boulevards had been piled high with garbage, as well as a sad array of human flotsam-and-jetsom. These sad-eyed creatures sat or sprawled on the steps, or stood stooped over, hunchback-like.

Surrounded by bodyguards, the small party marched on past the sad-faces, degenerate bodies, and wasted lives. The people peered up at Frank and Charlie in awe; at the female companions in anger. *Were we only as beautiful as you,* the eyes of these desperate females suggested, *then we would be the ones proudly trailing along behind such men of power.*

Without glancing sideways, the Americans and the expensive whores made their way into a club, past a long line of heavy smokers hanging out in the hallway. Charley's bodyguards shoved stragglers out of the way. Charley and Frank headed down dimly lit stairs. Once at the bottom, they arrived in a loud, lavish private cellar club, full of elegantly adorned patrons.

"Hello, and welcome!" The men of respect were greeted by the owner, a short, barrel-shaped native in a simple white suit, his jacket stained tan under the armpits from constantly flowing sweat. Obviously, Frank mused, this guy knows Charley. The man bowed low, as if acknowledging royalty, then trippingly escorted his visitors to a prime table beside a small stage, set down in a pit under a single low-hanging light. Other customers, barely recognizable as men and women much less Cubans or Americans in the semi-darkness, hurried aside or shuffled out of the way to make room for what were clearly privileged guests.

55

Seated beside Charley, the man whom Sinatra in his dreams most wished to be, Frank took in his first cockfight. He cheered along with the crowd as blood flew through the air, splattering onto their clothing. Their faces, too, as the struggle in the pit below grew even more fierce. The sensation felt good: hot, decadent, vaguely immoral. Later, two crazed-looking local women, wearing black leather boots, matching gloves and nothing else, wrestled.

Their bout concluded, the women engaged in sex with a black male giant, decked out in white fur, silver fox-tails hanging from his bejeweled belt. The Colossus wielded what might have been listed in the Guinness Book of World Records as the largest cock on the American continent. This finely muscled figure wore a matching white mask during the hour-long specialty act, which concluded with his sodomizing in turn each of what he loudly referred to as "bitches." All the while the Americans drank down the best rum this infamous Havana house had to offer.

"Like I said: some fun, eh, kid?"

"Charley, I bow before you, as always."

When, shortly before dawn, Sinatra crawled back to his suite, he found three expensive (though he was not expected to pay) courtesans from Casa Marina, the city's best brothel, patiently waiting. Frank greeted them with mild enthusiasm.

Shortly after the foursome slipped between the sheets, he again fell fast asleep. As had been the case with his previous companion, the three ready, willing, and able women remained silent, wondering if they ought to wake him or let the great man snore the night away. On consideration, they chose the latter.

*

During a late breakfast the following morning, respite from the way of all flesh came in serious discussions with Charley about mob business and its political backdrop. With an official okay from the man who gradually emerged as the reigning figure in the syndicate's stateside operations, Sam Giancana, Luciano and Lansky planned to fulfill Meyer's dream from nearly two decades earlier. They had even agreed on their choice for Cuba's next president: A military martinet, former president Fulgencia Batista (he the very same personage who had requested American participation back in the 1930s) held that post from 1940-44, after defeating Grau at the polls. Since then, Batista lived in the U.S. He'd dumped his aging first wife, married an exotic young beauty, and set up residence in Florida.

With the Mob's tacit backing, Batista would the following year run in absentia for the Cuban senate. Once he returned to

Havana to fill that seat, plans would be carefully arranged for an upcoming presidential bid.

"Nothing against Grau, mind you. I like him."

"Yet you prefer Batista."

"He's tougher on the people. Hungrier for money and power. I admire that in a politician."

A *golpe*, or military coup, would soon set Batista back in office, a fixed election to follow. "We'll share the casino ownerships with him. Everybody makes money. Everyone's happy."

"It all seems too good to be true," Sinatra sighed, sipping his rich Cappuccino.

Well, Luciano admitted, there was a serpent in the garden. A group of radicals, having headquartered at the university, infiltrated unions of cane cutters and banana harvesters. This revolutionary faction had recently tripled in number. These anarchists, or whatever they considered themselves, threatened to overthrow the apple-cart. Luciano laughed as he told Sinatra what such left-leaning subversives called their own movement: *gangsterismo*, a term borrowed from old black and white Hollywood crime films of the 1930s.

In the minds of such self-styled idealists, those onscreen mobsters had been modern Robin Hoods, reacting against a failed capitalist system. Now, these sons of well-to-do Cubans, their parents despising what their educated offspring were up to, planned a revolt, likely of hard-edged communist orientation. Luciano and Sinatra laughed out loud. What the Made Men in Chicago, New York, and other places depicted in those films had wanted was money. They were not opposed to capitalism, American style. The Mob embodied capitalism on its most elemental level. How fascinating these delusional fools could get everything wrong!

Gradually, the mood turned serious once again, as the old friends finished their breakfasts of eggs and a tasty, spicy meat Frankie could not recognize, bathed in some sort of bright red sauce that reminded him of the rooster's blood flying about the previous night. Well, he suggested, these gnats likely would not be much of a problem for the well-trained soldati Luciano would import as a counter-measure.

Charley nodded grimly but said nothing. Perhaps he saw more difficulty on the horizon than did his guest.

*

Before the limo headed out to the airport, Frank Sinatra's first of many visits to Cuba nearing its end, the man who would owing to the enormity of his talent rightly become known as The Main

Event ordered his driver to swing by the Malecon for one final glance at this twisting street and adjoining cityscape. Gaily dressed Cubans proudly marched up and down, as if in a constant state of celebration. Every day in this city seemed a spontaneous carnival, the excitement infectious to all who came to visit from the U.S. or any faraway land. Here, people danced rather than walked along the streets! How wonderful ...

Sinatra gazed over the rough sea wall that, back in the halcyon era of pirates several hundreds of years earlier, had provided a natural fortress straddling Havana's northern rim. The sight remained as awesome now as it must have been then, to the eyes of people whose exploits had become the stuff of rich legend: a mean-looking yet assuring buttress of rock, able to withstand any assault by man or the elements that happened to drift this way.

Exiting the limo, Sinatra again stood, as he had on his second afternoon here, on the storm-shattered precipice. A south-bound wind carried brine across the bay, up to where he'd positioned himself, feeling for the moment like some ancient conqueror of an unknown kingdom, all things possible. The smell of sea-salt seemed appealingly fresh here, not mingled with trash and dead fish, the case back on his beloved Jersey shore.

Breathing deeply, Sinatra enjoyed the rich aroma and its perfect symbiosis with those vast indigo waters that eventually segued with the soft turquoise skyline, the two blending into a shade every bit as seductive as Frank's infamous bedroom eyes.

He hated to leave. Then again, nothing lasts forever. When he did return, as Sinatra knew he would, here is where he would come first. A sentimentalist at heart, for Sinatra Malecon would always represent the essence of Havana. Not that he'd overlooked much of what the island offered.

What had Charley said? Bring Nancy and the kids along! Hell, no; they won't go. Frank hoped instead to escort Norma Jean, her name recently changed by the Fox studio to Marilyn Monroe, down to stroll alongside him by the sheltering pines.

As soon as possible. Hopefully, those insurgents Charlie mentioned would not interfere with Frank's plans for seduction.

CHAPTER FOUR:
SEMPER FI

"The Marine Corps wants a few good men!"
—recruiting poster, 1957

The sunny day of October 24, 1956, just three months shy of a decade before The Voice arrived in Cuba for the double duty of performing a concert and acting as Mob courier, a then-17-year-old boy marched back and forth across a small stretch of cracked pavement right outside the U.S. Marines Recruitment Office in downtown Dallas.

I think I can, I think I can. Isn't that what a character in some book Marguerite read to me as a child tells himself?

At last, Lee summed up his courage, opened the glass-and-steel-frame door and, pushing his shoulders back and upward in hopes of appearing taller than his 5' 8" frame, stepped inside.

Frankie? Stay with me now, will you?

Though Lee had been concentrating on a favorite moment from a Sinatra movie to inspire him, *Suddenly* was not it. Instead, nearly 2 1/2 years following his earlier attempt to enlist, Lee focused on *From Here to Eternity*. Compared to the larger men in Angelo Maggio's company, Sinatra's character appeared something of a runt. That didn't prevent the soldier from being popular, thanks to his good-natured humor and a basic sense of likeability.

This is my chance! Re-invent myself, turn my life around. Put the old Lee behind me. Step up to the desk where that all-American Tab Hunter type sits, banging away at his typewriter.

All this is a living movie. I am its star. Can I write, direct, produce this scene so that it turns out the way I want?

Lee had expected to encounter a lieutenant but the sergeant seated here would do. "Hello there, you fightin' leatherneck!"

Before Lee could stop himself, the words were out. He'd twisted his face up into an imitation Humphrey Bogart, drawing back his lower lip, extending his teeth forward. The marine raised his head from the paperwork, coldly considering Lee.

"Hello," the sergeant responded. "What can I do for you?"

Dropping the gag, Lee drew himself up straight and tall, as high as his 135 lb. body would reach. "I'm here to enlist."

Apparently unconvinced, the marine sergeant slowly rose from his seat behind a functional, non-descript office desk, looking Lee over. "Is this some sort of a joke?"

"Not at all," Lee whimpered, any energy he'd been able to muster draining out of him. "I want to be a marine," he added with a touch of desperation. "More than anything."

Realizing that this boy was sincere, the sergeant, sorry now he'd assumed this to be some wise-ass Beatnik, nodded affirmatively while bringing up his hand for a shake.

"I'm Lee Oswald," the would-be recruit smiled, noticing the firmness of the sergeant's grip. "I'd like to serve my country."

"Sit down, please." The sergeant indicated a chair adjacent to his desk. Lee pulled it up and did as told. His host eased back down into his own chair, Lee wishing he'd navigated his own move with such relaxed grace.

"Tell me as simply as you can why you want to be a marine."

I can't tell him the truth, about the Sinatra movie back in New Orleans. Johnny Barrows got his gun and I want one, too.

"My brother Robert enlisted right out of high school," Lee began. "So it's something of a family tradition."

*

That much was true. In 1952, Lee then twelve and a half, Robert joined the Marines. Two years earlier, half-brother John Pic had enlisted in the Coast Guard. He was now married to Margy.

Could there be something to John, who so feared and dreaded Marguerite, marrying a woman with the same name? Coincidence or ... What's the phrase ... the Oedipal Complex?

*

"Guess what? Lee and I are moving to Manhattan!" Marguerite had jovially announced in an impulse phone call. Mother and son had been back in New Orleans for several months. As always, she became antsy, obsessing on another move. Cross town or cross-country. Anywhere other than wherever they were at the moment.

"Why?" John asked, stunned, from the small, neat, cramped Brooklyn apartment that he and Margy shared.

"Why not?" Marguerite followed this with a mad laugh.

"Well, my wife and I will be glad to have you stay with us until you can find a place of your own."

That was only half true. John's bride detested Marguerite. Margy insisted they live in the New York City area to keep her new husband apart from what his wife considered an evasive, intrusive, unhealthy influence. Wasn't it just like that crazy harridan, damn her self-important hide, to follow them north?

"That will be wonderful," Marguerite said.

When she and Lee arrived, a myriad of luggage including the TV set Lee had grown addicted to, following, Margy gasped. No matter what John had explained, however clear he tried to make himself, the Oswalds had arrived for a long stay.

"Our family, together again. I've dreamed of this!"

Marguerite made no moves to find a job to help pay for groceries or locate their own apartment. For a while, John tried to make the best of it, more with Lee, whom he adored, than his mother. John knew Lee to be what the military referred to as the walking wounded, those who silently suffer from some invisible hurt. The kid had been dragged from the solid middle-class home of Lee's late father, who passed of a heart attack months before the boy was born, to a virtual slum. After that, hurried off to an upper-middle-class existence when Marguerite up and married Mr. Ekdahl, an electrical engineer. Originally from Boston, the fellow re-located them near Fort Worth, Texas.

Momentarily it had appeared that all truly was well that ended well. This guy was great to Lee and the boys when they returned home from a military school he'd sent John and Robert to and which they loved. Shortly, Marguerite, being Marguerite, decided that her husband was a philanderer. True or false, she divorced him, receiving a little more than a thousand dollars as a settlement and no future support.

How could this sad little kid, John mused, *establish a solid personality when one moment he was wearing decent clothes, the next reduced to hand-me-downs from Marguerite's older sister?* Earlier, John, age ten, had cared for Lee when all three brothers lived in Bethlehem Orphanage. John cleaned up three-year-old Lee's mess when the child lost control and went in his pants. As he had no kids of his own, John determined to treat Lee now as if his brother were his own son.

"Just you wait and see," John assured Lee the moment they were reunited at the subway stop. "We'll have a great time!"

So off they went to the Museum of Natural History, which Lee liked a lot. And the Bronx Zoo, which the boy delighted in. John could tell that Lee had an affinity for animals. Sadly, that was not the case with neighborhood kids. On the second day after arrival, John walked Lee over to where a bunch of boys played stickball in a corner lot of Yorkville. As man and boy approached the noisy group, Lee froze up, panic-stricken.

"What's wrong? Lee, these are 'the guys.' I'll—"

"Please! Can't we just go home?"

Stunned, John tried to draw Lee into the crowd, but it was too late. The other boys, pausing in their sport, witnessed Lee writhing in desperation and laughed. Minutes later Lee and John were back inside the apartment. Lee ran to the room he and his mother shared. He turned on the TV, then spent the rest of the day watching his favorites, old movies and live news: a frozen idealization of the past alternating with today's passing parade.

John learned from Marguerite that, after the Fort Worth disaster, on their return to LA she landed a managerial job at Everybody's Department Store, making $25 a week. This required her to be there full-time, six days a week. The room Marguerite had found for them was located in a crime-infested area, so Marguerite instructed Lee to run home from school every day.

"Tightly lock yourself inside, and wait for my return."

That's when Lee's TV addiction begun. During commercial breaks he would tip-toe over to the window and peek out at other boys, playing on the street. More than ever, Lee sensed his own difference, for the first time wondering why that was so. He was a freak, like those he had once observed at a circus sideshow.

Different, or ... dare he hope? ... *special!* Unique, and meant for more important things he had yet to discover.

Yes, that must be it! I'll just have to wait, bide my time, learn my higher purpose. Or maybe I could kill myself ...

Soon the show resumed. Lee would rush away from his window on the world, back to watch, sitting on the edge of the bed he and Marguerite shared each night, glued to the grainy black and white image. At the next advertising break he would return to the window. This became ritualistic, Lee not yet aware of that term. Though Lee could hardly guess it at the time, from that point in his life, his future was forever set in cement.

However addicted to TV he might be, Lee found one show repulsive. *The Adventures of Ozzie and Harriet* featured members of the Nelson family, mom and dad and two sons, all playing themselves. They lived in a wholesome looking neighborhood, got along great. No one ever raised a voice. Lee smelled a rat.

People weren't like that. How dare they put on a show that dangled an ideal family in front of the eyes of all those who could barely, and rarely, achieve even a little happiness?

He abruptly turned the channel and never watched it again.

*

On one of their sojourns into the affordable fun places in and around the New York City area, John had offered to buy Lee a souvenir. The boy picked out an inexpensive pocket knife. Sheer horror would result from this seemingly innocuous incident.

Over the past two weeks, Margy had grown frustrated, then furious, with the intensifying realization that Marguerite had arrived with plans for her and Lee to become permanent fixtures. Not that Mama ever said this outright; Marguerite's manner of dealing with situations was to remain silent and hope, even assume, what she wanted would transform into reality.

Margy set out to do something about that. She began dropping hints that the apartment was too small. Marguerite responded that in time "we'll get a bigger one."

We? You were invited for a few days!

Margy complained that Lee ate a lot for a skinny kid, hoping Marguerite would take the hint and offer to find work. "He's a growing boy," Mama shrugged. That *did* it! Margy wandered around her limited space, only days earlier her domain, now clearly her mother in law's, ever more depressed.

One day shortly thereafter, Margy stepped zombie-like into the kitchen area and happened upon Lee, sitting at the table, dutifully employing his new penknife to carve a miniature ship.

"Look!" Margy over-reacted, pointing at a small mess on the floor. "You're getting wood chips all over *everything.*"

"I'll pick 'em up when I finish," Lee shrugged, not bothering to look up. He failed to grasp any immediacy to this minor situation. Emitting a sound just short of a banshee's shriek, Margy slapped the boy across the face. Her open-hand blow landed so hard it sent the child flying across the room.

Shocked at the impact of her swing, already half-wishing she had not done it, Margy nervously stepped over toward Lee, concerned as to his welfare. As she approached, the boy leaped to his feet, bringing the pen-knife forward in self-defense.

"Do that again," he screamed, "and I'll *kill* you!"

Lee had never spoken in such a way to anyone before. He'd heard it in an old Allan "Rocky" Lane B Western that ran on TV's *The Gabby Hayes Show* the previous week. If Rocky said it ...

"That's *it*!" Margy hissed, knowing full well that if she hadn't checked her own forward movement she might well have run into the knife and been killed. "You two are *out* of here!"

Upon return from work, John tried reasoning with Margy. To no avail. She may have been glad the incident occurred; at last, she had an excuse to send them packing. John assured Lee he'd regularly stop by, wherever Lee and Marguerite settled in the area, continuing to take him to the movies. Lee would have none of it.

So far as he was concerned, John had betrayed the family by siding with Margy. Lee never spoke to John again.

Not even when John and Margy were invited over to the new apartment Marguerite had located in the Bronx, just off the Concourse, for Sunday supper a month and a half later. Robert, on leave, had come up to visit. The moment Robert appeared in their doorway, wearing his marine dress uniform and beaming proudly, Lee knew this was what he hoped to one day become.

*

"So you respect your big brother's choice?" the marine recruitment sergeant asked after Lee described that reunion.

"You can't imagine. So *very* much!"

"My great concern, Lee, is that you have a dangerously romanticized view of what the Corps will be like—"

"If I may interrupt?" Lee leaned forward, anxiously.

"That'll be fine."

"Actually," Lee continued, "I know *everything* about the marines. Your history, the code of conduct—"

"My turn to interrupt. Where did you pick this up?"

Lee explained the circumstances of Robert's visit, leaving out as much of the personal stuff—those bad feelings between himself and John and Margy, Marguerite's over-the-top act for everyone, as if all their world were a stage, she the designated lead player— as he dared. There had been a family Sunday supper, quite elaborate in light of Marguerite's modest means.

All five, the Oswalds and the Pics, seated together at her dinner table in a mutually understood state of truce. Marguerite wore her finest dress left over from those brief upscale Fort Worth days. Everyone might have relaxed, even grown comfortable, if she hadn't gone into her infamous Southern Belle routine.

"Mom," John made the mistake of saying, "would you please just be yourself and stop putting on airs?"

In a grand gesture, Marguerite fell with a theatrical faint into a nearby stuffed chair, then began bawling. "I'm sorry if I try to add a touch of quality to my surroundings, humble as they may be." Tears rolled down her aging cheeks.

Robert tossed John an angry look for spoiling everything, though he'd been thinking the same himself. She reminded him of Vivien Leigh as Blanche du Bois in the movie *A Streetcar Named Desire*. He'd joined the corps mainly to get far away from Mama.

Two years earlier, John had enlisted in the Guard for the same reason. The two often talked about their difficult home situation at night, when neither could get to sleep, at the orphanage. Even as other boys might fantasize about a life of adventure, they shared their desperate dreams for normalcy.

"I'm going out," Lee announced. No one said a word as he pushed his half-finished plate away, rose without making eye contact with anyone. He slipped on his jacket and left.

"Where will he go?" Robert worried.

"My guess is to the Bronx Zoo," John shrugged. He and Marguerite, speaking alternately with Margy throwing in side comments, related Lee's problems. Shortly after the current school year commenced he began attending P.S. # 117. Other boys picked on him. Some gave Lee a hard time owing to his outdated clothing. Others viciously mocked his modest southern accent. All sensed something irregular—"queer," a few ventured— about this new kid. The girls picked up on that and avoided him.

Sickened at the thought of enduring such humiliation, Lee would each morning wait for Marguerite to leave, he pretending to be on his way as well. Once she was gone he'd stay home. All morning Lee watched TV. At noon, he would take a break, make himself a sandwich, meanwhile turning on the radio. That's where his appreciation for Sinatra began. In early afternoon Lee would shove off, most days heading back to the zoo via the subway.

When the principal realized this new boy had attended only fifteen of the first forty-five school days, he sent a truant officer out looking for Lee. The man found him at the zoo, exchanging smirks with the monkeys. He grabbed Lee by his ear, twisting it cruelly. This immense bully then dragged the pained, humiliated kid back with him.

Lee tried to suffer through school, actually enjoying social studies and English literature classes, if miserable again when the bell rang. For the three minutes allotted to changing class-rooms, he felt alienated from all others in the crowded corridor, sometimes harassed by bigger boys.

Soon Lee headed back to the monkey cage.

*

The truant officer, figuring where he'd find him, came by. After that, Lee spent afternoons riding the subway, across and under the great city above. He made it a point to learn every stop and the precise distances between them. Lee appreciated such minutiae; a sense of power flowed through him knowing that he possessed myriad details that other people lacked.

I'm invisible to them. Someday, they'll see me ...

Lee most enjoyed those rare occasions when he had a car all to himself. Then it was as if the entire New York subway system operated for that brief interlude for Lee alone. When a car grew crowded, sometimes Lee would get off, go up, tenuously exploring the real world. Most areas were too crowded with Normals for Lee to feel comfortable.

One place he did appreciate was Greenwich Village. Lee loved the huge arch, done in an ancient style, at the entrance to a park where the Beats congregated, strumming their guitars, spouting incomprehensible poetry.

"The times, they are a-changin'," one bearded boy, no older than Lee, warbled mournfully.

Mostly Lee was fascinated by the chess players, a unique breed of societal drop-outs. They sat on benches, challenging passers-by to pay for a chance to match their skills. Whenever he had a little extra money, Lee would give it a try.

He came to know some of these fascinating characters, wondering if this might provide a possible career. Though Lee never beat any of them, on more than one occasion he came close. An elderly black man, whom Lee believed possessed all the wisdom in the world, winked and assured Lee he was good. Damn good!

Black people appreciate me in a way whites don't. As to chess, I'll bide my time, practice, and maybe someday ...

At a book stall, Lee picked up a home-printed pamphlet that had a major impact on his vision of self. Called "The White Negro," the piece had been authored by Norman Mailer, a scribe whose WWII novel *The Quick and the Dead* had elevated him to the level of celebrity author. The seller explained to Lee that this brochure had been produced by something he referred to as The Underground Press, an indie publisher called 'City Lights.' Lee hadn't heard that term before. He wanted to learn more soon.

Naively, Lee expected this to be about black people born with paler-than-expected skin. Instead, Mailer wrote about Anglos who had fallen in love with black culture, everything from jazz sounds to interracial romances. These were the Beats Lee had heard about, both here in The Village and haunts in San Francisco's Haight-Ashbury. Hipsters, Mailer called them.

Subterraneans, not suburbanites. They played bongo drums, danced the night away, and rejected contemporary Christian conformity to celebrate dark and ancient gods. They believed in free love and free thought, freedom for the body and the mind.

Could Mailer be talking directly to me, showing me the way?

One point that mesmerized Lee was Mailer's distinction between the psychotic and the psychopath. The former would be identified by society as a menace and incarcerated. The latter could pass unnoticed, a face in the crowd, until some day he, without warning, exploded with violence.

That second type of person ... that may just be me.

Lee spent an hour reading the piece on a bench. On future visits he would purchase the novels of Jack Kerouac and poems by Lawrence Ferlinghetti and Allen Ginsberg. "Coney Island of the Mind." "Howl." A whole new world opened up to Lee.

This continued until Lee was picked up again, now by a different truancy officer, nastier even than the first. Lee was summoned to appear in Children's Court, Marguerite required to take an afternoon off work to accompany him.

"I have no authority over the boy," she wailed to the judge. "I make him promise to attend school, but he runs off anyway. I have to work. What am I to do?"

"Madame," the judge snapped back, "if you cannot control your child, I will deliver him to those who can."

*

Shortly after turning thirteen, Lee was bundled off to Youth House, a horrible refuge for abused and/or disoriented children. Lee guessed the place was worse than any environment these kids may have come from. The other boys, all misfits too, taunted and bullied Lee. He withdrew to any private place he found, reading. Dickens; *Little Dorrit.* Sharing the suffering of others helped Lee survive. At least he wasn't alone.

He loved escapism as much as realism, so Lee grew ecstatic when he saw a volume called *Invisible Man* in the library. He'd caught the old Universal horror movie on TV a few years earlier and looked forward to H.G. Wells' original. To Lee's surprise, this turned out to be a new novel. Not *'The' Invisible Man* but simply *Invisible Man,* by Ralph Ellison. From page one L.H.O. realized this was penned by a man of color. The title did not indicate science-fiction but social status.

"I am invisible," Ellison stated, "simply because people refuse to see me." That, Lee could sympathize with. As he walked the crowded streets, people passing by made eye contact with every other stranger except him. He could almost believe there existed a confederacy of silence to avoid and isolate L.H.O. He and of course all the black people in America as well.

During Lee's term of residency, a psychiatrist named Carro observed the boy on several occasions. He alone among the staff doctors was able to persuade this particular boy to open up and talk. Lee's chaotic behavior, Carro insisted, stemmed directly from a sense of impermanence as to any place he might inhabit, any status he temporarily possessed; always believing if these were decent, they'd soon be taken away. If not, things could only get worse. Frequent moves in class and place had long since fractured any sense of personal identity, perhaps beyond repair.

"In my mind," Carro wrote in his official report, "there developed over time an inability to adapt to the changes ... Normally, a person meets these kinds of situations. Either you face them head on or you retreat. Perhaps Lee did the former for a while, trying his best to make do with an ever shifting reality. But the frequency, and drastic alterations as to lifestyle, may have proven too much for him to handle."

As a result, Carro came to believe Lee had without being aware of the process created an invisible shield around himself; a protective cocoon which the world, however oppressive, could not penetrate. Inside that invented, imaginary safe place, Lee designed and inhabited an alternative reality, one in which he existed as an all-powerful being. Different became superior.

Lee "feels as if there is a veil between himself and other people through which they can't reach him," Carro stated. If at some time in the recent past Lee had hoped to join, he "feels as if there now exists a veil between him and other people through which they can't reach him." Carro concluded that, if previously Lee had even remotely wanted to rejoin the brotherhood of man, The Normals, any such desire might be gone and forgotten. Now, Lee Harvey Oswald "prefers this veil to remain intact."

Robert, who had no idea of how terrible things had become, gasped. What had an uncaring world done to his kid brother?

"I only wish I could help," John explained, "but he'll have nothing to do with me since 'the incident.'"

"If you like," Robert suggested, "I'll try to get him to open up to me as soon as he returns."

"That," Marguerite announced, "would be wonderful!"

*

"I was a little mixed up a few years ago."

"Most kids are at that age," the sergeant responded.

"Robert said to me, 'Look, Lee, you can surrender to chaos or you can learn discipline. If you do the former you may have a wild ride for a while but you'll end up lost and alone. If you opt for the latter, you'll earn yourself a satisfying life.'"

"Your brother sounds like a very smart man."

"Of course he is," Lee gulped. "Like you, he's a marine."

The sergeant smiled back. For the first time, the recruiter actually believed that this kid might just have a shot.

"You want to know what Robert said the last time I saw him?" Lee—realizing he was winning the marine over—asked in a rhetorical manner. "Boy, if you ever get into the marines, you are going to end up a *general!*"

During the next half-hour, Lee continued his story about Robert's visit. How he read over the marine manual with his brother. When Robert left, he allowed Lee to keep the book. The boy read it over and over until he had it memorized. To prove himself, Lee ran through a litany of details—care of the M1 rifle, the philosophy of martial arts, the *esprit de corps* necessary for absolute commitment—stunning the sergeant as to Lee's veracity, comprehension, and passion for the Marines.

Lee didn't mention some of his other reading matter for fear the sergeant would send him packing. During one of Lee's visits to The Village a stumble-bum struck up a conversation about communism, insisting it would replace our own capitalist system, and there was nothing anyone could do to stop that. Lee had conversed with the elderly fellow calmly for a while, then began ranting about the true greatness of democracy.

About a week later, as Lee ascended from a subway stop, he came face to face on the street with a dreary woman, handing out pamphlets about the immorality of the Rosenbergs having been convicted and executed as spies on flimsy evidence that they'd sent atomic bomb secrets to Russia. Initially, Lee brushed past her; then, something snapped. He turned, headed back, took one.

At the apartment, where he lived alone now since Marguerite had disappeared again—she would return sooner or later, acting as if this were completely normal—Lee read it with interest.

As it happened, WOR-TV in New York, Channel 9, re-ran on weekdays a half-hour filmed series called *I Led Three Lives*. The show had been based on a bestseller by Herbert J. Philbrick. This advertising executive balanced his home life as an average white-collar worker and devoted husband with secret activities as a member of a clandestine Commie cell planning to overthrow our government. Perceived as a traitor by neighbors who learned of his double identity, Philbrick kept a greater secret, one he would not share even with his distraught wife: he happened to be a special agent working for J. Edgar Hoover. A patriot, Philbrick was willing to go down in history, if need be, as the worst traitor since Benedict Arnold in order to serve his country.

Over 23 weeks, Lee watched each of the 117 episodes, believing what he was told by the ever-ultra-serious announcer: every case presented here was true. Philbrick, played by Richard Carlson, discovered seemingly nice, normal citizens—from high school teachers through household-maids to local politicians—who, deep inside, were Red to the core.

It never occurred to Lee, nor to most impressionable viewers watching every day at 4:30 P.M., that the scripts were fictional, including one about a Harriet Nelson type housewife who transforms her vacuum cleaner into a bomb launcher, planning to initiate a bloody revolution from her own living room.

The show offered arch fantasy done in the style of docudrama, as such convincing to the innocent audience. This was the period during which Lee was ordered to Brooklyn's Youth House. In the TV room he watched the series. And the news as well. So there was Joseph McCarthy, the mean-bully of a senator from Wisconsin, staring into the camera, announcing that "the State Department has been infiltrated by communists." He held a paper high, insisting: "I have in my hand a list of 205 members of the communist party that are nonetheless still serving in the State department." He then hinted that the army too might be 'pink.'

How hard it was to tell where the fiction of *I Led Three Lives* left off and the reality of 'Tailgunner' Joe began! Lee decided he had to learn more. In *Invisible Man*, Ellison had insisted that the communist party was as corrupt as any other institution, promising to help the black man while exploiting colored people for the party's own ends.

On the other hand, Ellison defended pure Marxism. At once Lee took *The Communist Manifesto* out of the lending library. When other kids, bad to the bone, caught him in the act of reading it they taunted Lee even more viciously. One called him a Red, as such worse than the boy who had murdered his father.

"I'm not a commie," he tried to explain. "I'm a Marxist."

They didn't get the subtle distinction. In response to the next round of beatings, Lee flashed them that twisted, cynical smile, which he was even then in the process of perfecting.

Gradually, I am coming to understand my mission in life. I will be to the next generation what Herb Philbrick was to the previous. Like him, lead a seemingly normal existence. I will do so not as a civilian but as a marine. As such. I will let it be known to all I read Marx. I'll subscribe to the Daily Worker *so 'they' have an address at which to reach me.*

Sooner or later, I'll be contacted by a commie agent. I'll join them, only to betray their plans to the authorities, doing my country a greater service even than Philbrick. Like him, I'll write a book exonerating myself. Hollywood will do a TV series.

Who would I like to have play me? That's easy: Sinatra!

*

"I tried signing up two years ago. They said come back in a year. After that, I forged my mom's name on a paper saying it was okay for me to join up but they told me to go home."

"How old are you now, Lee?"

"I turned seventeen six days ago." Lee reached into his pocket and pulled out his birth certificate for proof.

The sergeant glanced over it, then eye-balled Lee. "No matter how tough your brother told you Boot Camp can be, it's tougher. They'll put you and all the others in your outfit through hell. Some will not be able to take it. Bigger guys than you have washed out. Do you want to go through with this?"

"Sergeant, it's what I was born for!"

*

Precisely as that marine said earlier, Lee arrived in San Diego for Boot Camp two days later. And, likewise, the 17-year-old learned the hard way that everything he'd been told at the Dallas Recruitment Center was true. Within minutes of arrival, the routine began: there is a right way and a wrong way *and The Marine Way* to make your bed, eat at mess, erect a pup tent, march in close order drill, wear your uniform, share a squad encampment, salute a superior officer, speak only when spoken to by your Drill Sergeant, clean your assigned piece, crawl across a three-rope bridge, sit on a stool at the PX while off duty (rare!), clean a latrine when that is your assignment, peel a potato, run in place when you believe it's impossible to take a step further, employ a knife during training for hand to hand combat; rapid disassembly of a .30 caliber machine gun, the proper means of thrusting forward with a bayonet, preparing your piece for inspection so perfectly a stranger could comfortably eat off it.

And, perhaps most important, fire that weapon from a prone position during hours of target practice. Lee had so completely memorized the details about corps rituals that from the moment Basic began he excelled all in his group at every aspect of marine life but one: firing the leatherneck's second spine, his M1.

"You are the worst shot I have *ever* seen," a freckle-faced instructor shouted one day in early November, 1956. "Damn! You couldn't hit the broad side of a barn from five feet away."

Lee mumbled some sort of apology but feared this might be his downfall: his aim remained terrible and likely always would.

"What kind of *marine* are you? What kind of *man* are you?" the instructor wailed a week later when Lee, unnerved, scored worse still. Those words hurt the most; the idea that Lee's poor aim somehow disqualified him as a man. After that incident, Lee—who had remained anonymous among the grunts until then—found himself once more marginalized. There was some razzing during the time spent in Basic. No matter how hard he tried to change, he was still Lee Oswald, not 'Angelo Maggio.'

Things took a turn for the worse once the group moved on to Camp Pendleton for full-scale combat training. A fellow grunt named Perry Sommers made it a point to chat with Lee, a rarity among group members. Timid to the point of near-total silence when not spoken to first, Lee at last opened up. He chatted with Sommers over a Coke during evening break, believing he'd found a friend. When the subject of women came up, Lee shyly admitted that, much as he thought about sex, he'd never actually "been with" a female. The moment those words were out, Lee knew he'd made a mistake. The grin on Sommers' face turned ugly.

The following day, fellow marines razzed Lee about being a "cherry virgin." he had no idea as to how he ought to respond other than force a shit-eatin' grin and pretend this was all in good fun, they laughing with, not at, him. Inside, he knew that wasn't the case. "Ozzie the Rabbit" became his corps nickname.

It would not go away; not here, not after that ordeal was over and Lee moved on to the specialty he had requested, radar control school in Jacksonville, FL and later Biloxi, MS.

At all four of his stateside bases, Lee was also kidded, sometimes hassled, about something far more disturbing. Copies of communist publications regularly arrived in the mail. Lee could have hid them for private reading; instead, he left such stuff strewn all over his bunk where others could observe what they considered radical material. Two muscle-bound jerks began to turn the screws whenever an occasion arose.

Worse, Perry Sommers, Lee's supposed friend, joined with them in harassment. More than once they tossed Lee in the shower after he finished dressing for dinner. None of this bothered Lee as much as the derisive humor about his sexual status.

How perfect! This is all fitting into my master plan ...

*

One day, early in January 1957, Ozzie was sitting around, playing chess with a fellow fan of the game, when another marine entered the barracks and whispered that Lee was required at headquarters. That seemed odd to everyone but him. Lee smirked, muttering under his breath that it was "about time."

Upon arrival, Lee was curtly escorted down a long hall into a large holding room, empty other than himself, then summoned by several M.P.s to step sharply between them down yet another long corridor, directly to a room at the far end.

"Sit down," a medium-build man in a dark civilian suit commanded. Ozzie did as told, glancing around the tight room.

"Yes, of course," Lee replied, his voice barely able to rise above a whisper. "I take it you're from the FBI?"

"What makes you say that?" The man curiously eyed Lee.

"In all honesty, I thought you would arrive some time ago."

"Explain, Private Oswald."

Lee, feeling more relaxed now that he could momentarily control the narrative, crossed his legs. "This is about the Red literature I receive in the mail, right?"

"As a matter of fact, it is."

"Some of the boys complained to higher-ups, and they thought it best to call you?"

"From the manner in which you speak," the FBI agent sighed, "it would appear that I'm here less by a natural chain of events than your conscious desire to summon me."

"Sir, that is precisely the case."

For the next hour, Lee rambled semi-coherently, the wild words augmented by grand hand gestures that left the agent too stunned to respond. No one was more dedicated to the United States than Lee; he would kill, even die for his country. But how could a no-one like himself make a contribution? Then he watched *I Led Three Lives* and felt inspired to follow suit: read the enemy's books, subscribe to the papers, figure sooner or later, once they had his address, someone would contact him.

He'd learn all their buzz words so that when this happened Lee would know precisely what to say, putting down "American Imperialism" in the post-war world, waxing poetic about power to the people. He'd earn their trust, learn what such traitors and spies had in mind, turning everything over to the government.

Only problem was, Lee had no idea how to contact the right people. He had spent considerable time considering this.

Suddenly, it struck him. All Lee had to do was make known his supposed commie leanings and sooner or later one of the boys would do Lee's job for him by contacting the FBI.

When Lee finally ran out of words and breath, the agent sat completely still, considering all he had been told. Several thoughts passed through the man's mind. First, this scrawny, shrill, excitable marine was nuts. Certifiable, no question about it. Then again, the agent had no doubt that Lee qualified as sincere, his bizarre plot so outrageous that someone in his own profession could not help but admire its carefully conceived madness. Anyone so dedicated, as Oswald clearly was, might have value not to the FBI, their main job to seek out the radicals. However, another arm of the government ...

"Mr. Oswald," the agent explained, "the FBI would not be the proper agency. Still, there are others in our information-gathering community who might wish to speak with you."

"It's an honor just to be considered. Who should I contact, and how do you—"

"That will all be taken care of," the agent said, rising. "I will contact them. They will contact you, *if* they believe it in everyone's best interest to do so."

"They?"

"The Central Intelligence Agency. If they do decide to go ahead, you will be approached by a man called George."

CHAPTER FIVE:
ANY ENEMY OF MY ENEMY

"Political solutions don't work."
—Woody Allen; *Sleeper*, 1973

Having recently returned to the CIA office in Miami following one of his frequent sojourns to Cuba, on January 10, 1957, agent Frank Sturgis, aka George, busied himself with typing a report on the status of Fidel Castro's desire to seize control of the island's politics with his guerilla force. Then the phone on his desk rang. Answering in hopes of keeping the conversation brief, George was pleasantly surprised to hear a familiar voice on the other end, causing him to smile.

"Hey, 'George'? Welcome home. 'Dick Tracy' here."

That could be only one man: Bob Maheu, a former FBI agent now serving several A list companies as a private contractor. Also Maheu performed a variety of chores for the CIA, making key connections between Company agents and potential operatives. He received his nickname owing to an uncanny resemblance to an ever popular square-jawed honest-cop comic-book character featured in the Sunday Funnies and B movies. Flattered by the comparison, Maheu had taken to sporting a yellow hat with black band similar to Dick Tracy so as to heighten the comparison.

"Hey, Robert. What have you got for me this time?"

The disembodied voice explained he'd been contacted by a field agent who had recently completed a routine investigation on a marine, seemingly of Red leanings. Instead, Lee Harvey Oswald turned out to be a super-patriot, if an odd one, as such perhaps of potential use to the U.S. government's information-gathering community. The FBI agent contacted the CIA; the top brass there tapped 'Dick Tracy' to get in touch with George and request he look into it, see if there might be something here.

"Of course," George said. He and his old pal chatted for a few minutes, George jotting down the essential information before returning to more pressing matters. The conclusion of his findings dealt with a Cuban whose friendship George cultivated while in Cuba, a valuable contact named Manuel Artime Buesa.

*

Buesa had been with Castro from the very beginning: i.e., the middle of March, 1952, following a military coup in which Fulgencio Batista seized control of the government and augmented an authoritarian regime to the benefit of Cuba's small moneyed classes if at the expense of the poverty-level multitude. No matter how exploited the dirt-poor masses were, Batista's new regime offered them less; so little that, as always happens when people no longer can feed their families anything but garbage, lacking even that, the likelihood of revolution increases.

Though born to the middle-class, the university educated Castro brothers, Fidel and Raul, felt the people's pain and set about organizing potential rebels in hopes of ousting Batista. Buesa, hearing Castro speak on a Havana street corner, had been attracted by his hulking presence and lawyer's ability to bandy about words, inspiring all who had gathered to listen. That very day Buesa offered his services. For the next year and a half, Buesa and other volunteers trained for the coming day of revolutionary fervor with whatever rifles they could get their hands on, mostly outdated Springfields and Winchesters. In time they came to number more than 160, mostly drawn from the lower-classes. Buesa noted five university-educated intellectuals among Castro's followers. To Buesa's surprise, Castro, despite his own academic background, appeared uncomfortable around such supporters. Several years later, Buesa would learn why.

Just before daybreak on the 26th of July, 1953, as the entire country readied for summer fiesta, a caravan of rickety cars roared down the highway toward the Monacada Barracks in Santiago de Cuba. Each was filled with stalwarts certain that, before the noon hour, they would capture the military compound.

Then, everything that could possibly go wrong proceeded to do precisely that. Unprepared for such an ambitious undertaking, the men ecstatically leaped out of the transports before Castro gave the order to do so. In moments, they were overrun by forces that outnumbered the rebels ten to one. During this skirmish, fifteen members of Batista's army were killed, as were nine of Castro's men. Others were captured. All were tortured, this including castration with rusty razor blades. Some were executed immediately afterwards, most imprisoned.

Fidel and Raoul managed to make their escape into the Gran Piedra mountains, hoping to re-organize there. These survivors were all captured by government forces three days later. In the early fall of that year, the rebels were tried en masse by an Urgency Tribunal. Castro, with his considerable argumentative skill, managed to wrangle his own separate court case at which he belligerently defended himself. No matter; after being found guilty, all were tossed into Presidio Modelo, a noted hellhole, each man sentenced to serve a one-year term there. This, supposedly, to teach each and all a lesson. In the case of Fidel Castro, the miserable food and filthy surroundings had the opposite effect.

During that horrific year, Castro—sometimes in a group cell, on other occasions relocated in solitary—constantly read. At this point democracy, which he expressed interest in as a university student, disappeared from his writings, the theories of Karl Marx coming to dominate his world-view. Buesa, on the other hand, was not won over. As he and Castro had discussed earlier, Buesa preferred to oust Batista, then call for open and honest elections so as to create a democracy, much like the one in the U.S. The now radicalized Castro scoffed, assuring his comrade that in time Manuel would see the error of his ways.

When Batista staged a fixed election in 1954, winning the popular vote overwhelmingly, Castro now had tangible evidence to convince his comrade that the right to vote clearly did not insure that the people would be heard. Buesa did take that into account, still continuing to believe the problem lay not with the idea of elections, rather the patent dishonesty of this one.

The turning point for Castro came from a source closer to home. Mirta had never bought into her husband's revolutionary fervor. She married Castro in 1948 owing to his advanced degrees, believing her husband would soon get over such youthful idealism and set to work earning a living as a lawyer. With Fidel behind bars, she set out to obtain a divorce. Worse, Mirta accepted a job in Batista's government, offered if she would publicly reject her husband's radicalism. Worse still Mirta openly raised Castro's son in Havana's most solidly middle-class neighborhood, as if to announce her subscription to the consumer-values of those rare few able to afford an American-like lifestyle.

Now Castro abruptly turned against the U.S., less for its democratic system than its economic base. If capitalism had corrupted his Mirta, it might do the same to anyone. Communism took on a lustre in missives Castro released from behind bars. Nonetheless, Batista, believing the revolutionaries must, after suffering constant torture, be sufficiently humbled, announced that all would be released on schedule. Batista guessed that the Castro brothers would crawl off into oblivion like whipped dogs.

Upon release, a hardened, bitter, more extremist Castro began sending loyalists out to bomb strategic Batista posts. As innocent citizens were harmed and in some cases killed, Castro insisting this was regrettable but unavoidable, he incurred the wrath not only of their fascistic leader but also moderate liberals and progressives who likewise opposed Batista but still subscribed to non-violent methods. Police were instructed to shoot down Movement members on sight. The Castro brothers, realizing they might soon be dead, quickly decided a strategic retreat was in order. On July 7, they and Buesa slipped away into Mexico.

"I shall return," Castro called out over his shoulder at the moment of departure, the bearded giant who now held the U.S. in contempt ironically echoing a famous American general.

Once in Mexico, where the right-wing government wanted no part of Castro and his insurgent force, the fugitives created a secretive cell dedicated to waging warfare against all dictators everywhere. As a result of this broadening policy, Argentinean doctor Ernesto "Che" Guevera arrived in the mantis-green jungle, joining a burgeoning force that now included several Mexican revolutionaries and people from other Third World Countries. Plus several Americans, claiming to support The Cause.

Among these came a man known only as George. In actuality, this was Frank Sturgis, sent down to infiltrate the guerillas by the CIA. The U.S. had grown concerned as to whether these rangy troops might constitute a viable threat to U.S. interests in the area. Corporations had recently poured immense amounts of money into Latin America, perceiving these as potentially lucrative sites.

Trained in the art of duplicity, George quickly won Castro over. He not only had been accepted into Castro's force but soon became an officer, always at The Beard's side in public, seated beside him at strategy meetings held in the leader's tent. Soon George made it a point to get to know as many other volunteers as possible, hoping to find some weak link in Castro's chain-of-command which he could then manipulate in favor of the U.S.'s crusade against communism. The moment that George first shared cigars with Buesa he knew that here was the man he'd been looking for, quickly cultivating a relationship. The soft-spoken Cuban shortly admitted his discomfort with the manner in which Castro had grown as authoritarian as Batista on the right.

At long last, Manuel grasped why Castro had distrusted the educated members of his group from day one. Any time one would suggest a democratic election of leaders, Castro tore into a fury, disappearing into his tent where his latest young mistress awaited. When Castro finally stepped out into the day-light, he sullenly stalked about camp, staring down whoever dared to speak such sacrilege. Now, it was Castro's way or the highway, not that there were many of those near their hidden enclave.

Buesa was, as George could clearly tell, wavering. Good!

Seven months later, Castro decided the time had come to strike. He secured a leaky leisure-craft, the *Granma,* capable of safely carrying twenty men at most. Castro crowded 82 followers into the time-worn hull, Manuel and George among them. Chugging along, the antiquated boat quietly passed along the river during the late-night hours of November 25, 1956, then slipped out into the gulf unseen by Mexican shore patrols.

During the next several days everyone complained of hunger and filth. One man fell overboard and nearly drowned. They were supposed to land at a designated beachfront in Oriente Province, where comrades would be waiting with provisions, weapons, and trucks. Together all would move in-land, the revolution about to ignite. But when a Cuban army surveillance helicopter spotted them below, plans had to be swiftly altered. The *Granma,* about ready to soon sink anyway, came ashore ten miles away from their mark, swiftly descending in a swamp near Los Colorados.

When the men tried to disembark, some drowned in the bog. Those able to crawl up onto land attempted to push inland only to come face to face with troops, ready and waiting; Batista had been informed of the coming invasion by some traitor in Castro's midst. Castro turned to his trusted officer, George, swearing that when he found out who had done this terrible thing he'd personally strangle the man. George nodded, apparently in solemn agreement, though not making eye contact, offering no reply.

For the next several days, remnants of Castro's ever diminishing guerilla force fought its way from one ambush to the next, trying to reach the Sierra Maestra mountain-range. There, Castro knew, like-minded supporters waited. When the two groups combined, this rag-tag army could disappear into the natural camouflage. Federal troops would be afraid to follow into what might turn out to be an ambush behind every tree. Castro counted noses; including his brother, the men numbered fourteen.

Even George was gone now, apparently killed in one of the fire-fights, though no one had actually witnessed the American going down. Likely, his body lay somewhere back there in the brush, among the dead and dying. The loss of so trusted a man only made Castro all the more determined to eventually win.

"I have not yet begun to fight," he promised, echoing yet another war-hero from the America he ironically despised.

When Batista, sipping wine in his Havana mansion, heard reports of this boast, he laughed out loud, calling Castro a bearded clown. Did this scraggly buffoon actually still believe he could topple a military dictator? The *fool!*

*

In the epicenter of Havana, a huge building constructed in the manner of an ancient Spanish fort rises above the diverse buildings that compose this age-blighted metropolis. Cut from stone, the imposing city-within-the city can be seen for miles by any resident who glances upward at the high-stretching rock on which the prison was long ago painstakingly erected. Since the first day of its existence, this dark, ominous tower has cast an ever-shifting shadow over Ciudad de las Columnas, the city of columns, Cuba's most formidable outpost of civilization.

Initially a humble village, Havana had been founded in 1515 by a loose confederacy of conquistadores and priests. For the better part of five centuries, the heart of Cuba's social and political systems withstood tests against its permanence by natural calamities and man's ongoing strife with his fellow man. Such people enjoyed victories and suffered defeat; won, lost, lived, loved and died; come and gone as if blown in and out by trade-winds. What remained was Havana itself, some days gay, at other times sad. Always lorded over by that black needle, the initial sign of the city any approaching visitor observes.

Adding to the medieval aura, two wide moats circle this edifice, one midway up the incline, the other closer to the top. Each remained crossable only by the wood-and-iron drawbridges that clank up and down following orders from the bastion's current commander, whomever that might be. This position of power had for centuries remained subject to change, no matter how solid any reign appeared. El Castillo del Principe was its name, the one-foot-thick walls dating almost as far back as the first crude mission, located several blocks away. Those who over the ages were interred here, like others living in daily fear of at some point doing or saying something that might cause them to be condemned to this ghastly place, refer to it as El Principe.

Until January 1, 1959, the thousands of prisoners held inside during those middle years of the 20th century were suspected revolutionaries. All had been rounded up by strong-armed military envoys and rudely escorted from their homes—enclaves within the city, small farming villages spread across the 761 mile long island —to this dreaded place. Once inside its clammy structure, they were starved, beaten, interrogated and tortured. In some cases, innocent and guilty alike were dragged back out, forced into canvas-covered trucks, the weeping victims, who grasped their coming fate, carried off to stretches of open land ten miles south of the city, there to be executed.

On several occasions, victims of such mass killings were buried. More often, corpses were allowed to rot in the fields so passing farmers and humble tradesmen would bear witness to what might be their future if they were to join, or even offer tacit support, to the insurgents. See and fear. Fearing, continue to work the fields without question.

Conventional wisdom in Cuba prior to '59: Do not mention democracy, American style, much less the communism spreading across the post-WWII world. To be heard whispering about such things, even in casual mid-day street conversation or after imbibing too much at some crude cantina during evening hours, might well chart a one-way route to El Principe.

No man in his right mind wanted that!

Everyone in Cuba knew that their current leader maintained friendly relations with the U.S. They also understood Batista had no interest in altering his corrupt state by adapting such a constitutional government. The Americans were to be tolerated as they feared those communists that posed a threat to Batista's power. The U.S. government not only closed its collective eyes, allowing vicious tyrants to rule in global hot-spots, but supported them. In some cases, openly; in others, covertly.

Dictatorship, Hitler style, which America had not so long ago opposed, was upheld. That was then; this, now. Anything, according to foreign policy, John Foster Dulles style, was better than communism. In the end, it all came down to a simple philosophy: Any enemy of my enemy is my friend.

*

The situation in Cuba in general, El Principe in particular, altered on a New Year's day that opened the final year of the 1950s. The tower of terror would remain filled with prisoners. What altered was the make-up of those held in the assortment of small, filthy cells, modeled on the interior of a bee-hive. In a period of 48 hours, the constituency in El Principe reversed itself. One American journalist who witnessed all that occurred, Lee Lockwood, immortalized the event in photographs and words.

Batista-friendly American political advisors and Mafia casino owners deserted by plane on December 31, 1958 when their New Year's Eve celebration degenerated into a bloodbath. The dictator absconded in the darkness as his armed forces hastily threw down their weapons, running away to hide in the hills or reversing loyalties, joining the guerilla invasion. Though Castro remained in the Sierra Maestra range, hundreds of miles away, his 26 de Julio Movement swarmed into Havana's streets.

The rebels waved red banners, wielding rifles above their heads, shouting "Down With Batista!" In the early hours of the following day, droves of humble citizens threw open their doors to the motley crew, offering what little beer and wine they possessed to the guerillas now heralded as 'liberators.' Those few who owned cars drove around an open city, honking their horns in unison, eager to let the rebels know that, despite their ownership of such luxury items, they too supported the revolution. It was a great day in the morning, all agreed.

Almost everyone. Ninety-plus-percent of the people had been living in near-starvation under Batista. Less pleased were the one in ten who had achieved middle-class or higher still status, desiring nothing more than to live like their American friends, reveling in the superficial joys of consumer culture. Their first and all-pressing thought: *How do I get the hell out of here? Next question: where in the name of God will I go?*

"We arrived at El Principe," Lockwood wrote, where "wives and mothers" of men long imprisoned "could already be seen struggling up the hill, hauling suitcases, shopping bags, and other containers stuffed with civilian clothing" to replace the filthy white cotton uniforms worn by prisoners. "A roar went up as someone found a key to the jail. A moment later, the prison's massive iron gate was flung open, releasing a hoard of inmates, who surged (out) in a white river, tumbling down the hill."

"Viva Fidel!" they shouted. "Viva Cuba Libre!" Others chimed in: "Viva la Revolucion!" The current Cuban revolution, also too the great world-wide revolution each present sensed must be right around the corner.

After all, considering what had happened here, who or what could possibly stand in their way?

By noon, those who'd served as prison guards found the tables turned, forced into recently vacated cells at gunpoint. In charge marched former prisoners, each with an ax to grind, in some cases literally. Shortly, the onetime oppressors would be joined in communal misery by wealthy citizens who had supported Batista. The wisest among them had already deserted by any means — planes, boats big or small—heading for Miami.

While all revolutionaries love to shout "Solidarity," always they prove incapable of maintaining that state for more than one glorious moment. In several days time, those favoring communism gained the upper hand. Recent comrades who now argued in favor of democracy found themselves in El Principe. From the moment that Castro arrived, it was the revolution according to one man, and only one: Castro. Get with him or get out.

Democracy? No. Moderately applied socialism? No. Hardcore communism immediately became the rule, Castro on the far left as totalitarian as Batista had been on the far right.

Communism, Castro style. Love it or leave it!

The majority of Cubans did the former, or at least accepted this as the new order. A minority, the latter. Cubans of means, favoring democracy and capitalism, embarked on an exodus to America. Among them, Manuel Artime Buesa, crossing the waters in a leaky rowboat with two other men, knowing that if and when he arrived in Miami, he would present himself at the offices of the CIA, offering his services. On that day when Buesa announced himself he was led down a hall to an office door identified by the name 'Frank Sturgis.'

Once inside, Manuel gasped at the sight of an old friend whom he believed had been killed somewhere in the jungle. Standing there with a welcoming smile stood ... George!

*

No one ever moved faster than Johnny Rosselli when he considered himself on a mission from God. It must be noted that the object of Rosselli's worship was not the wrathful Yahweh of the Old Testament nor gentle Jesus of the New but Sam Giancana, considered by others of a different mind-set to be the anti-Christ. Ruthless, intelligent, confidant, vastly experienced in the ways of the world, supremely in control of organized crime in America, hair-trigger quick to judge though slow to fire any literal or figurative gun, employing this as a final solution to serious problems, Sam 'Gold' Giancana possessed many aspects of some worldly-wise mystic, a contemporary Merlin of the Mob. As such, he sized up every situation with the hard, cold, calculated intellect of a Genghis Khan.

That well described what Sam had been contemplating as to The Cuban Situation since New Year's Eve, when Meyer Lansky called in a panic from the Riviera hotel to inform Giancana that Batista, along with his sycophants and all CIA personnel, were making hasty getaways. Concerned, Sam had instructed Lansky to get the hell out there fast. For once, Meyer steadfastly refused a direct order. He and his second wife Teddy remained until the bitter end, earning Sam's immediate gratitude for not doing as told and, afterwards, his lifelong admiration.

As rebels ran wild through the streets, firing guns in the air, shouting the slogans of revolution, drinking themselves into an alcoholic stupor, the hotel's staff deserting, Meyer calmly stepped into the kitchen and did the cooking himself. Teddy, displaying a facade of calm, pranced from table to table, managing a frozen smile while serving the few American and Cuban customers who hadn't yet fled. She and Lansky would shortly leave, with dignity intact. Another high-ranking mobster meanwhile slipped in to replace them.

The chaos continued. Giancana called Santo Trafficante in Tampa, since he was in charge of Cuba since Luciano, now living in Sicily, had decreed this in the 1946 Havana meeting. Clearly, the time had come for Santo to get on top of the Castro problem. As soon as he'd hung up the phone, Trafficante called Las Vegas and asked for Johnny Handsome. No one possessed Johnny's gift for pulling off the impossible.

Johnny? Get your ass to Havana and do so fast!

Three days later Johnny arrived, no one save Giancana and Trafficante aware that the man born Fillipo Sacco had even left Vegas. Johnny took up residence in the Hotel Nacional and held steady for orders. Johnny would wait, calm and quiet, until word arrived from Sam the Man, even now pondering what ought to be done. *We'll play it cool for the time being,* Giancana decided; *wait and see if Castro can be reasoned with. If not? In that case, the Beard must be whacked, and quickly.*

*

Rosselli did not have long to wait. On January 7, after Castro had arrived, headquartering himself on the 23rd floor of the Havana Hilton, The Beard ordered all casinos closed, all gambling banned. The United States, in his estimation, had turned his once clean Cuba into a decadent brothel. Shortly after this announcement aired on Radio Havana, picked up by the networks, a call came through from Santo, who had received one from Sam. Trafficante now reiterated Gold's orders to Johnny.

Minutes later, fully prepared, Rosselli set off on his errand. The streets seemed different than even a day or two earlier, the vivid sense of rich, colorful life that had filled them diminished. People were casting off their bright garb for drab fatigues. Instead of an ecstatic celebration of life Johnny had witnessed, most wandered about in a dull, serious manner. The good ol' days he had so loved to partake of were gone! Perhaps, though, this current assignment might bring them back.

Rosselli arrived at the Hilton, briefed by Trafficante as to what had already become Castro's ritualistic daily habits. Johnny took up a position adjacent to the main doorway. Panic overcame him when he felt one of his irregular asthma attacks coming on. As the mid-afternoon heat abated now that sweet breezes wafted in from nearby waters, Johnny spotted a sudden movement at the door. He reached under his coat for the weapon hidden there, a WWII-era German Luger, Johnny's pistol of choice since becoming one of the Mob's crack shots decades earlier.

Half a dozen figures drifted out of the building, Castro central to the group. Rosselli noted that in front of The Beard a large, rugged man with a Zapata mustache pushed forward. He obviously must have been the chief bodyguard. If only that important call from the states had come two days earlier!

Then Castro, believing himself to have the unanimous support of Havana's citizenry, dared strut about unprotected. That ended when a friend from college days, architect Enrique Avarez, hid in a high/wide modern building across the street from Castro's favorite dining place, the Casalta over on the east edge of town. Avarez planned to shoot his leader with a high-powered rifle, augmented by a telescopic lens, while The Beard gulped down shrimps, drenched in lemon and butter, roasted over coals, the house specialty. At the moment when he must squeeze the trigger, Avarez experienced a sudden failure of nerve and fled.

Spotted running away suspiciously, Avarez was captured. When Castro, face-to-face with the traitor but as yet unable to grasp what his comrade's motivation might be, demanded to know the reason why, idealistic Avarez defiantly shouted that he'd watched televised executions of confused citizens who, for one reason or another, Castro considered his enemies, in some cases rightly, with others wrong, operating as Batista had to supposed rebels. Viewing such brutality in his apartment, Avarez retched at the public spectacle, performed for a rowdy, delighted mob, French-revolution style. On-lookers cheered the flow of blood, purchasing beer and soda from street vendors who had rushed in to, in a capitalist manner, make a fast buck off the event.

Also Avarez complained that, winning over fellow students back in their university days, Castro had presented himself as an open-minded egalitarian. Now, he had revealed himself to be a Communist dictator. A communist, yes, Castro shouted at Alvarez. Not a fascist like Batista. *Do you think it makes any difference if authoritarianism comes from the left rather than the right?* Alvarez demanded. *Yes,* Castro blurted out. *That is where we now disagree,* came the answer, *and why I wish that I'd have had the courage to shoot you.* He spit on Castro and was summarily shot.

When Castro recovered from his shock and humiliation, he arranged from that moment on to be completely surrounded by hand-picked guards. While the big mustachioed man's formidable presence, stepping out of the Hilton as Castro's human shield, might have deterred any citizen-assassin, Rosselli was no such amateur. Schooled in the art and tactics of killing while an apprentice to Al Capone in Chicago, 1922, during the golden era of the Scarface Gang, the looker with thick oily hair and a strong Roman nose drifted around and past the bodyguard like a shadow passing through quick-silver. Rosselli closed in so quickly that no one alive could have stopped him. He whipped out the Luger, slamming its barrel against Castro's thick forehead.

"Do you want to die?" Rosselli softly said. For a moment, the Cuban leader could not form words. His bodyguards were at a loss; any movement might cause this Italian-American in a slick sharkskin suit to kill Castro. Each remained stock-still.

"No," Castro at last managed to whimper in reply.

God ... Gold! Please don't let me cough now!

"Then listen closely ..."

"Pull that trigger," the lead bodyguard ventured, certain he must do something, drawing his own weapon, a .45 automatic, leveling it at Rosselli's temple, "and you die as well."

"A-ha," Johnny laughed, eyes wild, "but there I have you. I don't care if I die or not. The same cannot be said of your glorious leader. Do you grasp my meaning? What's your name?"

"Pupo Valle."

"You cannot win, Valle. Ipso facto, I cannot lose."

"Remain calm, Pupo," Castro ordered, sweating profusely yet in control of his emotions. Then, furtively glancing to Johnny, he inquired, "What is it you want of me?"

Rosselli inched forward and for thirty seconds whispered into Castro's ear. Castro nodded in the affirmative. At that, Rosselli winked, returning his gun back to its leather shoulder-holster under his jacket, turning away from Castro, bodyguards, and a coterie of stunned onlookers. Valle continued to grip his pistol, glancing sideways to his leader for orders. Castro shook his head 'no.' He and Pupo stood together, watching as the man disappeared into a stunned crowd, gone like some bad dream that hauntingly seems all too real the morning after.

"I could have killed him easily as he left."

"Yes," Castro gulped. "And so 'they' would have sent another. Next time, they would finish me without a word."

"Next time, I would have been prepared—"

"No, Pupo. From those like Avarez, I have no doubt you can always protect me. From such as this? It's not your capabilities I question. Much as I hate to admit this, we must learn to live with the Mafia."

Pupo Valle wondered for the first time since the revolution if his exalted leader really was the absolute idealist he and so many other loyalists believed. Would a truly great man speak so? But Valle would keep his own counsel, for to speak such a thing to anyone would be construed as treason. At least for now.

*

The following morning, Castro called a special conference of political advisors, all aware already that their job was not to suggest varying approaches for severe problems to Castro but nod in agreement with whatever he proposed. Unexpectedly, he re-introduced the supposedly-decided issue of Cuba's American-owned casinos. After consideration, Castro pompously announced, he now believed that their country must not entirely isolate itself from the world. Also, the economy must not be allowed to fall into disarray before he developed future plans. With this understood, tourist money remained a necessity, if only for the time being. Of course, for Americans to continue to arrive and spend, they would require that the gambling houses awaited them.

No one in the room could believe what he was hearing. Still they shook their heads in unison, grinning like idiots. On January 17, 1959, all American-owned casinos could re-open. Johnny heard the news on Radio Cuba, grinned at his own effectiveness, and waited for word from the states. Within minutes, the old fashioned ornate white telephone, left over from those decadent days of the late 1920s, rang. This time it was Gold himself, the great one choosing to speak personally (a rarity) to a mob operative, congratulating his man in Havana on a job well done.

Johnny waxed rhapsodic in reply. Clearly, this had been a major upward career-move. He could hardly be held responsible when most American with money, deeply concerned about political unrest in Cuba despite the casino re-openings, turned their backs on Havana and instead flew west to Vegas, until then a gathering place for local rubes. Overnight, that changed. Johnny Rosselli/Handsome would be one Made Man who most profited from that new order.

*

To state that Fulgencio Batista Zaldivar, recently deposed dictator of Cuba, had long despised Rafel Leonidas Trujillo, self-proclaimed president for life of the Dominican Republic, would have been to put the situation mildly. The strong-arm politicians had throughout the 1950s waged a hostile competition for money and valued commodities, including military equipment, from the U.S. Each tried to persuade the American ambassador to his country there was but one true friend on the southern tier, now that the demon threat of communism had spread like prairie fire across Latin America, and that this—*he!*—was that man.

More than once, Batista and Trujillo had been on the verge of open conflict, American operatives intervening. It was in the U.S.'s best interests to keep both in power, armed and ready to train those weapons at the Reds when and if they came. Batista and Trujillo continued to harbor anxieties as to one another; so far as others perceived them, these were the Tweedle-dee and Tweedle-dum of the Third World: self-serving bullies with no concern for the people they pretended to watch over and serve.

Now, though, the Sixties were but a stone's throw away, a new decade ushering in an alternative sense of values. Even as Batista's power structure collapsed around him and on New Year's Eve he took flight for fear his very life was in danger, he knew from reliable sources that Trujillo suffered similar pressure from revolutionary forces in Santo Domingo. Perhaps communists in the Dominican Republican were in cahoots with the guerillas who had seized Havana two weeks ago, these part of an emergent international revolution. In this reconfigured world order, old animosities were forgotten, even as those between the United States and Germany or Japan had been when, after World War II concluded, the U.S.'s recent allies, China and the Soviet Union, waved red flags in defiance, inciting the bulls of the west.

Batista and Trujillo were dictators. If each man chose to posture and pose as a true democrat to appease the Americans, fascistic described their approach to stifling free public elections. Anything that threatened the one worried the other. This partly explains why Trujillo, upon learning of Batista's ouster, invited him to Santo Domingo until, with Trujillo's full support, Batista could convince the U.S. to, by any possible means, return their Cuban 'friend' to power in his homeland.

Today, Trujillo had decked himself out in full military uniform, boasting enough gold-braid to anchor a large ship. Batista instead wore a simple white suit. The two met on this sweltering early-afternoon at the Presidential Palace. Side by side, dwarfed by epic-sized paintings from the classical era, they spoke intimately about what ought to be done to keep the world, at least their corner of it, from spinning out of orbit.

Batista had been rushed to this meeting by a chauffeured limousine from his exquisite hotel. He had registered two days earlier as a paying guest. All financing for himself and his wife's stay, he'd been informed upon arrival, was required up front and in cash. Not a problem, as they'd carried a fortune along when the two scurried out of Havana minutes before the city fell to the rebels. The couple now enjoyed the finest accommodations available in this capital city, Batista's wife enjoying an elegant lobster salad lunch via room service.

Batista and Trujillo, no longer cautious of one another, casually exchanged information. Trujillo explained that he'd ordered Colonel Ferrando, his chief counsul in Miami, to sniff out the CIA agents there. What were The Company's thoughts as to a counter-strike? Would the U.S. openly support such a move or continue to offer only secretive aid? If so, in how long a time might that occur?

Batista, as Trujillo could not have guessed, harbored no interest whatsoever in such a victorious return. Following two sessions as Cuba's man with the iron fist (1933-44; 1952-59), he now only wished to slip away to Europe and live the good life in Rome, Paris, and other such exquisite cities. Certainly he and his wife had on their persons enough money to support such a high lifestyle indefinitely. Batista didn't dare admit this at the moment for fear of his host's wrath if Batista did not at least pretend to share the Dominican's hopes and schemes.

So Batista nodded, his gesture inhabiting some nowhere zone between affirmation and elusiveness, implying without saying so that he'd gladly serve as part of a coalition of Latin politicos opposing communism and seeking aid from the U.S. to defeat it.

Trujillo spoke at length about other countries most likely to fall in with the emerging plan, Nicaragua chief among them.

"You believe, then," Batista wanted to know, "that Nicaragua will allow Cuban exiles to train there, then use their airstrips for a launching point?"

"I do not believe," Trujillo answered with the supreme confidence that always characterized him. "I *know*."

They exited the sumptuous room, furnished with fine antique furniture and majestic statuary, from armless Aphrodites hailing back to the Greek golden age and bold Herculean warriors, their private parts hammered away by Puritan censors, that dated to the High Renaissance in *Firenze*. Each man, cradling a drink, stepped onto the balcony. From there they could observe the wide green fields, handsomely cultivated, stretching as far as the eye could see. How hard to believe, in this elaborately designed escape from the real world of excruciating poverty only a short distance away, that the privileged few inhabiting this palace might soon come under a deadly state of siege.

"When might such an intervention take place?" Batista, intrigued if disinterested, asked.

"Not any time soon, I assure you. The men for such an operation must be recruited, then trained at length, finally guided step-by-step by the CIA."

"Months?"

"If only it could be accomplished in so short a time."

"Years?"

"Several.

"Still, that is better than nothing."

"Amen to that."

"And as for The Company? You believe they can be trusted?"

"Always, you say 'believe'," Trujillo laughed. "Yet always I reply: 'know.'"

Momentarily, Batista stood silent, taking all this in. At last he felt comfortable venturing a conclusion. "Then it is what the Americans call 'a done deal', if in due time."

That gave Trujillo cause to wince. "Yes and no. You see, there is a wild card in our deck. A presidential election will take place in November 1960 in the United States. Already the leading candidates are pre-planning, raising funds ..."

"My guess? Nixon will be the Republican nominee."

"Agreed. A most unpleasant fellow! Still, one we can trust. If he wins, things will proceed as I outlined for you."

"If not?"

"A young senator named Kennedy is even now at work trying to corner the Democratic party's eventual nod. He has some competition: Stevenson once again; the Texan Johnson. Several others too. Still, a sense of inevitability has already begun to surround this young, handsome, charismatic senator."

"If he should succeed?"

"Perhaps he will set aside all the youthful idealistic nonsense he speaks to attract the country's young liberals to him. And, once in office, learn the politics of reality from his senior advisors, then continue in the path of predecessors as to the need for containing communism."

"Yet you imply, obviously, 'perhaps not.'"

"Well, you see, this I don't know. Or, as you would phrase it, 'believe.'"

"So?"

"So, we must both of us remain wary yet hopeful."

The two made eye contact, grimacing at the potential for danger, then accompanied each other back inside. In two hours, a state dinner would begin. Batista's wife Marta was by now preparing her wardrobe, hoping to captivate all attending.

If anyone had told Fulgencia Batista Zaldivar one year earlier that he would come to consider Rafel Leonidas Trujillo a close ally, Cuba's dictator would have laughed. Now? It was an old cliché, Batista well knew, but one proven true, over and over again in world history: any enemy of my enemy is my friend.

CHAPTER SIX:
THE TWINNING

"There are two governments in the U.S. today.
One is visible, the other invisible."
—David Wise and T.B. Ross, 1964

"Like presents?"

"Like 'em? I love 'em."

"Open the glove compartment and see what's inside."

Lee did as George commanded, as always. At this moment he occupied the passenger seat of a black Sedan, George behind the wheel, driving them away from Camp Pendleton, CA. Lee had been reassigned there on January 18, 1957, a year before that heady conversation between Trujillo and Batista would take place on the former's balcony. Lee began serving as a member of A Company, 1st Battalion, the 2nd Infantry training regiment, five weeks previous to this rendezvous with George. On February 27, L.H.O. left the base on an official two-week leave.

This was rare for a marine who had recently arrived and barely begun mastering the skills of Radar operation. None of the others in his company could come up with any logical reason why Oswald, or 'Ozzie' as they referred to the rabbit-like Lee, had been singled out for such sought-after special treatment. In truth, the leave had been arranged by George, he sending the word to the base's commander-in-chief, an officer who well knew that when a request arrived from some heavyweight player in the CIA, that was that. No questions asked.

"I will pick you up at the entrance to Pendleton at one p.m." George had told Lee in a furtive phone call three days previous. "You've been granted a two week leave. Officially, you will be going home to visit your ill mother."

As always, Lee replied affirmatively. The following morning he continued with his daily duties, pretending to be happily surprised when word reached him from headquarters about his upcoming leave. Now, George headed east along the highway.

"A book," Lee said, reaching inside the glove compartment.

"To fill your traveling hours. Recognize the author?"

Lee considered the cover: *Profiles in Courage* by John Fitzgerald Kennedy. Lee admitted to George that most of what he understood about the senator from Massachusetts was but common knowledge. JFK was reputed to have been a great war hero in the South Pacific. He saved his men after their PT boat was sunk by an enemy submarine, swimming in front of the survivors, doing so with one hand as he dragged along a seaman too badly wounded too continue. In the early fifties, Kennedy entered politics, basing his campaign in Boston where his prestigious family held court.

JFK married a debutante, Jacqueline Lee Bouvier, who had recently delivered him a daughter, the newspapers were full of this event owing to the attractive movie-star quality of each parent. Other than that, all Lee knew was that Kennedy had gone after the Democratic party's vice-presidential nomination, in hopes of running with Adlai Stevenson in the upcoming election. On August 17, 1956, this distinct honor had been denied him.

"A temporary set-back," George chuckled. "Believe me. This guy is going all the way to the White House."

"Seriously? But if his own party wouldn't let him—"

"Jack's father, Joseph, has a saying: 'When the going gets tough, the tough get going.'"

"I've heard that. And this book—"

"Ghost-written by a coterie of Ivy League brain-trust intellectuals who view JFK as their Great White Hope. Adlai losing to Ike again they considered a foregone conclusion. Kennedy's clique figures after another four years, the Dems will be ready to accept their boy with open arms. Meanwhile, Jack's at work building his coming campaign machine with a team of experts. Step by step, they're creating a myth around the man: macho in combat, intelligent in repose, gorgeous to look at, particularly when accompanied by his wife. She, by the way, is part of that master-plan, though I doubt the lady realizes it yet. She will! Jack's a womanizer, she his elegant cover-wife."

"If the Kennedys are so powerful, why was that necessary?"

"Now, you're being naive. The Kennedys, understand, are nouveaux riche. Their Irish working-class origins, along with their Catholicity, will cause dumb bigots to pause. The final thing Jack needs for the Total Image is a sense of belonging to an American aristocracy. That can only be achieved by marriage into such a circle. Jackie adds the necessary touch of class."

"But if Kennedy didn't really write this, why bother—"

"*Profiles in Courage* will provide the cornerstone of the emergent Kennedy legend. My outfit is eventually going to have to deal with that as well as him, the person."

"As one of your operatives, I will, too."

"Now you got it. However remote he may seem at the moment, Lee, believe me: in time, John Fitzgerald Kennedy will become the most important person in your life."

*

Lee first met George on November 22, 1957, six years to the day (and for that matter hour) previous to the assassination in Dallas of President John Fitzgerald Kennedy. Still quartered at the San Diego base if already in the process of readying himself for his transfer, Lee received a phone call while in the PX. He was alone there other than a girl on duty behind the counter.

"This is Lee Oswald. Who's this?"

"George."

For a moment the name didn't register. Lee ran through all the Georges he had ever encountered. Then, it hit him. *George!* The person that the FBI agent had told him about.

"Oh, yes. George. Of course! Hello."

"Lee, I'd like to meet with you to talk a bit."

"I'd be delighted." Lee was careful not to say too much while in hearing distance of the girl. However unlikely, she could be a Soviet spy. Lee knew that such things happened. After all, he'd watched each and every episode of *I Led Three Lives*.

"Jot down this address," George said. "Meet me tonight—"

"I'll have to see about a pass."

"Already arranged. Waiting for you at H.Q."

Lee yanked a napkin from a nearby container, then picked up a pencil stub lying on the counter. "Okay, ready."

Just as I guessed, the waitress mused. *That marine's a queer. Heading off now to meet the man he arranged with for a late-night tryst. As always I can spot faggots a mile away!*

*

As no direct bus line yet existed between the San Diego Marine Corps base and San Ysidro Port of Entry at the city's southernmost tip, Lee, in civvies, had to change three times. At the main bus depot he disembarked and hopped aboard the San Diego Trolley, which delivered him to the post. There, the guards awaited those wishing to cross over from the United States to Mexico's Northern-most city, Tijuana. Lee presented his identification to an uninformed Mexican who signaled him on.

That was easy!

94

Lee joined the gathered mass, sweating as he always did when forced to be part of a crowd. Among those also trickling into the foot walk from one country to the other was a mixed batch of Anglos and Latinos. Once in downtown Tijuana, Lee hailed a cab to drive him over to Rosarito Beach, a separate nearby community known for its red-hot row of clubs and bars.

Eventually they pulled up to the address. Lee recognized the name "Villa's Hideaway" above the door from George's call. Inside, the lighting proved dim but colorful, the walls crowded with Mexican kitsch including paintings of the country's own film and music-biz celebrities, Pedro Armanderiz, decked out in a Pancho Villa costume he'd worn in films on the folk-hero, prominent among them.

Lee pushed his way past low-hanging papier-mache renderings of blue bulls and bone-white models of the human skeleton, past scattered customers at the bar and tables, all the way to the back end. In an adjoining small room, set back in the furthest corner, sat an American in a beige suit with nondescript tie.

'George?' Lee mouthed the name without emitting a sound. A nod let him know that here was his coordinate. Lee stepped up to the table where the American signaled for him to sit.

"Hello," Lee now ventured to softly say.

"Lee Harvey Oswald, I presume?" George inquired, extending a hand for shaking. Lee responded in kind. "Everything you told the FBI man, I already know. I'd like to learn more about you. Any further details, please share with me now."

After a pretty Latina served Lee a beer, he rambled on. He could now accurately fire a rifle, if need be, in the line of service. Following his embarrassing moment on the range with that snarling sergeant, Lee practiced alone whenever he could until he became accurate enough to win the prized Sharpshooter distinction. Now, he rated as a *marine*; a man!

Lee had begun, in addition to leaving communist reading matter on his bunk, to openly spout phrases concerning "the disparagement of the common worker under a corrupt capitalist system" and the "obvious American imperialism taking place in the Third World." Most marines stepped away; a few threatened his life. On more than one occasion Lee was beaten by unknown assailants. All of this finally paid off: he had been invited to attend a meeting of San Diego's secretive communist cell.

Though people in attendance had only referred to each other by nicknames, leaving Lee unable to share with George their identities, he had taken close note of their appearances. Lee could relate these in detail to George if that might be of any value. Lee had arrived here to help his country, in any way he could, by creating an alternative Lee Oswald: a pinko facade that covered his real patriotism completely. When Lee finished, he knew from George's eyes that the CIA man had been impressed.

*

Three weeks later, an hour and twelve minutes after picking Lee up at the camp's entrance, George turned onto the well-traveled highway, abandoning it for a primitive road, clearly a forgotten relic of the 1930s. More surprising still, they later turned onto a rough dirt pathway from back in frontier days.

"My guess is that you'll finish the book by the time you arrive at your destination."

"Which means I'll be traveling for several hours?"

"Longer than that. You'll arrive tomorrow morning."

"Am I flying?" George nodded affirmatively. "Is there some secret CIA airport out here in the middle of nowhere?"

George glanced over, smiled, then returned his eyes to the path. "Assume whatever you like, Lee. No, there is no airport. I think you'd have to go a long way to even find some old deserted prospector's shack in this stretch of desert."

"It's like, if there's an edge to the world where people might drop off and disappear into a void, this is it."

"You got that one right." With that, George pulled over onto a long, flat stretch. In the moonlight, a few misshapen cacti located on the far side of a cleared-out square stretched toward the cream-colored moon, like the ghosts of some ancient Spaniards. Lee knew enough to step out without being told.

George, maneuvering around to the sedan's head lights, motioned for Lee to join him. A bit nervous, Lee did. "Lee, have you ever heard the term 'twinning'?"

Lee mulled that over. "I don't believe so."

"While we're waiting, let me explain. Twinning is the most extreme form of plastic surgery. 'Plastics', as medical people refer to it. Designed to restore a person's face to a normal appearance in the event a birth defect or accident."

"Sure."

"Well, twinning takes that premise a giant leap further. Eight plastic surgeons in the world, tops, are accomplished enough to perform this technique, though the concept is simple to explain. 'Twinning' means the making-over of one person's face in the precise likeness of another's."

"Wow. But how does this have anything to do with me?"

96

"In terms of the services you have volunteered for—and, Lee, let me remind you again, they are essential to the well-being of the U.S.—the Company requires that you have a double."

Lee took that in, stunned. "Someone who looks just like me? God, I wouldn't wish that on anyone."

George laughed. "Be that as it may, this is a necessity. Now, I must tell you too that you do not have to go through with it. If you wish, you may drop out of the program now."

Lee pulled himself up as straight and tall as he could. "I volunteered, didn't I?" George nodded. "I'm committed. Fully!"

"Glad to hear that," George sighed, relaxing. More than Lee could guess. Despite George's magnanimous offer of a moment ago, the CIA operative's orders were to, if Lee expressed hesitation, draw his .45 automatic from its shoulder holster right beneath George's jacket and execute Lee Harvey Oswald at once.

"I am interested to know, though: Why do I need one?"

"It has to do with your eventual planned defection to Moscow that I mentioned last time we met. At times, you might be needed back in the states. Whenever that occurs, your double will secretively enter the Soviet Union, assuming your place until you are able to return."

"Incredible," Lee responded, grinning with anticipation.

*

"So," George said in Villa's Hideaway in the late-evening of November 22, the first of three meetings there. "Now I know the life and times of Lee Harvey Oswald."

"If you want a dedicated American willing to go down in history as a traitor if need be, so long as he serves his country and serves it well, that's me."

One of the best at what he did, George had thoroughly researched Lee Harvey Oswald before this first meeting. Reports from sources as far-flung as Bethlehem in Louisiana to the Youth House in New York provided telling hints as to the personality of this over-anxious volunteer. George's job had been to take such jagged pieces and fit them into a revealing jigsaw puzzle.

One of the comments from Dr. Renatus Hartogs had far more meaning to the CIA agent than the good doctor likely intended. Lee "dislikes intensely talking about himself and his feelings." That ranked high among those traits any experienced CIA agent hoped to find in an inexperienced would-be operative. To Frank Sturgis, it was imperative that a potential operative be not only able to keep his mouth shut but be strongly inclined to privacy. Always there would be enemy agents feigning friendship to get a still-green operative to open up and spill his guts.

97

The word "feelings" struck George as the most important; stoicism was essential. The lack of such a trait made a man vulnerable, in particular to the beautiful women invariably recruited by the KGB to open up a naive man, he blurting out everything he knew once she tapped into his emotions.

Adding to this were the observations of a Youth House social worker, Evelyn Strickman, who had tagged Lee as "a rather pleasant" young man with an "appealing quality" despite his being "emotionally starved" and, as a result, an "affectionless youngster." The lady had not only reasserted Dr. Hartogs's statement about Lee's relationship to his own emotions, going a giant step further, implying he might actually be incapable of feelings. That, at least in the proper context, Lee could come off as "pleasant" and "appealing" was important if he were going to win over members of the KGB in an intricate plan that Sturgis and Company head-honcho Allen Dulles were developing.

Despite all these dark aspects, Lee had struck George from day one as naively innocent. An intriguing aspect of the mix!

One element troubled him, though: the fact that while attending school in the New York area, Lee flatly refused to salute the U.S. flag. This had provided incentive for several brutes to beat him in the playground during recess though that did not deter Lee from his decision.

"You tell me you are a patriot," George had asked Lee point blank, "and yet ..." He quoted the report verbatim.

"Show me the stars and stripes whenever you like," Lee responded. "I'll jump up and salute. See, that was at the time when my master-plan first began to take shape. I had to plant the thought in others' minds as early as I could that I was turning anti-American. At school, jobs, even the marines; always I had to do something to make people suspect I'm a Commie."

"So that they would contact you, then you'd contact us?"

Lee grinned, nodded, and told his inquisitor all about his experiences in Beauregard Junior High after Marguerite made the decision to abandon New York as a bad idea and return them both to New Orleans. For once, Lee actually found a friend. Fellow teenager Edward Voebel shared Lee's interest in aviation. They joined the Civil Air Patrol, a boy's club. Lee made sure his fellow fifteen-year-old saw copies of *The Communist Manifesto* whenever Ed visited. If Voebel were in the future questioned by any government official, he would verify that Lee harbored Red leanings way back then. Another friend, Palmer E. McBride, like Lee appreciated classical music, the only kind Lee listened to other than Sinatra. After Lee shared copies of the *Socialist Call*, a magazine Lee subscribed to, McBride's father said that Lee could never come to their house again. That was alright; Lee was establishing a false front which, as such incidents accumulated, would eventually bring party members around to meet him.

"Usually," George admitted, "we have to do a great deal of legwork in setting up a 'legend.' You appear to have covered most of the bases on your own."

"Legend?"

"Our term for the alternative you. The Lee Harvey Oswald of public perception as compared to the one who actually exists."

"I see."

Do you, Lee? I hope so. If you do, this could prove more important than you, or even I, can imagine at this moment. If not—if you ever make the ultimate mistake of confusing the one with the other—all hell could someday break loose!

*

"Lee, this is where I must leave you for now."

George, aka Frank Sturgis, stepped around the car and proceeded to slip back into the driver's seat, preparing to head off.

"You're going?" Lee asked in a panic. He glanced around. The desert now appeared as something out of a nightmare about the southwest: a vast, empty expanse in the darkness, where life consisted only of snakes, spiders, other unthinkable monsters dating back to pre-history. The land itself might swallow him up, so formidable was the white sand below, the black sky above.

"Yes. I must."

"But—" Lee gulped, panicky.

"No buts." Without another word, George smiled cryptically, waving his left hand in a circular gesture of farewell. Then he backed up the sleek Sedan, turning it around, heading back down the barely visible path. In a moment, man and machine were gone as completely as if neither had ever existed.

Now, Lee could make out sounds, somewhere in the far distance, moving his way: animal sounds, small feet whirring at rapid speed; something else leglessly swirling toward him in a serpentine fashion. Uncontrollably, he began to shiver and shake.

Maybe all that had gone before was only some carefully planned ruse to eliminate Lee Harvey Oswald from the face of the earth. Yes, that was it! First the FBI agent, then this CIA operative, decided Lee was crazy. Someone in need of elimination.

How could I have been such a fool? My God, I'm their patsy. Why wasn't it obvious from the beginning that—

At that moment, Lee heard something above, a loud, churning noise. Perhaps it was one of those flying saucers everyone was

99

talking about, the CIA in league with Men from Mars to destroy poor little ... as the clouds moved on and moonlight again rendered his surroundings visible, Lee spotted a helicopter as it descended onto that flat stretch of land. Once it was down, a young man in casual clothing waved to Lee from behind the control panel inside his thick glass and steel bubble. Relaxing at least a little, Lee stepped up to the whirlybird.

"Lee Oswald?" the pilot asked. Lee warily nodded. "Hi, I'm Bill. I'll be taking you the next stretch of your trip."

"To the hospital?"

"No," Bill laughed. "That's way too far for my copter. I'll drop you off at a small Company airport. There, you'll board a private jet, then be on your way to—"

Whirlybird? Secret airport? Private jet? Lee calmed down, thrilling to the cloak-and-dagger goings-on. He'd made it! For the first time, Lee Harvey Oswald knew what it was like to be one of the boys. And, beyond that, a Very Important Person.

*

On February 28, 1957, Dr. Angelo Martinelli, recently turned fifty but feeling ages older, rose as he did every morning at six o'clock. Leaning over in the darkness he gently kissed the cheek of his sleeping wife. Sara did not stir. Angelo rose from the bed, went through the process of washing, shaving, dressing, afterwards peeking on each of his sons, both asleep in their rooms. Not a worry in the world passed through those happy childish heads. Angelo attempted to recall a time when he had known such wondrous oblivion. An image began to take form in his memory of himself as a boy, fishing at a clean, clear lake, his dog barking nearby. Before that picture, real or imagined, could reach full fruition it disintegrated, falling away from Angelo's conscious mind, lost somewhere in time, space and imagination.

"See you all soon," he softly whispered.

Yawning, Angelo descended the stairwell of the handsome, tasteful, upscale penthouse suite he and his family owned in upper Manhattan. In the kitchen, Angelo brewed himself a pot of coffee, sipping a cup while reading the morning paper. Leafing through its pages, Angelo did not appreciate most of what he confronted. One bright spot: in Rome, representatives from the democracies were moving close to approving a treaty that would establish a European Common Market. This would further unify America's allies, which Angelo, a patriot, found promising.

Otherwise? Bleak! Down in Little Rock, AK a spokesman for the school board insisted that the following autumn their stand on segregation of the races would remain in place. Surely, Pres.

Eisenhower must move to break that stranglehold, employing military force. Good for him, and about time. Still, that could only weaken an already strained sense of solidarity in the U.S. at a crucial juncture when we needed just that more than ever.

The race for nuclear supremacy between our country and the U.S.S.R. continued as America and Russia announced plans to shortly test new, high-power ICBMS in the ongoing vicious contest for supremacy in our post-atomic-world.

Last, but hardly least, the military dictatorship of Gen. Marcos Pérez Jiménez in Venezuela had been sorely tested during the past week by open rebellion. The people, undernourished and now aware from independent news sources that well over fifty per cent of that nation's huge oil profits poured directly into the pockets of those at the top, were no longer willing to quietly accept their miserable lot in life. Who could blame them?

The problem, as Angelo saw it, involved a free and constant flow of Venezuelan oil into the U.S. If a revolution were to succeed and if it took on a communist attitude, favoring Russia over the U.S., the very sort of chaos ready to explode in at least a half-dozen other Latin American countries, this might limit the U.S.'s ability to buy all the oil it needed cheaply. That could put the U.S. at a huge disadvantage to the Soviets, perhaps turning the tide of world domination in their favor.

By five of seven, the doctor had retrieved his new Cadillac from an adjacent garage and sat behind the wheel, driving away from uptown New York to the George Washington Bridge, crossing over into New Jersey. This was highly irregular. On most days, Martinelli parked at one of three Manhattan hospitals where his skills were in high demand. Not today. He'd been informed by his Mob contact, Johnny Rosselli, that he would be required at their establishment, hidden deep in an all but unknown and virtually unapproachable stretch of Appalachia.

As a poor boy decades earlier, Angelo Martinelli, his desire to become a doctor and heal those in pain hardly a secret, had been approached by a representative of the Made Men: We'll take care of you if afterwards you take care of us. Your university and medical school bills will all be covered by a secret benefactor. When you graduate, most of your time will be your own. Here's the catch: you must earn a degree in the advanced study of plastics. At rare times, you will be called upon to perform operations for us; twinnings, as we refer to them.

Martinelli had requested several days to think it over. That was fine; if he chose not to take the offer, no problem. If he did opt to do so, he was 'in'. *Forever.* Two days later Angelo returned to the meeting place, a Jersey shore bar, presenting his own variation on 'the deal.' Yes, he would do that, so long as he was absolutely guaranteed of one thing: Never, under any circumstances, could he be used to create such a double if this 'twin' were to be employed for violent purposes of any sort.

That never even occurred to us, Angelo was assured. *Look, it's simple: Sometimes guys get in deeper than is good for us or them and need to disappear, go off and for the rest of their lives enjoy the suburbs. Maybe head to Europe, even back home to Sicily. The hard part is getting out of the country, or in the U.S. remaining unidentifiable to any enemies. So we have specialists, called in on such occasions, to alter his identity.*

Nothin' more, nothin' less. So! Do we have a deal?

That, Martinelli sighed, wishing there were another way to become a doctor, knowing there wasn't, I can handle it. He only hoped the Made Men meant what they now said, praying that they would not at some time in the future decide ... that was then, this is now—things change—all the old deals are without warning null.

Forty-two minutes after leaving home, Martinelli turned off the main highway, driving down a rock-formation road so outdated most Garden State residents were not aware of its existence. This led to a more primitive path still, circling around through a thick forest, nearly a jungle; similar to what Joseph Conrad, in Angelo's favorite novel, had tagged the heart of darkness. All at once, he was out in the open again, driving across a field of what appeared an isolated, innocuous farm.

*

"What's up, Doc?"

Judging from the look in the gaunt plastic surgeon's eyes, Lee guessed he had just committed a faux pax by trying to appear lighthearted as to this upcoming twinning process. The doctor, who had initially eyeballed Lee, turned away, glancing down at the floor, clearly not at all pleased.

"Hello yourself," he muttered.

Turning serious in tone, hoping this might possibly solve everything, Lee stretched forward his hand for shaking. "I'm—"

"No, please. I don't want to know your name. Nor should you be familiar with mine. The more hush-hush this remains, the better all around, for everybody. Particularly you."

They stood together in a pleasant waiting room, to which Lee had been summoned by a slick, handsomely oily fellow in a form-fitting sharkskin suit. The man known to Lee throughout his stay at the hospital only as 'Johnny.' He'd met Lee at 3:35 A.M. when the bumpy, late-arriving flight landed at this hospital, designed to appear from any angle including the air as a farm.

Johnny brought Lee to his whitewashed cabin, attractive and comfortable. Johnny returned to wake Lee at six-thirty with a knock at the screen door, apologizing for the early hour. Lee laughed, explaining that this was a gift. In the Corps, everyone had to rise and shine at five. Johnny seemed amiable though Lee sensed this ruggedly built Sicilian was not someone to underestimate.

Johnny accompanied Lee from the pleasant cabin to breakfast in a large, agreeable dining room. Several other people seated at white plastic tables on matching seats. An attentive waiter quickly arrived.

"Are they all here for 'twinnings'?" Lee dared inquire.

"No, no," his host laughed. "Only you, this time around. Everyone else, other than the regular doctors who work here, have arrived owing to ... well, you know ..."

"No. I don't know anything."

"Gunshot wounds. That sort of stuff."

"Oh, sure. Suffered in the line of duty. But ... why not simply take them the nearest hospital?"

Johnny considered Lee curiously. "Well, there *are* reasons sometimes why these things have to be kept quiet, Lee."

Lee didn't press the issue any further. The bacon and eggs proved perfect, an extreme contrast to what passed for breakfast on the base. God, almighty! Was that only three days earlier? It seemed an eternity, as if he'd passed into an alternate galaxy.

When Lee finished, Johnny gave him the look-over once more, than accompanied Lee to the meeting place. Crossing over a turf so green it resembled a plush golf course, Lee spotted a fellow of about his size firing an automatic rifle at targets.

As it happened, the shooter took a brief break in his practice as Lee and Johnny passed near to him. Smiling, he stared at Lee for a moment, then waved: "Hey, guy. What d' ya know?"

"That's him," Johnny offered, guessing Lee's thoughts.

"The man who's going to look like me?"

"Right. You've got the easy part. He's in for an ordeal."

"Why am I needed for two weeks, then?"

They'd reached the main building, the one that appeared an immense barn but which, on entering, Lee saw for what it was: a hospital facility as advanced as anyone could ask for. "It's a slow, painstaking process. The Doc will need to photograph and re-photograph you. He may not like the original mold and need to create another. When you do leave, the procedures on the other

103

guy will be complete. He'll of course remain here, bandaged and under 24-7 medical surveillance, for another three weeks."

Lee followed Johnny up a circular staircase to the second floor. "Then I won't be able to see the results—"

"Nah. You wouldn't wanna anyway. It's kind of eerie, y' know, looking at your own twin."

They reached the top of the stairs and entered the waiting room. An exquisite silver pitcher contained rich coffee. Servants had neatly surrounded this with saucers and cups that struck Lee as the sort that might be used for High Tea in some English manor.

If they could see me now! All of them, any of them ... the kids in New Orleans and Fort Worth ... the boys in the orphanage and later Youth House, the grown-ups running those places ... the marines back at base, others I trained with ... they'd never believe it ... me, Lee Oswald ... here! ... in a place catering to the special, the elite, the chosen few ... a place they'll never see, other than in the movies ... I'm here, now ... as if I've entered into a Hollywood film ... all my life, I've anticipated this moment ...

*

"What am I expected to do in my off hours?" Lee asked.

"Relax," Johnny told him. "Enjoy yourself. The dining room's always open. There's a game room if you enjoy pool, table tennis, that sort of thing."

"I like to read a lot."

"Fine. You can do that by the pool or in the privacy of your cabin, whichever you prefer."

Why had I worried that this might be an ordeal? Everything here sounds like a free vacation at a resort. The only thing confusing is the ornateness of it all. From what George has said during our meetings, I had the impression that under Allen Dulles, the CIA was not in the habit of throwing a lot of money around on luxuries for its agents. How do they justify this?

Lee's fascination with the place continued to mount during the following weeks. Initially, he read in his own room, feeling insecure about taking advantage of those amenities. On the third day, having finished *Profiles in Courage,* he moved on to *The Trial* by Franz Kafka, more in line with Lee's preferences in literature. Lee slipped into the pair of swimming trunks in his brightly painted room. Carrying a towel along Lee strolled over to the pool. On arrival he was stunned to see several of the most beautiful women he had ever observed other than in the movies stretched out on lounges. Each wore a bikini so brief they would have put the new French starlet, Brigitte Bardot, known for her daringly skimpy swimsuits, to shame.

One blonde, lying face down, raised her head, strands of hair whirling all over, signaling to Lee to come on over and take a nearby lounge next to her. Gulping, Lee did as indicated. He also fell madly in love with her at first sight.

"Hi, I'm Honey."

"I'll say you are! I'm Lee."

"Perfect timing, Lee. Would you please undo my top and rub some oil on my back? I don't want to burn."

"Sure," he managed to reply. Moving on to her lounge, his legs rubbing up against hers, Lee did as requested, snapping the plastic pieces apart, allowing the strings of her top to fall gracefully, one to either side. Lee reached for her container of lotion and squirted some on Honey's back. The blonde then shivered slightly and giggled. Lee rubbed it in, over, across, around ... every contour of her already tan and perfectly proportioned backside, augmented by the white material.

"Ooooh, Lee-eee," she whispered provocatively.

That pleasurable task accomplished, Honey smiled again and thanked Lee. Swallowing hard, he settled down on his own lounge and attempted to concentrate on Kafka. Suddenly, though, that surrealist's dark vision, one which ordinarily would click with his ever-depressed mind, struck him as ridiculously out of place in this wondrous playground for ... the CIA?

Johnny strolled up, wearing another slick suit, equally impressive to yesterday's if a slightly different shade of gray.

"Hello, Honey. Hey, Lee. What're you up to?"

Lee admitted he was trying to read but could not get into his book. Johnny retrieved a paperback from his inner pocket and tossed it over. "Try this. Just finished it."

Lee thanked Johnny and glanced at the cover. On it, the title was emblazoned in bright red lettering across the top: *Casino Royale*. The author's name, Ian Fleming, appeared at the bottom. The picture featured a rugged looking fellow with cold, hard, merciless eyes. A pair of beautiful, nearly naked women, one blonde, the other brunette, stood behind him on either side, nestled against the man's back shoulder-blades.

Lee considered the image; his dream vision of the way he, like any man, wished his life would be. Of course, this was only some paperback fantasy, concocted in the creative imagination of the author. Yet, Lee guessed, there had to be at least an iota of truth to it. Somewhere, *somebody* lived like this.

Why not me? Hey, I'm doing that right now! From the slums of New Orleans to ... this? My God! I'm halfway there.

"Agent James Bond, 007," Lee read from the prologue. "Licensed to kill."

"Great stuff," Johnny assured him. They made plans to shoot pool in mid-afternoon. How about that? This super-cool Sicilian, treating me as his guest of honor. Johnny asked if there might be anything Lee would like. Honey piped in that she could use a martini. Lee, wanting to be a part of everything, echoed that he'd very much enjoy one, too.

Johnny nodded, then left as quickly as he had come. A while later a brunette, also sporting a skimpy bikini, hers blue, marched up carrying a small tray. With a smile as sweet as Honey's she served the drinks, promising to be back briefly to see if there might be anything else they should desire.

A half an hour later, Honey requested Lee redo her back-strap so that she could head over to her cabin. That task accomplished, Honey rose, allowing Lee an ever better angle of vision on her remarkable body. Before stepping away, Honey mentioned that she'd be busy for the remainder of the day but, if Lee liked, she could stop by his cabin at midnight.

In a suddenly hoarse voice, Lee answered that he would be delighted. Brushing her long-flowing blonde mane against Lee's face, she winked provocatively and strutted away.

*

After the game of pool with Johnny, Lee had to report to the doctor for more photographs and the fitting of yet another mold. With Dr. Martinelli stood another surgeon, Dr. Joe Battle, considerably younger, also Sicilian, introduced as Martinelli's assistant. Following that, Johnny accompanied Lee to dinner. More beauties dined with middle-aged men in sharkskin suits.

"I tell ya, Johnny. Never in a million years would I guess that those guys are CIA agents. They just don't look the part."

"They're not. GoodFellas. Get my drift?"

Lee didn't, but he was too busy anticipating whether Honey would actually show to think much about it. Later, Lee retired to his cabin, passing the hours by trying to concentrate on *Casino Royale*. At the stroke of midnight there came a rapping from out front. Wearing the luxurious, plush white robe he had discovered in the closet, Lee opened the door. Honey, as good as her word, now wearing a golden wrap that fit her body like a tightly twisted piece of cellophane, entered without a word. The blonde slipped her arms around his shoulders and kissed him hard.

When Lee awoke the following morning, Honey was gone. With her lipstick she'd left a note on his bathroom mirror:

see you later by the pool?
—XXX! Honey

Feeling like a million bucks, whistling a happy tune, Lee shaved and shampooed. Somewhere between showering and brushing his teeth, Lee's ultra-logical mind, always sharpest in the early morning hours, returned to a topic that had been forcing its way into his consciousness: This hospital is not owned and operated by the CIA. The grounds here belong to the Mob!

Ipso facto, if that's the case, then the Combination is in bed with The Company. Which means I'm working not only for the U.S. government but also organized crime.

Jesus H. Christ! This is so freakin' cool ... .

CHAPTER SEVEN
CHANGING OF THE GUARD

"Every story must have a beginning, a middle, and
an end—though not necessarily in that order."
—Jean-Luc Godard, 1963

Midway through 1959 mobster Johnny Rosselli, aka Johnny
Roselli, aka "Handsome Johnny R.," aka "Johnny Handsome," aka
a half dozen other monikers (born in Esperia, Frosinone province,
Italy), then recently returned to the U.S. following the debacle in
Cuba, did something he'd never before considered: the 44-year old
asthmatic drove to an L.A. art house to catch a French film.

With *subtitles*, no less!

Previously Johnny had always guffawed at the thought of
watching anything but a Hollywood picture. He enjoyed the glossy
color items 20th Century Fox produced with that woman The Boys
liked to think of as 'their girl,' Marilyn Monroe. Also the sort of
cheesy crime flicks he'd overseen while executive-producing low-
budget items on Poverty Row during his brief turn as a co-
producer. Rosselli had been the executive who made certain that,
despite weak productions values, such B budget (at best) items
conveyed the flavor and heat of America's big cities.

Recently, some guy he knew whispered that one of those new
European films the intellectual set adored had been dedicated to
none other than ... Johnny! ... more or less.

*Wait a minute here. Aren't those frogs highbrow types who
likely never even heard of me? This, I gotta check out. God knows I
never thought I'd drive half-way across town to see somethin'
called* A Bout de Souffle *... what does that even mean?*

All the same, here he was: seated in a drab, clammy old bijou,
one of those places where movies were referred to as cinema. In
the lobby they served wine and cappuccino rather than popcorn
and Pepsi. Rosselli watched as the house lights dimmed and the
film's American title, *Breathless*, appeared.

*

When 91-year-old Robert Maheu attempted to rise up out of
bed on the morning of August 4, 2008 he felt a sudden sharp pain

tearing upward toward his heart and instinctively sensed that in a second or two he would be dead. Like a proverbial drowning man whose life passes before his eyes, providing just enough time to decide whether or not he can justify his existence, Maheu's mind flashed back to his education at Holy Cross, particularly those Jesuit values that he'd learned there. One stood out vividly: *Though Shalt Not Kill.* How could Dick Tracy resolve that ideal with his own involvement during the early 1960s in Operation 40, the plot to secretly rid the world of Fidel Castro?

Now, as always since that day of his recruitment, Maheu remained loyal to a theory that way back then allowed him to, if against his better judgment, accept an invitation into a complex spider-web of men, motives, and mechanisms geared to achieving a single goal. All the while hoping he'd been right in believing the greater good of America must remain his top priority. Maheu adhered to an attitude he'd learned from Johnny Rosselli, a questionable source at best, while each was operating out of Vegas. All the same, characters like that could sometimes come up with unexpected bits of worldly-wisdom.

Once, while sharing late night drinks in the neon-bathed bar of a Mob-owned casino, Maheu blurted out: "How do you go on living, believing as you say you do in a God, when you have performed acts that make even me, a former FBI agent who has witnessed pretty much all that's out there, cringe?"

Johnny switched positions, flashing a look of lizard-like comprehension. "Here, 'Dick Tracy,' is your answer. A Sicilian saying goes like this: The thief knows he is not so bad because he is not a killer; a killer knows he is not so bad because he is not a rapist; a rapist knows he is not so bad because he is not a child molester; the child molester knows ..."

Even as, in 2008, the elderly Maheu began a slow spiral to the floor, he attempted to offer up a combination of prayer and confession to the Catholic God he still worshipped. If Johnny had been right, the mobster's words recalled by Dick Tracy in the split-second he had left to live, no matter how terribly we sin, always there is someone else who has done something far worse. Might I then be admitted to purgatory, if not heaven? Otherwise, Maheu had just begun his long descent down to hell.

*

"It takes a lot to get Ike mad," Sheffield Edwards, CIA Director of Security, confided to Bob in the former's D.C. office, "but he's mad as hell right now."

"Understandably so," Maheu replied. Shef referred to Fidel Castro's ever more hostile statements about the U.S. in Radio

Havana broadcasts. Since seizing power a year and three months earlier, Castro had veered far from his initially hopeful stance as a democratic liberator to something more disturbing to the U.S.'s interests: a hardcore communist. As such Castro left himself vulnerable to what U.S. spies had decoded from messages between Havana and Moscow: the Russian premiere Nikita Khrushchev recently proffered overtures to the Cuban leader about setting up nuclear weapons, pointed at the United States, a mere 90 miles away from U.S. shores. In return, Cuba would receive more financial and military aid than ever.

Nothing, at the Cold War's height, could so swiftly spread fear through America's defense community. The existence of U.S. and Russian nuclear sites equally distant from one another had serious implications. But if this were to become a reality, a delicate balance would be diminished in Russia's favor.

"It'll come as no surprise to you that we've had our agents down there attempting to undermine Castro for the better part of a year. It hasn't worked. Now, we must kick it up a notch."

"And you believe I can be of service?" Maheu asked as he considered the situation on that second day of March, 1960. Though he'd left the FBI in 1947 to open offices as a private consultant and investigator, first in Washington D.C. and, after considerable success, California as well, Dick Tracy was often contacted by the CIA to make key connections owing to his great expertise as an arbitrator between difficult personalities.

"Yesterday, Dick Bissell asked me to come up with someone who might put us in contact with members of the corporation that owns the gambling casinos in Havana." By that, Maheu knew, Shef meant The Mafia. Even in the intimacy of his own security-savvy office, such a high-ranking government official hesitated to openly admit such a thing. As for Bissell, Maheu knew that any statements from the CIA's Deputy-Director for Plans would have reached Bissell from Allen W. Dulles, current Director of The Company; this only after Eisenhower ordered Dulles, through his higher ranking brother John Foster D., to 'do something.' "Anyway, I ran through some names of people I've relied on in the past. Yours, Bob, more or less jumped up and out at me."

That sounded reasonable. Once Maheu won over Howard Hughes, the bizarre megalomaniac of a multi-millionaire as a client, it became necessary to spend a lot of time in Nevada, all Hughes' business interests headquartered there. As one thing leads to another, during off-hours Maheu visited casinos along the Strip, operated by those same "businessmen" in charge of similar properties in Havana, Miami and Tampa.

Castro's rise to power, his backing down on the issue of closing casinos reversed owing to Rosselli's persuasiveness notwithstanding, led to the loss of one hundred million dollars a year from gambling. That didn't take into account lucrative returns from prostitution and drugs. Castro must be considered as intolerable to The Mafia as, if for different reasons, our government. While the old adage about killing two birds with one stone didn't apply, Shef Edwards suggested it might be possible, perhaps even necessary, to kill one bird with two stones.

No question about it, if such parties, unmentionable in public, were going to be brought in on this 'project.' Dick Tracy was the man who could cinch the connection. He alone, Shef reasoned, could bring together the opposites that might attract.

The problem: Maheu didn't appear convinced. "Tell me, Shef: up until now, have your strategies involved any of these 'other' people, or did you assign only Company men to the 'problem'?"

"Strictly CIA personnel, up until now."

"And aren't they the best at what they do?"

"Sure. Problem is, Castro's top security guys got their hands on a list of our best agents. They can spot one of our guys coming on down a mile away. We need to try something else."

"Truthfully? I think it's a bad idea. Do you recall what Scott Fitzgerald said about 'the very rich'?"

"Of course." Edwards, like Maheu, was a highly educated man. Each had enjoyed university courses in literature as much as those pertaining to political science. Such people could quote *The Great Gatsby*. "They are very different from you and me."

"Uh-huh. Anyway, that goes double for Made Men."

"You don't think they can be trusted?"

"It's not that. As I've learned, they consider themselves men of respect. That means they hone to a code of honor, no matter how far that may be from anything you and I believe in. Still, if they agree to something, they'll see it through."

"So? What's the problem?"

"We'd be setting a precedent here that I don't think is healthy for the country. Government agents in league with—"

"You've heard that 'any enemy of my enemy is my friend?'"

"In all honesty, once too often lately. And, in all truth, I don't necessarily believe it to be true. We're supposed to be shutting these kinds of people and their operations down, not—"

"That's the FBI's job. We're CIA."

Appearing uncomfortable, Maheu shifted in his seat, eyes penetrating Edwards. "Then it's okay to keep the governmental body's left hand from knowing what the right one is up to?"

"I know it sounds crazy. Particularly as, ever since the Kefauver Crime Commission began its hearings, there's been a concerted effort between all agencies to bring down The Mob."

"Finally!"

"'Amen!' to that."

*

By that, they referred to one of the government's best kept secrets. In 1933, when Franklin Roosevelt first assumed office, a cost-cutting committee during The Great Depression considered shutting down the relatively new Bureau of Investigation, headed by J. Edgar Hoover. That human bulldog guessed that the only way to head such a move off was to convince America all citizens were in grave danger from criminal elements, and only a federal police force could protect them. Hoover, then, required a worthy opponent. That wasn't difficult: organized crime, operating out of Chicago and New York City, fit the bill perfectly.

All Hoover had to do was appear on radio, perhaps the popular show hosted by his friend Walter Winchell ("Good morning, Mr. and Mrs. America, and all the ships at sea ...") and tell the truth about this viable threat.

One little problem prevented that. Hoover and his lover/ assistant, Clyde Tolson, had made the mistake of not only dancing together at a New Year's Eve Party at which liquor, still illegal, was served. They did so with J. Edgar decked out in a brightly-colored dress. Also, Hoover kissed his longtime companion on the mouth at the stroke of midnight. Unknown to them, a mob photographer had been planted in the boisterous crowd. He delivered the photos to Charles Luciano in Chicago, who roared with laughter, then had more copies printed, sending a batch to his friend, Meyer Lansky, in Manhattan.

During a phone conversation on New Year's Day, 1929, the child-hood buddies chuckled a lot about Hoover's tough-guy image as compared to his reality. Yet another set was sent directly to J. Edgar, who received them in a plain wrapper two days later. Staring at the photo in his hand, The G-Man gasped for breath.

"With love from Lucky" the accompanying note read.

No further explanation was necessary. If Hoover were to set his men against organized crime, copies of this picture would be sent to every newspaper and magazine in America. This, in those days before the invention of devices that allowed for the easy alteration of photographic images. Seeing, at least then, any photo meant believing. Even if the Bureau somehow survived, Hoover was finished, a laughing stock. That was considered intolerable.

Days later, Hoover did indeed go on the air alongside Winchell. When directly asked about the issue of a Combination by his host, the guest swallowed hard and lied: "There is no organized crime in the U.S. That is a myth spread by those who would like to undermine the stability of our country. In part by racists who want to discredit those wonderful salt of the earth people, Italians and Jews. Also by Communists, most likely."

Still, there had to be some reason for the Bureau, which even now Hoover was in the process of renaming The Federal Bureau of Investigation, to continue in existence. Something Hoover could convince the public was out there, menacing every American. By fate or accident, just such a scapegoat came to his attention. While escaping from prison, a minor bank robber named John Dillinger stole a car and crossed state lines. In so doing he had committed a federal offense, if a relatively minor one.

"No, Walter, the problem is not some imagined organized crime syndicate. It is the *dis*-organized crime even now wreaking havoc, destroying lives, causing ordinary people to fear for their life-savings which have been ripped out of widows' hands by members of this chaotic confederacy of amoral rednecks. John Dillinger, Pretty Boy Floyd, Babyface Nelson, Clyde Barrow, Machine Gun McCain. These subhuman monsters tear around the countryside in their cars, wielding Tommy Guns, raping, pillaging, taking what they want, leaving devastation in their wake. I plan a nationwide crusade to stop them in their tracks."

Actually, most of those rural bank robbers had never shot anyone. In comparison to the Mob, their impact on the American scene was nil. No matter. That was a reality which, if swept under the rug, did not weight heavily on the current vision of the United States as created and presented by the media, this mythic construction accepted by most citizens as the way things were. In those days before television, hearing was believing. Who would ever doubt anything broadcast on Winchell?

Hoover sent top agent Melvin Purvis and a well-armed task force out to round up or shoot down the rubes. Every time one bit the dust, the public cheered after learning the details from the newspapers or on the radio. Dillinger, who had killed only one man, and that in an accident he deeply regretted, would be posited as "Public Enemy Number One." FBI agents plastered his photo on the bulls-eyes of their targets for shooting practice.

F.D.R. sighed. The masquerade had worked. If he dared close down the FBI now, people would perceive him as soft on crime and likely he'd be a one-term president. He caved. Hoover survived.

Luciano and Lansky had what seemed to be the last laugh. Only that wasn't quite true. A quarter century later, J. Edgar had, like them, grown old. He might soon retire. Young turks were taking over the FBI, hoping for an Attorney General with guts. One who'd let them take on the Mob, Hoover be damned.

Things change. As Maheu and Edwards well knew.

*

"On some level, we'd be justifying the Mob's existence."

"Does that mean you won't help me out here?"

"Before I answer that, Shef, keep in mind, if they *do* pull this off, from that moment—actually, from the time you first have me, or anyone else, communicate with them—the CIA is in bed with the Mob. *Permanently.* Have you thought about that?"

"Of course," Edwards sighed, clearly displeased.

"Are you comfortable with it?"

"Hardly! Then again, these are troubling times. Survival is at issue. 'Comfort' is not then my immediate aim right now."

Glumly, Maheu took that in. "Well," he shrugged, "I'll do whatever you ask. For the good of the country, as always. And hope and pray your call is the right one."

"I appreciate that, Bob."

"But I have to draw the line somewhere and here it is. You must guarantee me that we—the CIA, the Mob, whoever else gets involved—remove Castro without 'eliminating' him."

Both men knew what Maheu meant: bring Castro down but not kill him. *Thou shalt not ...*

"Agreed." The two firmly shook hands across Edwards' desk.

*

Edwards instructed Bob Maheu to put the project on a back burner and go about his everyday business. Shef didn't inquire as to what Maheu's work for Hughes consisted of. Clean or dirty, the CIA honcho did not want to know. Dick Tracy did precisely as told. When work brought him to Vegas, he consciously cultivated relations with Mob boys, deciding on one in particular as his future contact when and if Shef eventually called.

That occurred several months later. Shef explained that he'd been going over plans with Bissell, Dulles, and J.C. King, Chief of the CIA's WH Division, ever since their meeting. When the first phase of what had now officially been tagged Operation 40 went into operation, things must run like clockwork.

Though Maheu knew King to be dependable, he was not happy that so many people had been brought into what in his view ought to have remained a secretive affair. An inner voice warned him to get out quick. But he, a man of honor, had given his word.

Nausea overtook Maheu when he learned that Gen. Charles Pearre Cabell, Chief of Air Force Intelligence, would also be briefed. When Maheu wailed that this widening circle of high-level participants must be curtailed, Edwards insisted "the Old Soldier is alright." Cabell had been persuaded to accept a key position as Deputy Director of the CIA while remaining employed as a five-star general at the Pentagon. With that two-pronged sphere of influence, he might just prove invaluable.

This whole thing is veering out of control! The CIA and the military? Once we also involve the Made Men, anything can happen ... and probably will ...

Like Maheu, James P. O'Connell had been a Special Agent for the FBI before becoming involved with the CIA. Unlike the now-entrepreneurial Maheu, O'Connell had joined up, serving as Chief Operational Support Division, Office of Security. Shef Edwards decided at this point to remove himself as much as possible from the work Maheu would be doing so as not to get his hands dirty. He appointed O'Connell as "case officer" assigned to facilitate the "special intelligence operation" in any way Maheu might find use for him. O'Connell enthusiastically greeted Bob Maheu at their first meeting, appearing completely sincere while offering to serve as Bob's right hand. Nonetheless, Dick Tracy did feel vaguely betrayed at having been passed off to someone else.

A short while after committing to the project, Maheu woke in the middle of the night with a chill running up and down his spine, thinking: *This whole thing is doomed to failure. If I could get out, I would. But I'm past the point of no return!*

*

"Johnny Handsome? That you?"

Rosselli knew the caller at once: Maheu, recognizable from his voice, at once scratchy, tinny, yet strangely sweet. Also, no one else ever referred to him by that nickname on the phone.

"Yeah. Dick Tracy?"

Other men called Bob that owing to his resemblance to the fictional character. Rosselli had a personal reason: besides the pop-art offerings, Maheu bore an uncanny resemblance to Ralph Byrd, the actor who played the comic-strip-cop, wearing the signature trench coat and perky hat, in several low-budget movies for producer Bryan Foy that Rosselli had overseen.

"It's been a while."

While the expression "what happens in Vegas stays in Vegas" had not yet been coined, that pretty much summed up the way things worked. A big small town, everyone got to know everyone. Not surprisingly, the former Fed and the active Mafioso shared the same watering-holes. And, in a couple of instances, women: those tall, stately, available showgirls who performed for the public, then went to bed with men of power.

"Too long."

"Thinking the same thing myself. Can we get together?"

As Maheu had to finish up some work at his D.C. office and Rosselli couldn't leave Vegas until Friday, they made plans to get together for drinks in Los Angeles Saturday night. Rosselli kept a suite in the City of Angels: Maheu, a business office.

Despite the casualty with which that invitation had been extended, Rosselli understood that something big was up. So Maheu, once in Rosselli's apartment, with a shot-glass full of prime Scotch in his hand, got right to it: he had been employed by several well-known legitimate business interests that dealt in varied goods and services, all partaking of the Cuban market previous to Castro. There appeared only one way to recover their losses and that was by figuring some way to put Castro out of power.

Maheu never mentioned the term "Mafia." No need to. Both men knew the score. Rosselli admitted the absence of Castro would be in the best interests of his business associates back east. Maheu then confided that the people who employed him would pay $150,000 if Rosselli's own "associates" could arrange for a "disposal." Rosselli admitted that this was an attractive sum but he did not have authority to accept the offer. This could only be settled by his superior. Before any details could be discussed, a top-level meeting must be arranged.

Maheu agreed, knowing precisely who he would have to speak with: Sam Giancana, aka Sam Gold, the mobster's mobster.

On November 23, 1960, Rosselli met again with Maheu in a quiet cellar club in downtown Manhattan's Little Italy. This time Maheu brought along James P. O'Connell. Though Rosselli had not previously met this man, he knew O'Connell's reputation as a former FBI agent. As an ice breaker, O'Connell half-kiddingly asked Rosselli if he were related to a guy who once worked in Chicago, "Johnny Roselli."

"Well, yeah, of course that was me. My parents lived in Boston; back in '22, a 'situation' caused me to hurriedly head West." Rosselli did not explain further; he had murdered a man and gone on the run. Maheu and O'Connell already knew that. "I decided to change my name. My saintly mother always adored art so I picked a Renaissance painter. We had a print of 'Madonna With Child and Angels' in our home. Cosimo Rosselli was the artist. Freakin' fool that I am, I mis-spelled it then."

All laughed genially. Though no money was exchanged it was decided that O'Connell, as Maheu's colleague, would attend to the business at their end of the deal, he far more astute at such delicate operations. Maheu would serve as the go-between.

Then Rosselli explained that he now felt comfortable enough with the proposed situation to go ahead and make arrangements to introduce Maheu and O'Connell to his boss. Later, Rosselli phoned Maheu to inform him that Mr. Gold had agreed. The meeting would take place on November 25 at Miami's Fountainbleau hotel.

Why there? The former Feds wanted to know. Mr. Gold wished to be in Florida as his unofficial god-son, Frank Sinatra, whom he had more or less inherited from his predecessor, Charley Luciano, would be performing. That sounded kosher. They agreed.

*

"Everything's changed," Sheffield Edwards, sweating in a way that was not characteristic of this ordinarily calm, cool and collected CIA executive, informed Bob Maheu on November 22, 1960, some eight months after their initial meeting, fourteen days following JFK's election, three days previous to the Miami meeting, and three years to the day before JFK's assassination.

"I'm listening," Maheu nervously responded.

"Ike was Ike and JFK is JFK. Nearly two months to go before he takes office and already he's making his iron will felt."

"You're scaring me, Shef."

"Brace yourself! Undermining Castro is no longer an option. Jack told Dulles, Dulles told Bissell, Bissell told me, and I'm telling you: now, the operative word is 'elimination.'"

Maheu had guessed from Edwards' appearance this must be what was coming next. "You swore that was not in the mix," he stammered.

"Times change, Bob. And things along with them."

Both knew without needing to speak the words that, under Kennedy's administration, their task would no longer be to find a non-violent way to dismiss Castro but to kill him outright.

"And it'll be Mob boys, the CIA farming the job out to them, who will be expected to pull it off for us?"

"Right. Though our agents will oversee operations."

"I must ask: have you've heard the same rumors as me?"

Edwards nodded 'yes'. Maheu could only be referring to a widely held belief that Kennedy's father, Joseph, had used his son's friendship with Frank Sinatra to connect with crime boss Giancana. Following a meeting between 'Mr. Gold' and the elder Kennedy, the Mob—*if* this rumor were true—arranged for JFK to carry several key Chicago districts, as well as another in West Virginia. This arrangement cinching JFK's electoral victory.

Closing his eyes momentarily, Shef nodded. "It's all over D.C., of course. No one knows for certain but—"

"I know Mob people, Shef. You don't. With them, a deal is a deal. There can't be any reneging on promises, not ever, or they might just ..." Maheu couldn't finish his sentence, so deeply concerned was he about the possible dire consequences.

"You know me, Bob. I'd never in a million years—"

"It's not *you* I'm worried about."

Edwards understood completely. Maheu harbored no concerns regarding Dulles, Edwards, Bissell, Esterline or any Company men. He was worried about the same thing as Edwards, already turning this possible problem over in his mind: The new wild card, that movie-star-handsome President-elect with a charming if slightly cynical look in those dazzling eyes, the killer smile that made the good grey men, quietly dedicated to the best interests of the U.S. at the expense of their own selves, wonder as to precisely what JFK was up to. And how far he dared go in manipulating people to Jack's own ends, whatever they might be.

"Got you. Still, there are some solid reasons why this might be to our advantage. If the process was undertaken by these ... *gentlemen* ... that would give us a ... how to put it? ... cover story. We want Castro gone; so do they. If your Vegas associates agree to complete the sort of job they are expert at—we would of course pay generously for them to do so—The Company could find ourselves in a no-lose situation."

"If any of their people were to blab that we were involved, we would simply deny, deny, deny."

"Who would the American public believe? Mobsters or a trusted government agency?" Edwards shrugged. "And, if they should fail, we'll be no worse off than before."

"If they succeed, everybody wins." Bob Maheu breathed in deeply. "Can I sleep on it?"

Sheffield Edwards rose and stepped around his desk, warmly dropping an arm around Maheu's shoulder as he guided his visitor to the door. "I wouldn't have it any other way."

*

Back in his apartment, Robert Maheu helped himself to a double shot of scotch and set a 33 1/3 L.P. of Strauss waltzes to playing. He remained alone in the dark for hours, sometimes sitting, sometimes standing, mostly pacing back and forth; half-listening to his favorite music, running through that heady conversation endlessly in his mind, trying to gain a sense of purpose. If he agreed, spoke to Johnny Rosselli about doing the job, and it went down, Dick Tracy must forever consider himself as guilty of Castro's death as if he had pulled the trigger.

Maheu had always been a supremely moral man. While a Georgetown law student he perceived litigation from such a point of view. There was the law and there was what he knew to be right and wrong. Whenever these concepts came into conflict with one another, his conscience suffered a total meltdown.

In the value system that this man had always lived by, there could be no more unforgivable act than the taking of another's life, other than in war or self-defense. Even if that man happened to be a threatening adversary. Then again, Castro, whom Maheu despised, appeared ready to allow Russia to install nuclear missiles pointed at the nearby U.S. How many American lives might be lost, if such a Fail-Safe moment occurred, so that this one person might go on living?

He deeply loved his country, adored its people. If only a single American life might be saved, how could Maheu say 'no'?

All night he wrestled with the complex issue. Perhaps the days when moral matters presented themselves in black-and-white ended with the crusade against Hitler. No matter how much Maheu longed for the return to such clear-cut simplistics he well knew all now inhabited a different world, were involved in a different sort of war. Still, war is war.

There was no doubt in Maheu's mind whose side he was on. When he finally called Shef the next morning, after taking a stiff swig straight from the bottle to fortify himself, there could be only one possible answer to Shef Edwards' request.

*

Maheu and O'Connell flew to Miami together but took lodging at separate hotels. At the scheduled meeting time a headwaiter who met the men at the entrance to the bar whispered that plans had been changed. The casually dressed, fleshy-faced O'Connell's presence would not be required. That could prove to be a deal-breaker. Any such last minute 'adjustment' sounded suspicious.

Concerned, Maheu and O'Connell drew back and discussed the matter quickly. One option was to walk away, for safety's sake. They didn't guess there would be trouble, much less a gangland execution awaiting them. But the Mob thought like an animal with a brain notably different from everyday people, so the remote possibility could not be discounted. The deciding factor that caused them to agree was the importance of their mission.

So O'Connell headed back to his hotel while Maheu followed the escort to a dimly lit booth at the furthest end of the long bar.

For a quarter hour, Maheu waited; then Rosselli appeared on the scene, ushering a now 52-year-old Sam 'Gold' Giancana into a seat directly across from Dick Tracy. This allowed the Mob boss to stare directly into Maheu's eyes, Rosselli slipping in right alongside Maheu. As Giancana glared at Bob for several minutes, the square-jawed cop took the opportunity to do the same in return.

In his dapper dark sports jacket, thin metallic tie, dark sunglasses and Broadway Fedora, Sam looked similar to Sinatra on one of his recent album covers. First came small talk, allowing Giancana to size Maheu up. He determined that Bob Maheu's was a sincere request, not some set-up to nab him. The air cleared; they spoke for an hour in hushed voices.

According to the unique protocol of such a meeting, "ugly" or "bad" words were never used. They discussed, like solid American businessmen, the "possible solution" to a "serious issue" that had been deemed "unacceptable" by both interests, calling for "a mutually planned solution" to the "problem."

As to the fee, Gold considered it more than fair. Rosselli explained that once their organization decided how this project ought to proceed. Maheu's people must be responsible for providing the means. Bob saw no problem there. Sam Giancana then pointed to a medium-sized bespectacled fellow, leaning against the bar, sipping his drink alone. Sensing that he was now being observed, the nondescript man glanced over, green eyes flashing.

Giancana nodded; the man nodded back, then turned away.

"That's Joe," Rosselli informed Maheu. "He's our top courier to Cuba, headquartered in Tampa with a second office in Miami. He'll transport any mechanisms we deem necessary, which you will of course supply. Joe will make the transport."

"Got ya," Maheu grimaced.

"I'm not sure you do," Giancana confided, speaking now the sort of no-nonsense language all had up to this point patently avoided.

"If you are hoping for some sort of gangland 'hit,'" Johnny continued, "forget about it. We might have considered that before Castro's protection developed from comical amateurs to qualified professionals. Mr. Gold will not send any of his men on a mission from which I know he cannot possibly return alive."

"What, then?" Maheu wanted to know.

"Poison," Giancana flatly stated.

"Botulin," Rosselli specified. "Joe will smuggle it into Cuba. We have a number of contacts there who can administer it."

Maheu thought that over before responding. "My clients don't care how it's done, just so long as the job's completed."

"You will supply the botulin to Mr. Rosselli, who will hand it over to Joe, who will deliver it to yet another 'operative,' who will then give it to the girl who will do the deed."

"Another operative?"

"One of yours," Rosselli explained. "This cannot and will not proceed without active participation from one of your own. Not somebody you farm things out to. A CIA man. Mr. Giancani knows that only if we hold hands, so to speak, can we be certain that one hand washes the other, if you grasp my drift."

"I do." Maheu understood that the Mob had no intention of being left holding the dirt-bag alone if things went south. A CIA man serving as connective tissue during the operation would assure there could be no double-cross, nor could the Company ever blow the whistle on La Casa Nostra afterwards. George would surely be the man for that. "You mentioned a girl?"

"Oh, yes. Quite irresistible."

"Alright, then. Done deal."

"Not quite," Giancana firmly asserted.

Uh-oh, Mahew thought. *Now comes the catch!*

*

On the morning of August 4, 2008, a moment before Robert Maheu's mortal coil ceased to exist on this earth, his fast-fading mind made one final connection. August 4 was the same day that, 46 years earlier, Marilyn Monroe expired in her West Coast apartment. Like pretty much every other man of his generation, Maheu had long harbored an extreme crush on The Blonde. Such a shame that she had to be eliminated. He of course had nothing to do with that. All the same, Bob continued to feel guilty over her death, along with all the others who, as part of the massive operation he knowingly and willingly participated in.

Marilyn's disposal? The last favor the Mob performed for the Kennedys before that tenuous relationship all at once blew up in everyone's faces. Could his oncoming death on that same day be mere coincidence, or was this some act of fate?

Dick Tracy never got around to deciding finally whether he, at the moment of end-game, believed in free will or predestination. A split-second later Bob Maheu's eyes closed forever without his having an opportunity to come down one way or the other on that all-important issue, once and for all, at least for himself.

*

In the first shot of *Breathless* some French guy, whose name Johnny Rosselli never could recall, wandered down a Parisian boulevard, pausing at a local 'cinema' to consider the image of Humphrey Bogart on a huge poster advertising the revival of one of that great screen tough guy's classic films. This frog—*Belmondo? Yeah, I think that's it*—unconsciously drew his hand up and over his lip in the precise manner Bogie always did when playing his most memorable gangland roles.

Unconsciously, at first, Rosselli followed suit, all at once realizing with a laugh that he had just imitated, in the reality of the theatre's auditorium, an actor in an artsy Gallic film imitating an earlier star of Hollywood film noirs.

At that moment Johnny Handsome was 'sold'. This movie, and the man who made it, were friggin' *alright*!

Rosselli had particularly appreciated the hand held camera-work and sudden, abrupt editing style. Apparently, this approach had been done on purpose in *Breathless*, borrowed from the unique style Johnny Handsome initiated at *Mascot* and *Monogram* twenty years earlier. That incidentally had been what Johnny's friend meant when he mentioned this film had been dedicated to Rosselli if indirectly: before the story started, the frog, a guy named Godard, paid tribute in a title card to those lowest of the companies. Their output had been considered so much junk—many critics didn't even bother to pay these pictures the respect of reviewing them *negatively*—when the little films were initially released. So now, they are ... what ... considered art? More influential on movies yet to come during the Sixties than respected big pictures from the likes of Warner Bros. and MGM?

Jeez! What goes around really does come around.

In Johnny's case, he hadn't had his crews film in such a manner owing to any desire to create a radical directorial style in defiance of a more sedate old Hollywood order. The case had been more simple and reality-bound: mostly, they couldn't afford tripods. Even when the Poverty Row filmmakers had them, there wasn't enough time to set the cameras on the devices, so tight were the shooting schedules. As to the 'aesthetics' of editing back then, this did not derive from an experimental artist's desire to break the rules, only the necessity of stitching a story together from bits and pieces of film.

The French guy who wrote and directed this new flick had obviously, in his impressionable youth, seen and adored the ones Rosselli and his gang haphazardly created; today, yesterday's lowbrow junk had been transformed into tomorrow's high art.

When the show let out, Rosselli placed a call to Bryan Foy, oldest son of the showbiz legend Eddie Foy, one of his famed

Seven Little Foys in vaudeville days. It was Foy who, as an indie producer, had helped Johnny get started in the business, before word reached Rosselli from Al Capone in Chicago to get to the Windy City fast, his unique services required at once.

Foy got a charge out of hearing about the tribute, then shared some good news of his own. If this Jack Kennedy guy won the upcoming presidential election, Foy would get to co-produce a movie about JFK's wartime experiences to be titled *PT-109.*

CHAPTER EIGHT:
FIRST BLOOD

"Alright, marines: *Saddle up!* Let's get back into this war."
—John Wayne as 'Sergeant Stryker'
in *Sands of Iwo Jima* (1949)

"Hello, fellas. I'm John Wayne! Pleased t' meet ya."

Momentarily, Lee believed he might be hearing things. Perhaps too many hours of mess duty scrambled his mind as Lee prepared eggs others would consume. To keep from going mad owing to the dull daily duty, the only work he'd been assigned since his outfit disembarked on Corregidor a week and a half earlier, during the pre-dawn darkness of January 15, 1958, L.H.O. applied arch rationality to turn drudgery into a game. 'Ozzie' devised a unique system, inserting one side of the large rectangular hand trays under bubbling eggs on the grill, flipping this concoction high into the air, catching everything as it fell back down without spilling a drop.

John Wayne? Here? I'm losing it! Maybe somebody dragged a TV set into the bombed-out WWII-era hospital we employ as our mess? I didn't know there was one on the island but ...

From his position in the adjoining kitchen where Lee had been supervising clean-up following morning meal, he slipped out the rear screen-door, ambling around to get a look inside the cavernous building. Incredible but true, the greatest movie star ever (the only exception, at least for Lee, Frank Sinatra) stood in its center, all 6' 5 ¾" of him, smiling graciously.

Yup. Hard as it was to believe, John Wayne held court to the delight of about thirty marines, mostly officers. The Duke jauntily shook hands with one after another. The majority made an attempt to present themselves with some semblance of normalcy in spite of this sudden happy shock to the system. Those still seated were uncertain as to whether they should rise in the presence of Hollywood royalty. Wayne would have none of *that*. Motioning for the boys to remain where ever they were he would humbly come around from table to table.

"Hello, marine. Great t' meet ya." Those majestic, world-weary eyes made clear Big John meant every word he said.

The star had never been a member of the military. Not even when others among Hollywood's living legends rushed to enlist in 1941. Wayne confined his fighting to the silver screen. A wide gallery of glorious portraits established him as the ultimate movie symbol of American patriotism.

"Hello, Duke. The pleasure's all ours!"

One marine hurried up with a breakfast tray. Wayne politely thanked the fellow, sitting down randomly beside two officers.

"Well, I'll tell you," Wayne explained when one asked how he happened to be here, "I was flying overhead, in a copter on my way to a location shoot for *The Barbarian and the Geisha*, when I realized: that's Corregidor below. I'd always wanted to visit the island since ... oh, I don't know, ten years now ... I did a film set there, *Back to Bataan*. Shot in Hollywood, as we mostly did it back then. Ever since, I wanted to visit."

Everyone smiled and nodded, reiterating their admiration and appreciation. This was something each would tell his kids about. Their grand-children, too, if they lived that long.

Part of Lee burned to step in, head on over, introduce himself. Mention he'd prepared the food, hoped Mr. Wayne enjoyed it. Explain that he, Lee Oswald, worshipped the ground Wayne walked on. Yet he held back, hovering in the doorway as others took advantage of this once-in-a-lifetime opportunity.

The problem was, the other marines knew Lee not as the super-patriot he was but as the communist sympathizer, according to Lee's "legend," he performed at all hours of the day. What if one said something to The Duke about Ozzie being the squadron's Soviet Fifth Columnist? Why, Wayne might slap him around, as he had done to more than one commie in his 1952 film *Big Jim McLain*.

If Lee were to say, 'Oh, how I loved *Hondo*!' others might realize that what Lee offered was nothing but a created character. Everything he and George had developed could be lost.

I'm wearing only a T-shirt, whereas the men in there look natty in uniform. I don't smell so good. So near, so far ...

"Hey, Mrs. Oswald. What's a matter? Not man enough to go on in and say 'hi' to John Wayne?"

Lee turned to see Perry Sommers hulking behind him, flashing the nastiest grin he could muster. Sommers rudely brushed by, purposefully banging against the slender marine.

That's it. The final straw. A man can take only so much!

*

Lee had hated Corregidor from the moment the marines first landed. Almost every waking hour was spent on mess duty while others set up a radar command post, spending free time swimming or sunbathing. Even George could not, from behind the scenes, do anything about that. This bored Lee worse than the routine in Atsugi, where he had been assigned to stare into Crystal Balls. That was their nickname for radarscopes, the basic equipment for men assigned to this specialty. Every radio communication from base to a flyer had to be carefully monitored. Their duty was to oversee the area stretching from the South China Sea to Korea and ascertain that things above remained normal.

If any questionable plane, perhaps a MIG flown by some Red Chinese pilot, was spotted, popping up first as a dark glitch, this followed by a loud beeping sound, Lee alerted the Tactical Air Control Center at Iwakuni. Moments later, interceptor jets would take off to head-on meet any potential threat.

All had not been easy there, however. Perry Sommers was the catalyst for friction between Lee and the others. Relentlessly, Sommers questioned Lee as to his status: "Still our 'cherry virgin?'" In response Lee grinned, saying nothing.

Mostly, in situations involving Lee with the squad members, including those who treated him with respect, he remained mum as to his personal life. Which only piqued their interest.

On other issues, Lee proved to be the most talkative guy around. He would leap whole-hog into rap sessions on movies or music. When talk turned to politics, Lee would suddenly tear off on a tirade against the American right wing.

Most bizarre were those occasions when the marine called Oswald the Rabbit would transform himself into an imitation of an even more famous cartoon bunny. At odd, unexpected intervals, Lee would step into their work-bubble and shout, "What's up, Doc?" Some marines began referring to him as Bugs.

Initially, Lee laughed along with them. Things took an ugly turn when Sommers, having appointed himself Lee's nemesis, decided that "Mrs. Oswald" ought to be his new identity.

*

"We gotta get you laid," Gator Daniels announced two days later. By 'we' he referred to himself and two other marines who had befriended L.H.O. These were Gordy Wilkins, an upstate New York native whose sophisticated views were obvious whenever he spoke, and Wilkins' foil, Zack Stout, a lovable rube from the heartlands who joined the Corps less owing to patriotism than boredom. As for Gator, he had wrestled with the beasts deep in the Everglades since childhood. They were the four musketeers, Lee functioning as the innocent young D'Artagnan.

Oswald and Gator constituted the unlikeliest of odd couples. They first became chummy while crossing over from California to Hawaii aboard USS *Bexar*. That transport departed San Diego on August 21, 1957. Assumed by most onboard to be a moronic giant, Gator-—who had never even heard of chess—was impressed that Ozzie, the undisputed champion, would take time out from reading his latest favorite, *Leaves of Grass*, to teach this supposed Neanderthal how to play.

Lee's initial fear of another betrayal proved unfounded, as he would soon discover. Not only did Gator turn out to be a true friend; he also happened to be as innately intelligent as Lee. Gator's ignorance was due to an upbringing in which he'd barely been taught to read and write. Though Gator's language remained modest and crude, his thoughts at last began to take shape.

"Y'know, Lee, yer right. This Marx makes some sense."

Following a brief stay, The *Bexar* left Hawaii and continued on to Japan, arriving there during the first week of September. As all the men learned upon arrival at Atsugi, directly across the rice fields from the base, several night clubs beckoned to marines when they secured passes. There they could enjoy liquor, gambling, and the flesh of Asian 'hostesses'.

"Whether you partake or not," a lieutenant explained, "is your business. Understand this: under no circumstances should you talk with any of the girls about anything that occurs on base. Most of them are precisely what they appear to be; whores who want only your money. On the other hand, one in a hundred is a spy for the Reds. It's impossible to tell these apart from others who hope to trade their bodies for American dollars."

Initially, Lee let on that he was too shy to go along when his buddies headed out. Radical politics aside, Lee remained an old-fashioned moralist who didn't approve of giving in to one's vices. Sommers stirred the others up against Lee. If at first the term "cherry virgin" (now applying only to Lee's "legend," not his secret self, thanks to Honey and other willing teachers) irked Lee, his nemesis pumped up the volume on his harassment.

"The problem with Mrs. Oswald ain't that he's a cherry virgin. It's that he don't wanna do nothin' about it."

Why do some men assume I'm a queer? A cherry virgin is bad enough. Until not so long ago, that's what I was. But how does that translate into homosexual? Why would they suspect me?

I've been with Sara, the best-looking woman on this base. Honey, the Mob's dream girl. A Marilyn Monroe look-alike. If only I could tell them ...

Funny, as this is what I wanted for so long. Keep a veil between me and everyone else. Now, I'd love to tell all. The real L.H.O. is not only a highly accomplished cocks-man but has bedded some of the most beautiful women in the world.

Yet that must remain secret, the legend—based on the L.H.O. I once was—accepted by all as my reality.

Oh! The irony of it all ...

*

Perhaps the ugliest moment for Lee occurred shortly before Christmas. Marguerite had sent him a Care Package filled with assorted goodies. What Lee most appreciated were the red and white holiday candies, round little suckers that tasted like candy canes. Minding his business, Lee sat on a bunk, sorting them for himself and friends. Sommers happened by and, with a ham-like fist, smashed them into bits. Lee snapped.

"You bastard. You no good freakin' son of a bitch!"

As Sommers attempted to force Lee into a corner, Lee's giant of a protector hurried over. "You wanna hit Ozzie," Gator howled, coming up from behind and slugging Sommers hard on the spine, "why not start with me, you friggin' prick?"

Once recovered, Sommers quickly backed off, trying to make light of the whole thing. "Hey, Gator, I was just joshin'—"

"Josh with *me*," Gator continued, closing in, Sommers now backed against the barracks wall. Gator shoved his huge chin forward. "Take the first shot. Go on! Then it'll be my turn."

"I got no gripe with you," Sommers whined, crouching in fear. "You're a regular guy."

"Yeah? Well, so's my pal Ozzie. You frickin' un'erstan'?"

"Sure, sure," Sommers awkwardly agreed, darting away. There would be no further such incidents, not that the ribbing—now mostly behind Lee's back—abated. At least not yet.

Meanwhile, a well-intentioned sergeant sat Lee down for a talk. He explained that Lee brought a lot of this crap down on himself by talking like a communist.

"Let me give you a bit of advice, Ozzie. There's nothing more stupid in life than doing the same thing over and over again while always expecting different results. Remember that!"

*

The days spent by those marines serving in the Air Control Squadron operations room were tedious, exhausting, depressing, and utterly unrewarding. The base, built in 1938, occupied by

128

Americans since 1950. The sprawling set of structures were located halfway down the island's westward-stretching curvature, in a south-eastern area known as the Kamagawa Pefecture, straddling the twin cities of Yamato and Ayase. As to radar specialists, during work-hours they found themselves confined within a tight compartment they, on arrival, nick-named The Bubble: a glass-enclosed top-of-tower circular room. A continuous succession of seven-man-teams occupied the claustrophobia-inducing area, machinery and other technological devices taking up the lion's share of space, for five to six hour stretches. Then one group would be replaced by the next shift. Always, and without fail, the bubble must be manned.

As a member of the Coffee Mill, his outfit's logo, Lee spent what felt like endless hours, employing an MPS-11 radar height-finding-antennae to determine what passed by. Fully dominating the enclosed area spread an immense plotting board, translucent and, in the dim light, ghostly. Here marines would mark with grease pencils the intercept route of anything above.

If a single thing always took the men's minds off such everyday miseries, this was the presence of an unknown flying object that, from time to time, appeared down there on the mile-long runway. In time they learned its name: the U2, kept in a special hangar built some distance apart from those which housed routine planes. Rumors spread about what might be the function of this large, strangely shaped, blue-black device. Descending from a flight the U2 had to be supported by jeeps on either side to keep its awkward wings from dragging. Afterwards, tractors would haul the U2 back to its private place, where a coterie of fully armed guards oversaw its exclusivity.

The jet, if that's what this bizarre creation was, could reach altitudes of more than 90,000 ft., one Coffee Mill member insisted after charting the U2's course. Nonsense, others piped in; that's not possible. You've been watching too many science-fiction films. It's our state-of-the-art reconnaissance air-craft, another ventured, tested in secret here before flying high over Russia on spy missions.

Lee never joined in any of these discussions, acting as if he did not know any more than the others and that he could care less. Actually, nothing on the base intrigued him more. The U2 was the reason why he, and for that matter all in his unit (to cover Lee's "legend"), had been assigned to this specific job in this particular place. The military had received word from high- ranking members of the confederacy of departments known in the postwar world as the intelligence community—the State Dept., the Defense

Intelligence Agency; the FBI; the Office of Naval Intelligence; G-2; the National Security Agency; the CIA—that this assignment must be made at once and without question.

George had informed Lee as to what was coming in one of their private meetings several weeks before Lee and the other marines shipped out on August 22, 1957, disembarking at the port of Yokosuka on September 12. From there they were transported by truck to this base. For reasons the two would discuss at length upon Lee's return, he was assigned to, from time to time, be seen in the vicinity of the U2's hanger, even though this area was off-limits. To make Lee's "interest" more widely known, he was to purchase a camera and stealthily snap photos of the U2.

*

When Lee agreed to accompany Gator, Gordy and Zack to the Bluebird so as to complete "the final rite of manhood" (Gordy's words), Lee's only friends were stunned when he, after a few drinks, ran off at the mouth about the presence on their base of this nearly-fantastical piece of flying equipment. The others made it a point to confer with Lee about this on the way back, requesting Lee not allow himself to be singled out as some sort of loose-lipped fool or, worse, a traitor.

Lee scoffed, insisting that word had long since leaked out and these hostesses knew more about it than they did.

During that first visit, Lee drank but refused to gamble. That would come in the carefully schematized narrative he now controlled while seeming to be a powerless tag-a-long.

I'm a chess-champion, the puppet-master. Just like George!

Best of all, in the minds of his buddies, Lee rose to the occasion after slipping into a narrow room with a whore. After some coaxing, Ozzie did her proper, then marched proudly into the club's main cooridor, flashing that insane grin. Every marine present, with the exception only of Sommers, cheered him on. The men did not call him "Mrs. Oswald" ever again.

Initially, though, rumors as to Lee's sexual preference did continue. Whenever he traveled the further distance to Tokyo for a weekend, Lee always insisted on going alone, even if his best friends were also headed there. Talk had it, initially at least, that he visited several of the male prostitutes who haunted that city of shadows. Others, now convinced of Lee's masculinity, had another theory; he was off to visit Communist headquarters there, passing information about our latest radar-height finding antennas to the enemy and, worse still, his photos of the U2.

A third possibility trickled down to the enlisted men from a surprising source: their officers. Word leaked out that Lee had been in Tokyo frequenting a high-class (i.e., expensive, with truly beautiful women) brothel known as The Queen Bee. Most men below the rank of lieutenant never went near it less owing to restrictions than cost: more than $100 for the night, hardly affordable for men whose pay ranged between $70 (Buck Private) to $90 (Sgt.) a month. Yet according to several officers able to afford a visit, one PFC had been in attendance on Friday *and* Saturday during a single weekend. Where did the money come from?

Some marines did not believe Ozzie could get near, much less handle, the most attractive prostitute: The Dragon Lady, her nickname hailing from the seductive Asian villainess in the popular comic strip *Terry and the Pirates*. It was rumored that even the most tight-lipped of johns spilled all to this dark beauty while in her elegant boudoir. Everyone gasped with disbelief when, one day, the Dragon Lady traveled down from Tokyo to Atsugi to spend a weekend with L.H.O. Majestic, at least an inch taller than the runty marine, the spectacular beauty proudly marched around the base, gripping Lee's arm as if he were ... Sinatra. Lee showed her 'the sights'.

I need a favor. Come on down to the base so I can show you off. When you do, act like I'm ... I don't know ... have you read the James Bond novels? 007; Yes? Great! I'll act nonchalant and you as if you can't keep your hands off of me. In return I will provide those pictures of the U2's interior ...

Yet whenever one among them marched over to headquarters and requested to file a report, nothing ever came of it. As for Lee, he continued his tirades. Gator shocked everyone when he, finally growing uncomfortable with Lee, admitted during a late-night poker game that Lee had actually suggested defecting.

*

On October 18, 1957, his eighteenth birthday, Lee strolled from the wooden two-story barracks in which the 117 man MACS-1 unit was quartered, this located on the easternmost perimeter of the Atsugi base near the main entrance, to the compound's far side. None of the others had ever gone over there, though Lee visited the 'compound within the compound,' as some referred to the two-dozen non-descript buildings, on a daily basis. Officially referred to as "The Joint Technical Advisory Group" (most marines did not have a clue what that meant), this secretive area housed the CIA's headquarters in Japan.

Here was where Ozzie arrived each morning to pick up his encoded messages containing the latest orders from George. These pertained to his weekend passes, Lee enjoying prostitutes on The

Company's tab (the CIA, not his assigned company) while passing disinformation George knew would confuse Soviets once Lee's false 'facts' were added to the KGB's mix on the U2.

"Hi, Lee," the pretty brunette known only as Sara brightly said. "No message today. But you're to call George. The cable-connection is set up and all ready to go."

This surprised Lee if only because it had never occurred before during the two months he'd served at Atsugi. As Lee and George had carefully planned, Lee earlier arrived at the Naval Air Technology Training Center in Jacksonville, Florida in late March, 1957. There he was promoted to Private First Class, soon cleared to handle documents marked Confidential and/or Classified. This to the dismay of Allen Felde, a squad member who had been with Lee since San Diego and was fed-up with Lee's rants.

"I don't get it," Felde openly stated, sometimes in front of Lee. "If they'd clear this Red bastard, they'd clear anyone."

As for Ozzie, he in response simply lowered his head slightly and drew his mouth into that twisted half-grin ...

It's working. My "legend" is established. Word will spread, and in due time, the Commies will contact me ... and believe all I tell them about our secrets ... my disinformation ...

"Did he say what it's about?" Sara shook her head while raising her eyebrows and gritting her teeth, the brunette's manner of communicating 'I don't have a clue!' She escorted Lee into a small, tidy office, the only adornments a pair of old photographs, one of Pres. Eisenhower in his WWII dress uniform, the other that famous shot of marines raising the flag atop Mt. Surabachi during the battle of Iwo Jima. Sara handed Lee a tattered *Life* to read, then left, providing total privacy.

Lee flipped through the magazine, particularly interested in the cover story about John Fitzgerald Kennedy, his lovely bride Jackie, and their children. It wouldn't be hard to mistake either husband or wife for a movie star, so picture-perfect were they. Lee chuckled, recalling what George had confided during their drive to the desert; fascinated by the sedate, sincere, sweet smiles on their faces. This was how the public at large was allowed to see the likely next occupants of The White House. Lee and a few others knew the truth behind that dazzling façade!

When the phone rang, its brittle sound shook Lee out of his reverie. He answered; there was George's voice, barely audible.

"Lee? We have a problem. Good Karma!"

After a moment's hesitation, Lee replied: "Bad Karma!"

That constituted The Company's password for, and required response to, any discussion of Achmed Sukarno, the now 56-year-old president of Indonesia. Highly educated, fluent in numerous languages, the area's Javanese-born power-broker since 1945 did not sit well with those who ran America's Invisible Government.

The first issue against Sukarno was that, during WWII, he aligned with the Japanese. Now, of course, that country was an ally. Sukarno, however, did not subscribe to the idea that the U.S. ought to be welcome to enter and establish military bases. He accused America's current world policies as "fascistic" and spoke positively about "New Emerging Forces" in the Third World.

Whereas in those situations the U.S. tacitly defended right-wing dictators against rebels, here America took the opposite approach: as Muslims instigated a possible coup against Sukarno, U.S. forces were readying to back up any such action.

Not that the CIA and others of their ilk were comfortable with these insurgents. Far from it! As always in the Eisenhower era and, perhaps more significant, the age of John Foster Dulles as the key to foreign affairs, one rule was repeated over and over.

Any enemy of my enemy is my friend ...

For what it was worth, the name Sukarno roughly translated in English to 'Good Karma'. At any rate, George explained that the area was heating up. The marines were about to ship out and possibly participate in a violent invasion via a route through Borneo. If that occurred, the likelihood of combat in question but placement of marine divisions in strategic areas certain, Lee's radar unit MACS-1 would accompany them as a communications team. Which meant Ozzie would go along for the ride.

This, George had not anticipated and did not appreciate. Lee Harvey Oswald was needed right where he was: in Japan.

"Isn't there anything you can do about it from there?"

"Believe me, Lee, I've looked into it. Of course I could arrange an immediate transfer. But that would stick out like a sore thumb. Chances are, your cover would be blown. Forever."

With that, as Lee well knew, he would become dispensable. All he'd achieved gone like a wisp of smoke. That must not be allowed to happen. He could certainly ship out with the others.

"What should I do?"

"You're a big boy now. On your own. Your call."

*

Nine days later, at eight-thirty on the evening of October 27, 1957, Lee sat in his barracks on a lower bunk assigned to Robert Augg. That marine was at the P.X., enjoying a Coke and a burger. Even as Augg strolled back at a swift gait to hit his bunk before Taps, a shot rang out, discharged by a small weapon.

133

As Augg darted inside he spotted Lee, his right arm bleeding, grimacing in pain. Beside Lee on Augg's bunk lay a .22 caliber silver-plated derringer, a thin coil of blue-gray smoke circling upward. Already, a Navy corpsman had appeared.

"What happened?" Augg wanted to know, none too pleased that this took place on the bunk he would sleep in that night.

"Crazy accident," Lee mumbled. "I shot myself."

"Don't look like no accident to me," the corpsman hissed while bandaging Lee, his own fingers now bathed in blood.

"Hey, come on," Lee laughed. "You don't think I was trying to 'off' myself, do ya?"

"No," the corpsman insisted. "When a marine wants to commit suicide, he generally succeeds. All you wanted was a flesh wound serious enough to get you off active duty."

"You have no proof of that."

"I know all about you, Oswald, and your commie leanings."

Later that night Oswald was attended in the base hospital by several nurses, one of them attractive. Ordinarily she might not have given this scrawny runt a second glance. But she had heard all the rumors about Oswald's reputation as a lover who had conquered Tokyo's Dragon Lady and Sara, the best looking secretary on base. Wanting to know what all the shouting was about she whispered in Lee's ear that she'd return at midnight.

Fortunately, Lee had been assigned a single room. *Or did George somehow arrange that for me from stateside?* On other nights Sara visited Lee, she apparently possessing authority to go wherever on this base she chose. In addition to providing sexual favors, Sara brought messages from George and picked up ones from Lee which she would send out in the morning.

Initially George expressed elation that Lee had been willing to go above and beyond by actually wounding himself to avoid the scheduled November 8 shipping-out. Unfortunately, though, that massive move was pushed back several weeks.

The doctors, certain Lee's wound had been self-inflicted to avoid leaving, made certain he was discharged on November 18, two days before the new date of departure. The USS *Terrell County* carried Lee and other radar experts toward the northern tip of the Philippine's archipelago for Operation Strongback.

Everyone noticed Lee's terrible depression, assuming it had to do with his not wanting to fight and hesitancy to leave those beauties. None guessed that he terribly feared his use as a CIA operative might be compromised, his run as a spy now finished.

Shortly after their arrival the men were rounded up again and shipped out once more. They incorrectly assumed (and Lee desperately hoped) they'd head back to Japan. Instead they joined thirty other transports deep in the South China Sea, waiting for orders. Lee perked up a bit as he shortly became the squadron's clear-cut chess champ. He also began to gamble; this, and his glorious conquests, caused Lee to become fully accepted by the men around him for the first time in his life.

Lee enjoyed this experience so thoroughly that he failed to set himself up as a target as often as he ought to by spouting Red propaganda. People actually seemed to like him. For the first time ever, Lee Oswald finally began to like himself.

Then, whistles blew, men rushed to ready themselves for what might come, and they approached the island of Corregidor. Where, as punishment for a fake suicide, he worked mess duty.

Things calmed down in early March and, to Lee's delight and relief, they returned to Japan, arriving at Atsugi, Lee later re-assigned to Iwakuni. He received word from George, through Sara, that Lee would resume his three lives as hard-working marine, traitor, and double-agent. While in Tokyo he learned more from The Dragon Lady than she did from him. He actually was turning into a real-life incarnation of fictional James Bond.

Owing to the medic's charges and illegality of the self-owned derringer, Lee went before a court martial on April 11 and was found guilty. In addition to constant kitchen work while on Corregidor, an unofficial advance punishment before Lee even had a chance to defend himself, now he was sentenced to twenty days at hard labor.

Wait a minute, here. I'm experiencing déjà vu ... this is the From Here to Eternity *scene when several MPs escort Frankie to stir. At this moment, I finally am 'Angelo Maggio.' Meaning I've become Sinatra. Will Ernest Borgnine as 'Fatso Judson' be waiting for me on the inside? Whatever! It's finally happened: my pitiable life has become one and the same with my favorite movie ...*

When this ordeal ended, Lee returned to his outfit. He struck everyone as a changed man, no longer spouting the joys of communism but bitterly, even viciously attacking America.

It's working. I'm fooling them all again ...

In so doing Lee followed to the letter a script George had prepared and transferred to Lee through Sara. In terms of plans George scripted for Lee following his tour of duty, it was necessary that Lee accrue a terrible reputation, a number of verifiable outrages appearing on his permanent record. The worst being his threatened defection to Russia. Lee basked in the possibility; his adventures as a secret agent were not about to come to an end but only just beginning ...

*

Three nights following John Wayne's unexpected visit to Corregidor, on January 29, 1958, Perry Sommers arrived to take his turn at guard duty on the outer limits of a temporary base at Cubi Point. He carried a shotgun, the weapon of choice for such an assignment; communist Fillipinos were known to search the area, looking for stray Americans they might murder. Also Sommers had in his possession a canteen full of hard alcohol which the men fermented from leftover potato and orange peels.

In Sommers' shirt pocket a hundred dollar (American) bill had been tucked in place.

The agreed on time was one a.m. Where the fuck are you? Come on ... I'm tired of waitin'. You're gettin' paid plenty.

The man Sommers none-too-patiently awaited was a young Fillipino, extremely pro-American, who had taken to serving homosexual members of the company. Mostly this occurred when they were alone on guard duty, the least likely time anyone might discover them in the act.

All along, Sommers had carefully kept his secret from being known to the others, so extreme was the harassment a "faggot" received in the armed forces, particularly tougher-than-leather marines. He lived in denial about this elemental truth except when the urge grew too strong to resist. Then, hating himself for what he considered a weakness, Sommers would arrange such assignations on the fringe of any military base, where shadow men would service so-inclined soldiers, sailors, and marines.

One of Sommers' key strategies to maintain his man's man image was to pick on some small, shy, therefore suspect person. By identifying such a fellow as a "queer," he the "man's man" least able to tolerate homosexuals, Sommers believed he might create the perfect cover. No matter that most such victims did happen to be heterosexual; in the late-1950s an abiding myth insisted that men of a certain type-—big, boisterous, bullying-—must be straight while the smaller guys, particularly those who had not yet shed their virginity, were "queers."

From their first days together in San Diego, Sommers had sensed Lee would be the perfect scapegoat. There, at Pendleton, Jacksonville and Biloxi, Sommers set Ozzie up as "suspect."

Here he comes at last. Friggin' little Fillipino shrimp.

Kim, the diminutive 5' 4" 21 year old with facial features as delicate as a lovely woman and skin softer even than most females, warily slipped into sight. Sommers took a quick glance around to ascertain no one else had wandered into this barren strip where a recently erected stretch of barbed wire separated flat open-ground from surrounding jungle. Excited at the prospect, Sommers set down his shotgun against a fence pole. Kim following fast behind, Sommers disappeared into the bushes.

Not a word passed between them. Sommers rapidly undid his belt, dropping the fatigue pants and under-drawers. Kim fell to his knees, arching his head up, opening his mouth.

With both hands, Sommers reached forward, seized Kim by his black hair, and pulled the boy's face upward toward an exposed crotch. Sommers roughly pushed forward, downward, eyes closed, grunting with immediate pleasure and a mental backlog of shame. Kim sucked and slurped, accepted the whole wad, gulping it down.

"Well, isn't this a pretty sight, now."

Both men, one standing and the other kneeling, felt a surge of horror pass through their systems like electric bolts. As each pulled back, they simultaneously glanced to another nearby bush where a man, in fatigue pants and T-shirt, quietly stood. Over his unrecognizable face, a stocking had been pulled tight. This intruder now cradled Sommers' shotgun, both barrels cocked.

"Who goes there?" Sommers gasped.

"Your worst nightmare," the interloper replied. He stepped forward, the weapon leveled at Sommers mid-section.

"Please, don't kill poor Kim!" Terrified, the Fillipino rose, sobbing. The unknown man, who could not have been more than 5' 6" tall, indicated for Kim to leave. Kim nodded his thanks.

"Didn't you forget something?" Kim, confused, spread his arms wide to suggest 'I don't understand.' The unknown person nodded for Kim to re-approach Sommers. "You haven't been paid yet." The interloper motioned for Kim to retrieve what he had earned. Kim reached into Sommers' shirt pocket and drew out the hundred dollar bill. The man holding the shotgun motioned for Kim to scat. A second later he was swallowed up by darkness.

"Now," the visitor informed Sommers, approaching with the gun pointed at the guard's belly. "What shall we do with *you?*"

"Please, no. No, no!" Sommers wailed, tears rolling down his cheeks. Without realizing it, Sommers dropped to his knees, raising his arms, joining one hand with the other as if praying.

"Not so tough now, are you?" The unknown man brought the shotgun up beneath Sommers chin, forcing the marine to peer up.

"I'll never kid you again," Sommers pleaded. "Never!"

"That's right. You won't."

With that, the stranger pulled the trigger, unleashing first one, then the other blast, afterwards hurrying off.

Seventy-five-feet away, Lt. Hugh Cherrie, in the process of inspecting another guard-post, heard the double-boom followed by a bloodcurdling scream. Freezing up, he tried to tell himself the former was lightning, the latter a harsh wind coming off Subic Bay. *No, it's a marine. And he's in* serious *trouble.*

Leaving his post technically qualified as dereliction of duty but there was no stopping Hugh when a comrade in arms might be in danger. Arriving simultaneous with a medic who also heard the sounds, the lieutenant spotted Sommers, head all but blown off, lying in a thickening pool of his own blood.

Another marine, Peter Francis Connor, was assigned to the remainder of that night's guard duty. Several others were called to remove Sommers' dead body. The experience was eerie, but no detail-—not even the blood, dark brown in the moonlight—struck Connor as bizarre as what he noticed throughout the area: bits and pieces of red-and-white Christmas candy everywhere.

Accident or suicide, the word eventually came down, and likely no one would ever know which. Case closed. All the same, a rumor spread throughout the base that this had been a murder, with but one suspect. Marines looked suspiciously at Ozzie from then on. But no one kidded him ever again. When any marines did speak to him they politely addressed him as Lee.

Also, Oswald struck the marines as different from that day on. "A completely changed person from the naïve and innocent boy" was how Joseph D. Macedo, another member of Coffee Mill, recalled Lee, as understood through his attitudes and actions beginning the following morning. Others would, in retrospect, particularly after the events of 11/22/1963, remember that Lee had grown "cold" and "bitter," yet conversely more outgoing than before. He joined the guys (not only his three friends) for drinks, gambling, and whoring sojourns.

On one occasion, at the Enlisted Men's Club, Lee picked a fight with a larger guy, Miguel Rodriguez, though this Mexican-American from Texas had never given Lee a problem. Not wanting any trouble, Rodriguez refused to meet Lee outside for a fist-fight, even after his tormentor had flipped a full measure of booze all across Rodriguez's clean shirt.

An official complaint was filed. Lee again stood Court Martial, this time for behavior unbecoming a marine. He found himself locked in The Brig for a month. When Lee stepped back out into the light of day, everyone could tell the treatment behind bars, known to be brutal, had not caused this difficult marine to mend his ways. Rather, imprisonment had the opposite effect. His eyes had turned mean, ugly even; the shoulders were pulled far back, head held high as if to announce what he soon put into hysterical words: L.O.H. had gone all the way over to the other side, hating everything his country stood for.

Beautiful! Everything according to our scenario ...

Lee would rant and rave, occasionally quoting Shakespeare, which he had focused on behind bars: "Oh, how all occasions do inform against me!" Additionally, he put in for a hardship discharge. If granted, following return to San Diego, he would not be required to remain in the reserves. Lee could go off to attend his sickly mother. He had, in the short time between leaving Corregidor and finishing his tour of duty, come full cycle: the perennial outsider accepted as one of the guys, then through seemingly stupid mistakes back to the barrel's bottom.

They're actually buying it. I hoodwinked everyone.

One day, a month and a half later, Gator—figuring that their continuing friendship entitled him to ask what none of the others dared—questioned his pal over beers at the Bluebird.

"Lee, just how angry are you?"

"Want to know the truth?"

"I'm almost afraid to say this, but ... yes."

"I'm considering defecting to the Soviet Union."

After a long silence, during which he recovered, the gentle giant spoke: "There's something else I have to ask."

"Mmmmm? I think I know."

"You can tell me, Lee. You know I'd never rat you out."

"I trust you, Gator."

Hesitantly, Gator closed the remaining space between them so Lee could whisper. "Did you kill Sommers that night?"

Lee's smile turned laconic. "That, my friend," he replied, "is one of those things you never will know, not for certain."

CHAPTER NINE:
STRANGE BEDFELLOWS

"Make no mistake about it: espionage is a dirty business!"
—Robert Maheu, 1963

An eye for an eye, the Mafia code of honor insisted, a tooth for a tooth. Hardly, though, in the Biblical sense, the phrase originally intended to keep capital punishment at a minimum. La Casa Nostra read those words less mercifully:

Vengeance is mine, sayeth the Made Men.

Resulting in that final detail to be agreed on before Bob Maheu and Johnny Rosselli could cement their plan to assassinate Fidel Castro as a joint venture by the Mob and the CIA ...

Whenever Sam Giancana was not absorbed with his "family" business, Gold spent his hours banging the beautiful recording star Phyllis McGuire. With her older sisters Christine and Dorothy, she had created a sweet-spirited form of pop music back in the pre-rock 'n' roll era of the early 1950s via songs like "Sugartime" and "Sincerely." When the bright-eyed ladies would appear onstage or on television, they appeared to be the old-fashioned all-American girl next door, multiplied by three.

Pretty as they all were, Phyllis rated as 'the looker.'

Why such a woman would allow a morally reprehensible man like Sam to be in her immediate presence, much less touch her, remained a mystery. The sisters had begun their careers by singing in rural Ohio church choirs and, when asked to play Vegas, refused to wear overtly sexy costumes.

Nope! This is who we are. Take us or leave us. Your call.

As to her adoration of Sam the Man, some speculated that Phyllis sold her soul, along with her body, to The Mob. This, in exchange for a high-finance recording contract which called for the most prominent of the sisters to 'service' Giancana at his whim. As for Phyllis, throughout her life she consistently kept to a simple line: Giancana, while perhaps not the handsomest fellow, had been a true gentleman; she had no conception as to his 'business' until years later; the relationship remained platonic, a series of delightful dinner dates.

Whoever, and whatever, one believed, this "relationship" continued into the early 1960s. Then Giancana found himself unable to spend as much time with Phyllis owing to pressing problems, most immediately the huge amounts of money Castro cost his Syndicate. Meanwhile, Giancana soon came to believe Phyllis to be cheating on him.

A deeply paranoid personality, he would rush into her apartment at odd hours, expecting to find the great love of his life in the arms of another man. Her *lover*.

Who could it be? I'll know when I catch them in the act. Then ... Heaven help him. I'll castrate him first, then—

That never happened, no matter how carefully and often Sam re-adjusted the hours of his surprise visits. Some observers, around at the time, insisted no such competition ever existed, except in the hard, cold, threatened mind of Old Sam Gold. Others claimed McGuire, aware of Sam's jealous rages, used her brain. She never brought her boy-toy home (if he existed), fucking him in secret at his own place.

Six of one; a half dozen of the other. In time, the fear of her infidelity, initially a preoccupation, developed into full-blown all-encompassing obsession. Sam would smile at colleagues attending a top level/closed-doors meeting, nodding in agreement at suggestions about the Castro problem, secretly focusing on Phyllis: Those lips, those eyes; that hair, that *body* ...

Like most cold-blooded 'tough guys' when in the world of men, Gold was too terrified of the elegant beauty to broach the subject directly with her. Instead, he grew ever more moody, silent, sullen. Something was clearly wrong, but what? Phyllis wondered. When she asked, Sam glumly turned away. Eventually, he decided that the best way to solve this problem would be to have her possibly non-existent lover whacked. But who was he?

*

Though ever-rising issues kept Sam hurrying back and forth between Chicago and Miami, Phyllis' career had her heading off once more to Vegas. Desperate for even a quick glimpse at her, Giancana learned that Phyllis would appear on a TV interview show from Sin City. He worked his schedule around the broadcast. As it happened, Phyllis shared airtime with a jovial, handsome, mustachioed comedian, Dan Rowan, of the Martin and Rowan team.

"And now, live from Las Vegas, here is ..."

In what may have been an innocent gesture, the most elegant if enigmatic McGuire sister, hoping to offer viewers a sense of the camaraderie among show-biz types, took hold of the hand of

Rowan. They smiled and made small talk. Giancana, ever on the lookout for any sign or signal, interpreted this gesture as evidence.

"It's him. He's the one! I'll fuckin' kill him!"

Faithful attendants, fearful he'd suffered a stroke, rushed in to see if they might help. The crazed mob boss stomped his feet, pointing to the small black and white screen. The others stood there, with no idea what had set him off. Sam, like most paranoid personalities, never shared his conclusions with them, preferring to simmer until the proverbial pot boiled over.

Dan Rowan must die!

*

The timing of this epiphany struck Giancana as marvelously appropriate, considering the CIA's offer to join with The Mob in killing Castro. *Fine! But to do that job for you might make us vulnerable, particularly if anything goes wrong. That's why we need one of your guys, this 'George' of whom you speak, to be the middle-man. And why we now ask you to honor our request for something totally unrelated to Fidel Castro ...*

"See, right now, in Vegas," Johnny Handsome explained to Dick Tracy, "there's this *bum* ..."

Maheu's jaw literally dropped. He tried to control his body which had begun to shiver and shake. Initially, he had agreed to be part of the plot to destroy Castro just so long as it didn't involve the leader's death. That had been reconfigured with the appearance of Jack Kennedy on the D.C. scene. Somehow Dick Tracy found a way to justify this additional moral conundrum which ran counter to his essential Jesuit values: *Thou shalt not ...*

Now, the circle of guilt widened. He was asked to join in a conspiracy to whack an ordinary guy who had done nothing but sleep with some beautiful woman—if he had even done that.

God, almighty! Where do I draw the line? Or do we, in this new decade, the Sixties, inhabit a world in which there are no lines anymore, and anything goes?

Excusing himself abruptly, heading for a phone booth in the hallway, hands sweaty, Dick Tracy slipped in some coins. Maheu called Edwards; Edwards called Bissell; Bissell called Dulles (Allen); Dulles called Dulles (John F.); Dulles (John F.) called JFK; JFK gave the word to Dulles; Dulles passed the answer down to Dulles; Dulles to Bissell; Bissell whispered the decision to Edwards; Edwards told Maheu ... without anyone actually saying the precise words per se ... kill the fuckin' bastard.

My country, Maheu repeated over and over again in his mind, right or wrong! *Heaven help me if it, and now I, fall into the latter category, for some day there will be a final reckoning ...*

But I can't think of that now ... I must live in the moment ... and as always in my life do what I consider best for my country ... even if at the price of my immortal soul.

Maheu returned to the table. Barely able to speak, he at last muttered what Giancana and Rosselli were waiting to hear: the deal had been finalized. The CIA would become involved, if only "peripherally," in the murder of a goofy, non-political stand-up comic. This, to prove to Sam Giancana, that the CIA was now aligned, and permanently so, with The Mob.

Who was it, Dick Tracy tried to recall, *first pointed out that politics makes for strange bedfellows?*

*

Hours after the Fountainbleau meeting, Maheu sent O'Connell packing back to Washington. He boarded a plane headed for Vegas in the company of Johnny Handsome. A luxury suite awaited Maheu at the Sands hotel and Casino. After a troubled night's sleep he joined Rosselli for breakfast in a private meeting room though Dick Tracy, ordinarily a big eater, couldn't swallow anything.

"To show your absolute loyalty," Rosselli had explained en route, "Sam Gold would like you *personally* to ..."

The scheme would go down this way: while Rowan was out of his suite, Maheu would slip in, planting a small microphone. This would allow Rosselli to tape anything that occurred there and report to Giancana whether his beloved was or was not a slut. If the latter, no problem. Then, back to Castro.

If, on the other hand, Rowan and Phyllis were 'involved,' Rosselli must arrange for the entertainer to be whacked or do the job himself. The CIA need not dirty their hands further.

Shaking, Dick Tracy explained over his untouched plate of eggs and bacon that he had wrestled with the issue all through the night. Finally, he could not bring himself to do it. The wiretapping would be simple for someone with his experience to perform; he'd done this sort of stuff often during his days of government service and, more recently, for Howard Hughes as to business associates. In such cases any information collected would result in fortunes lost or made.

But with Hughes there had been no blood. *Thou shalt not—*

"It's a deal-breaker," Johnny reminded him.

"I understand. So, after realizing that I could not do it myself, here's what I came up with, God forgive me."

To try and make things work, without sticking his own hands directly in the muck—*the thief knows he is not absolutely evil as he is not a killer; the killer knows he is not absolutely evil as*—Dick Tracy would bring in someone more expert than himself. Arthur J. Balletti, now Maheu informed Johnny, was already on his way.

Balletti would do the microphone plant that night while Rowan performed. That was the best Bob Maheu could offer.

Johnny excused himself and made a call back east to Sam while Maheu glumly sat, sipping his coffee, half-hoping his compromise would be rejected. If that were the case, he could walk away and not have to suffer guilt, even by such remote association. The aging Cold Warrior felt sick to his stomach when Rosselli jauntily returned. Sam had agreed.

God, I hope for Dan Rowan's sake that he's not banging this bitch. And, of course, for the preservation of my own soul ...

Rosselli and Maheu shook hands. Minutes later, Maheu headed for the airport, on his way back to Washington even as the plane that carried Balletti touched down in Vegas.

*

At first all went according to plan. The small, ordinary, nondescript Balletti patiently relaxed in his own room, watching TV, eating a club sandwich from room service. When evening set in, shows opened all along the Strip. Balletti then drew the needed materials of his trade from his luggage and rode the elevator up to what Johnny had informed him was Rowan's suite.

An expert at lock-picking, Balletti entered seconds after his arrival, no one else in the hallway. A moment later he slipped into Rowan's bedroom-area. There Balletti inserted a miniature microphone into the telephone on an adjoining table.

His work completed in less than two minutes, Balletti then prepared to quickly disappear into the night.

End of story.

Only, it didn't turn out that way ...

As Balletti exited the room, after peering out to make certain no one happened to be in the hallway, a maid at that precise moment finished cleaning the room two doors down. Such an intrusion rare at this hour, but necessary as the occupants had remained inside all through the day. Balletti had calculated the likelihood of his running into anyone just now would be miniscule. Maybe a million to one.

However, as anyone who has ever played the odds knows, that unlikely number can come up when one least expects it. Balletti stepped into the hallway and came face to face with the maid.

"Oh!"

144

Trying to cover for himself but shocked by her presence, Balletti stammered something absurd on the order of "How are you?" and "Nice evening!" Had he simply kept his trap shut and refused to make eye-contact, Balletti likely would have escaped unnoticed. His awkward speech and nervous gestures did cause the maid to grow suspicious. Besides, she recalled that this room was occupied by the comic even now performing downstairs.

Why should a stranger be in there, and alone? Clearly, something wasn't quite right here.

The maid made some feeble excuses to remain in the hallway, assorting towels on her mobile rack to appear busy, until this possible interloper stepped into the elevator. The moment he was gone, she used her master key to enter Rowan's room. Though the phone wire had been planted so effectively she could not spot it, the woman felt vaguely uncomfortable with the situation. While no tangible evidence existed, she relied on her woman's instinct and decided to do something about this immediately.

She might have called hotel security. If that had been the case, nothing more would have come of the matter. For this was a Mob-owned casino-hotel and such employees would have known what to do. Instead, for reasons she was not able to later explain, the maid reached for the phone and dialed the sheriff's office.

Within minutes, lawmen swarmed all over the Sands. They quickly uncovered the wire, a federal offense. Through the maid's vivid description, they targeted Balletti and headed for his room. He was not there, but they did discover his technical apparatus, strewn over the bed, the culprit clearly in no way expecting anything like this.

All they needed to do now was find the man, the maid certain she could positively identify him. If not in his room, however, where might he be?

In fact, Balletti was even then in the showroom, enjoying Rowan and Martin along with other visitors. He'd heard that Dan Rowan was an incredibly funny man. Guessing that this might be the last opportunity to catch the fellow's act, Balletti had joined the crowd. They found him laughing the evening away, assuring himself that more likely than not, the maid would not think anything of it and all would be fine.

Assumptions, however, are dangerous. Lawmen stuck their noses into every restaurant, bar, and gambling nook before, as a last resort, they decided to check out the Sands' own showroom. The maid accompanied them. From the rear of the auditorium, she pointed out the nonchalant man seated in the jovial crowd.

Moments later Balletti was under arrest. Also attending that evening's show was Johnny Rosselli, his motivation for being there pretty much the same: catch this acclaimed act before it was over and done, if indeed Rowan proved to be guilty.

No one would ever determine that. It turned out to be one of those things in life that you never do know. Not for certain.

*

Realizing that everything that possibly could go wrong had proceeded to do just that, Rosselli—sweating heavily, rare for so cool a character—rushed to his office and called Giancana. Stunned to hear that something which had sounded so simple could without warning turn into a potentially disastrous situation, Sam—when able to form words—decided he would have to consider this carefully before making any decision as to what they might do next. As always, Giancana operated like a stealthy jungle cat.

Meanwhile Balletti, from his jail cell, called Maheu in D.C., pleading for help. Stunned, Maheu phoned Rosselli in Vegas, catching Johnny a few seconds after he'd hung up from his call to Giancana. Learning that Old Sam was going to sit back and wait to see what transpired, the two confederates decided that, as a back-up plan, they ought to cook up some sort of scenario which each would stick to, whatever might happen next.

Johnny, they decided, would at once pay a "friendly visit" to the local authorities, arranging (owing to the influence he and his organization had in Vegas) for Balletti to be released. That would not be too difficult to manage, so each blew a sigh of relief as Rosselli headed over to police headquarters.

Things might have quieted down then except Maheu's own phone had recently been tapped by the FBI. This, owing to the continued diminishment of Hoover's influence there, the Bureau turks peered into dark corners of Mobdom that J. Edgar always insisted must go un-inspected. As a result, they had commenced with keeping a close eye (and ear) on former FBI personnel who were rumored to now be in league with members of the Mafia.

Convinced this was the case with Maheu owing to what he'd heard through the grapevine, a young agent had decided to stake out the supposedly cleaner-than-clean cop. Maybe something ugly had been going on with him lately; hopefully not. Either way, it seemed an imperative to this agent that he know for certain.

Listening in on that call between Maheu and Rosselli, realizing the dirty business involved not only Maheu and the Mob but at least indirectly the despised CIA, the agent figured he'd struck gold. Immediately he rang up his immediate superior. As this man listened to the agent's account of the bizarre incidents, aware too that the agent had been smart enough to tape-record these clandestine conversations to have unassailable if less than legal proof of whatever charges might be leveled, the two decided they had no alternative but to request an indictment against the former agent and his correspondent, a Made Man.

In an irony the two agents were perhaps not fully aware of, they planned to use their own illegal wiretapping to arrest, then convict, Rosselli and Maheu of ... illegal wiretapping.

In the wee small hours of the morning, the FBI men arrived at Maheu's apartment. They confronted him with the evidence. As would happen again in 2008, when Dick Tracy fell to his death in a Vegas motel, his life flashed before his eyes. Maheu glimpsed a career dedicated to public service going down the drain, he spending the remainder of his years in prison. As a good soldier, Maheu seized control of his strained emotions. He forced himself to speak with quiet dignity and an impressive air of authority.

"I've just talked to my superior, Sheffield Edwards, Director of Security at the CIA. On his authority I will reveal to you what we had hoped would not need be revealed. Pretending to represent a number of business people, I have in fact been, for the past several months, an unofficial Company employee. My task has been to off-the-record deal with a number of men who, to be as honest as I dare be, are regarded as Mobsters.

"Yes, as I know, members of the criminal organization that you have recently set out to bring down. No question this is an awkward situation. Please be aware, none of what I've embarked on is self-serving, motivated by personal profiteering. Other than a small fee for my services, which I can assure you is less than I would require from private businesses, the sole reason I am involved in any of this, at obvious risk to myself and my reputation as your presence here now makes all too clear, is a desire to the serve the best interests of the United States."

Maheu cleared his throat as the two FBI agents stared on, dumbfounded. He continued ...

"If this entailed doing things that ... how to put it ... might not be considered 'strictly kosher,' then my view had to be, so be it. All of this relates, if in a serpentine manner, to the issue of national security. You have our permission, my own self and that of Shef Edwards, to relate all this to J. Edgar, as well as suggest Mr. Hoover discuss everything I have said with Attorney General Robert Kennedy, he also aware of what we've been doing. That, gentlemen, is all I have to say."

The agents stood stock still for a while, unable to offer any coherent response. This was beyond their comprehension. They asked Maheu to take a seat, which he did, while they scurried off into a far corner to discuss the can of worms they'd opened.

One possibility was to contact someone higher up in the Bureau, perhaps Hoover. That did not strike either as viable. After all, they had, like everyone in government service, heard the rumor, around for so long it had been generally accepted as fact, that the Mob held in reserve a picture ... That didn't mean they should not now report their findings of a CIA-Mob connection, only that the old bulldog was not that person.

"If not J. Edgar, who, then?"

"Give me a moment to think ..."

Another element had to be taken into account: the recently strained relations between the FBI and the CIA. From the start of the latter organization's inception, Hoover clearly felt threatened that his Bureau might soon play second-fiddle to the Agency. Since the election, JFK clearly preferred the jet-age cowboys to those now stodgy agents best remembered for gunning down the Dillinger gang, back during the Depression.

Then the first tangible blow-up between FBI and CIA had occurred. A ranking KGB officer defected from the Soviets. He presented himself directly to the CIA, as if unaware the FBI still even existed. Worse, CIA members who had taken the man into custody, immediately informing both Kennedy brothers of this potentially explosive event, only approached the FBI as an afterthought. Hearing this, Hoover hit the ceiling.

For Hoover, here was a sign that he and the Bureau now rated as minor-league citizens. And would continue as such so as long the Kennedy clan ran things. An angry complaint was lodged. As a result, JFK did tell Allen Dulles that from now on, the CIA really ought to inform J. Edgar about such matters. Jack did so in such a contemptuous manner that Hoover became hysterical, though Dulles and Helms agreed to keep him in the loop.

The two agents now in Maheu's apartment recalled all of this. They agreed that if anyone higher up in the Bureau were to be informed, Hoover would catch wind of it in a matter of time. When that happened, holy hell would break loose. Both men were, like Maheu, the most dedicated of patriots, more concerned about what was best for the U.S. than themselves or the particular venue in the intelligence community they happened have joined.

"We're agreed, then?"

"I believe we are."

The agents re-approached Maheu. They explained that, for the time being, they would not mention this to anyone. While they would not agree to Maheu's request to destroy the tape, the agents promised to keep it locked away to avoid precipitating a commotion that would reflect negatively on both their agencies.

"Well, I appreciate that. *Very* much."

Maheu breathed a sigh of relief. For the moment, at least, things would likely remain under control.

*

Meanwhile, Sam Giancana prepared himself for the likely possibility that Phyllis might hear about his attempt to have Dan Rowan whacked. Terrified at the thought of now losing her forever, whether she had cheated or not, his fears and anxiety proving to be a self-fulfilling prophecy, Sam determined to let the matter of infidelity, real or imagined, drop.

Also, Old Sam knew that he would have to provide a gift so spectacular that Phyllis could not bring herself to refuse it. And, as a result, would take him back. Diamonds the size of the Ritz wouldn't work this time, nor would the most expensive mink coat for sale on Fifth Avenue. He had to outdo himself and, once that cunning mind went to work, Sam managed precisely that.

Already, he had made a top recording, radio, TV, and stage star of her. More of the same was not enough, not now. Phyllis wanted more. She had always wanted more. If she craved something, Sam would get it for her. And, as soon as he did, whatever this may have been struck her as meaningless. Always she wanted more.

In show business, 'more' could only mean one thing: Phyllis wanted to stop being a celebrity and become a movie star.

So Sam phoned his unofficial godson, Frank Sinatra, in L.A. Now nicknamed The Chairman of the Board, as such not only a super-star but a paragon of the entertainment business, Frankie could do pretty much anything he chose as to upcoming projects.

"Not a problem, Sam. You know me. As with Charley, any favor asked is a favor honored. It'll be taken care of."

Shortly thereafter, it was announced that recording star Phyllis McGuire would co-star with Sinatra in his upcoming big picture, *Come Blow Your Horn*, which would start shooting soon.

*

Even as Bob Maheu had breathlessly related his impromptu but convincing speech to the pair of disbelieving FBI agents, Johnny Handsome in Vegas hurriedly packed a few essentials into a suit-case. Shortly he headed for the airport where he caught a plane bound for Miami. Sam had suggested Rosselli disappear for a while. He should assume one of his many aliases—*you haven't used 'James Stewart' in a while, have you?*—while in Florida.

There, Johnny would help CIA agent 'George' and the Mob's own Santo Traffacante, Jr. to pick and choose among men then being recruited to fly missions over Cuba. Such operatives had, for some time, pretended to defect, then operated as 'moles' and on occasion agents provocateur to try and bring down Castro.

The previous operatives sent on such perilous missions included George's favorite, young Lee Harvey Oswald.

Yet even as Maheu and Jim O'Connell had been preparing for their all-important meeting in Miami with Sam Giancana, Shef Edwards, who had initiated the project at least so far as Dick Tracy was concerned, began harboring second thoughts. He did consider the Mob connection a necessarily evil. Still, those words of warning Bob offered, kept out of Shef's conscious mind during his waking hours, now haunted his dreams. Also there was his own moral conscience which, like that of Bob, resoundingly warned him of that Biblical commandment: Though shalt not kill.

Such nightmares only increased after Edwards gave Dick Tracy the go-ahead to call Johnny Rosselli and start planning a final solution to 'the Fidel problem.' Realizing that time still remained to complete this business without an execution, Shef called an emergency meeting of the CIA's top agents.

One man came up with a bizarre scheme that held everyone's attention. The CIA would send an operative down to Havana, have that person convince Castro's minions he had defected and wished to serve The Great Leader. The volunteer would claim to be an expert at broadcasting and offer to work for Radio Havana.

Sounds like a perfect chore for Lee, George mused.

As an American, the Cubans would naturally be wary, always searching the agent for hidden weapons before allowing him anywhere near their leader. Of course, he would carry none.

The plan: destroy Fidel Castro's credibility with the Cuban people. Before some upcoming public address, the agent/defector would offer to thoroughly clean the studio where Cuba's great man would shortly speak. No one would ever suspect anything as he darted about the area, spraying air freshener.

Only this would be no ordinary can. Inside, CIA experts at such secretive matters would have inserted some substance that could cause Castro to grow disoriented. Cuba's leader would make a fool of himself, live on-air. This would set into motion the beginning of his end. Meanwhile, the perpetrator would have hurried away to some waiting escape vehicle and be long gone.

"Seems reasonable. What chemical did you have in mind?"

"Lysergic acid is the official name. The government agency that's been testing this synthetic concoction calls it LSD."

"We'll have to check, make sure it's dependable. If we do go with this, how do you suggest we get the stuff down there?"

"It'll be tough. Castro has appointed a truly brilliant guy, Fabian Escalante, as his new head of security."

"How about this?" someone suggested. "Suppose we stage an air-jacking. The pilot must appear to be an average guy. With him would be a recruit, not officially CIA, so no record with us Escalante might come across. Some obscure man who'd like to do his government a big favor, wants the money, and hungers for some adventure in his life. You know, fame and fortune?"

"Great. Only, where do we find such a man?"

"I know precisely the right guy," Frank Sturgis piped in.

*

Knowing time was of the essence, Edwards reached a decision that day. LSD had to be abandoned owing to its unpredictable impact: Castro might experience a heightened clarity rather than disorganization. The notion of an air-jack remained very much alive, that device in use already as a means of delivering CIA operatives down to Cuba. Shef liked the concept of transforming Castro into a clown in the eyes of his people and had discussed this with Jake Esterline, head of the Cuba task force.

The whole business came down to finding two individuals who were willing to try just about anything and able to pull off the near-impossible. Sturgis had already suggested Lee Oswald as the likeliest candidate for that element of the job. What they needed now was someone willing to fly the plane down.

Needed too was a top gun, someone with prowess at shooting his way out of any impossible situations if it came down to that. Owing to the reconfigured relationships between the CIA and the Mafia, this meant bringing one of their boys on board.

"I think I've got it," Edwards announced. "Since Bob Maheu has already begun the process of establishing a Mob connection, in my mind the third man ought to be one of theirs. A mobster known for his derring-do. Preferably one who already has a Cuban-connection, knows the lay of the land, so to speak."

"Alright," Esterline countered, "so who comes to mind?"

"Maheu says that one of their top boys in Vegas, Johnny Handsome, fits the bill. The man Giancana dispatched to kill Castro unless he re-opened the casinos back in January '59."

Esterline considered the possibilities. "Won't that make him immediately recognizable if captured?"

"Castro only saw him for a few seconds. With a thick beard, a change of hair-color, and contact lenses to alter his eyes? I think Johnny can get away with it."

Maheu was at once contacted as to whether this approach might serve as an intermediary attempt to come up with a solution to the Castro problem. Meanwhile, the conversation pertaining to the Mob whacking the Cuban dictator via some pretty girl continued. For the better part of a month, Frank Sturgis had begun processing just the person to take on the role of Castro's assassin. Occasionally, the girl was called 'Lolita' referring to her child-like appearance. On others, The Kraut, referencing her ethnicity.

Maheu called Rosselli, Rosselli called Giancana, and Old Sam said sure, why don't they try that approach during the brief time remaining before the all-important Miami meeting in which a more permanent solution would be discussed. Rosselli got back to Maheu, Maheu called Edwards, and he contacted Allen Dulles.

They agreed to try this route, doing so without informing Kennedy. They were fearful that JFK was out for blood and might say 'no: I want you to whack the Beard and that's that.'

When Lee first heard the plans from George, he all but did a dance of joy. Johnny Rosseli had mightily impressed him during the twinning process. The idea of heading off on such a top secret mission with the greatest CIA operative and the deadliest of the Made Men thrilled Lee to the bone. It was like ... being the star of a spy movie.

A CIA private jet flew Lee and George to Tampa. There, Santos Trafficante Jr. had several *soldati* pick the boys up at the airport in a sleek limo. At Crisco's, a Mob owned and operated restaurant in downtown, the two CIA operatives met in a quiet corner with Johnny, his code name now 'Jimmy Stewart,' after the all-American movie star, an irony Rosselli enjoyed.

*

"My beard," Fidel Castro had swaggeringly stated in a TV interview, "means many things to my people."

Though he did not choose to offer specifics, most listeners in Cuba grasped what he meant. Shaggy, unkempt and possibly dirty, perhaps with a horde of microscopic bugs nestled deep within the twisted strands, Castro's facial hair represented, at least in the late 1950s, an open rebellion against all those white-bread values America held most dear during the Eisenhower era.

Here was a rebel, maverick, non-conformist. The Third World equivalent of one of those Beatniks in Greenwich Village, who inhabited cellars instead of apartments. Or in some cases lofts;

anything that did not fit into the mainstream style of living. These were self-consciously squalid drop-outs from society who had, like Castro down south, grown disenchanted with the U.S. postwar policy toward Third World nations. Every upstanding suburbanite considered these characters a threat to everything they held dear. As most of the males wore beards, that caused them to be suspect as Communists, perhaps pro-Castro.

What better, then, to turn Castro into a figure of ridicule by eliminating this signature item? A beardless Fidel would look naked in a manner of speaking. And, as such, humorous. No one can take seriously a giant who, like Samson, existed without hair in Gaza or Havana. People could not respect or fear what they found funny. Here was a curious means of dethroning the target.

So began a brief-lived crusade to de-beard the Beard. The trio of Lee, Maheu and Johnny was not the first to depart. Even as they were readying to board their aircraft, another ascended to begin the hour-and-a-half journey south. Hidden aboard, to be passed to an operative there who would then turn the cargo over to the musketeers, was a box of cigars laced with thallium salts. These, the CIA's scientists insisted, would do the job.

The perpetrator would land his supposedly high-jacked plane, send the pretend-kidnap-victim-pilot flying back home, then surrender himself to authorities as a defector. This would put him in the position to pass the cigars on to another CIA agent already planted in Castro's organization. This man would sneak the box to Lee Oswald after his arrival.

Always, the Company worked in a serpentine method. The CIA doctrine held that the more complex any such operation became, the less likely any specific member of their task force would be apprehended. If they were confused, the enemy must be, too.

Initially, the plan appeared to be working. No one however had taken Castro's considerable sophistication as to tobacco into account. Oswald, employed in the radio station, offered his new leader a cigar. The moment Fidel locked his teeth onto the strange smelling tube, he sensed something wrong. Castro spit out the initial whiff of smoke to enter his throat, shouting for guards to drag the CIA plant off to El Principe. Lee, Maheu and Johnny spent several miserable nights there before release.

The plot didn't end there. The operative who had flown in previous to Lee had accepted a lowly job at the Havana Hilton. Despite Castro's supposed nonchalant attitude toward fashion, it was well known that Fidel always left his shoes outside of his suite door every night to be shined, this (and the fine silk underwear he secretively slipped into every morn before pulling his ragged fatigues on over them) one of his few decadences. The agent requested the honor of doing the shining. In the process, he would scatter thallium salts in the shoes.

The plan held that such toxic chemicals would be absorbed through Castro's socks, into his skin. The salts weren't strong enough to kill, but the specialists insisted that his beard would shortly fall out, and that would be the end of that.

This was not to be the case. The following morning, Fidel took one look at his shoes, saw white powder spread all across their insides, and yelped for the employee responsible to be arrested. El Principle now held another lodger. From then on, supposed defectors from the U.S. were no longer greeted with a hero's welcome. Instead, all would be closely scrutinized.

Here ended the last great hope of ridding the world of Fidel Castro without killing him outright. From then on, it was do or die, the hope being that Castro would do the dying.

Several days later, Santo Trafficante, aka Joe the Courier, passed the botulin pills to Frank Angelo Fiorini, aka Frank Anthony Sturgis, aka George, the CIA operative. He in turn handed them over to Lorita Morenz, aka The Kraut, aka Lolita.

She failed so totally in her attempt to kill Castro that Sam Giancante, aka Sam Gold, sent word through Rosselli, aka Johnny Roselli, aka Handsome, aka John F. Stewart, to Maheu, aka Dick Tracy. He passed Sam's message to Edwards, who passed it on to Jake Esterline. He then turned it over to Dick Bissell, who whispered with Allen Dulles, who huddled with John Foster Dulles.

He in turn reported to President John Fitzgerald Kennedy. La Casa Nostra, working with CIA operative George, had to take some time if they were to plan a more effective assassination for Castro. The word went back through the grapevine that George had another solution to the problem in mind. No longer would he rely on giddy girls who thought they'd mastered the skills of a female agent in a James Bond book. This must be accomplished by some man, a nondescript face in the crowd. Already, George had picked out the precise person he wanted for the job.

*

JFK, unable to grasp why the task couldn't be completed as fast and clean as it would have been in one of those Ian Fleming novels he daily devoured, howled that heads would roll if this was not accomplished. Shortly, Chief of TSD Cornelius Roosevelt okayed yet another box of cigars, this one containing fifty Havanas laced with the deadly botulin toxin. These were passed on, once the lab had completed their latest offering, to Dr. Edward Gunn, Chief of the CIA's Operations Division.

Why cigars would work this time around, at least in the minds of those who conceived the plan, was anyone's guess. Apparently none had ever heard the old adage that the dumbest of the dumb were those who steadfastly continued to try and attain a goal by the same means that had failed in the past.

Lee Oswald could have told them that. But they didn't ask.

On February 13, 1961, Gunn passed the cigars to an unknown CIA operative assigned to deliver the box to some unspecified Mafia runner, who would then give them to the courier assigned to smuggle the cigars into Havana, these to be handed over to the CIA's operative, already smuggled into Cuba by submarine.

Whether they arrived but were never employed, or failed to make it there, remains unknown. Two months later, though, the CIA and the Mob received word that any such attempts on Castro's life must cease, at least for the time being. This edict came down from the highest level of the U.S. government.

The reason? Between April 15 and 18, 1961, the Bay of Pigs disaster transpired. In its aftermath, America appeared shamed in the eyes of the international community. The last thing that anyone wanted now was for Castro to die as a result of what would obviously be an American instigated assassination.

For the time being then Fidel would have to be tolerated.

At least until the world began the process of hopefully forgetting about the fiasco that was the Bay of Pigs.

CHAPTER TEN:
HARD TIMES AT HAPPY VALLEY

"If the press had been doing their job, the
Bay of Pigs would have never happened."
—John Fitzgerald Kennedy, 1962

Shortly after midnight on April 15, 1961, a long black limo, six CIA agents seated inside, slowly pulled up to a nearly deserted airstrip in Puerto Cabezas, Nicaragua. Dressed in all but identical dark suits, each man wore a thin black tie and sun-glasses despite the late hour. Such cryptic attire caused the agents to appear less what they were than stereotypes from some Hollywood movie. Each cradled a submachine gun under one arm. Reaching an empty parking lot, they exited their vehicle and marched up toward the hangers, the buildings' curved roofs appearing silver in the stark moonlight.

Awaiting them, having patiently remained silent in one of the hangers for an hour, 17 Cubans stood at the ready. For the past six months, they had been living in Miami, training and planning for this moment. Now, the Cubans impatiently held their collective breath, anticipating such members from The Outfit, aka The Company, aka the CIA. Compared with these tall, slick Americans, the Cubans appeared bedraggled, wearing rough khaki pants and worn leather flight jackets. All of those gathered together here had only one thing in common: they wore cowboy boots, natural enough for the scruffy Cubans perhaps, less so for the suited CIA agents. Nonetheless, such foot-ware served as a special sign among these uneasy allies. When these men did on occasion speak of it, they used a phrase that had naturally developed among those united in the international fight against the spread of communism: Cowboy Politics.

Initially, though, no one spoke. The Cubans eagerly nodded to the Americans who returned that gesture, if in a more restrained manner. In the cool of the night, the two groups stood, wordlessly facing one another under what appeared a huge vanilla wafer pinned to a black satin backdrop up above. Some intruder on the scene, failing to grasp what was about to take place, might have mistakenly thought that at any moment the Cubans would reach under their jackets and pull out pistols, the CIA boys responding in kind. Then the two groups would fire at one another in the manner of an Old West shootout, America's wild frontier days re-staged in the 20th century. The gunfight at the O.K. Corral, circa 1961. But that was not to be the case.

For one thing, the Cubans didn't carry guns. Also, these men had gathered to confer, not fight. At least not yet. And certainly not with each other.

"We're on?" croaked Mario Zuniga, titular leader of the Cubans, as well as the person who one day later would land at the Miami airport, receiving a hero's welcome, he afterwards subject to softball interviews by the press. There, Zuniga would speak eloquently about a great adventure over Cuba, everything he said dutifully reported by journalists working in broadcast news and the print media. As a result, most everyone in the U.S. would learn about a thrilling escapade that, in actuality, had never taken place. In truth a far greater, if also considerably more frightening, event, had: a daring if disastrous misfire of an invasion that would swiftly alter world history.

Zuniga's CIA counterpart, known only as George, nodded. "Yes, clearance completed," he formally announced. George held high, then waved official papers signed by his boss at the CIA, the Joint Chiefs of Staff, and John Fitzgerald Kennedy, sitting President of the United States. Which meant too, as all were aware, America's Commander in Chief. The man who, if things worked out the way they should, when all was over and done, would stand up boldly, like good ol' Harry Truman nearly twenty years earlier, insisting that whether the scheme had gone well or badly, the buck stops here ...

Therein lay the problem. John F. Kennedy was no Harry Truman, nor had he ever longed to be. Perhaps what happened next proves that the right man for that big job may not be one of "the best and brightest" with an Ivy League degree, a ghost-written Pulitzer prize winning book, an upscale trophy wife and a lofty reputation for heroism in naval combat that didn't come close to what it was cracked up to be. Maybe far better suited was some former soda jerk from Grandview, Missouri; a simple man who knew and understood people, in particular this nation's people, thanks to constant contact with them every day of his life.

'An egg-cream? Yes, sir! Coming right up!' A man who respectfully listened to what such heartland types had to say, deeply respecting the common man in all his glory and misery. An ordinary guy doing the best he could, with the common sense of those who work hard, as well as a commitment to standing behind one's word. Or, if things fall apart, taking it on the chin.

*

"On, then!" the Cubans chanted, like a group of little boys playing games despite their menacing appearance in full combat gear. The great moment had arrived at last. The one they'd planned and prepared for in such detail. Zuniga stepped forward and accepted the three pieces of paper, impressed at the notion that he now fingered letters from a triad of the most powerful men in the world. Zuniga then breathed in deeply as, after reading them over, he now passed them back again to George, the American who had recruited the Cubans in Florida, then oversaw their thorough training, mostly in Miami, the final lessons in airborne war, guerilla style, taking place here.

"It's official," George declared without emotion.

"Alright," Zuniga cheered. "Let's do it!"

As had been carefully pre-planned, and rehearsed more than once, the Cubans, moving in unison, shuffled off to one side. There they, hushed, observed while the CIA men, pairing off, entered the hangers. As the automatic doors rose, each pair of agents re-emerged, seated in the cockpit of a readied and running B-26. The planes slowly wheeled out to a waiting area adjacent to the runway. At that point, the CIA men braked, shut down each plane's twin engines, and descended.

"Stand back," George commanded the Cubans.

As they obeyed orders, anxiously waiting and watching, the CIA agents aimed their submachine guns at one of the planes and let loose with a hail of gunfire. This was the B-26 Zuniga had been selected to pilot, Number 933 painted on its nose. This bit of artwork had been applied the previous morning, while the letters FAR were emblazoned on its tail. Zuniga observed his craft while each of the other planes awaited their turn under the gun.

"Perfect," George wistfully sighed.

As the shots resounded through the night air, Mario Zuniga felt a sudden chill pass over him. At hand was the event he'd been dreaming about, hoping for, their moment of truth. The CIA and other organizations had carefully outlined every move the Cubans would make. The time had arrived when they'd initiate the task of bringing back the good ol' days that abruptly ended in 1959. With a little luck, the Mob would return, re-opening the casinos three months from today.

American money would once more pour into the economy. Cuba would be liberated from its supposed liberator, who had proven as authoritarian as his predecessor. Reclamation of the homeland, at last, would take place. Normalcy would return.

Viva Kennedy! Down with Fidel! Up with a free Cuba! A Democratic Cuba. A capitalist Cuba. An American influenced Cuba. An anti-communist Cuba.

A Mafia-controlled Cuba.

George approached Zuniga. "Run it by me again," he barked. "The whole story, from start to finish."

One last run-through? Sure. Can't be too careful, particularly when considering the stakes. After all, Zuniga—whom George had deemed the smartest of the group, also the most mature at 35 years of age—was the one who had been picked to sell their story —"legend," actually—to the American public. This had been scheduled to take place at the precise time when his companions performed the considerably more dangerous grunt work.

So here was how it must go down ...

*

Zuniga would wait until each of the other eight B-26 planes had in turn taken off, this procession beginning promptly at 1:40 a.m. They'd ascend in as rapid succession as possible.

Once airborne, the flyers would divide their crafts into three pre-arranged groups for the trip to Cuba. Code-named "Linda," "Puma," and "Gorilla," each would fly in a direct route, every mile to be crossed significant since each plane was weighted down with extra loads of fuel as well as ten bombs, 260-pounds each.

There could be no margin for error.

Hours later, their timing must be precise: even as dawn broke, the three formations must simultaneously sweep down on their assigned stretches of the unsuspecting homeland, doing as much damage as possible to Fuerza Aerea Revolucionaria below. Take out as many planes as they could. Kill the pilots, many of them former friends, if they should dash out of their barracks, trying to speed their planes into the air, hoping to save them from destruction. Pave the way for the coming armed invasion by sea so that in 48 hours Castro would be a fading memory.

The first formation to rain down bombs and bullets was commanded by Luis Cosme. Though Cuban-born, he could have easily passed for Dobie Gillis, the all-American boy next door played by Dwayne Hickman on a popular TV show that the Cubans enjoyed during the eight months they spent in the Miami area. His "Linda" force, augmented by two other planes piloted by Alfredo Caballero and Rene Garcia, both of whom like Cosme were Cuban Air Force veterans who had also done commercial flying for Cubana Airlines, would sweep down on San Antonio de los Banos, located southwest of Havana. Their job was to take out the wide array of crafts, including B-26s, from back when the U.S. thought of Cuba as a likely ally. And Russian MIG fighters, more recent contributions from the other side, in the brief moments before daybreak.

Minutes later, Jose Crespo's "Puma" formation would circle Camp Libertad closer to Havana. This small squadron included B-26s piloted by Daniel Fernandez Mon and "Chirrino" Piedra, each accompanied by a co-pilot dedicated to carrying out the mission should the man in charge be maimed or killed owing to ground-fire.

A final task force consisted of two planes, flown by Gustavo Ponzoa and Gonzalo Herrea: "Gorilla," the only unit assigned to knock out grounded aircraft in a far distant location. At Santiago de Cuba in Oriente Province where the revolution originally simmered five years earlier, a small, significant airport hidden away in the bleak Sierra Maestra range housed the second largest formation of planes. This reserve could, if undisturbed, be called upon a day later when armed forces, pro-American Cubans even now huddled on six U.S. troop-carriers surrounded for defense purposes by a full array of smaller battle-ready warships, initiated their attack.

With Castro's air force knocked out, the invasion would face no harsh strafing from above. They ought to easily push forward so as to take the high ground while encountering little if any resistance. The Cuban patriots, even then waking from an uneasy sleep aboard such transports as the *Houston*, had spent the past two months in Guatemala. There, American trainers ran them through the most rigorous program the U.S. military, operating in full accord with the CIA, George also the genius behind all this, ever devised. Recruited from the anti-Castro Cuban population that flooded into Miami two years earlier, these men now possessed not only the will but the know-how and equipment to get the job done.

As the three squadrons whistled across the night sky above, each man aboard the boats took pride in the knowledge that some 24 hours hence, he would hear the order "hit the beach!" Then swiftly, violently, proceed to complete through hand to hand combat what their airborne allies earlier began.

Their landing would take place at Bahia de Cochinos, soon to be known worldwide as the Bay of Pigs.

*

George smiled, even as the first plane roared down the runway before slowly tipping upward. Several seconds later, the sleek craft punctured the vast blackness above.

"Now, your personal, specific role in the operation. Tell me slowly. We still have time before your scheduled 1:40 take-off. Be thorough. Leave no detail out."

"Very well," Zuniga said, beginning the story he would tell a day later first to reporters who would gather at Miami's main airport, unwitting pawns in our Invisible Government's grandest scheme to date. Zuniga would fly the 830+ miles from Puerto Cabezas to Florida's southern tip. Owing to the minute planning and exquisite timing, he would arrive over U.S. soil simultaneous with the release of the first bombs down toward the island nation of Cuba.

Approaching Florida, Zuniga would then call in a sudden distress signal to the control towers at the Miami International Airport. His rehearsed pleas for help would begin with a barrage of lies, Zuniga's fanciful scenario serving as a cover-up for the planned invasion. This had been planned by members of the CIA but would be carried out by a motley group of Cubans composed of true idealists as well as jaded opportunists, transported by U.S. military ships. The attack force itself would consist of citizens of a foreign country with which America was not at war, for the purpose of attacking their own home-land.

He had just defected from Cuba, Zuniga would explain after touch-down. There, his plane had been shot to pieces by Castro's gunners. He would reach into his jacket pocket for the pack of Cuban butts George had planted there, another small but convincing detail; this, taken together with other such touches, would allow the ruse to appear convincing first to the officials and later in the day to journalists. Zuniga would light up the cig before explaining that an internal revolution had begun.

When members of the press heard, an hour or so later, from Radio Havana that Cuban airfields were under attack, the natural assumption would be that these raids were being carried out by those very friends Zuniga had spoken of: Two men who like him stole the planes they had up to then been flying for Castro, boldly turning their guns against the communists in an act they hoped would initiate a major counter-revolution. They were, in theory, firing the contemporary equivalent to the first shots heard at Lexington Green at the onset of America's Revolution.

With one major difference: None of this had any bearing in reality, as the pilots flew to Cuba from Nicaragua. What Zuniga delivered was not The Truth, rather 'a truth.' This, everyone in the

Douglas Brode

anti-Castro force of Cubans and the United States' government wanted the world to accept as reality.

A myth—or in CIA terms a "legend"—its source stretching all the way up to the highest power in our country.

The chain of events was supposed to work this way: When other like-minded Cubans on the homeland learned that the first salvo had been fired and heard 'round the modern world, they would declare that enough was enough, take up what-ever crude weapons they could lay their hands on, and strike. That was the "foregone conclusion" (in the words of the then-current CIA head) on which this air raid and subsequent invasion were based, the essential motivation for carrying the plan out.

*

Still, why Miami, of all Florida cities? the press might ask Zuniga. Ah, but that two was part of the scenario ...

Because here, beloved American friends and allies, my dear wife Georgina and our four darling children—the two boys, Eduardo and Enrique, and the girls, Beatriz and Maria Cristina— live. Don't take my word for it. Contact them at south West 20th Avenue. They'll back up everything I have said. Just don't print their names, please! Or mine, for the time being. You see, that might endanger our relatives still in Cuba. You cannot imagine the wrath of Fidel when he learns what I have done, and his immediate reaction will be that I have betrayed him, and Cuba.

I, and you, know better: To "betray" Castro and his odious communist/authoritarian regime is to prove my ongoing love for Cuba and my prayers, as a devout Christian, that we will take our home-land back from his godless regime and begin to build a 'little U.S.,' so to speak, with a democratic system of free elections and an economic base in capitalism.

For now, we must trust that you will be kind enough to host us, the pro-American Cubans, and others like us, until our country is freed from the oppression of Castro.

"Very good," George said, impressed by the thoroughness of Zuniga's soon-to-be-delivered plea and the sincerity of his tone. "And, finally: Your ultimate order?"

"Under no circumstances whatsoever must I tell the truth about what is going on, not to anyone, not for any reason."

Even as Mario Zuniga finished relating his plan of action to George, who beamed with approval, another limo, smaller but far more elegant in design than the one in which the CIA men had arrived, cautiously approached. Once the driver had glided his vehicle to a halt, the driver servant-like bounded out, hurrying around to open the passenger's door. A tall man, silver-haired and

162

impeccably dressed, stepped forth, holding his head high, his body moving in what struck both George and Zuniga as an aristocratic manner.

This regal fellow approached, offering a hint of a smile, the trio a few yards from the final plane, readying to depart.

"I was growing nervous," George admitted.

"My sincere apologies," the new arrival sighed, bowing graciously. Though Zuniga had never before met this exalted personage, he knew from pre-planning this must be a high-ranking member of the Nicaraguan Government. The U.S. had secretly, and from the start of this long-in-embryo operation, worked closely with the powers-that-be. On day one, George had negotiated full permission for the training and eventual take-off. The U.S. intelligence community and military considered this a necessity. The upcoming incident would lead to acts of blood-shed which would have grave international repercussions if the truth were discovered. All hoped that would not be the case.

No matter how much money the U.S. delivered annually to those in office to keep Nicaragua from falling under Russian influence, such clandestine permission had to be secured before the mission could be launched. Though that had been set in cement months earlier, a government official had to be on hand at this juncture, just in case anything went wrong.

But what possibly could? Everything had been planned down to the minutest detail by brilliant strategists. This ought to play in a clockwork manner owing to such thoroughness.

Only something did go wrong. In truth, everything that could possibly go wrong almost immediately proceeded to do so. As a poet once put it, the best laid plans of mice and men failed to produce the desired results. There would be the Bay of Pigs invasion as it already existed in the minds of all involved, a great victory for the U.S. and all pro-American Cubans. And then there would be the Bay of Pigs invasion as it played out in reality.

Which as all would discover can turn out to be something else entirely.

*

Precisely at their scheduled time, the "Linda" and "Puma" squadrons began dropping bombs on Camp Libertad near the Miramar suburb of Havana and at San Antonio de los Banos. For a brief glorious moment, success seemed imminent as a half dozen planes—MIG fighters as well as U.S. B-26s and T-33 jet trainers from the United States—were consumed in flames. Surprisingly, ground forces responded with anti-aircraft fire far more furious than had been expected. Mon's plane took a bad hit,

163

swiftly whirling high into the sky, then back down hard toward the sea with the speed and intensity of a rocket. Emitting a long tail of black smoke, the B-26 would have crashed had it not exploded.

The charred remnants of a once formidable aircraft dropped piecemeal to waiting waters, along with scattered bits of flesh and bone from the deceased Mon.

The sight of one of their fellow airborne cowboys blown to smithereens, not part of the game-plan for instantaneous success, set waves of panic tearing through the other flyers. Though the pilots did manage to resume their mission, the aim of their bomb-drops from that moment on tended to be way off. Fewer of the targeted planes down below suffered direct hits. Castro's pilots, now awake, rushed out of the barracks, hopping into the cockpits of their planes as anti-aircraft guns covered them with rapid-fire. This made it impossible for the two remaining "Pumas" to effectively strafe the scene below.

At that moment, Crespo's engine began emitting weird sounds. At first he assumed he had been hit though he'd heard no noise, felt no impact. As he soon grasped, Crespo's engine had simply malfunctioned. Realizing that he might at any moment lose control and crash, Crespo made the decision to pull out of the formation at once. Knowing that it was not likely he would be able to fly all the way back to the Happy Valley base in this out of control plane, Crespo made an on the spot decision to turn abruptly and fly toward Key West, Florida, a much closer destination, hoping for the best. He and Perez did manage to bring their shaky B-26 down at the Boca Chica Naval Air Station there at two minutes after seven in the morning; precisely one hour before Zuniga, who had no knowledge of Crespo's situation, sent out his first call to the towers at Miami International.

Neither Zuniga nor Crespo could have guessed that the problems back over Cuba were rapidly multiplying. It was as if the mission had been exposed to a fast-spreading disease that, once contamination began, consumed all their hopes and dreams like wildfire. Alfredo Caballero of the "Linda" formation, after dumping his first round of bombs, glanced with a pilot's instinct at his control panel. He noticed that his fuel tank was rapidly approaching empty.

Abruptly, Caballero aborted his mission, turning his plane south toward Grand Cayman Island. On their way to that new destination Cabellero and his co-pilot Maza discussed how they ought to handle what would likely be a difficult situation once they landed. Since Grand Cayman Island fell under British jurisdiction, and that country had not been informed of this American mission, so secretive that even the closest allies of the U.S. were left blithely unaware as to what was going down (or more correctly failing to go down), this could turn ugly.

As no one involved in the planning process figured on anything like this, none of the Cubans had been briefed as to what they ought to do or say in such a situation. They panicked.

*

JFK had, from day one, viewed the Bay of Pigs invasion in precisely the same manner that he, in the recesses of that man's uniquely functioning mind, perceived everything: a no-lose situation. This ought to benefit him if it worked, leave the president as unscratched as Teflon should it fail. This helped explain why, after approving of the final strategy as submitted to him days earlier, JFK made plans to be away for the weekend. He would travel to Middleburg, Virginia, there enjoying the relaxing atmosphere of a luxurious home he had rented.

Shortly before lunch-time in Washington on Friday, April 14, JFK addressed an African Freedom Day celebration held at the State Department. JFK basked in applause as a civil rights crusader, the hero of all ethnic minorities. No mention was made of the fact that several years earlier he, as a senator, during the Eisenhower administration blocked the passage of key civil rights legislation which that president had attempted to pass, eager to have the fight for racial equality become a part of Ike's own legacy. But when Ike had attempted to push important bills through congress, JFK led the fierce opposition. His prominence insured the reforms would die in committee.

JFK did so not because he opposed the proposals, the very sort of anti-racist legislation his administration would put in place and, after 1963, President Lyndon Johnson would continue to uphold. Why insure the defeat of what he then did believe in? JFK wanted to convince white southerners that he was not hostile to them, thereby making it easier for him to win the next presidential election. Give them some early evidence that he was not as liberal on this issue as had been reputed and, in fact, actually was.

Some might consider it cynical that, once in office, he planned to perform a total turnabout, championing such bills in the congress, then take the credit for this himself. In the minds of those who did not feel comfortable with JFK, even if they happened to agree with most of his political positions, the idea was to double-cross those southern citizens he had courted. As the reliable saying goes: That was then; this, now.

Within minutes after concluding his inspiring speech, JFK was swept by limo to the D.C. airport. In Air Force One he flew off for a much-needed vacation. Lyndon Johnson, who had been added to the ticket as JFK's vice-presidential candidate only because this would allow JFK to carry Texas—both Kennedy brothers were openly contemptuous of the "ignorant cowboy"—had been purposefully kept in the dark ("black," in CIA lexicon, for anything secretive) about the operation's existence. Johnson had been shuffled off to some insignificant speaking engagement so that, with JFK out of town, Johnson would not be able to claim executive privilege if anything went wrong.

That left Richard M. Bissell, Jr., the CIA's DDP (deputy director for plans) in charge of Washington, America, and by implication the world. Bissell would remain in close contact with the president as to how details proceeded.

*

To a large extent the Bay of Pigs invasion had from day one been Bissell's baby. He was the one who had approached JFK time after time, fervently requesting permission to officially begin work on this covert operation against a foreign land that, so far as the press was told, we were attempting to diplomatically woo over to our side. Not that Bissell was some maverick; he broached this subject with full authorization from his own boss, CIA director Allen W. Dulles, the brother of Secretary of State John Foster Dulles, who also believed that such a move was not only advisable but necessary.

So that no one would suspect that the CIA might be involved as the longest weekend proceeded, Allen Dulles flew off to Puerto Rico. While the attack took place, he'd meet with pro-U.S. business people, a perfect cover. As for chain of command, Allen Dulles knew precisely how to delegate responsibility. As to Dick Bissell, there was no one person Dulles trusted more. Rightly so. JFK himself admitted to having been highly impressed by Dick's tall, angular frame and his knowledgeability from that day the two men met in the Oval Office, shortly after JFK assumed the U.S. presidency on January 20, 1961.

After much careful consideration, JFK concluded that if this idea came from such a source—Ivy League Bissell had been a professor of economics before accepting a government position—chances are everything would work out fine. Even if, when push finally came to shove, it wouldn't be men like Bissell who'd mount an attack on the current equivalent to San Juan Hill but a coterie of cowboys—CIA operatives and anti-Castro Cubans—doing so without any equivalent to the daring, fearless, inspired leadership

166

of Teddy Roosevelt. That battle's in-front-of-the-troops commander had insured their earlier operation's success, its legal questionability notwithstanding.

How can I say no? JFK mused. *They succeed, I take the credit. They fail, I blame the CIA Either way, I win.Make a public appearance with Jackie by my side, basking in the glory should we conquer Cuba, expressing my wrath if we do not. Either way, I come off smelling like roses. Then ditch the bitch, meet Marilyn for some secluded sex. Or, if she's too drunk or drugged up, Jayne, Mamie, Angie ...*

*

"Hello, Mr. President," Richard Bissell said to JFK mid-afternoon, Saturday. "Enjoying your vacation?"

"Lovely down here in Virginia, Dick. Tell me some good news. I'm put off by a few things I heard on the radio."

"Several planes shot down. In my mind, Mr. President? So long as we remain on course, the outcome will be as planned and expected." Bissell paused, then spit out the next words, hoping and trusting JFK's answer would be what he so needed to hear: "I have your assurances, Mr. President, that you'll allow us to continue according to our scenario?"

"By all means, Dick. Why did you think you had to ask?"

Relieved, the CIA man breathed in deeply. Until, that is, JFK followed his initial statement with a disclaimer: "Unless, of course, you hear different from me."

The president replaced his receiver on its base, leaving Bissell as uncertain in Washington as Adlai Stevenson then felt in New York. He, of course, was the man Bissell must call next.

Adlai sat in his office, shaking, waiting for the phone to ring. The moment of truth had arrived, as he knew during those three months following his meeting in the Oval Office that in time it would. He had yet to decide what to say when his name was called to approach the podium at the General Assembly Political Committee's upcoming emergency meeting at the United Nations. There, he was expected to deliver the United States' official statement as to what was going on down there in Cuba.

What's a man to do? Adlai Stevenson wondered.

The time was precisely two p.m. Less than an hour from now he would address the gathered diplomats. Should Adlai offer the usual disclaimer, muttering something to the effect of "so far as I know ..." hoping that would be enough to squelch this tense situation? And the world's wanting to know if America was, in any way, shape or form, mixed up in whatever this might be? Or would he do what he knew those in the chain-of-command—up from Barnes through Bissell to Dulles to JFK—had begged for: his insistence in public that we absolutely were not involved.

Throughout the day Dick Bissell had fought to restrain himself from calling either JFK or the U.N. ambassador. He knew what everyone else following the story did and little else. Bissell did hear first, if only by minutes or in some cases a matter of seconds, before the latest release of what had just occurred hit the media. The first reports had been encouraging. Bombs were dropped, several enemy planes knocked out.

Still, Bissell held out, not wanting to jump the gun. In time he was glad he had taken such a cautious approach. Later reports made clear that gunfire from the ground had brought down one, maybe two of the planes that had attacked from Nicaragua. Others veered off course. This worried Bissell, but not much.

Not yet. Perhaps the initial bombing accomplished the necessary damage to curtail Cuba's air force. A second scheduled air raid ought to knock out the remaining opposition even as the anti-Castro Cuban volunteers began their sea-to-land invasion. The progress, if limited, appeared to Bissell as acceptable.

Then came word that Mario Zuniga successfully landed at Miami airport. After disembarking he swiftly launched into his fully rehearsed lie about how he and his companions bravely stole several planes from their hangers in Havana, headed up into the wild blue yonder, thereafter bombing their own base. Could this be considered a perfect morning? Perhaps not. Still, Stage One, Operation Mongoose, had more or less proceeded according to plan. There was every reason to believe Monday's sea-to-land attack, Code Name: Operation Zapata, would cinch the victory.

That meant Bissell could call ring up Adlai. First, though, the man at the top. So Richard Bissell, Jr. placed that initial call to JFK, the president then relaxing with a cool drink and a hot blonde at Glen Ora. This conversation concluded, Bissell dialed up Adlai, while JFK set about fucking the movie star, who had recently appeared with his sometimes pal Frank Sinatra in one of the popular Rat Pack films. In later years she would sarcastically refer to the experience as "the best seven seconds of my life." Precisely what she also secretly whispered about JFK's world-famous entertainer friend.

The subsequent phone conversation between Richard Bissell and Adlai Stevenson lasted less than three minutes. This took place between 2:47 and 2:50 p.m., moments before the latter exited his office and proceeded to the special suite where the political committee would meet. Bissell would listen to the broadcast on his radio, nervous as to Adlai's famed idealism.

Trusting though that, however much a milk-toast liberal Stevenson might be, he remained at heart a patriotic American, and would come across for his country and president.

Before the debate began, Bissell rearranged paperwork on his desk, hurriedly reading through notes, preparing to spend the hour listening to all that was said while checking each new report as it trickled in. Also, he'd try and keep track of what was going on down in Miami as Zuniga schmoozed with Ed Ahrens, in charge of the International Airport, then a bevy of reporters who were quickly invited out for an official press conference.

Bissell felt a little like a juggler, attempting to keep three balls in the air at once. Difficult, but not impossible. And, in truth, he loved that sort of thing. This explained why he'd left The Ford Foundation for the U.S. secret intelligence community after his World War II spy unit, then known as the OSS, evolved into the CIA. In so doing, Bissell had situated himself at the cusp of contemporary history-in-the-making; the very thought of his eminence provided a sudden rush.

Still, now, his mind kept returning to the question: Would Adlai do the right thing? Hardly superstitious, Bissell crossed his fingers as the three o' clock hour approached, then silently prayed. He wasn't much on religion. But as someone noted back in WWII, there are no atheists in foxholes.

Well, here was a whole new kind of war. And foxholes, if not always visible, still existed.

Half an hour later our American ambassador to the U.N. concluded by insisting those Cuban planes which landed on American soil would be impounded, and under no circumstances would the pilots be allowed to take off again.

Zuniga was, in fact, already readying to leave. Early the following day—Sunday, April 16—he, Jose Crespo and Lorenzo Perez departed in a C-54 on their way back to Happy Valley in Nicaragua to rejoin their anti-Castro Cuban forces and members of the CIA. The following afternoon, the two were off and flying again as part of the air command scheduled to give full support to those sea-to-land troops readying to attack. Crespo and Perez were shot down, dying on April 17 as Bay of Pigs turned from a no-brainer success into an unprecedented disaster.

Momentarily Richard Bissell, Jr. relaxed. So Adlai Stevenson had, as hoped for, proven himself a good soldier. Thank God for that! A God, of course, that loves America.

*

From day one, the success of the Bay of Pigs invasion had been pegged on one vital element: those air strikes carried out by

Cuban pilots, flying out of Nicaragua on American planes. Even as back home knowledgeable Bissell and the unwitting Stevenson provided an elaborate cover, further bombings insured a victory by taking out the FAR, assuring no airborne counter response could be mounted two days later as sea-to-land forces swept up from the beach. Though our traditional military brass agreed with little that the CIA chiefs, who now co-opted many decisions which in the past were theirs to make, believed best, everyone involved in the long, elaborate planning process, JFK included, agreed that eliminating the FAR was essential.

This accomplished, it seemed impossible that the wave of well-armed, carefully-trained fighters could be halted as they marched on Havana. Even as dawn broke on Monday, 1,447 patriots prepared to disembark from the safety of seven U.S. ships and attack.

How could they—we—lose?

True, there had been mis-haps, Bissell knew. But he was a realist. When he called JFK, then Stevenson on that Saturday afternoon, Bissell had learned from his information sources that his pilots reported knocking out at least two dozen planes; earlier bulletins warned that there weren't that many T-3 jets, B-26 bombers, English-built Sea Furies and recently arrived aircraft from Russia in all of Cuba. Nonetheless, this meant at least some, maybe most, of Castro's air force no longer existed. When our Cuban pilots, after returning to Nicaragua for fuel and a brief rest, returned on Monday, they'd complete the job.

Exhausted, Bissell headed home for some much needed sleep. Here was a done deal/political coup America would approve of if one which, at least for the record, we'd had nothing to do with.

Yet during the night, Bissell found himself plagued by a series of dark dreams. In them, the operation went terribly awry. Burning pilots dropped from their planes, whirling without chutes to the ground below. Armed men in camouflage were mowed down on the thin green line separating thick jungle from white sand. A few survivors hurried back to the big blue only to realize their landing crafts had returned to the convoy, leaving them trapped, helplessly and hopelessly awaiting their deaths.

Bissell irregularly woke from the oppressive nightmare. He felt chilled to the bone each time, sweating profusely as he made a valiant effort to force such horrific images out of his mind. He'd roll over, soon drifting back into a sullen sleep.

When Bissell did at last rise the next morning, he felt more exhausted than when he'd retired. The first thing he did was reach for the New York *Times,* hoping the headline might make a mockery of his fantasies.

To his surprise, even horror, the newspaper confirmed them. Questioning whether Adlai Stevenson's statement before the United Nations the previous day had been true, hinting that Honest Adlai had been sold a bill of goods by the State Department or, for the first time in his life, set integrity aside, becoming complicit in an obvious con job. Other articles, scattered through the thick black-and white encyclopedia of the week's events, deconstructed the U.S.'s official position.

Bissell felt faint. Any person who read this would know that the whole shebang had all been a ruse.

Some time later, as a special news service truck rolled up to his home with papers from all across the country, Bissell took heart from what he found there. Most featured nothing on the Cuban crisis other than an Associated Press summary of what our government had told them. How reassuring it was to know that ninety per cent of loyal Americans would read only this today.

Bissell, however, was far too savvy to continue for long in this cushion of denial. Only a small number of intelligentsia would see today's *Times*; tomorrow, though, other reporters would have devoured it, harbored second thoughts, composed better-late-than-never follow-ups. There was no way to head off the coming storm. Still, Bissell might yet minimize any problems this might create and inflate. There was indeed a way!

A Connecticut born-and-raised member of the unofficial U.S. aristocracy of Ivy Leaguers, this old school blue-blood had earned his straight-A grades at Yale by studying seriously in a way he knew the nouveau-riche upstart JFK only pretended to do a generation later at Harvard. It all came down to one inviolable rule: History is written by the victors. So what if word leaked out about what we'd done? So long as those in charge reassured the American people that victory loomed on the horizon, a grave threat eliminated, the vast majority would accept whatever had happened. With victory, the ends would justify the means.

Richard M. Bissell, Jr. believed that to the marrow of his bones. Things would work out so long as the president backed him one-hundred percent. Bissell could not allow himself to even consider the odious possibility that JFK might blink.

Such a notion was unthinkable. He had JFK's word, didn't he? Even if the promise had been followed by a phrase that did not sit well with Bissell, whose hand shook as he reached for the phone to once again make contact with JFK ...

BOOK TWO:

THE IDES OF TEXAS

"Why are we always attracted to innocence when we ought to be repelled by it? Innocence is like a dumb leper who has lost his bell: wandering the earth, meaning no harm, endangering us all."

—Graham Greene, 1948

CHAPTER ELEVEN:
LICENSED TO KILL

"I always felt that the Cubans were being pushed into
the Soviet block by American (foreign) policy."
—Lee Harvey Oswald, 1962

So where was Lee Harvey Oswald when Bay of Pigs went down? According to official records, in Minsk. Lee had arrived in Moscow on October 16, 1959, announcing to Soviet officials there and the American ambassador his plans to defect. Russian authorities sent him to Minsk in January, 1960; Lee had lived there ever since. On March 30, 1961, complaining of an inner ear infection, he had been admitted to a hospital. During his twelve days there he was often visited by his latest girlfriend, a pretty if none too bright young thing named Marina. On April 11, Lee would be discharged.

Most of this was "legend," a cover-up for what Lee had been assigned to try and achieve during this time period. George had remained in contact on a regular basis since the defection, via several couriers, while Lee divided his stay between two Moscow hotels, later via a single go-between once he reached the smaller provincial city. The assigned courier appeared on Lee's first day in Minsk. An elderly American had approached him on the street, mentioning that he too had defected. They genially shook hands. When that was done, Lee walked away with a piece of paper in his hand. The following morning when the men passed each other again, they stopped, chatted, and shook hands once more. This time it was Lee who passed a message through this intermediary back to George. And so on and so on.

On March 28, the brief note from George instructed Lee to enter the hospital within two days, complaining of unbearable pain in his right ear. Admitted on March 30 and putting on a convincing performance, Lee noticed in the midnight darkness a male coming up the aisle to his bed. This shadowy figure stepped close, whispering in Lee's ear. Finally Lee got a good look at the intruder's face, a duplicate of his own. Realizing that what George had explained to him would be a transfer was occurring, Lee slipped out of bed even as the twin took his place. Quietly Lee exited. As he left the hospital a car pulled up, the driver signaling to Lee. Two hours later he was dropped off in a remote field where a plane awaited. Once aboard Lee found himself headed to Helsinki, transferring there to a jet bound for Miami.

Lee stepped off that craft four hours later and, exhausted, headed into the main terminal. George and Johnny Rosselli were waiting for him. They greeted the bleary-eyed arrival, took Lee out for breakfast, and described the upcoming mission. Something big was about to go down in a week and a half. Lee was not to be briefed about any of it for fear that if captured by Castro's forces he might be tortured into talking, so the less he knew the better for all. George would only say that in less than 24 hours Lee would be off to Cuba, there to serve as part of a three-pronged assassination attempt on Castro. Johnny would be one of the other two operatives, as would a sometimes employee of the government to be known to Lee only as 'Dick Tracy.'

Just like in the James Bond books ... and the upcoming movies based on them, which I read are already in pre-production ... my private fantasy is about to become public reality ... 007 and, now, Lee Harvey Oswald are ... licensed to kill!

Kill, but not drive. As Sinatra would say, now ain't that a kick in the head? I doubt I'll ever master it. Something comes over me every time I try. I shake and shiver and give up.

Killing? Ah, that's easy. Driving? Difficult!

*

The following day, according to plans, Lee arrived at the Tamiami airport at precisely six a.m. He waited in the lobby, miniscule compared to the one in Miami's International Airport, until Johnny Handsome stepped alongside him, motioning for Lee to follow. At the ticket counter stood a young attendant, the only person on duty so early. Johnny explained that he and his friend had paid in advance for the rental of a Cessna 172, the three-year-old model most popular with amateurs who wanted to take flying lessons. A pilot had been arranged for as well. She checked over their identification, with a smile instructing them to pass through the lobby and onto the runways out back.

A pilot, wearing the traditional brown-leather jacket that had been popularized during the war by the Flying Tigers, smiled broadly, waving for them to board. Johnny slipped into the back while Lee hopped in next to the flyboy. Several attendants on the ground scurried about, making the final checks. These men stepped back and signaled for what was to be a conventional take-off. Each was shocked to see that the man in the backseat pulled out a pistol, crammed it into the pilot's right cheek, and roared:

"We are defecting to Cuba. You will fly us there at once."

The pilot, appearing panicky, nodded. They cruised down the runaway and rapidly ascended. The mechanics hurried back into the building, calling to the young woman to report another skyjacking of the type that had recently become frequent.

Once airborne, the three jet-age cowboys had a good laugh. The ruse was necessary so that word of the hijacking would be spread all over international radar. Those in Cuba assigned to monitor such airwaves would pick up on this, which ought to prove helpful once they landed, as heroes, outside of Havana.

"Well, so far, so good," Lee smirked.

"We've only just begun," Dick Tracy reminded him.

During the first third of the flight they ran through their operation. In three days time, each man working on his own would try to kill Castro while he dined at his favorite restaurant. Their approaches were so drastically different that it seemed impossible all three could fail when the tactics were carried out simultaneously. This would make the situation all the more favorable for their side on 'D Day,' a term Dick Tracy used, Lee aware the flyer knew more about the coming Big Event than he.

"Well, I trust and believe that we're going to pull this off and maybe with a little luck all three of us will live to tell our grandchildren about it," Lee said.

"The odds are in our favor as to the first part of your statement," Dick Tracy explained, "less so as to the second."

"Most likely one of us will go down," Rosselli added.

"Maybe two? Well, as I said that first day when I signed up for the marines, I'm willing to give my life for my country."

"Let's hope it doesn't come to that," Dick Tracy replied.

"Still, I've got to say, while all I know about Castro is what I read in the papers, and while my impression is mostly negative, I've got a feeling in my gut that says all of this crap might have been avoided."

Dick Tracy turned to Lee briefly, studying the man who sat grinning smugly in the passenger seat. "I don't get your drift."

"Well, I keep as close an eye as I can on everything that's happening on the international scene. So I can't help thinkin' that things didn't have to reach such a ... how would you put it ... crisis point between the U.S. and Cuba."

Dick Tracy, checking out his flight panel once more, solemnly shook his head. "How could we have avoided it, Lee?"

"After the take-over in '59, the only thing I think Castro really cared about was his own survival. If I'm right, that means he had to be open to all offers which might benefit him. Including any overtures from the U.S."

"You're forgetting," Rosselli said, "Castro was a Red."

"Right. But also an American. A Latin American, a Third World American. But an American. Don't you think he might have opened his arms to U.S. aid if we'd offered to pour money and goods in, rather than assuming a bunker mentality toward us? I mean, think about it. A lot of blood got spilled during that New Year's eve revolution, but no Americans were harmed."

"You sound soft on communism," Dick Tracy remarked.

"Better dead than Red," Rosselli added.

"Well, yeah. Sure. Hey, I like American style capitalism as much as either of you guys. But that doesn't mean we can't live with a Marxist state, so long as it isn't openly hostile."

"You're claiming then that Fidel might have been an ally?"

"I'm saying that I believe he left that route open until we started playing dirty tricks, like cigars to destroy his beard."

"You yourself were in on some of that stuff."

"I know, Johnny, I know. And glad to do it. My country calls, I answer! All I'm saying is—"

"—we might have tried extending an olive branch first."

"Right, Dick Tracy. I mean, the Soviet Union likes to come in and swallow things whole. Maybe Castro would have preferred to be our ally, however uneasy, if only we gave him a chance."

"Yet you're going down there to kill him at this moment?"

"I sure am, Johnny. Like Alfred, Lord Tennyson said about those who serve their country in the military or any other such capacity: Ours is not to reason why; ours is but to do and die."

"Could all those months in Minsk, when you were pretending to be a true believer in communism, have turned you around?"

"No, no, no! Believe me, if there's one thing I learned over there, it's that their supposedly left wing government is as authoritarian as Batista's fascist Cuban state before the revolution, and Castro's left wing authoritarian regime now."

"How about the U.S. of A.?" Dick Tracy wanted to know.

"We may be far from perfect but so far as I can see we've got the best of all possible governments in an imperfect world."

"Now you're talkin', pal!"

"Still, any government is only as good as those people who are running it at any one point in time."

"Are you referring to Kennedy?" Dick Tracy wanted to know.

"Yes. But Eisenhower, too. I mean, he may not have been out for Castro's blood, like JFK. Still, maybe he over-reacted a bit by trying to rid the world of Castro by non-violent means."

*

They said little else during the remainder of the two hour seven minute trip. Lee wondered if he might have spoken out of turn, even as he had back during his first days as a marine when he opened up too soon to a seeming friend.

Yes, these guys were fellow members of a mission, but not my best buddies. Well, too late now to do anything about it. Just hope they took my words as intended: small talk.

Dick Tracy, clearly a skilled flier, kept their positioning at 210 degrees, straight on toward Havana. Some twenty minutes north of Cuba, Lee spotted a pair of MIGS out his window, but they roared off in the opposite direction and did not turn around at the sight of this American craft. Shortly the plane crossed over and away from The Big Blue, crossing over sandy browns of the rugged beaches, then wildly diverse greens of adjacent rolling hills, fully visible, absolutely breathtaking.

"Here we go," Dick Tracy sighed, nosing the plane downward. All had been briefed as to the swiftly-evolving defense system on the island, posts strung out at regular intervals so that any air invasion attempt could quickly be detected. Dick Tracy circled twice, checking his controls, over toward a medium-sized compound: a dozen rusty tin buildings circling a larger, older wood-frame structure. A quarter-mile northward, a landing strip extended eastward, little more than a primitive field cut from waist deep weeds, shoulder-high cane, and an encroaching mantis-green jungle. Descending the Cessna, the pilot likewise released the wheels. Minutes later, they landed without a bump.

"We're here!" Lee shouted, excited to once again be in Cuba, which he had adored during his previous brief stay.

"Do precisely as you are told," a firm voice commanded in thickly accented English, "or we will shoot. Do you understand?"

"Oh, shit!" Lee gasped. A squad of eight men rushed toward them, all wearing drab olive fatigues, crouched low, pointing submachine guns directly at the recently airborne intruders. Burning eyes suggested none had any hesitations as to shooting the Americans on the spot rather than assume any risk.

"We're defectors!" Johnny called out, standing still in the spot where he had leaped down seconds earlier. Dick Tracy, just then jumping down from out of his own doorway, repeated that in Spanish.

"Step away from the plane. Quickly!" One bearded Cuban, obviously the leader, barked orders while waving sharply, his other arm cradling his weapon. Never having felt this close to death before, Lee's body shook so hard he feared that he might not be able to comply, however much he wanted to. The leader then nodded for them to proceed toward the main building.

A not inconsiderable arsenal of weapons remained trained on the three as the Cubans roughly escorted them to G-2, the local office of Castro's secret police. That imposing Cuban squad leader verbally accosted and accused the men, insisting that they were CIA agents. All denied, denied, denied, pleading to be taken to Havana to where they could present their case to the authorities. The inquisitor's eyes suggested that he might possibly believe Lee and Johnny were defectors, Dick Tracy the hapless pilot they forced at gunpoint (Johnny's weapon long since seized by guards) to fly them here.

The interrogation at last over, they were held for several hours in one of the windowless tin shacks which, as the middle of the afternoon encroached, came to feel like a crude oven. As evening wore on, a guard approached, informing Dick Tracy that he was free to go but must immediately return to Florida. Not glancing at the others, he exited the building and headed back to the plane. Shortly Lee and Johnny heard the motors roar as he took off. This was precisely as they had hoped things would go. Their confederate would proceed to a hidden airstrip not far from Havana, meet them at an appointed time and place, so the three-pronged assassination attempt would proceed on schedule.

Several hours after Lee and Johnny had fallen asleep on the dirt floor, each stirred as there came a dull noise at the door. They rose without exchanging a word. This, they knew, was the pre-planned escape; one of the supposed guerillas in the squad would be a CIA plant. As the scenario dictated, the lock had been removed. Cautiously, they slipped off into the night and started on their long walk to Havana.

So far, so good!

*

Two days later, everything quickly turned to shit. Dick Tracy was the first to fail. Since he had never before come face to face with Castro, he'd been assigned the task of doing just that. As Castro sat down at one of Casalta's outdoor tables, always preferring to catch the first breeze from the sea rather than swelter inside, Dick Tracy stepped up, thrusting forward a pen and paper, humbly requesting Fidel's autograph. Though two guards stepped between their leader and this sudden interloper, patting the man down as they checked for weapons, Castro nodded magnanimously; happy to oblige! As the American set a pen and paper down on the table Castro yanked a pen from an inner jacket pocket, writing:

> If only more U.S. citizens would come to visit all would know that we are not your enemies!
> —Fidel Castro

This left Dick Tracy, recovering from his surprise, saying thank you to Castro, hastily picking up the autographed paper and his own pen, then departing. This pen contained a secret syringe filled with poison. The plan had been that, as Castro completed writing a message, Dick Tracy would reach to take back his pen while thumbing the lever, releasing botulin, pricking Castro's skin, and injecting poison into his system. He hadn't guessed Castro would have a pen of his own. Phase one had failed.

Lee, across the plaza, was already in position with a Browning FN High Power Bolt Action Rifle, the 1959 Safari Grade Model, SN L7168, peering through a telescopic sight, aiming at the guards. Having achieved sharp-shooter rank in the marines, in the South Pacific proving to George back home that he had no compunction killing someone who needed killing, Lee had received this assignment. When Tracy bolted and ran, Lee would, employing smokeless-powder cartridges so as not to give away his hiding place, take both the guards down.

Within seconds of Dick Tracy leaving, out of the restaurant ambled Johnny Rosselli, carrying a hot plate of grilled shrimps, the dictator's favorite, which he ordered every Wednesday night. These, Rosselli had drenched in botulin as well as lemon and butter, adding the third element while easing out the door. Despite his face-to-face confrontation with Castro in mid-January, 1959, Rosselli had no fear of being recognized. His hair was now light brown instead of jet black, he wore contact lenses to change his eye color to a shade of sea-green, and he kept his head tilted to one side while setting down the platter.

There was only one problem: an old friend of Castro's, to whom the dictator recently extended a favor, had sent precisely this dish over to the dictator's offices for lunch, accompanied by a bottle of white wine. So now Castro was in the mood for something else, perhaps a rare steak. He pushed the plate over to a cabinet minister seated at his right, whispering in the waiter's ear that he wanted a different dish. Maintaining his low profile,

Rosselli nodded, turned as if to step back inside Casalta, then slipped off into the crowd. Like a wisp of smoke, Johnny was gone, even as Castro's doomed associate swallowed a mouthful of the delicacy and, gagging, fell to the ground. He rolled about, his face at first crimson, then ashen, dying.

Lee was to have shot down the guards if Castro ate and died, covering Johnny's escape. Such tactical work was no longer his concern. Now, all he had to do was pull the trigger, bring down Castro, and hurry off, meeting the others at the Cessna in a pre-arranged place. Lee's finger tightened on the trigger. Even as he began to squeeze, in the slow and efficient manner mastered at Boot Camp, Castro stood up and stared straight at him as if the dictator knew precisely where Lee had hidden himself. Lee was gripped by shock and confusion: How and why had Castro glanced this way? Lee could not know that toward the end of January 1959, this was the spot from which Enrique Avirez had tried, and failed, to pull the trigger on Castro.

The dictator experienced a sense of déjà vu, fully expecting to die this time around. Perhaps that explained why he did not. Lee saw such passion, fury, desperation, and intense longing to live in the eyes of the man across the way, his finger momentarily froze. Lee blinked, then quickly regained composure, readying to shoot. In that split-second the guards had thrown Castro down on the ground and leaped on top of him, shielding his body with their own. Someone in the late-afternoon crowd spotted Lee and pointed, shouting. Dropping the rifle, Lee rose, turned, and ran for his life.

Twisting his way up and down narrow boulevards, Lee almost immediately crashed headlong into a police officer summoned to the scene. Assuming this panicky fugitive must be guilty of something, he grabbed Lee by his short hair, yanked him up, and hurried to nearest police station. Once inside Lee bleated his innocence, halting in mid-sentence until he saw Johnny Rosselli and Dick Tracy in handcuffs, these now placed on his wrists.

*

The prisoners bounced up and down, driven over roads bumpier than any Lee could remember. They sat on a hard metal bench, handcuffed, in the back of a filthy police truck. Three guards squatted across the way, glumly staring. Each cradled a Thompson submachine gun. None spoke during the fifteen minute drive. Each guard's eyes suggested they secretly hoped for some small gesture to justify opening fire. There wasn't enough food in Cuba to go around. Who wanted three more mouths to feed?

Furtively, Lee glanced at Johnny on his left, Dick Tracy to the right. The latter stared ahead as if willing himself into oblivion, Lee guessing this was Company policy. Johnny hunched over, shoulders downward, likely the Mob approach. As the truck at last slowed, the guards broke their silence, conversing in ecstatic Spanish. Something major was about to happen.

"You will disembark immediately," the one in charge, at last making eye contact, commanded. The incessant whirring of the vehicle's motor ceased, the scent of hot oil from its timeworn engine engulfing them. "Now, do you hear?"

As when they'd disembarked the Cessna, Lee hopped down first. On the street, many Cubans paraded by, a few in the rich colored clothing from pre-revolutionary days. Most men now chose military fatigues, signifying the preferred no-nonsense style of a regime that condemned any personal pleasure as political decadence. With of course Fidel's secret exception: fine cigars, grilled shrimp, beautiful women. Johnny Handsome and Dick Tracy dropped down beside Lee, the constant flow of Cubans considering these handcuffed Americans with curiosity. A ragged man, face full of hatred for anyone from a country arrogant enough to send armed men here to kill their leader, spat in their direction.

God help me! Please? I'm begging you ... Please give this one a happy ending. Get me back to Minsk and beautiful Marina?

Glancing about to get his bearings, Lee's attention was drawn to something on high. They stood, he realized, in the shadow of a looming hill topped by a dark fortress, something right out of the middle ages. Then he recalled seeing it on his previous secretive visit: El Principe prison.

"You will be our honored guests," the lead guard announced without emotion, "in our own great castle."

With that stout fellow pompously leading the way, Lee and the others shuffling behind him, the remaining guards holding tight on either side, they trudged up the hill. Minutes later they approached the first of two immense drawbridges, its thick, splintered plank surface slowly lowering over a winding moat.

"This is bad, bad, bad," Lee whispered, any bravado that he had felt setting off on their mission long gone.

"Stay calm," Dick Tracy whispered.

"All they can do is kill us," Johnny Rosselli laughed. "Hey, everyone dies."

"No talking," the lead guard called over his shoulder. Another jabbed Lee in the belly with his gun barrel, a signal to cross over at once. The wood bridge, with its metal bindings, creaked as the party stumbled across. When they at last reached the incline's halfway point, nearing the second drawbridge, another group of guards awaited with three more prisoners, these appearing more bedraggled than themselves. Lee guessed them to be Cubans captured during a counter-revolutionary demonstration. The two trios merged, making silent eye contact, saying nothing.

At least I'm not alone. My guess is that they'll be worse off than us. Castro won't think twice about executing some of his own people. U.S. Citizens? Maybe that will give him pause.

Once beyond the building's looming entrance they were guided down a narrow corridor. Everything smelled stale, as if old, unwashed clothing were piled high nearby. At last reaching their journey's end, the entire party entered a cavernous room. The only pieces of furniture were a large desk and accompanying chair. In it, a big man with a barrel-like torso sat, reading reports Lee assumed contained all the known facts about the six.

Additional guards circled, grunting for the prisoners to step in the seated man's direction. When Lee hesitated, one nasty looking guard shoved a gun barrel against his back.

"My friend," whispered the burly, red-headed prisoner just beside him, "as Sophocles said some two thousand years ago, 'the greatest gift would be to have never been born.'"

He quotes a philosopher? In English? Oh, that's right. George told me: educated citizens are always suspect in Castro's Cuba. They think too much, fail to follow the party line. And speaking of George: where are you when we most need you?

For the following quarter-hour, the commander lectured his prisoners about El Principe, afterwards sharing his resume. A thirty-something man with black eyes set deep in a flat frying pan of a face, the commandant's other features camouflaged by a huge Zapata mustache, his unnaturally round head perched without a noticeable neck atop an unusually thick body.

"Comprehend, uninvited American guests, I am Captain Pupo Puerta Valle, supreme commander of El Castillo del Principe. Before accepting this position I had the honor to serve as group leader in Fidel Castro's personal bodyguard. We wore civilian attire so as not to be easily recognized by those hoping to harm our leader. Every man carried a .45 automatic with orders to shoot first, as your American cowboys say, ask questions later. These were replaced by more sophisticated weaponry, the Belgian-made 9 mm automatic 15 shot pistol, our new arsenal provided by a European nation sympathetic to our cause." Everyone sneaked a quick glimpse at Valle's holstered gun. "In time, the personal bodyguard was disbanded, the Party assuming responsibility for

Castro's continued safety. I was given the honor of serving in any other capacity and picked the position in which you now find me. Traitors among our ranks are summarily executed. Americans who have arrived without invitation are held until we can determine the best manner of dealing with your situation. Some are returned home, others allowed to stay, and a few executed. Only time will tell as to your fates. In the meantime, you are under my jurisdiction. No matter how brave and bold you might consider yourselves, I will learn precisely who you are and who sent you. As someone once put it, 'there is an easy way to do things and a hard way.' Only fools choose the hard way. Shortly, I will learn which of you happen to be fools."

Torture! He means torture if we don't break down and talk.

Captain Valle whirled his head as a signal to his men. With weapons still held ready, the guards pulled backward. A moment later a dozen uniformed men, brandishing rifles with bayonets in place, hurried in from the corridor.

"You six will strip down," Valle ordered. "Now!"

The prisoners hurriedly removed their clothes, standing in this clammy room in their underwear. "I said strip," Valle continued. Each prisoner allowed his drawers to drop. Glancing down, Lee noticed that the grey stone floor had over the years been bloodied, leaving a ghastly purple stain.

Once they were naked, two enormous guards stepped up alongside each of the six. They lowered their rifles so that a pair of bayonets touched up against each man's scrotum. As if part of a choreographed routine, one guard extended his blade forward until it pricked the flesh of each prisoner's limp penis. His partner simultaneously jabbed at each prisoner's sad hanging sack. In precise movements, this bizarre ballet of bayonets continued. Guards toyed with the men's masculinity, always on the verge of castrating them, barely holding back.

Please, God, not that! Just let them kill me.

"Any questions?" Valle demanded in an irritated tone that made things abundantly clear: no response need be offered.

No, no, no. I don't want to say this. It's just like the first day at Boot Camp when I tried to become 'Angelo Maggio,' Sinatra's adorable runt who had a gag for everything. I tried doing that and it didn't work. Some sergeant told me, during one of my low ebbs, that nothing is more stupid than doing the same thing over and over again, always expecting a different result. I only wish I could stop the words before I speak them—

"Captain Valle? Where do babies come from?"

*

183

"I'm sorry," Lee wailed, cocking his head toward the jail cell's bleak ceiling. "I didn't mean to say it."

"Why the fuck did you?" Johnny demanded.

"I don't know. It kinda slipped out."

"It must've come from somewhere."

"Jerry Lewis."

"What?"

"It was in a Jerry Lewis movie. He and Dean Martin were in the army. A top sergeant bawled them out. Then he asked, 'are there any questions.' So Jerry—"

"That's only a movie!" Johnny shouted.

"George warned me about you. Said you could be our top operative if it weren't for something crazy deep down inside."

"I'm sorry. Sincerely! I'll try—" Then, Lee wept.

How often in my life have I wished that I were dead? And considered suicide? Those were "the good ol' days" compared to this. If only there were a way out, I'd take it. Something I might use to end it all. But there's nothing ... nothing!

Now Dick Tracy began to feel sorry for Oswald, who during this reprimand had shriveled up before the agent's eyes. Lee literally fell down into a corner of their small cell.

"Marguerite!" Lee sobbed. "Marina ..."

I never realized it 'til now: The names of my lover and mother begin with the same three letters. What might that mean?

Following Lee's bizarre bad joke, Captain Valle ordered the self-styled clown tied to a rack against the wall, arms forcibly stretched outward as guards primitively bound his hands.

"I was only kidding. Can't you take a joke?"

Valle turned and stepped around to his desk, taking a whip from the central drawer. He returned to where Lee helplessly hung and administered five harsh lashes. Lee yelped each time the thick strand of leather tore down on his milky flesh. The other five, forced to watch, had to struggle to keep from vomiting. This included Rosselli who, while working for Capone in Chicago, had seen, even done, pretty much everything. Yet nothing came close to this. The smell of torn flesh ...

When the ordeal finally ended, Lee, initially standing, hung by cuffed wrists, semi-conscious, like a side of beef in a slaughterhouse. Valle signaled his minions; one rushed out of the room, returning with a metal tub. He splashed water across Lee's back. This brought Lee out of his stupor. Valle ordered Lee released and, wobbly though he was, the humbled prisoner managed to stumble back in the line with the other prisoners.

184

The two original groups, during their march through the corridor to the cells, had remained separate. During the ordeal a sense that they were developing into one amorphous community gradually overcame everyone. The trios were forced into adjacent cells at bayonet point. In the confines of their 25 by 20-ft. cell, Dick Tracy inspected the wounds on Lee's back. His partner would live, though infection might become a problem.

All had to urinate and defecate in a single hole. They slept on hard stone as there were no cots. The two sets of three men remained in their cells 24 hours a day, except when guards arrived to drag someone down the corridor for interrogation. The victim would be solemnly greeted by Valle and returned an hour or so later, badly beaten. Why are you here? Valle demanded. Who sent you? Lee, like his two companions, had been fully briefed by George during planning session as to how to answer if things came down to this: I acted on my own accord. Yes, the other two men were my co-conspirators, but that is the limit of guilt. We are American patriots. Right or wrong, we arrived to eliminate our country's greatest threat in the Western hemisphere.

Beat me, whip me, kill me. All I can do is admit my guilt, accept any punishment. But you cannot break me, cannot force me to lie and say that the United States government had any part in this. I'll go to my death assuming full responsibility.

I will die lying to protect me country. I am a patriot. This is what I promised George at our first meeting in Mexico.

No matter how badly the Americans were tortured, the Cubans in the adjoining cell had it worse. If for the first two days an invisible wall of secrecy separated the cells, a camaraderie gradually developed. Men from one group exchanged words now and then with the others. The conversations continually expanded in length and intensity. Essential to such talk was the reality that Valle had spoken of that first day: Fidel Castro feared nothing more than allowing the U.S. government some excuse to send in the marines, which might occur if the Americans were to be summarily executed despite their assassination attempt. Even a long stay in El Principe for them could lead to an invasion.

No doubt Castro wondered if that might be a pre-planned narrative, the three sent down to purposefully be arrested, this allowing the U.S. an excuse to do what the administration most hungered for: a full scale invasion of Cuba, motivated by the need to "save" the "innocent" U.S. citizens held there.

As for the Cubans in the next cell? That was something else entirely. They awaited execution at Fidel Castro's whim.

*

Located in the center of each cell, a ragged hole had been cut into the stone. When a prisoner needed to relieve himself he rose and approached this spot, then squatted over it. Lee had heard the expression "shit-hole" before but never had he seen, much less used, one, not even at the makeshift camp back on Corregidor. Also there was what the men referred to as "the other hole," this one located closer to the entrance. Twice a day, emissaries would arrive and, while guards kept guns trained on the prisoners, poured muck into this cavity. After, each prisoner had to scoop his food, if one chose to call it that, up from this reservoir with his bare hands. No one ever cleaned the space or explained what it was they ate. Lee guessed it to be a stew of bananas and meat from some animal. Rats? Ugh!

He, Johnny Handsome and Dick Tracy initially preferred to go hungry, so putrid was the slop. The Cubans in the adjoining cell glutted themselves. In time, hunger took its toll, and the Americans ate. Lee's stomach refused to accept the concoction. He hurried over to the other hole and puked, groaning like a sick beast. The next meal Lee skipped. Starving, he tried once more, somehow holding the stuff down. No sooner had he finished than a case of the runs set in, leaving Lee unable to leave the shit-hole for more than an hour. Toilet paper, a necessity back home, the Americans recalled as a luxury. Old newspapers lay scattered around for the prisoners to wipe themselves.

"Who sent you?" Captain Valle screeched into Lee's ear, he seated in a rough wooden frame chair, hands bound behind his back, unable to even wriggle when the lash came down again.

"No one. I swear, it was our own crazy idea—"

Once more, Valle slashed the whip against Lee's naked back.

I must not break, I must not break, I must not ...

*

To keep from screaming while incarcerated, particularly on occasions when Johnny Handsome and Dick Tracy were escorted out for joint interrogation and torture, Lee made conversation with the Cubans. The red-bearded shrimper, an odd fellow, marched around his cell's borders, reciting poetry. He introduced himself as 'Cavarez,' an ardent anti-Castro democrat. Though he now worked as a cleaner of fish at the docks, he'd been educated at university and briefly employed as a grade-school teacher before the revolution. Cavarez, if that was his name, insisted anyone whose eyes and mind had been opened by a wide array of books could never be seduced by simplistic Red propaganda.

"And you? I hear your companions refer to you as Lee. I thought you might be Chinese. What brought you here, my friend?"

Even as Lee opened his mouth to speak his mind he realized what was going on. These men were plants! The coincidence of them brought to El Principe precisely as the three Americans were interred strained credulity. At that moment when they were at their most vulnerable, these Cubans—doubtless spies for Castro, so loyal they were willing to undergo torture if that proved necessary to cultivate the attempted assassins and seduce one into spilling the beans—were government agents.

His eyes filling with anger, Lee turned and stepped away. When his companions returned, Lee disclosed his suspicions.

"Of course. How did I not see spot that at once?"

"Great goin', Lee. You just saved our friggin' necks!"

They rolled over and went to sleep. When the Americans woke the next morning, each privately wondering how he could possibly make it through another day here, all noticed that the adjoining cell was now empty. Whether the Cubans really had been anti-Castro and were taken away for execution, or as spies for Castro they had passed on word to Captain Valle that their cover was blown and so excused, Lee would never know for certain.

Shortly eight guards, wielding rifles, arrived. The leader unlocked the cell door, signaling for all to follow. Out they went, back down the hallway, then the huge corridor, finally out of the fortress into the morning air. They marched back down the path, crossing both drawbridges, then were loaded into a canvas-covered police truck similar to the one they'd arrived in.

This is it! Either they take us out to a field and shoot us down or they bring us to the Cessna and let us go. Hey, I'd even prefer the former if it means leaving this prison forever.

It proved to be the latter. They were ordered to step out of the truck in the field where Dick Tracy had left the plane a week earlier. At gunpoint they were ordered to board. The Cessna had been refueled. Their pilot started up the engine.

"Goodbye," the squad leader waved with an ironic smile that made clear it would not be wise for them ever to return.

Two hours later they descended to Miami's Tamiami airport.

During the flight, Lee wondered if either Dick Tracy or Johnny Handsome had during their previous joint interrogation broken down and admitted they were CIA and Mafia, this reported to Castro who, fearful of both, decided that discretion had to be the better part of valor, as the Bard had written 350 years earlier, and set them free out of fear. Still, if Lee learned anything at all from the ordeal, it was to keep his mouth shut.

They reported to George, apologizing for the mission's failure. He poo-poohed such talk, insisting their attempt had been noble and had been considered unlikely to succeed if well worth the try. They were heroes and would be treated as such.

*

Following five days of R and R in Miami, during which time Lee fell in love with the city, particularly after making the rounds with Johnny Rosselli, he began his trek back to Russia. This time he followed precisely the same round-about route that brought him here only in reverse. Late at night on April 19, 1961, he secretly entered his apartment. Everything appeared normal, his double having effectively covered for him, apparently leaving shortly before Lee arrived. Exhausted, he slept soundly.

The following morning, Lee woke to a loud knocking at the door. He pulled himself together, opened it, and saw his current girlfriend Marina, laughing and crying at the same time, all excited, her body shaking, apparently with joy.

"Yes!" she shouted.

"Yes, what?" he yawned.

"Yes, silly, I'll marry you."

As Marina leaped forward and threw her arms around him, kissing Lee on his cheeks, his lips, his forehead, he silently cursed his double, who had indeed left Lee returning to a big surprise! What did that jerk do? Propose to her while assuming my place in the hospital? Then, Lee realized that perhaps the twin had been ordered to do so by George as part of a CIA plan.

Marina, meanwhile, rambled on about wanting to stop by here ever since Lee's release on April 11, though she had to be absolutely certain this was the right thing. That's why she'd stayed away until now, when it came to her all at once: *I want to be his bride more than anything in the whole wide world.*

She entered, they locked the door, and the couple made love with great passion and a touch of fury. Ten days later, on April 30, they were officially married. In between, the two barely left his rooms. In addition to the sex, they spent a great deal of time together, he on the couch, listening to radio reports concerning the then-underway Bay of Pigs invasion.

Wow! So that's what 'Dick Tracy' meant when he used the phrase 'by D-Day' back in Miami!

CHAPTER TWELVE
THE HAPPENING

"When it comes to leisure reading, I prefer the
James Bond novels of Ian Fleming."
—John Fitzgerald Kennedy, 1962

Miami had always been a contradiction in terms, a point noted by Pedro Menendez de Aviles when he first discovered the area, claiming it for Spain in 1566. How could a single stretch of land alter so drastically, from mellow Biscayne Bay just off the east coast to the treacherous Everglade swamplands near the western border? By the mid-20th century, even the architecture featured not one style but two: ancient stone buildings dating back nearly 400 years in tandem with steel-and-glass needles stretching upward as if longing to touch the clouds.

Such a contrast held true for the population: half Anglo, half Cuban, this mix salted by Tequesta Indians, peppered with African-Americans, spiced too by assorted people of color.

To the city's immediate east, separated from Miami proper by the Bay and from there edging toward the Atlantic, sat the community of Miami Beach. Incorporated and independent, here was a demi-monde with its own unique appearance, people, and values.

Structured over a set of strangely shaped barrier islands, some natural, others man-made, there one discovered a smaller world within the self-contained universe of Miami. Most unique among its neighborhoods: South Beach (SoBo as locals called it).

This area overwhelmed Lee with its odd, appealing buildings, described by the ever-knowing George as Art Deco: a throwback to the late 1920s and early thirties. The New Yorker Hotel, where Lee stayed (courtesy of the U.S. government) during those heady five days in early April, 1961, captured the spirit of this playground for adults. The building's extended horizon gradually curved so as to give the impression of a large land-bound leisure-boat of the type Cole Porter envisioned for his long-ago musical *Anything Goes*.

Of course, Lee had never seen the lavish show performed onstage. As a boy he had watched the movie on TV, imagining himself transported to such an alternative domain in which men wore tuxedoes, women elegant gowns; everyone was beautiful, the surroundings lavish. Always soft jazz played in the background.

I did it. I made it. I'm here! At this moment, I'm living inside a Hollywood film ... Three days ago I ate garbage in a filthy Cuban prison cell. Last night I dined on lobster ...

Hot chicks were twisting on the corner of 79th Street as Lee roared by in Johnny Handsome's Corvette, The Muse seated in-between them. They were off for a drive as Johnny and his young beauty, who appeared as if out of nowhere, informed Lee. He detected a European accent when the young woman spoke, likely from Germany. He couldn't be sure. She said little as they drove west from Miami, as if this 'muse' were a beauty object, not some real person with a history, feelings and ideas all her own.

It's as if I'm living out a scene from some fantasy ...

The trio enjoyed their quick passing glance at the girls, none over the age of seventeen, breaking into the latest dance craze, The Hully-Gully. These real-life Lolitas wore bathing suits so brief that, had they dare appear in public so flimsily attired two years earlier, the authorities would have had them arrested.

That was then; this, now. The Eisenhower era, dominated by such solidly old-fashioned icons as *I Love Lucy* and the Davy Crockett Craze, had given way to the Kennedy Years: a jet-set sensibility that incorporated something called The Sexual Revolution.

Motored by everything from the advent of The Pill, which freed casual sex from the stigma of unwanted pregnancy, to *Playboy*, around since 1954, suddenly part of the mainstream.

*

The political scene had altered, too. Cuban exiles living in Florida, for the past year busying themselves with handing out anti-Castro literature, had turned militant. Lee could detect that in their eyes and body language as the Corvette cruised down Biscayne Boulevard. All along the main drag he observed a striking contrast. For each street corner peopled with giddy, wild, oblivious kids arriving from all over the country for their annual spring break, on the next there would be a plank table, manned by refugees from the revolution.

Angry, intense, ever more open and aggressive, the Cubans and a smaller coterie of Anglo supporters wanted to share with passersby what they considered the absolute need for America to join them in opposition to that bearded tyrant, Castro. As Johnny pulled to a halt at a stop-light, Lee heard the talk between pamphleteers and the locals and tourists who happened by. What had once been a carefully kept secret could now be spoken of openly: an armed invasion of their homeland.

"Shortly a secret brigade, 'Freedom Forever!,' will launch an attack," one man insisted to Lee, leaning close to Johnny's sleek Corvette, before the light changed and they drove off.

The trio zipped onto the highway. Everything struck Lee as clean, fresh; palm trees, soft green at the top, dark brown on the base, swaying slightly in the mid-morning breeze.

It doesn't get any better than this! If they could see me now ...

*

The city now behind them, Johnny explained to Lee and The Muse what George and Dick Tracy had told him: there had until recently been more than fifty organizations, each with a small membership, between five to twenty volunteers tops. That old adage—too many chefs, too few cooks—applied. Not only did the groups fail to unite; some expressed hostility toward others.

To George's disappointment, the leaders mostly turned out to be egomaniacs, jealously viewing counterparts as competitors. Angry statements from any one patriotic group were more often directed at neighbors than Castro.

Clearly, they could never get together to achieve something of value until a single leader emerged. Representing the CIA, George initially assumed that role. He knew, though, that only a fellow Cuban, one with much charisma, could fill the bill.

Meanwhile, George had ordered an ongoing series of B-26 raids, kept secret from the American public, assigned to drop bombs over Cuba. Once, for kicks, The Muse flew alongside the pilot, she dazzled by the yellow, orange, red explosions below.

"How beautiful it looked, Lee. Like fireworks—"

"But people on the ground ... were killed?"

"Hmmm? Oh, yes. Of course."

When Castro screeched over Havana's radio network that such illegal, immoral actions were taking place, and that some of his citizens died, the U.S. government denied any involvement.

Who would people in the heartlands believe: JFK's Secretary of State, or the ugly, swarthy bearded giant down south? They believed their movie-star handsome president to be a hero. Cliff Robertson even now prepared to play JFK in a film.

It's as if we're all at once living in a movie. Let's call this film The Sixties. A Beach Party flick. Beautiful girls in bikinis, twisting away their afternoons. Political activists, readying for a Crusade in Cuba. Our gorgeous leader in his American Camelot with that perfect queen-like wife beside him.

The bearded, unclean enemy, whom most Americans hoped would drop dead, howling somewhere to the south.

We, the good guys; about to wipe out the bad guy. Then "the End" appears over a screen as we live happily ever after.

But that's only in The Movies. Life isn't like that. JFK can't be as perfect as everybody wants to believe. Nor can Fidel Castro be the simplistic villain he's made out to be.

This is real-life. Complex, not simple. Which means sooner or later, the shit must hit the fan. It's only a matter of time.

*

Without warning, the highway ended. They passed onto an old road. That in time gave way to a dirt and pebble path. No others were traveling in this direction today. Lee recalled the back-roads George once drove him down. Now, in a different part of the country; yet everything looked the same as it did then.

The Everglades! We're approaching the swamps. But why head here? Not exactly right for a spring afternoon picnic, what with all the snakes and other beasts crawling about ...

As they proceeded along a barely visible trail through foliage so thick it appeared black rather than green in the increasing brightness of an early-afternoon sun, Lee spotted a guard station ahead. Manning the small outpost, three scruffy fellows, each brandishing a large pistol in a holster by his side, lolled about chatting until the Corvette cruised up.

"Hello, Le Muse," the trio's leader called out.

"Buenos dias," she answered with a Cheshire cat smile.

"I hoped to show my companion here the outpost."

"Any amigo of yours, Johnny," the man responded with a pleasant smile, "is our friend as well."

This man in charge nodded to one of the guards. He pushed a button, bringing the metallic gate up so that the car might pass into the compound. On Lee's passenger side, a long stretch of barbed wire, naturally camouflaged by the twisted overgrowth, could barely be detected. Deeper inside the hidden camp, Lee spotted several groups of young Cubans, all in para-military fatigues, training under similarly attired Anglos.

Johnny swerved his car off the trail, up onto the gravel, so they could watch experts instructing Cubans in martial arts, the handling of heavy and light weapons, and a guerilla tactic in which scouts slipped up behind an enemy, shadow-like.

"Hello," one instructor, his face shrouded by the brim of a fatigue hat pulled low, called out. At once, Lee recognized the voice: *George!* He allowed his trainees a ten minute break and sauntered over, pulling away his cap to reveal the face of Lee's CIA mentor. "Welcome to Operation Vaquero."

Vaquero? Lee thought. *Isn't that Spanish for cowboy?*

"I might have known you'd be in charge here."

"Actually, I'm only assisting. I found a Cuban national to handle that job. That's why you're here: to meet him."

Lee gradually put the pieces together. This had to do with the upcoming D-Day he'd heard Dick Tracy mention during the flight to Cuba. Apparently, now that they were back—mission *not* accomplished—no longer did the brass have to fear Lee breaking down and talking under torture.

"That'll be my pleasure," Lee said.

Johnny pulled the car back onto the muddy dirt road and continued on past flat fields. Lee assumed these to be take-off and landing points for airborne arrivals and departures. Most intriguing: the Company made no serious attempt to conceal this place from the public. Yet few if any in the nearby city knew of its existence. Nor, apparently, did they care. If the media were aware, few reporters felt any compunction to report on it. The attitude trickled down from the government: ignore everything.

Seeing was believing. People believed what they read in the papers and watched on TV. There, they perceived none of this.

Ignorance was bliss. Until something unexpectedly went awry.

True, the New York *Times* had printed probing editorial pieces, insisting those in authority in D.C. should be called on to explain what was taking place. That small percentage of the public labeled the intelligentsia, which read this paper, mostly agreed. The other ninety-percent of Americans were happy to remain blissfully ignorant as to pretty much everything.

Their attitude? What we don't know can't hurt us. Those in charge know what's best. Anything they do is for our benefit.

The mainstream press in those pre-Watergate days? Their job was to rubber-stamp anything the government said, pass it on to readers and listeners, mostly without comment. Already, the newspapers and TV networks were doing precisely that as to yet another theatre of war then developing: Vietnam; southeast Asia.

And, for the time being at least, the majority of Americans believed whatever they were told. As Lee's mother liked to say: If it weren't true, they couldn't put it on TV.

At the compound's main building, an ebullient Cuban came darting out to greet the trio and shake Lee's hand.

"Meet Manuel Artime Buesa," Muse said. "George's hand-picked choice for this all-important task."

"Oh? This one actually has a full name?" Lee asked, the other Cubans at the guard post having remained anonymous.

Buesa laughed heartily. "We all do, amigo. But it would prove difficult for me to try and keep mine secret. You see, I am Miami's secretary general for the MRR."

Lee knew that to be the abbreviation for *Movimiento de Recuperacion Revolucionario*, an umbrella title for all those splinter groups that manned the Biscayne recruitment tables; originally united by George, now fully overseen by Buesa.

*

"How did they ever make a movie out of Lolita?" billboard advertisements and media commercials for the first controversial film of the new decade asked. There was Sue Lyon, the unknown child-woman picked to embody onscreen the perfect nymphette in red plastic heart-shaped glasses, sucking provocatively on her drink from a straw. Based on a much-banned book that had been subject of heated discussion during the previous decade, *Lolita* had been considered unfilmable then. No self-respecting L.A. producer was willing to consider such an explosive property.

Now? This was The Sixties. Things change ...

Johnny had received a pair of passes to a preview of *Lolita* and swung by The New Yorker to pick up Lee. In the Corvette, which caught the eyes of every female the two men passed, they headed downtown, arriving early to be sure to secure seats.

Lee, who had read the book, swept up by its artistic sensuality, wondered how close this commercial project dared approximate the power of Vladimir Nabokov's prose-poetry. The work analyzed an older man's fascination with an under-age female.

James Mason, as Humbert, takes one of Sue Lyon's adorable little feet, gently holding her steady with his left hand while applying nail polish to the other. What a marvelous way for a filmmaker to suggest the man's obsession that Nabokov relayed in words ... That's *how they made a movie out of 'Lolita!'*

"I've got a surprise for you," Johnny said as they exited.

"I'm almost afraid to ask 'what'?"

"How would you like to *meet* ... 'Lolita'?"

Lee stopped in his tracks. "The actress is in town?"

"Not her. Something even better. The *real* Lolita."

*

"Absolutely true," the beautiful twenty-year-old blonde, wearing the satin gown in which she'd performed as headline singer at one of Havana's night spots, explained after exhaling a mouthful of cigarette smoke. "*I* was supposed to play Lolita!"

"What went wrong?" Lee asked, sitting opposite the slender beauty at a prime table while Johnny made the rounds.

"The whole idea was, Errol would play 'Humbert Hubert', and I'd be Lolita. Reflecting, of course, our actual relationship."

Johnny says she started sleeping with Errol Flynn in 1958. That would make her fifteen at the time. Lolita's age, in the film. I gotta admit, she does look the part.

"Incredible. So?"

"Just before shooting was about to start, the law came down on us." She paused for a long swig of her double-Scotch. "Errol was charged with statutory rape with me being so young. His mug was on the cover of every tabloid in the country. No major Hollywood company wanted anything to do with him after that."

"But even if they dropped him, why didn't you—"

"A package-deal. Without him, I was persona-non-grata."

"Such a shame! How amazing it would've been for people to see a *real* Lolita and the real Humbert together onscreen."

"Well, actually, they can. I mean, we did make a movie, if not so big a one." Surprised, Lee asked her to explain. As an inveterate movie buff, he could hardly believe a film had been shot with such a major star that he'd never heard about, much less caught. "It's called *Cuban Rebel Girls*. Shot on location!"

"Must've been only a short while before Mr. Flynn died of that heart attack up in Canada."

"Bullshit! Errol didn't drop dead. He was murdered by the Mob. My guess is, your pal Johnny over there likely did it!"

"Please continue," Lee begged. "I'm all ears ..."

*

The Tasmanian-born, Australian-raised devil-may-care star had always been a closet lefty. Following the war, his Warner Bros. contract finally exhausted, Flynn became an independent producer. For fifteen years he labored, trying to get a film made about William Tell, the great peasant-rebel from Swiss history. Flynn would have starred in the screen-play he co-authorized concerning the overthrow of a tyrant, Gessler. In the film, this would directly parallel current Latin American rebellions against corrupt dictators.

When Castro, whom Errol adored, appeared likely to succeed, this inspired Flynn all the more to create his movie-metaphor. He hoped his film would win over the American people, terrified of communists, to see the Cuban situation in a positive light.

During that final year of planning, Beverly Aadland was to have been the female lead. Then, funding dried up in the light of the Errol Flynn/Bev Aadland scandal.

195

"Incredible! I'd heard that Flynn was a right-winger, even attracted to Hitler during the late 1930s."

Bev roared at that. "No one in Hollywood hated the Nazis more than Errol. He never made a big deal about it because he believed stars should keep their politics to themselves, when speaking in public if not as to what they might slip into any film. Go back and watch *Robin Hood* from 1936: it's no accident that the peasants carry hammers and cycles into Sherwood."

Of course! That was purposeful. I never realized it until now but, they do just that. Robin Hood as Red propaganda!

"So one day, Errol got invited to the White House for a special secretive meeting with F.D.R. The German bund was just then forming. The president asked Errol, owing to his Aryan appearance, to join. You can't imagine how many American lives were saved by information Errol picked up as a secret agent."

"He did that, knowing he might later be considered a Nazi?"

"Errol believed the good of the country was more important than any man's reputation. Even his own."

Just like me! Defecting to Russia, as George requested.

Acknowledging in late 1958 that the big William Tell epic was never going to happen, Flynn—now nearing fifty, looking decades older owing to years of wine, women and song—decided to use whatever box-office clout he might have left to realize his dream movie, a cinematic tribute to Castro, if on a considerably less spectacular scale. What mattered most, he believed, was the message: To paraphrase FDR we had nothing to fear from communist Cuba but fear itself. Fear would drive them into the enemy camp as a self-fulfilling prophecy.

One night, while lying in bed with Bev after sex, his mind already off and wandering in search of a first tentative step, it dawned on Flynn: Why not go down there, improvise a movie on location? Perhaps even convince Castro to play himself! Such a trip would cost money. Lots of money. Once wealthy, Flynn didn't have any, his fortune squandered on what he referred to as 'my wicked, wicked ways.' Then he admitted to Bev that in his secret life Errol Flynn had always wanted to be a journalist. She gazed on as his eyes, red and blurry, lit up as a scheme hatched.

Right-wing newspaper magnate William R. Hearst, unaware of Flynn's fellow traveler sensibilities, worshipped the star. The publisher, an extreme right-winger, had like many others heard of Flynn's pre-WWII era "legend" as an ardent Nazi sympathizer, Hearst secretly supporting Hitler in the days before the America entered the war.

"You're not thinking what I *think* you're thinking?"

Indeed he was. Flynn called Hearst. Could they meet in the publisher's office to discuss a unique project? In a half-hour session, Flynn convinced Hearst, in those days leading up to the New Year's Day takeover of Havana, to send him down as a reporter. Flynn promised to glorify Batista at Castro's expense while planning to do precisely the opposite.

Delighted at the prospect, Hearst tipped the CIA off. Aware of the star's previous Secret Service work, the Company approached Flynn with the idea of assassinating Castro during an interview. They too were unaware of Flynn's far-left leanings.

Devilishly delighted at how things were progressing, Flynn gladly agreed. He even went through several weeks of special training, planning to instead kill Batista, who would surely invite the Hollywood star to dinner upon arrival.

The CIA meanwhile put Flynn in touch with The Mob, already fearful of what would happen should Castro pull off his coup. Knowing the amount of money that the Made Men possessed, and that some, like Johnny Handsome, had once been involved in the movie business, Flynn came up with a far more bizarre concept, one that would realize his secret cinematic project: Talk the Mafiosos into financing a B-budget anti-Castro film while preparing to kill Fidel for the CIA. The idea flew.

Amazed at how beautifully all the pieces were falling into place, Flynn accepted the deal, writing a script that would instead glorify Fidel. He and Bev left for Cuba and, shooting on a shoe-string, did precisely that.

*

Lee finally caught the flick about a year and a half later as the third feature on a triple bill at a Texas Drive In. He was with Marina and their daughter June, seated in an old jalopy, never mentioning that he'd met the female lead. So far as anyone could see, they were one more white trash family, out for the night.

Bev played Bev Woods, a typical American teenager who can't grasp why her boyfriend would ditch her to run off and join the Cuban revolution. She follows and, shortly after arrival, meets a Vodka-guzzling American movie-star-turned-war correspondent, Flynn as Flynn in a script written by Flynn, he starring in a project produced by Flynn. The old rogue raises the nymph's political consciousness as together the two trek off into the hills. She strips down to short-shorts, whacking away at jungle foliage and fascistic forces with a machete.

Flynn planned to end his story with a fictional projection of he, Bev, and Castro making ready for the invasion of Havana. Then he would rush home, edit the film, and release it so the American public might see the event before it could occur.

Instead, the New Year's Eve attack took place while Flynn and Bev were still shooting. Improvising, Flynn filmed Castro's motorcade entering Havana, Bev sitting up on a tank, waving a red victory banner. Bev playing Bev while, adjacent to her, Fidel embodied himself, fact and fiction mingling, blurring, coming together as never before on celluloid.

The image cut away to Flynn, happily glancing down from his hotel room window. In a voice-over, he explains:

Well, I guess that winds up another stage in the fight to rid Latin America of tyrants and dictators. The spirit started by this wonderful band of rebels is speedy and growing stronger every day. And all you young men and women fighting for political freedom, your beliefs?

I wish you good luck!

Shortly after returning home, having tried but failed on several occasions to shoot Batista, carrying several cans of film under each arm, Flynn was dead.

He and Bev had on October 9, 1959 flown to Vancouver where Errol hoped to lease his much loved yacht, the *Zaca*, on which he had spent so many happy days with his underage mistress. Now he desperately needed money so that he and Bev could continue to lead 'the sweet life': that emergent 1960s fast-lane style.

On October 14, the two attended a party at the West End apartment of Dr. Grant Gould. Errol knocked down drink after drink. Shouting "I shall return!" an unbalanced Flynn waved bye-bye and stepped into the adjoining bedroom to crash.

After an hour or so, Bev—who had spent that sixty minutes conversing with an Adonis-like suited Latin named Johnny—began to worry. She excused herself, rose, and headed into the bedroom to check on her lover.

Flynn's face, red as a beet, stared up at her from the bed, his wide-open eyes utterly devoid of life.

"Oh, my God," she wailed. "Johnny, I think he's dead!"

Johnny, who had followed Bev, leaned over Flynn's body to check. "Yep," he said, cradling Bev under his arm. "Errol is with the angels now. Or, heaven forbid, down below."

That struck her as a strange comment. Still, Bev needed to be held that night. She went home with Johnny, who made love to her almost as fiercely as her legendary paramour had often done.

Shortly, all known prints of *Cuban Rebel Girls* disappeared. Until one eventually surfaced at a rural Texas Drive-In.

*

"Hey," Johnny suavely said, swinging back to the table where Bev held court, Lee gazing at her adoringly. "Shall we go back to my place and pick up where we left off in Vancouver?"

The heartbreaking blonde considered Rosselli long and hard. "No," she finally quipped, rising. "I think I'll go home with Lee. Thank you anyway, though, for a lovely evening."

The following morning, after Lee and Bev shared coffee together on his balcony, she prepared to leave.

"One last question. You said early in the evening that you believe Errol was ... murdered?"

"I don't believe. I know! Look, Lee, he took Mob money to make a movie they believed would work to their benefit. Then he went and shot precisely the opposite."

"They'd actually kill a guy for making a pro-Castro movie?"

"Never in a million years. Live and let live. So long as someone does something on his own, that's his business. This was different. He lied to them. Took their dough and then betrayed their trust. It wasn't the movie so much ... as ..."

"I get your drift."

"Do you? Then always keep this in mind, particularly if you're going to hang out with Johnny Rosselli, whom I now hold responsible for the poisoning of Errol's drink. I never would have gone to bed with him that night if I'd had any inkling—"

"As you were saying?"

"Oh, right. Listen to me, Lee, and listen good. You don't want to play ball with the Mob, you don't have to. That's up to you. On the other hand, don't ever fuck 'em over."

"I hear you."

"Good! Because no one can get away that. Understand? And when I say no one, I mean *no one*!"

*

When Johnny swung by to pick Lee up the next evening, the Mafioso found his unlikely pal reading yet another James Bond paperback. Unconsciously, Lee crammed it into his jacket pocket and they took off. Lee felt a little nervous there might be some friction with Bev choosing him the previous night. Rosselli laughed at the idea. He'd spent the night with the Muse, and few women could compare to her. Matter of fact—*hey, this is quite a coincidence!*—her CIA code-name used to be *Lolita*.

"Okay. So where we headed for tonight?"

"Guess you could call it a party. More like what the kids these days call 'a happening.' Pretty cool. You'll see."

They cruised down The Strip, that stretch of high-rent property where enormous hotels and glitzy bars awaited the arriving upscale visitors. At least those who hadn't yet abandoned Miami for Vegas, where gambling, the final necessary ingredient in such an adult entertainment mix, was legal.

Feeling like a million bucks, Lee observed in passing 'The Big Five,' as the prime resorts were known: The Americana, Carrillon, Deauville, Eden Rock, and Fountainbleau. Sinatra, Ella Fitzgerald and Sammy Davis all put in regular appearances. Johnny pointed out another attraction: a houseboat docked at the canal. This was used for all the exterior shots on Warner Bros.' TV series *Surfside Six*. Twice a year, sandy-haired youth-idol Troy Donahue would show up and film here for two weeks.

As to what transpired next? When Lee thought back on it later he could not tell what had actually happened and how much must be relegated to a fantasy concocted by his brain. They arrived at one of The Big Five. As an attendant parked Johnny's car the two were ushered by a pair of beautiful women in elegant satin sheaths into a large, crowded private hall.

Before he knew what was happening, Lee had been handed a drink. He sipped it. A double-scotch, of the highest quality. As soon as the glass' level had diminished, yet another gorgeous hostess appeared, refilling his glass.

Within minutes Lee felt under the influence. Johnny stood beside him, for the moment. The crowd grew ever thicker.

"How do you like it?" the man Lee was supposed to address as 'James Stewart' while in the Sunshine State asked.

"Excellent Scotch."

Johnny laughed. "I meant the L.S.D. it's spiked with."

Now Lee understood why his head felt as if screwed on backwards. He'd read about the experimental drug known to alter and intensify one's perceptions. The room appeared to whirl around him, though a strobe up above in the semi-darkness, projecting harsh rays of white light onto each of the party-goers, added to that effect.

Lee's rational mind told him to stop drinking. But there was nothing at all rational about the situation he found himself in: a phantasmagoria of lights and shadows, time and space now dissolving; everyone before him moving, as if in a film, in slow-motion one moment, terribly speeded up the next.

Any final sense of reality dissipated when Lee stumbled into ... himself. For a second, he thought he was about to walk into a mirror and, perhaps Alice-like, pass into a Wonderland.

There was no mirror. The image facing Lee, a man with his face, sported a different jacket. Unlike lee, he wore no tie.

"Hi, guy. What d'ya know?" Lee's twin joked.

Lee couldn't speak, partly out of the shock of confronting his double, also as he'd momentarily lost the ability to do so. His tongue felt frozen, yet dry.

"The sneer was the most difficult part to master," the twin explained. "Took me many hours of practice to perfect *that*." He broke out in the snide, cynical grin Lee had developed as his shield against the world. "You have quite a surprise waiting when you get back, Lee Harvey Oswald," the twin continued.

Before Lee could respond, another voice pierced the lights and colors from behind them. "Which of you is which?"

Lee turned and found himself face to face with Robert Kennedy, the president's younger brother and Attorney General of the United States. Or did he? Was this real or only imagined?

"I'm ... me," Lee gasped. He tried to imagine how they three might appear to others: Robert Kennedy, with a Lee Harvey Oswald standing on either side. Then Lee recalled everyone else in the room must be as spaced-out as himself, hallucinating in Technicolor.

"Good to finally meet you in person, Lee. George has been telling me great things about your devoted service."

One thing that couldn't be denied: When all of this was over, Lee's copy of *From Russia With Love* was nowhere to be found. Only a recollection of, during the time Lee spent with Robert Kennedy and the other Lee—seconds, minutes, hours—wanting more than anything to give the great man a present.

But here, in the crowded room, what could he offer ...

"Mr. Kennedy, I've heard that you and your brother love the 007 novels." Lee pulled out the paperback, handing it to Bobby Kennedy. "Have you had a chance yet to read this one yet?"

"Yes, Lee, I have. Been recommending it to Jack, though he's been too busy to get around to it. Maybe someday."

Ecstatically, Lee responded: "Take my copy, sir. Please pass it on to the president." Then Lee realized he also had a ball-point pen in the same pocket.

He drew it out and on the first page wrote:

To President John Fitzgerald Kennedy
From your greatest fan!
Lee Harvey Oswald

"Thank you," Bobby graciously responded, sticking the book into his inner jacket pocket. "I'm flying back to D.C. tomorrow. Jack will have it later in the day."

"Wow! From Lee to Jack, me to the president."

Bobby nodded, then mentioned he had to be moving on, greet other guests. Before doing so, he shook hands with Lee, who later recalled this as the greatest single moment in his life.

If, that is, it ever actually happened.

*

"Hey, I see you finally met Bobby," Johnny Rosselli said, joining them as Lee's twin soon disappeared in the crowd.

"He and his brother are my heroes. Civil rights—"

"That's all well and good." A frown lined Johnny's brow as a dark cloud passed over his face. "Let them do whatever they want for the niggers. They'd best not fuck with *us*."

Lee mulled that over, recalling something on the radio or TV about Bobby possibly employing his office to finally go after organized crime in America.

Lee was on his fourth drink when a hush fell over the room. The strobe light whirled across to a stage on the far side. A woman stepped into view there. Apparently, someone played a record of "Diamonds Are a Girl's Best Friend," the number Marilyn Monroe had sung in *Gentlemen Prefer Blondes*.

Then there she was: Monroe, under the stultifying white light, wrapped from neck to toes in that hot pink dress she'd worn. The diamond tiara, clasped chokingly tight against her chin, with matching elbow bracelets; waving the jet-black fan that reflected the outfit's dark borders. A white fur trim completed the illusion.

A Marilyn impersonator! And talk about a twin! This blonde looks as much like the real thing as my own double resembles me. She's even lip-synching the words to the song with perfection.

The proverbial pin could have been heard dropping as the blonde went through the precise motions of choreography Lee and everyone else in the room had seen in the movie. It was as if that sequence now came to life in front of their eyes, a dream from Hollywood transcending into actuality ...

"She's so beautiful," Lee whispered to Johnny.

"I know," Johnny grumbled, "but I'm worried for her."

"Huh?" However swiftly the room had been whirring earlier, this latest drink caused Lee to feel as if he'd lost all touch with gravity, free-floating through an alternative universe.

"Too brazen about 'doing' Jack and Bobby. The girl's a loose cannon. That's dangerous. To her, unless she shuts up."

Lee tried to take that in but nothing made sense anymore. Johnny was talking about the impersonator as if she were ...

The infamous number finally reached its climax. To ecstatic applause, The Blonde stepped down, into the crowd. Like Moses leading the way through the Red Sea, she parted the human waters as awestruck partygoers stepped aside, allowing the fantasy-come-to life to drift by, eyes half closed, her mouth smiling dazzlingly.

As she swept past Lee, it suddenly occurred to him that this might be the girl he had bedded during the Twinning. She had struck him as Marilyn-like. Could it be … ?

"Honey?" he called out as she breezed by.

"My name's Norma Jean," she cooed over her shoulder, "but you can call me 'Honey' if you like."

*

When Lee woke on the couch of his suite at the New Yorker, he had no idea what day it might be or how he had come to be there. The last thing he recalled was a sense of free-falling.

Lee had dropped into a strawberry-tinted, banana scented tunnel, sliding down, and further down, with the possibility that no end awaited him.

But that was not true. Only a nightmare. For here he was, waking to a new day, if a bit worse for wear.

Lee had to be certain, though, make sure he was the person he believed himself to be. He grabbed for his jacket, whisked out his wallet, flipped through his identification.

The passport made clear that he was indeed Lee Harvey Oswald. So that much seemed certain.

Moreover, the photograph next to it proved that his life had, up until this strange sojourn in mid-April, been what he believed it to be.

For there was Marina, the girl with the flashing eyes, waiting for him even now in Russia.

All at once, he could not wait to be with her again.

CHAPTER THIRTEEN:
PHANTOM LADY

"Marina liked Italian cinema, loved Fellini films so much.
Those movies certainly gave her ideas!"
—Norman Mailer, *Oswald's Tale*; 1995

"Can we go to the movies?" Marina asked when Lee Harvey
Oswald picked her up for their first date on March 19, 1961. The
two had met five days earlier at a social function in Minsk, a gala
prelude-to-spring celebration at the Palace of Culture.

"Sure. Anything in particular?"

"*La Dolce Vita*. The Soviet censors have finally allowed it to be
shown here without cuts."

"Who's in it?"

"I don't know. It isn't like one of those Hollywood films where
you can identify a movie by the stars."

"Who, then?"

"The director, of course. In this case, Federico Fellini."

"I heard of him back in the states."

"I've seen every one of his pictures. I believe him to be a true
genius. So?"

"Your wish is my command, lovely lady."

"Precisely what I hoped to hear, Alik."

From the moment that film began, Lee, aka Alik, knew that he
was witnessing something special. In the opening, a plane carried
a statue of Jesus out of the city of Rome, off to be repaired. Over
the rooftops they fly; down below, beautiful young women, in
daring bikinis, sun-bathe on top of apartment buildings, their
radios turned to stations that play American rock 'n' roll. The pilot
waves; they respond in kind.

But it appears as if they're waving 'bye-bye' to Jesus.

A metaphor, just like my English teacher used to say. This is
about life not only in Rome but any modern city. Christ is removed.
All that's left below is hedonism: 'The Sweet Life.'

*

Though she didn't appear in that movie, no single person more
perfectly captured the essence of 'La Dolce Vita' than the French

actress Brigitte Bardot. Lee, like most every other male in America, rushed out to a theatre to catch her first important film ... *And God Created Woman,* when released late in 1957.

Previous to his first view of 'Bebe,' Lee had, like pretty much all American men, considered Marilyn Monroe The Dream Girl: sweet, flirtatious, kookie. For five years Marilyn defined what sexiness meant in the late-Eisenhower era, via onscreen roles and a 1954 nude lay-out in *Playboy.*

Already, though, the fifties were moving toward end-game. This newcomer from France stole away much of Marilyn's steam.

Bebe flaunted all the conventions. In several films, the character Bardot played, based on herself, casually married. Soon she engaged in adulterous affairs. Not out of some deep, uncontrollable passion. On a whim, just for the hell of it.

"It is better for a woman to be unfaithful by choice," the Gallic beauty stated without shame, "than faithful and unhappy."

Here, Lee knew, falling madly in love with her precisely as several million other men simultaneously did, appears the shape of things to come.

Bardot is not some aberration, rather a role model for a New Woman about to emerge. Girls will see her and imitate her, even as only a few years back they did M.M.

My guess: by 1960, every female in every remote corner of the world will mimic Bebe's swagger, her smile, that casual display of her body. They'll dress like her, talk like her.

And style their hair in the careless, devil-may-care way Bebe's blonde locks fall down all over her face.

*

"You look just like Brigitte Bardot," Lee Harvey Oswald, calling himself Alik, said to Marina the first time the two met. Each had arrived separately at the dance, Lee showing up early, anxious as always to meet women. Marina waltzed in three hours late, only a short while before the party was about to conclude.

This was entirely deliberate on her part, planned as if Marina were a military leader executing a strategy planned out far in advance. As she drifted in, dream-like, wearing a heavy black overcoat, a cowl covering the top and sides of her head, all eyes turned to consider the late-comer: those delicate near- perfect facial features and intense eyes initially demanded the crowd's attentions. Then, with the precision that can only be achieved through hours of rehearsal, the actress (for that's what Marina was in this theatre of life; character might be a better term still, as Marina was not this woman's actual name but the role she had agreed to play) drew her shoulders inward.

205

As she did, the cowl fell back, the coat slipped off her deliciously slender frame. Anatoly and Sasha, two young men enamored of Marina, had waited patiently for her to arrive. Each had grown fearful Marina would not show. At once they rushed to grab her wrap before it could reach the floor.

Marina meanwhile stood, like a professional fashion model, still as a statue, posing, preening, glamorous in a bright red Chinese brocade dress, white slippers out of some old fairytale adorning her tiny feet. Her bright eyes were overly made up, midnight-black Mascara adding a dark, decadent aspect to her otherwise pert, Lolita-ish girl-woman's facade.

Perhaps most breathtaking was Marina's hair, precisely styled like that of Bardot in glossy magazine lay-outs that first appeared in Paris, then the U.S. and free world, finally here in the Soviet Union, even provincial Minsk.

"Your accent is strange," Marina answered the intense young man. "Do you hail from one of the Baltic regions? Estonia—"

"I'm an American."

Lee noted that the young beauty lit up at this statement. She could not, he guessed, know his secret: that, in his youth, other boys wanted nothing to do with him, so atypical was Lee of what a U.S. male was supposed to be. Yet as is the way of the world she would assume he represented his homeland. For those living in Russia, dissatisfied with the ways of communism and its dull lifestyle, America provided a dream of excitement, fun and wealth. The grass is always greener, as the cliché goes.

Marina fell in love with Lee, or Alik, or whoever he was at first sight. What she fell in love with was not the person but her idea of him: the American male, *her* American male, the long hoped for example of that seemingly glimmering culture, arriving on the scene none too soon. The longed-for prince approached the unappreciated princess, he a half-formed idea out of her wildest fantasies. If she played her cards right, he might whisk her off to his American castle, where they would live happily ever after.

Take me away from all this. Please? I've been waiting!

Lee fell in love with Marina at first sight. What he fell in love with was not Marina the person (who did not exist now and never had) but an idea of her: the enchanting European dream girl, slim yet with lush, upturned breasts beneath that exotic costume, hungry to be touched by the right male. And the hair! Free flowing, seemingly unkempt, carefully fashioned to allow for that impression. A princess, lost here in the outer reaches of her world, longing for a prince among men to appear ...

There must be a dragon to slay; merely tell me where it is and I'll rush out to conquer the thing and win you forever...

All those boys, those Russian boys, some wealthy as far as was permitted in this communist state, most far more appealing than this scrawny youth before her, fell away in comparison.

He had said the magic words: 'I am an American.' Where do you keep your Bowie knife, your Winchester repeater? When do I meet your faithful Indian companion? Why are you not wearing a buckskin jacket? Where do you stable your great stallion?

Lee fell in love because everyone wanted her and no one could have her, as the situation made clear. Marina fell in love because here was her American at last.

Your shortness, that in-truth homely face, the leering grin are all wonderful, though I would reject any Russian boy with any of those defects.

You are you; or, at least, my dream of you.

I love a man who exists only in my imagination. My vision of him, I impose onto whoever might be standing here now ...

I love a woman who exists only in my imagination. My vision of her, I impose on whoever might be standing here now ...

That night, Marina and Lee each fell in love with a persona rather than a person; an image, not a reality; a projection of each individual's needs, these rightly or wrongly conceived as belonging to the imperfect person standing there. Love at first sight, if with an already existing fantasy the dreamer falsely believes has miraculously become actualized. There is, in the world, no more certain a formula for disaster, though neither would have believed so during this spectacularly silent moment.

The world appeared to open as their oyster. The future would be a great mutual adventure. They would share everything, their love a great novel, each day the next chapter.

How could anyone doubt it? For they had fallen in love at first sight.

*

Nineteen months earlier, on August 18, 1959, a beautiful seventeen-year-old girl, worldly beyond her years in emotion and intellect if not experience, stepped into Moscow's KGB headquarters. To her surprise, she was ushered into the office of the director as though a Very Important Person had just arrived. This, she had not expected. She was, after all, only an ordinary girl, other than her remarkable looks and sharp mind; from the most average sort of family.

She had applied in May to the Leningrad KGB post offering her services as a spy, was accepted into their program, and went through extensive training. She had no idea what sort of mission she might be sent on. She didn't care; anything to break the monotony of her boring life. *I'll take anything!!*

After all, she'd seen movies. And in movies, particularly Hollywood films, young women, born bright and beautiful, got to live exceptional lives. Not your average marriage and/or job; something ... Romantic! Yet her outstanding attributes aside, that hadn't happened. As a result, she determined not to settle but venture out in the world, or her corner of it; make her own fate, seeing as it had failed to come and find her.

Recently, she'd caught a spy film, knowing that it was only a movie. Still, it had to be based on something real. There were spies. Everyone had heard of Mata Hari, the German seductress from World War I who almost changed the conflict's outcome and the course of world history owing to her irresistibility, which allowed her to draw secrets from formidable enemy officers.

So this young Russian woman had decided to give it a try.

On a whim, of course. Most things that most women do are whimsical. Beautiful women? Their very lives are whimsy!

"The situation is this," Alexander N. Shelepin, head of the country's KGB, a bloated middle-aged man who looked more like a butcher than a high-ranking government official, explained: "We received word only a few days ago that a young American, just now returned to California from service with the marines in the South Pacific, has filed for permission to withdraw from any further duty to care for his ill mother. In fact, this is but his cover. He plans to leave for Europe under the auspices of attending university in Helsinki, upon arrival there applying for a six-day Visa to visit Russia, intending to defect."

"And your correspondents believe him sincere?"

"We can never know such a thing for certain. But our agents in the U.S. followed his course of action for some time. Since late childhood, he has expressed serious interest in communism. While in the service he condemned American imperialism in the Third World while secretly joining our secret cells, passing along classified information he'd obtained on his base."

"It doesn't smell right to me. If he feels so for our way of life, why would he join an elite fighting force?"

"There's the question we must attempt to answer," piped in the other man occupying the room. Yuri Nosenko, the KGB agent assigned to Lee Harvey Oswald, even now had that American's file open on his lap. "It could mean that he is a plant, an agent for the CIA, sent here as a spy."

"Precisely what occurred to me as you were speaking."

"It's also possible he's the real thing," Shelepin added. "We can't ignore the possibility this may be the case and pass up information he apparently has about America's new super-spy plane, the U2, as well as other significant military details."

"What makes me believe this could be the case," Nosenko said, flipping through the file, "is that he has a history of strange, self-conflicting activity. Our agents who have been in contact with him in the U.S. and Japan during his tour of duty suggest that once a person comes to terms with his own self-contradictions, it's logical, at least according to this man's unique logic— the world as it exists in his individualistic vision—he'd volunteer as an American warrior, simultaneously dedicating himself to the seeming opposition of communism."

"It's not unheard of," the young woman, extremely well-read and university educated, agreed. "One of their greatest generals from the Second World War, Carlson, was a dedicated communist."

"True. Which of course explains why the public does not know his name as they do Eisenhower, Patton, or MacArthur."

"My assignment then will be to seduce him in order to learn one way or the other who he is and who sent him, if anyone?"

"More 'involved' even than that. You will marry him."

Her jaw dropped. "I didn't expect anything so ..."

"If you wish to back out," Nosenko offered, "you may."

"When I committed, I did so with the understanding my mission might be ... how to put this ... 'extreme'."

"*Why?* Of course. You have a right to know, and in fact must know if you are to fully grasp what is expected. If this fellow—Lee Harvey Oswald is his name-—turns out to be what he says he is, marriage will allow you to draw from him all he knows about rockets, radar, other bits and pieces of information we can fit into the jigsaw puzzle that we daily attempt to complete so as to achieve a full picture of America's defensive and offensive capabilities. Even if he agrees to speak with the KGB, as we imagine he will in exchange for Soviet citizenship, a wife—you—will on a daily basis be able to learn considerably more."

"Supposing he knows nothing, says nothing?"

"A quick divorce could be arranged. You would not be stuck with him permanently, if that's what concerns you."

"Precisely! I want to pursue this career—"

"And you will, particularly if he turns out to be not what he claims but an American agent. If that's the case, Oswald will want to remain here just long enough to learn as much as he can while spreading disinformation. The CIA understands that to mis-lead us about, say, the U-2 will do more harm to our side than any secrets he might share. At any rate, if that is the case, he will, that job accomplished, decide he is not as happy here, choosing to return to America. That's where you come in."

"Now, I'm confused again."

"In-between attempts to achieve his aims and a departure, you seduce and marry him. Then, you will return with him to the U.S. There, you will be in a position to observe and provide us with up-to-date reports even as you spread disinformation."

This is even better than I thought! The one thing I always dreamed about, even more than an exciting life as a spy, was to go to America. I can either do what the director asks, serving in the U.S. Or, if I do fall in love with this man, and his country, cut off all communications.

What can the KGB do other than brood? In that case I will become, in time, what I initially pretend to be: an emigrant housewife. There is no need for any rush as to deciding.

"That certainly sounds an effective strategy."

"As we discussed earlier, 'you' will cease to exist. A missing person who will never be found. From this moment forth, no communication at all with family or friends. Hoping that you would accept, we have already created your new identity."

Excitedly, she said: "I can't wait to start."

"Then we'll start now. Here is your 'legend,' as our CIA counterparts would put it. You come from poverty, born out of wedlock on July 17, 1941, in the remote town of Molotovsk."

"By the seaside, in the province of Arkhangelsk? Oh, but I went there once on holiday."

"We know. That's why we picked it. At any rate, you never knew your father, not even his name. Your mother—we've decided to call her 'Klavdia Vsilyevna Prusakova'—couldn't care for you and so turned you over to her grandparents to raise."

"Interesting plot point."

"More than merely interesting. This Oswald experienced something similar as a child. When the two of you meet according to our schedule, this creates an immediate symbiosis. Besides being entranced by your beauty, he will see you as his soul-mate. To further this, we have included in your 'legend' that when your grandfather died—you were four at the time—you rejoined your mother, now living in Zguritsa near the Rumanian border, she re-married to an electrical engineer. The family soon moved to Leningrad."

"My home city. Of course! That way I can speak fluently of where I recently lived. Now, this again parallels ... what did you say his name was, the man I am going to meet and marry?"

"Lee Harvey Oswald. Yes, his mother remarried. Constant moving about appears to have had a significant impact on the boy, creating disorientation, as we know from reports written by various doctors. One more thing you will have in common."

"Will all this happen in Leningrad, or Moscow?"

"Neither. Minsk."

She was flabbergasted! *Minsk?* "So out of the way ..."

"Precisely as we wish. No question that he will request to live in Moscow. That's where he could be the most dangerous to us, if Oswald is what we fear instead of what we hope for. By relocating him in Minsk, Oswald will be temporarily diverted into a holding pattern while we determine which side he's on."

"Minsk will render him harmless. When am I to leave?"

"Three days. As to your motivation: Your mother died, your stepfather remarried. You no longer felt comfortable there. You have an 'uncle' in Minsk. A charming, gruff old Colonel, Ilya Vasilyevich Prusakov. He and his wife share a comfortable, large apartment in one of that city's finest areas, Kalinina Street."

"As to this 'uncle': Who is he, really?"

"Officially, a high-ranking official in the Ministry of Internal Affairs. Secretly, the top KGB agent in that sector."

"Why, you've worked this out to perfection!"

"Thank you for the compliment. As for your personality, you must strike Lee Harvey Oswald, when you meet him, as none-too-bright, despite some upward aspirations toward gentility. You know nothing much about classical music, but are enthusiastic as to learning. This will allow him to perceive himself as your mentor as well as lover; that he, however superficial his knowledge of such things, can lead this beautiful girl into a more sophisticated realm that they, together, will share."

"*Naïve.* That's what I'm to be?"

"I hadn't thought of it, but you are absolutely correct."

"As for your 'look': On that day when you first come in contact with him, your hair should be styled in the manner of the French actress Brigitte Bardot. You are familiar with her?"

"Yes, of course. Rather decadent, don't you think?"

"Absolutely. But our agents in America who are in contact with Oswald made clear he, like most men, is enamored of her. You see, sheer beauty, which you already possess, is not enough. We want you not only to be 'a' dream girl, but 'his' dream girl. The character you will play—*become*, as the Stanislavski method would have it—must not only be highly attractive to all men but Oswald's vision of the perfect woman. That way he can't resist."

"So thorough! And my new name will be?"

"We gave that much thought. Apparently, young Mr. Oswald has all his brief life been involved in a bizarre love-hate relationship with his mother. That's something we can make use of. Her name is Marguerite. The only other thing he appears to have ever truly loved is the marine corps. So we have devised a name for you that partakes of both. From now on you are Marina."

*

For their second date Lee, or Alik as he insisted everyone address him, escorted Marina to yet another dance. Her earlier boyfriends Anatoly and Sasha, both anxious for her to arrive, saw her enter with the American and realized both were lost as to ever winning Marina. The former competitors found common ground for friendship and left to drown their tears in vodka.

Marina agreed to go to Victory Square with Lee later, the two slipping into a booth at one of the coffeehouses so popular with the elite of Minsk's youth: Those attending the university, mostly boys, and girls pretty or bright enough to be escorted here, where everyone talked politics and culture late into the night. Marina spoke plainly about her current life. She worked at the pharmaceutical section of the Third Clinical Hospital, in the city's central hub. As she lived with her uncle and that man's wife, who did not charge room and board, Marina was able to spend most of her 45 ruble salary on clothes, explaining why a woman of such modest means could always appear so striking.

Lee talked openly about himself and his current situation, or more correctly presented Marina with his "legend," then only recently re-aligned with current realities. Each, oblivious to the other's play-acting, hoped that the person seated across the table would accept fantasy as reality.

Lee, according to his tale, had arrived in the Soviet Union full of high hopes, these gradually dashed. In America, he had devoured the works of Karl Marx and Vladimir Lenin, drawing from the philosopher who had crystallized the communist manifesto and the revolutionary who put those values into action back in 1919.

Lenin: a pure idealist! All men could be equal; everybody must share and share alike. In time, experiences in Moscow and Minsk made all too clear that the dream did not transfer into reality. High-ranking Party members enjoyed all sorts of special luxuries that were obviously denied the common man and woman.

"Oh, Lee! That is so true, so true ..."

Worse, instead of having more than the average American, the working poor possessed considerably less. Lee rambled on and on about the lack of bowling alleys and nightclubs, the déclassé entertainment enclaves where blue collar workers congregated on Friday and Saturday nights in America to spend however little they had on simple pleasures. These did not exist here and, had they, the masses would not have been able to afford them.

Even the movies, which almost every U.S. citizen could enjoy owing to low ticket prices, were here mostly attended by the elite, as their date to see *La Dolce Vita* made clear.

"Back home," Lee/Alik waxed rhapsodic, "there is so much more democracy. Every person can say what he wants in the press, radio, TV. Censorship here is worse than I expected. Not that my country is perfect. All in all, though, I'd have to say that ordinary people have it far worse than where I come from."

"I'd like to see America for myself someday."

Lee eyeballed the ravishing young beauty as her eyes danced at the thought. "Maybe we could do that together, you and I?"

"That would be ... a dream come true, Lee."

"Sometimes dreams do come true! Or so Americans like to believe. If we strive, perhaps you and I can make that happen?"

Her eyes remained locked with his. "Do you know what I like most about you?" she finally asked, smiling like some Sphynx.

"Uh-oh! I don't know if I want to hear this."

"Well, you shall. There is a quality of innocence to you. So much passion in your voice. I am very attracted to that."

"I see. Do you know what I like most about you?"

Marina laughed: "That with my hair styled is this manner, and my dark eye-make up, I look like Brigitte Bardot."

Lee laughed too. "No. That's what first attracted me to you and what I like second-best. Beyond that, there's a quality ... not 'innocent', as you said of me ... for there's a kind of quality to you ... how shall I put it ... a naivete?"

"You think me a silly girl, not a true woman?"

"I think you are quite remarkable. The ultimate female I have searched for all my life. To me, you could be wife, lover, sister, mother, friend, comrade—"

"Alik! You are moving far too fast."

"Sorry. I hope I didn't spoil everything."

"Not at all. Come, walk me home. Meet my aunt and uncle."

Lee feared they might resent any American. Certainly they would express concern if he dared admit that any loyalty to Russia was fast-fading. To Lee's happy surprise, they enjoyed him, commenting on Lee's excellent manners, as compared to many of the local boys whom Marina brought home. In addition to being polite to a fault, Lee was provocative, interesting to listen to and converse with. Clearly, they heartily approved.

"Come back soon, and often, Lee. Always a pleasure."

Within a week the family extended to Marina her freedom to visit Lee at his apartment, with the understanding Lee would behave as a perfect gentleman. The two kissed on the couch and stood together on one of the twin balconies, holding hands, her head on his shoulder. They watched the ships slowly move up and down the river, from and to the sea.

Hours were spent listening to records, Tchaikovsky Lee's favorite. He would, between movements, explain details about the work. Marina said that she had listened to such music before, enjoying live performances in Leningrad. Now, through Lee's mentoring, she truly understood them. He introduced her to Sinatra, opening up a whole new world for the wide-eyed girl.

In between passionate kisses, though no more than that as promised, each revealed his or her own inner lives, or at least the "legends" concocted for them, to the other.

Your mother abandoned you? So did mine!

You never knew your father? Nor did I!

You were moved from place to place until you believed that you belonged nowhere? Me, too.

Why, we are soul-mates! This is not merely some temporary attraction. I believe we were made for each other!

In a bizarre sense, that happened to be the truth.

*

Another date was set for March 31. To her surprise Marina received word Lee would not be able to keep it. Suffering from an ear-ache, he had admitted himself to the Fourth Clinical Hospital, where he was to undergo an operation on his adenoids.

Lee hoped she would visit, mentioning that he would be stuck there for two weeks. Marina rushed to his side, her big eyes full of concern for her skinny American. The doctors told her that they were having difficulty locating the infection, though the patient continued to complain of insufferable pain.

While with Lee, who certainly looked none the worse for wear, Marina was taken by a sudden personality shift. When Lee spoke, his voice sounded ever so slightly different than before. This she wrote off to his throat problems.

Far more perplexing was what he had to say. Her Alik seemed tougher, which impressed Marina. If there had been anything lacking in him during their time together, it was masculine assertiveness. Gone, though, was a certain quality she adored, in Lee's words and his eyes; that innocence she had mentioned.

In its place, a jaded element appeared. So when he without warning proposed, Marina could not answer at once. Back in the apartment, likely she would have capitulated while in Lee's arms. Instead Marina insisted she had to think about it.

Still, she came to see him every day. For whatever reasons, Alik chose not to discuss intellectual matters, as before. Now, he spoke of mundane things, like the quality (or lack thereof) of food here; which nurses were pretty, which were not.

Previously, she'd had the impression that when with Marina, Lee remained oblivious to other woman.

So what am I to do now? At first, I felt myself falling in love with my prey, though as a secret agent that is verboten. *That caused concern; such emotions leave one vulnerable. I could easily have said 'yes,' traveling with him to his wonder-land, sharing his bed, as my orders insist I must.*

Now all of that is changed. I don't love this man as I thought. Me, the real me, that is; not Marina. She must. I can pretend to do so, despite a sudden hardness in his character.

I will do whatever I decide is best for me *... or, more correctly, Marina will do whatever I decide is best for her and me—the real woman who performs that character daily, but never forgets that beneath Marina's persona, there still exists an entirely other person, filled with hopes all her own ...*

Though every day I play this role, I lose a little more of her ... of me.

*

As Lee and Marina exited the theatre, she anxiously tried to get him to talk about the film. The two headed to their favorite coffee shop, taking their regular booth. But while she rhapsodically recalled the contemporary clothing the women had worn, and the wild, decadent parties—the men literally forcing women down on all fours, riding them about a huge chateau like horses—Lee remained silent for the longest time.

When Marina asked if something were wrong, fearful this intriguing American had grown bored with her, Lee snapped back into the moment. He assured her that that was not the case.

In truth, he'd been so engrossed with *La Dolce Vita*'s implications he found it necessary to think them through before responding. Now, he was able to do so ...

The main character, Marcello, was the first true paparazzi ever to appear on screen, photographing superficial/celebrity Beautiful

215

People on their late-night odysseys through Rome. The city's classical architecture served as an almost surreal foil for the ultra-contemporary goings on.

In the most memorable scene, one tall, busty blonde movie star, Anita Ekberg, drunkenly sloshed her way into the Trevi Fountain, her jet-black gown soaking through, shimmering in moonlight as her impossibly long, tangled mane of blonde hair, seductively wet and messy, fell across her oblivious face.

Marcello pursued her throughout this momentary madness, hoping to seduce an icon of The Sweet Life. She laughingly dismissed him and all other men. Untouchable, yet at the same time available, Ekberg captured the essence of this still new decade, the Sixties, a lifestyle emergent; she like Bardot (and Sue Lyon as *Lolita* when Lee eventually saw that film) served as replacements for Marilyn Monroe and all those other blondes of the Fifties. They suddenly seemed outdated, nostalgic even.

This Marcello was one of the jet-set yet always there existed the possibility that he, and he alone, might prove capable of something better—an earlier sort of traditional life these others abandoned in their hungered search for immediate gratification, their senses all important, anything spiritual out of sight and mind—like that removed statue of Jesus; Marcello alone capable of a return to simpler times, before life roared out of control and nothing signified anything of lasting value.

The world, Christ removed, belonged to those young girls who wore bikinis while listening to rock 'n' roll: The Moderns.

In the middle of the film, when Marcello's father arrived to try and persuade his son to return with him to their small village and the values still existing there, Lee had, on the edge of his seat, hoped Marcello would do so. For the old man offered earthy salvation from such superficial pursuits.

Throughout the film Marcello regularly came in contact with a lovely girl, not one of the In Crowd, the last old-fashioned female in all Rome. She happily did laundry while singing a folk tune, her smile sweet, genuine rather than cynical or sardonic.

Always, she beckoned for Marcello to join her. But to do so he must abandon his current companions.

In the film's final shot, Marcello and the party-goers, hung-over from the most perverse of all orgies, drifted down to the beach at dawn. There they discovered the grotesque remains of a fish consumed by nuclear waste that had been dumped into the ocean, the nightmare aspect of our modern world destroying all that is natural and best.

Those with Marcello took perverse delight in viewing this monstrosity. Only he seemed unconvinced this was 'fun.'

Then, far down the beach, he spotted that girl again, she once more washing sheets, humming that ancient ditty, smiling. Recognizing Marcello, she waved to him, hoping he would leave the others, join her. For one moment, his eyes grew thoughtful, mournful, simultaneously sad and happy. Some capacity he once possessed for living in the fast-fading old world order, put aside for contemporary kicks, rose again in his consciousness.

Momentarily, a hunger for tradition appeared ready to reach the surface of Marcello's mind. By her very presence, she offered him a return to the way things were, before the world went mad, embracing nihilism rather than fighting against it.

Marcello appeared about to desert his current company, as she cooed: "Come! Come to me!" Then their howling at the sight of the all-too-real monster drowned out her voice. "I can't hear you," Marcello apologized, any recollection of an earlier sort of knowledge, about to be reborn, disappearing from his eyes.

He shrugged, turned away, rejoined his companions as they moved on to their next round of drinking, drugs, sex.

Down the beach from this representative gathering of La Dolce Vita, the girl, knowing on some non-intellectual, deeply spiritual level that Marcello was lost to her, now and forever, smiled sadly. Then she returned to her work, humming again.

Marina, in her naïve way, had accepted the film's gaudy details at face value: the gowns, the diamonds, sleek cars, rock 'n' roll, casual sex. Lee, in the darkness of the theatre, experienced one of those epiphanies he, on rare occasions, did when he had just seen a movie that spoke directly to him.

The film, he grasped, was not a celebration of The Sweet Life but a condemnation of it; a profoundly traditionalist work, a warning to each Marcello out there in the audience. If given this hero's final choice, we ought to accept that gentle girl's offer, flee from La Dolce Vita, re-embrace the Good Life of hard work, a man and a woman sincerely, simply surviving together.

Finally, Lee shushed. Locking eyes with Marina he feared he spoke above this beautiful but none-too-bright girl's level. Here she was, with her Bardot hairstyle, her enthusiasm for fun and pleasure. What was the title of a Bebe film he had seen? *A Ravishing Idiot*. Yes, that was her. And Marina as well.

He dared not reveal just how 'square' he himself was deep down. Yes, the traditional life had always closed him out. But what did someone once say in a movie? *Just because you love something doesn't mean it has to love you back.*

Lee did not want to lose her, not this one; couldn't stand the thought of Marina heading back to other boys, they more open to the swinging style. Reveal too much of his own sentimental soul and Marina might dismiss Lee as a hopeless innocent.

If Lee Harvey Oswald, the homely runt most men thought of as beneath them, even "queer" perhaps, had worked his way up the shimmering rope ladder this high, there remained a part of him that did not want to lose everything by opening his mouth and saying something ... embarrassingly innocent. Then he would never reach the top rung and sleep with ... Brigitte Bardot.

Still, such a reasonable facsimile as he gazed at now was more than most men could or would ever know. These included many who had laughed and scorned him, but now led the most ordinary lives with the most ordinary wives. Like James Stewart in another of Lee's favorite films, *Vertigo,* he could at least embrace the twin of his dream girl. That would have to suffice.

Always, though, there would be the other Lee. The Lee who, like Marcello in the movie, wanted to abandon superficiality. Embrace something true. Hold on to that. Who knows? Perhaps Marina could be both, the Beautiful Person, glimmering in the moonlight but also a substantial young woman, able to boldly move in daylight, solid, strong. The woman who could bear him children, turn Lee into ... a Normal.

Was it possible for any woman to be first one, then the other? Or perhaps better still both at once, the hard-working life's partner by day, the elusive, alluring mistress when the lights were turned low? Was every woman all women? Or was this only what Lee, like every other male who had ever walked the face of the earth, most wished?

However impossible it might be, however unfair to the woman in question to expect so much, he wanted all that.

Terribly, completely, heartbreakingly wanted it.

Lee didn't know, couldn't answer that one. But he would know. In time. For he had determined already that Marina would be the one. The girl he would try to "have it all" with.

Marina, Lee grasped, was the woman he must marry. Yes, they truly were soul-mates, made for each other, as the saying goes.

Marina. The woman he fell in love with at first sight.

CHAPTER FOURTEEN:
COME SPY WITH ME

"There is the distinct possibility that an imposter is using Lee
Harvey Oswald's passport in Russia."
—J. Edgar Hoover, head of the FBI;
Memorandum to the State Department's
Office of Security, April 1960

In truth, Marina was far from the first woman Lee had fallen in love with at first sight. An unabashed sentimentalist, he had experienced just such a sensation whenever Lee gazed at a lovely woman. This was not confined to reality. The first time Lee saw Marilyn on the screen, he flipped. Then came Brigitte.

However intense Lee's one-sided romances with movie dream girls may have been, they were also, essentially, superficial. 'Love at first sight' did not necessarily imply 'ever after'.

As for his Russian sojourn, Lee first met with George in Tijuana. Things were proceeding smoothly. In Japan Lee had established ties with communists, spread disinformation among them, and established his pinko "legend." Upon return, George guided Lee through two and a half months of strategic moves that would conclude with his arrival in Moscow during mid-October, 1959. First, Lee requested that the Corps grant him a hardship release from further duty to care for his sickly mother. A routine check would have revealed that Marguerite was able of body if not mind. But behind the scenes the CIA signaled the military brass to take Lee's claim at face value.

Lee received his dependency discharge on August 17. He then applied for a passport in Santa Ana so as to attend the College of A. Schweitzer, Switzerland. Before Lee left Santa Ana by bus on September 11 for Fort Worth, he and George met at Villa's.

"First, Lee, I want you to boil down all key classified information about the U2 into a single brief statement."

Lee did not hesitate: "When ready, 'The Race Car' will cruise high above the Soviet Union, reaching altitudes that may exceed 100,000 ft. This will allow the U2 to fly undetected over Russian radar, incapable of spotting an object at such a height.

Cameramen inside will capture detailed images of Soviet military and industrial positions below, the Soviets completely unaware."

"Correct in every detail. Other than aspects of nuclear weaponry, this is America's most classified information today."

"Of course."

"When we originally planned this mission, the idea would be for you to openly offer the KGB such classified information in exchange for citizenship. Then you were to ...?"

"Spread disinformation," Lee chimed in.

"Precisely." George sighed, growing intense, leaning in closer. "Only that aspect of the plan has been altered. You will now do the opposite: reveal *everything* about the Race Car."

Lee found himself unable to reply. Nothing of the sort had ever been suggested. Momentarily, he wondered if perhaps George might be a double agent, working for the Russians, about to turn Lee, the patriot, into Lee, the patsy—a traitor to America.

"Calm down, Lee. It's all kosher. I've told you on more than one occasion the CIA's most important goal."

As if brainwashed, Lee responded: "The United States wants to create a viable, continuing state of world-peace, no matter how tenuous it may be. We must avoid an atomic war that would obliterate much of America even if we 'won.'"

"Again, absolutely right. You are a most apt pupil."

"This, however, must be done without our being reduced to a second-rate nation in terms of our power to respond or, as a last resort, make the first strike. In the atomic age, this can only be assured if we, to borrow from Theodore Roosevelt, speak softly but carry a big stick—bigger than the other guy's."

"Better still. Now, Lee, figure this out yourself: Why do we no longer want 'the defector' to spread 'disinformation'?"

Lee paused, taking a swig from his beer. "We do not want the confrontation to occur. Therefore, the big stick—the U2—only works if the other guy knows it exists. Not being fools, they can then do only one thing: back down."

Maybe I underrated this guy. Lee actually could become one of our top men, the agent to whom I will someday assign the most difficult, dangerous mission of all—whatever that might be.

"Congratulations, Lee. You *get* it!"

Realizing he was on a roll, Lee couldn't stop the words from pouring out. "My job: make certain they know everything. Their possession of such knowledge will serve as deterrence. Yet our security forces must appear to be effectively protecting such secrets. If not, American citizens would panic. On the other hand, if some rogue-traitor turns over such information ..."

"And you will be that rogue traitor. Or pretend to be."

Lee's eyes lit up brightly. "Meaning I'll do more good for my country than perhaps anyone ever has before?"

George smiled. "A wonderful thought, isn't it?"

"Wonderful, yet horrible. To achieve this in reality I must go down in history as the worst villain since Benedict Arnold."

*

On September 16, 1959, Lee bid farewell to his mother and brother Robert and boarded another bus, this one to New Orleans. On arrival he was met by George. With money supplied by the CIA, Lee booked passage on a small freighter, the *Marion Lykes*, paying $220.75 (cash) for a one-way-ticket to Le Havre, France.

Subsequently, a letter was mailed to Fort Worth only after George carefully edited Lee's words down to an absolute minimum: "It is difficult to tell you how I feel. Just remember this is what I must do. I did not tell you my plans because you could hardly be expected to understand. Love to you both, Lee."

Four other passengers traveled aboard the small boat. They took meals together adjacent to the galley. Lee's fellow travelers wanted to learn all about each other, but Lee offered no details as to his reason for making the journey. When one woman asked him to join them for a group photo before disembarking, he refused.

Without so much as a farewell, Lee took the boat-train to Southampton, England. Once there, he booked a flight from Heathrow Airport to Helsinki, remaining there for five days.

At the Soviet Consulate Lee obtained a travel visa (# 403339), allowing him to visit Russia for six days.

On arrival in Moscow, Lee checked into the upscale Hotel Berlin. Shortly, he was met by Rima Shirokova, a pretty employee of Intourist, the relatively new organization created to aid foreigners. (The Soviets had just relaxed their previously tight standards, encouraging more visitors).

The moment Lee glimpsed Rima, it was love at first sight.

*

Considered the most personable of all those hostesses at Intourist, Rima also happened to be the most beautiful. A natural blonde, she boasted a tight figure and dancing eyes. Fluent in English, Rimma was assigned to greet rare American tourists. Lee had purchased a five-day DeLuxe ticket; Rimma assumed 'Mr. Oswald' must be wealthy. As such he intrigued her.

But when Rima arrived for their initial meeting in the hotel lobby she found herself face to face with a short, sad-eyed youth. He wore ordinary clothes. Lee, simply, was nothing like what she expected. Moreover, he remained surprisingly quiet during their morning odyssey around the city. Rima attempted to make all her carefully rehearsed anecdotes about Red Square, the Bolshoi, and other places of interest sound spontaneous.

Hard as she tried, she could not get a response. Lee only stared straight ahead, occasionally considering the sights.

"Mr. Oswald, I fear I am boring you."

"No, no, no. It is not you, Rima. It's *me*."

However, she could not help but notice Oswald cautiously checking out her feminine attributes. Rima did not join him at his hotel during the lunch break; that was considered intrusive on a visitor's privacy. When she returned at two p.m. to pick Lee up for his tour of the Kremlin, he asked if they might take a walk instead in the nearby park. Fearful that what he really wanted was to invite her back to his room, Rima tried to dissuade Lee. But he remained insistent and she agreed.

To her surprise, Lee, seated beside Rima on a bench, grew teary-eyed: he hadn't come to Moscw to visit but to defect. "I've had it with America, Rima. I want to become a Russian citizen. Don't try to convince me otherwise. I've made up my mind."

Taken aback by his passion, Rima agreed to help Lee in any way she could. They spent the rest of that first afternoon composing a letter from Lee to the Supreme Soviet. In it, he requested political asylum, in time Soviet citizenship.

"Don't try to dissuade me. I know what I'm doing. I've thought it through and this is the right thing for me."

They parted three hours later, Rima again wondering how such a seemingly ordinary fellow could afford a two-room suite, with attached private bathroom, in Moscow's most splendid hotel.

During the next two days, Rima continued the tour. Lee bounced back and forth between periods of elation—he would soon be a part of this mighty union!—and sudden bouts of depression, fearing he would be told to pack.

Rima repeatedly made clear that while she had personally approached Alexander Simchenko, head of the IVIR/Passport and Visa Office, the routine treatment of such a request was to explain to any would-be defector that he must go back to his homeland and there apply for Soviet citizenship at the Embassy.

"Rima? I think I love you."

"Lee! I'm doing this as a friend. Please? Nothing more."

On Lee's fifth day in Moscow, Rima appeared in the hotel lobby at nine p.m. sharp, as per schedule. Lee, anxious as ever, had been waiting for an hour. Turning to greet her, Lee noticed that

Rima was now accompanied by another young woman, also from Intourist. Rima introduced the brunette as Rosa Agafonova.

One look at this shorter, darker, charmingly lush beauty and Lee Harvey Oswald fell in love at first sight.

*

"You know," Alexander Simchenko told Lee after listening to the earnest (though in Simchenko's perception unbalanced) young American's pleas for citizenship, "we're not able to do anything here." By that he meant his division, the IVIR.

"Isn't there *anything* we can try?" Rima asked.

"Someone you might call for help?" Rosa added.

"I'm being honest with all three of you," Simchenko said. They sat close together in his medium-sized office, adorned only by a framed photograph of Nikita Khrushchev on one wall. "I have only so many 'special requests.' My superiors do not like to be bothered by ordinary, doomed appeals. Can you understand?"

At that moment, Lee changed tactics, much to the surprise of the two women, one seated on either side, who had thought of him up to this point as something of a milk-toast. "How's this? I am a former United States Marine. I studied radar, worked at Atsugi aircraft base in Japan. While there, I passed on military secrets to Red agents in Tokyo. Contact them; they will vouch for me. Most of the classified information was relatively minor. That's because I was saving the big stuff for such a crisis as this. I can provide the KGB with photographs of the U2 that they have been so desperate for. I know everything about its inner workings and surveillance capabilities. I am in possession of dossiers of classified information about placement of Allied nuclear weapons in Europe. I know where the Naval fleet is and where it will be routed next. All this information is yours. In return I do not want rubles, only to be allowed to remain here."

Simchenko, whose throat had gone dry, did not hesitate to reach for the phone, dialing his immediate superior. Momentarily that executive called the KGB. Lee grinned from ear to ear.

That night, October 18—Lee's birthday—the two beauties celebrated with him in his room. Rima brought Lee a copy of her favorite Dostoevski novel, *The Idiot,* as a present. They drank champagne and toasted what they hoped would be his welcome to the Soviet Union. While speaking so, Lee had become 'sexy.'

*

Lee spent most of the next several days in his room, at times reading *The Idiot*, occasionally growing so frustrated with the extended wait for a phone call that he couldn't concentrate. Every afternoon after lunch at the hotel's restaurant, Lee would exercise

223

by taking a walk. Exiting the lobby he turned right and continued on for five blocks, turning right again, following this pattern to create a perfect square. Twenty-five minutes later he arrived at the spot where he began.

On the first day Lee was approached by a tall man with a severely rounded face and big hound-dog eyes. The stranger wore an expensive black fur over-coat and, atop his head, a ragged peasant's cap, presenting an incongruous image. He stopped Lee and asked if he were an American. Lee said he was, but hated his country. The other fellow roared good-naturedly, explaining he achieved Soviet citizenship five years earlier. As he strolled this area daily, they would chat again. The two shook hands.

Lee walked away with a missive from George in his palm, passed along by his assigned CIA contact. Likewise, the other fellow now had in hand a piece of paper in which Lee reported back to George. No sooner had this secret agent returned to his apartment than he drew out his concealed high-tech radio and sent a coded message to America, waiting for a reply.

"What am I to do?" Lee asked George on his contact's radio set several nights later, supposedly arriving to share a cup of tea. Earlier, he had been informed by Rima that his request was denied. A police officer had arrived, insisting Lee pack and leave the country immediately. Rima felt deeply for the American and couldn't grasp why his potential had been rejected.

She could not know that those in power were eager to have Oswald remain. However, they'd agreed on the likeliness that he might be a CIA plant. So they must take every precaution. And so the chess game continued. Refusing Lee constituted a feint, a decision arrived at to discover what he would do next and, based on that, allow them to consider this man's dubious sincerity.

"Stay, stay, *stay,*" George insisted, his voice barely audible. "Whatever it takes, whatever you have to do: Stay!"

Lee returned to his hotel room and sat on the bed, trying to determine his course of action. Clearly, George was not going to move Lee, his pawn; he had to play the game himself. Only an extreme gesture would serve this purpose. That had to be suicide.

I've considered it so often. Now, it's natural ...

The Soviets must be made to believe he earnestly would prefer to be dead than not Red. Lee would slit his wrists, allow his blood to trickle into the bathtub. But he must be careful so as not to actually end everything. Rima was scheduled to arrive in the lobby for a sad farewell at eight. If he were not there, she would sense something wrong and alert the manager.

First, Lee scrawled on a note pad:

October 21, 1959; 7:00 P.M.
My fondest dreams are shattered ... I decided to end it.
Soak wrist in cold water to numb the pain. Then slash my
left wrist. Then plunge into bathtub of hot water ...
somewhere a violin plays as I watch my life whirl away ...

The final line, Lee borrowed from an old movie. When he heard
the orchestra playing down below in the tea room, that sequence
came to mind. He appropriated it, giddy at experiencing a
transcendence between a classic Hollywood scene and real life.

Lee applied all the skills he had learned in the service so as to
prick himself slightly, drawing blood, careful not to come near the
vein. He did this at 7:45. That way, he should survive, if only
Rima followed her usual pattern of promptness.

At ten after eight, having borrowed the master key, Rima
entered and saw Lee. He played his role as if going for an Oscar,
twisting up his body into a pretzel-like shape, gasping
incongruous words. Rima screamed for help.

An ambulance arrived minutes later, speeding Lee off to
Botkin Hospital. The doctors took one look at the cut, three
centimeters in length, and laughed at the idea that anyone might
seriously take this as a suicide attempt. They packed Lee off to
the insane ward. Rima remained with him that night, stroking his
hair, attempting to comfort this sad man-child.

The honesty of her concern never in doubt, Lee resented that
Rimma repeatedly uttered the word *svaie.* That indicated, from
the little Russian he'd learned, a baby brother—hardly how he
wanted to be perceived by this beautiful blonde.

Though Lee appreciated Rimma's arranging for him to shortly
be transferred to, in Lee's own words, "an ordinary ward," he
asked if she could send Rosa around to visit him next time.

*

Upon his dismissal days later, Lee transferred to the Hotel
Metropole, Room 233. His suite at Hotel Berlin had been assigned
to an arriving tourist the morning after his 'suicide attempt.' Even
more spacious, the rooms were full of antique furniture,
apparently left over from before the Revolution; remnants of an
age known for luxury for the elite, poverty for all others.

Lee spent much of his time waiting to discover the impact his
supposed little theatrical piece would have on those who made
decisions. He devoured *The Idiot,* heading off to purchase other
books by Dostoevsky. *Crime and Punishment* turned out to be one
of those rare volumes that change a person's life.

The notion of a murder committed by a man who sees himself as 'above the law' spoke directly to Lee. He had after all been licensed to kill. The author's questioning of moral issues in a modern, amoral world proved impactful on Lee, who realized great literature could speak to him even as a Sinatra film once had.

Then a missive from George was passed to him on the street. His contact, aware of Lee's change of residence, had altered his daily walk-route to pass by the Metropole. They nodded, shook hands, and Lee walked away with a note from George.

Shortly after noon on October 31 Lee caught a taxi, rode to the American Embassy, entered, and told the receptionist that he demanded to speak with the Consul, Richard Snyder.

"Mr. Snyder? There's a man here who needs to talk with you at once on a most pressing matter." Lee was ushered into an old-fashioned American style office adorned with Oak furniture.

"I am a Marxist," Lee, standing, announced as he raised a finger in the air, considering the 'decadence' surrounding him.

"You'll be a lonely man as a Marxist," Snyder cynically replied, remaining seated. He then explained that the values of Karl Marx, so altruistic, had precious little to do with the harsh realities of life in Khrushchev's current corrupt state.

"Don't try and talk me out of it. I know what I'm doing."

Officially, as Snyder's office mate John McVickar noted, the Consul continued to attempt to reason with Lee. From time to time their visitor, refusing a seat, grinning maniacally, interrupted with such pat phrases as "I hate America."

Exhausted, the Counsul rose, came around, shook Lee's hand, wished him well, then led this acerbic young man to the door. As Lee left, Snyder agreed to initiate the arduous process.

"Thank you, Consul. I'll be waiting to hear from you."

All of this had been carefully scripted by George. McVicar was not in on the scripted if unrehearsed little piece of life as theatre. Snyder had a double identity of his own, he also the top CIA man in Moscow. His position as Consul had been arranged so that while seeming to serve in an acceptable capacity Snyder could secretly oversee all plans to undermine Russian security.

"As I said, Mr. Oswald, this will take time."

As for Snyder and Lee, each had been instructed to say precisely what they did owing to George's concern the office had been tapped, the KGB listening in. If this were true, what the operatives heard would help convince the Russians that Lee was what he claimed to be. It certainly couldn't hurt.

"The sooner the better. I *hate* America!"

When they shook hands, each passed a note to the other.

*

As for the KGB, they were not convinced the suicide attempt had been for real. Still, there remained the possibility that Oswald was what he claimed to be. So what to do?

For a stop-gap measure, they extended his Visa indefinitely and put Lee up, at governmental expense, at his hotel. During the following two months, KGB agents checked with every possible source, relying heavily on statements from communist agents in California and Japan who had been in contact with Lee. Missives came back commending his passionate speech but some questioned his supposed "wide reading" of communist theory.

Lee would express himself in brief phrases—"All power to the people!"; "Death to capitalism!"—that sounded borrowed, trite, and tired. Lee, clearly a bright enough fellow, would have had more command of the political theories than that if, as he claimed, he truly did study book after book.

"So," Shelepin asked one after another of his co-workers, "what are we to do in the case of Lee Harvey Oswald?"

Many an hour was spent discussing 'The Oswald Situation.' As top KGB man, Alexander N. Shelepin would have to make the call. He favored sending Lee home, less owing to any concern Oswald constituted a serious security risk than to maintain his position. If Shelepin were to stamp Oswald's file as a 'non-threat,' and Lee turned out to be a plant, not only would Shelepin lose his prestigious position but likely end up in Siberia.

On the other hand Yuri Nosenko, specifically assigned to monitor Oswald's file, leaned in the opposite direction. There was so much potential here to acquire information that any possible risk should be considered a minor issue.

As the American waited at Hotel Metropole, the hefty head of KGB and his thin assistant pondered Oswald's file.

"Whatever we decide, our careers might be ruined."

"True. Then again, our reputations might be enhanced."

Unknown to them, a similar file had been established in Washington, D.C. at the offices of the FBI. As competition between that venerable information gathering service and the newer, more aggressive CIA intensified, each became ever more interested in its own survival than in its assigned security goals. Each arm of America's source of national protection set out to keep its competitor from knowing what it might actually be up to. The immediate effect? A decrease in the effectiveness of both as to national interests.

Not only had George and his superiors made no attempt to share Lee's status as a spy with J. Edgar Hoover; rather, the CIA attempted to cover up all traces of his mission. The FBI, understandably blindsided, could only consider this defection a serious threat as news reports of Oswald's activities trickled in. At George's request, Snyder had filed an obligatory report to the U.S. naval attaché in Moscow. This man had in turn passed the report on to the Commander of Naval Operations in D.C.

"Lee Harvey Oswald," this official record stated, "has offered (the) Soviets information he possessed on US radar."

Later that day, this report reached Hoover. He decided this might offer an opportunity for his Bureau to re-assert its authority.

Assigned to study the materials, Col. Thomas Fox, chief of Clandestine Services for the Defense Intelligence Agency, summed it all up: "The possibility that Oswald had been recruited or had prior contact with Soviet intelligence while in Japan would have to be fully explored. A net damage assessment, indicating the possible access (that) Oswald had to classified information" would commence immediately.

Confusing matters further, several FBI agents reported to Hoover that Oswald had been simultaneously spotted in various locations in the U.S. This caused Hoover to wonder if the ex-marine might be here, someone else meanwhile posing as Oswald.

File 301 was established at FBI headquarters, agents sent out to interview fellow marines, old friends and family members. John W. Fain, special agent assigned to speak with Marguerite and Robert, arrived in Fort Worth in late October. Marguerite, upon hearing the agent's polite but concerned questions, threw herself onto the nearest couch and wept. Robert, working a milk route to cover their expenses, showed up a later in his white suit. Balding, Robert appeared considerably less impressive than he had several years earlier in full marine dress garb.

"Yes, sir. Actually, I expected to hear from the FBI much sooner. I'll be glad to cooperate in any manner that I can."

Calmly, Robert explained things to Fain. The moment Lee's defection hit the airwaves Robert sent a telegram to his brother by way of the American Embassy: "through any possible means, keep your nose clean!" Not only had Lee failed to respond but, as Robert learned through Western Union, when a secretary at the Embassy contacted Lee, asking him to stop by and pick up the message, Lee refused. The FBI man thanked Robert for his cooperation and took his leave.

*

As per George's orders, Lee turned down most interview requests from American reporters in Moscow, each hoping to nail a scoop. A key exception: Priscilla Post Johnson, ostensibly in Moscow to cover the Russian news-front for the North American Newspaper Alliance. Like Embassy boss Snyder she served as a CIA plant. Previous to this assignment, Johnson worked for Senator John Fitzgerald Kennedy, he even then readying his presidential bid. Since JFK favored the CIA over the FBI, Johnson —ever loyal to JFK—made herself known to Allen Dulles, who introduced the young woman to George. He had taken care of her arrangements with the newspaper syndicate to place Johnson in this position.

"Hello, Lee Harvey Oswald. Thanks for agreeing to speak with me." (Be careful what you say: someone may be listening!)

The moment Lee met Priscilla Post Johnson it was love at first sight. Unfortunately, this turned out to be a one-way attraction. She left two hours later, her joint missions accomplished. As a reporter, she came away with a routine story. As a "mole," Johnson's more significant task had been to slip a message to Lee from George and carry one away as she left.

"Thank you, Mr. Oswald. Perhaps we'll meet again."

God, I hope so. You are so gorgeous ...!

All the while the KGB officials pondered, argued, stalled, agreed, disagreed, decided, re-evaluated. Lee remained free to come and go as he wished. Rima had offered to spend New Year's Eve with him but, convinced the relationship would not lead to the romance Lee longed for, he asked if Rosa might be his date.

They attended the ballet, dined on caviar, retired to his room. He could not guess, much less know, that what he thought to be his own decisions had been orchestrated by the KGB, Rosa one of their top agents.

"Oh, Rosa. I'm so crazy about you. Please—"

"Relax, Lee. Let me get to know your better as a person. Tell me 'the Lee Harvey Oswald story.' Who are you, what—"

On New Year's Day, however, Rosa could only relate to her superiors what they already knew: This man seemed sincere; an almost ethereal element of innocence surrounded his presence.

Then again, this might mask a brilliant, devious mind.

*

"I've got good news and bad news," Lee told George in a frantic phone call from Moscow to Miami on January 4, 1960. This took place from the apartment of Priscilla Post Johnson, which she daily scoured for traces of listening devices in her rooms or a wiretap on her private radio-phone.

"Hit me with the good news first."

"My Visa will be extended for at least a year."

"Terrific. And the bad?"

"They're sending me to Minsk! That's off in Byelorussia."

"I know where Minsk is, Lee."

"That's like one of theirs hoping to mole himself into Washington and learning he'll be sent to Dubuque Iowa instead."

"Will you calm down? This has to be a Sheletin decision, and I believe I understan how the man arrives at his decisions. You are being allowed to stay on because they assume you probably are what you claim to be. But they aren't certain. By sending you to a far-off city, they're placing you in a virtual test-tube. Agents will be watching from every angle, pretending to be ordinary citizens. They'll report every move you make. In time, Sheletin will make his decision. If they come to disbelieve your 'legend' they'll oust you. If they buy it, you'll be back in Moscow. Then you'll truly be our key mole there."

"If I'm sent home ... I won't be 'dumped'?"

"Jesus, Lee. When will you relax and realize you're 'in'? Now, here's what I want you to do. Go with the flow but insist that you want to be assigned to some sort of radio job when you arrive, based on your marine expertise. This will put you in a position to learn about technology outside of Moscow, which we know precious little about. Everything may work out for the best."

George read Sheletin correctly; this double-decision did constitute a temporary holding pattern. Lee took heart at the realization that his ongoing status as a secret agent would continue in some form or another. He received the substantial sum of 5,000 rubles, supposedly from the Red Cross, as well as the government's promise that they would pay him an additional subsidy of $700 a month while in Minsk.

A four day train trip brought him there. Lee was greeted as an arriving hero at the station by Mayor Sharapov. He offered a fine rent-free apartment for this American who had dared speak out, condemning his country's imperialism. Two local Red Cross nurses accompanied Lee to the city's leading hotel, more upscale than he had expected.

"Hello, Mr. Oswald. Welcome!"

I never thought Minsk would be so full of pretty girls.

As Lee checked in, young females crowded around outside, peering in windows, for a peek at the young American they'd heard about. Lee basked in the realization that these teenagers saw him as a sexy celebrity.

Again, he thought: *if they could see me now ...!*

The next day, Lee rose early and left room 453 to make a tour of his surroundings. He wandered down Sverdlov Street, peeking into a butcher shop on the pretext of taking a glance at what meats were available. In actuality, he passed a note for George to the pro-U.S. Russian who owned the place. Lee checked out GUM department store, then reported to work as a fitter-trainee at Gorizoni (Horizon). There he would be employed as a "checker," or metalworker, allowing him access to all the radio equipment and communications technology the firm developed.

He did grasp that the friendly workers who smilingly welcomed him to the Radio Factory were likely assigned by the local KGB chief to befriend him and report back daily.

"Thanks. Nice to meet you. The pleasure's all mine."

One uneducated oaf, named Viktor, took an immediate dislike to Lee solely because he was an American, Lee's pro-Soviet views be damned. They came close to fighting once, though several of their comrades rushed over and tore the two apart. One, Stepan Vasilyevich, fluent in English, offered to give Lee Russian language lessons so that he might converse in the native tongue.

As Lee guessed, Stepan's generosity was not precisely what it seemed. This late twenties fellow would at day's end report to Igor Ivanovich Guzmin at the plant. He filed summaries with the local KGB. Here, they were further edited before operatives sent them to Moscow. By the time such missives reached Sheletin, they were completely garbled and totally inaccurate.

Still, the desire to know for certain who and what Lee was weighed heavily on all. This explains why he was not assigned work at a less sensitive job than experimental radio. Only by setting him down in a position where Lee might reveal himself via a simple slip could the KGB learn what they needed to know.

Again, life came to resemble an elaborate chess game. What appeared simple, obvious blunders were sophisticated feints.

On March 16 Lee moved into his Kalinina Street apartment, he appreciative of the exquisite columns on building number N4's exterior. These allowed for a high-tone appearance. So much the better if Lee should bring girls here. Also appealing was his view of the twisting Svisloch River from the private balcony.

Each day, Lee took a trolley to and from work. People got to know him and, in time, Lee was invited to parties at the home of Don Alejandro Ziger, a thick-necked, furrow-browed, curly-haired emigree from Argentina. This fellow's wine, like his spirited conversations, proved splendid.

Also, Lee appreciated the intellectual university crowd he met here. He joined some on outings to theatre Central, which played imported movies from all over the globe. The smart set enjoyed their complex visions. Then, on to Café Vesna for cake, coffee, and heated discussions of any particular film's merits.

"But Fellini is so decadent. All style, no substance."

"I beg to disagree. His very style is his substance."

"I prefer Rossellini, with his crude use of camera. This allows an audience direct immersion in his political agenda."

"A movie must not be judged by what it has to say. If film is an original art form, the aesthetic for criticism must be the manner in which a filmmaker employs his camera to communicate."

At work, Lee found himself situated near Ella Germann, "a silky black-haired Jewish beauty with fine dark eyes, skin as white as snow, and a beautiful smile," in Lee's words. It was love at first sight: Rima and Rosa, whom he missed terribly at first, flew out of Lee's mind once he and Ella began to talk and take lunch breaks together. Ella intrigued him; she hailed from a theatrical family. Also, as a free thinker, she dared question her government's anti-American propaganda.

"I know, Ella. Some of my enthusiasm for Soviet citizenship has been severely strained by inequities I see in the system."

Always remember: She may be yet another spy!

At twenty-three, Ella proved more mature than most of the other girls. She balanced daily work at Horizon with night school classes at Minsk University, determined to get ahead of her current status. This revealed an ambitiousness that struck Lee as essentially American. One class dealt with the English language. Ella mentioned this to Lee, guessing he would offer to help her with such studies.

"I feel your pain, Lee. Open up. You can talk to me."

As a Jewish girl, Ella knew that what was best for herself would be an eagerness to prove her loyalty to the motherland. Her people experienced discrimination still, if nothing so arch as in the old days. A half-century earlier, Cossacks would boldly ride through the narrow streets of a Pogrom. The flamboyantly costumed cavalrymen would playfully employ their long, curved blades to slice off the heads of Jewish women and children as they, terror-stricken, attempted to scurry away and hide. Beneath huge, hanging black mustaches, the Cossacks would loudly laugh at the sight of what appeared to be large balls rolling down the alleyways. Here was a sport they relished practicing on random occasions, particularly when bored and drunk.

That was then; this, now.

Anti-semitism, over the decades, grew more subtle. Certainly, though, it had not gone away. If a Jew hoped to succeed in the modern Soviet Union, then, it was necessary to prove oneself to those in authority. So as to the case of Lee Harvey Oswald, Ella perceived him strictly as prey, cultivating the relationship in hopes of scoring points for herself.

"You are so vague about your motivations for leaving the United States. I so want a better sense of you as a person."

Together at his apartment, the couple remained chaste on her insistence. She claimed to be a virgin, saving herself for marriage. On May 2, they sat side by side, spellbound by radio reports concerning the shooting down of an American spy plane that had been illegally circling the Ural Mountains. An anti-aircraft missile slammed into the U2 piloted by Francis Gary Powers. He parachuted down into a gap between the rugged Asian steppes and the Soviet Union's easternmost European perimeters.

"He and his plane, both captured?" Lee gasped.

Ella noticed that Lee's mood changed during the course of listening. He began silently wandering around his room as if a stranger there. He stepped out on the balcony, gazing off into the distance.

"What's bothering you? Tell me ..."

If only I could. But I can't let myself trust you, even if I'm falling in love. Are you 'you'? Or merely a 'legend?'

Their relationship altered. Instead of suggesting marriage, and the beginning of a life together in Minsk, now Lee, clearly enamored of the pretty girl, would suddenly blurt out statements like "If I were to go back home, would you agree to go with me?"

After months of platonic dating, Lee now complained that perhaps he deserved a kiss goodnight. But Ella was not willing. Then, it dawned on him: She does not find me attractive, yet goes out with me. There can be only one explanation. She is a plant, here to coldly discover what she can for her own benefit.

Without warning, Lee broke off the relationship, refusing to see Ella again, much to the young beauty's surprise.

For the better part of a year, Lee did not date, so furious was he at her attempt to turn him into a patsy, the last thing in the world he ever wanted to be reduced to. Lee now once again disappeared into the darkness of movie theatres.

To his delight, Lee learned that the Mir movie house would be showing a film called *Babette Goes to War*, a comedy about a beautiful French girl who joins the Resistance to fight the Nazis. She was played, naturally, by Brigitte Bardot.

The best thing about women in movies was that they cannot betray you as so many do in real life. They are frozen onscreen like the maidens on that Grecian Urn in a poem by Keats. What did the

poet write? 'Heard melodies are sweet; those unheard, sweeter ..."
How true! Bebe, perfect forever on film ...
So near and yet so far ... wondrously frustrating.

A few nights later he went to see the film again, though it had been mediocre. No matter: Just the opportunity to look up at the blonde for ninety minutes, with that hair flying across her face, momentarily obscuring the overly made-up eyes ...

*

On March 17, 1961, several friends insisted that Lee join them for a pre-spring celebration. That night Lee was introduced to Marina, the only local woman—at eighteen, a girl really—who dared to style her hair in the manner of Bardot.

Not surprisingly, Lee fell in love with her at first sight.

CHAPTER FIFTEEN:
HOME FROM THE HILL

"Not even Marina knows the real reason why
I've returned to the United States."
—Lee Harvey Oswald to Marguerite;
Friday the Thirteenth; July 1962

A little voice inside Lee had told him that were he to marry Marina they would, as if in a fairytale come true, live "happily ever after." That phrase, though, hardly described their existence once the two made their way to the U.S., settling in the Dallas-Fort Worth area. Their very living conditions revealed the extreme contrast which Marina (or the woman playing a part called 'Marina') experienced between her earlier existence in Minsk and current situation in Texas.

In the U.S.S.R., everything was supposed to have been functional, non-luxurious, anti-decadent. Yet she'd resided in an elegant (at least by Russian standards) suite with her 'uncle and aunt.' Marina moved into Lee's smaller but pleasant rooms.

Coming to America turned out to be a revelation and shock to her system. As it turned out, the land of plenty, at least for the Oswalds and their baby daughter, proved anything but.

One person who visited them often, G. De Mohrenschildt, described a visit to one of the Oswalds' living place: "the atmosphere of the house and neighborhood (are) conducive to suicide. The living room was dark and smelly, the bedroom and kitchen facing bleak walls ... the place spruced up by lovely photographs of the Russian countryside." These were taken by Lee during his travels through thick forestlands adjoining Minsk.

The photos, De Mohrenschildt decided, constituted a visual plea for help; an admission of the mistake she made; evidence of her dream to return to Russia, at any cost, by any means.

De Mohrenschildt decided on the spot that he would do all he could to facilitate that unarticulated request. Yet while he served the KGB, and had been assigned as this beautiful spy's contact, De Mohrenschildt had trouble grasping whether such nostalgic melancholia came from the created-character called 'Marina' or the woman who had been assigned to play that part.

In truth, Marina herself could no longer be certain where the one left off and the other began.

*

This G. De Mohrenschildt had sought the Oswalds out soon after their arrival in Texas on June 13, 1962. In actuality, plans for Lee's return to the U.S. began on May 2, 1960. Lee then still hoped to win the mysterious dark-haired Ella. On that day when Gary Francis Powers had been shot down, Lee made some feeble excuse to leave Ella and proceed to the local bakery.

"Hello, Mr. Oswald. Fascinating news, yes?"

"That, Yuri, is putting the situation mildly."

This was, like the butcher shop he entered on his first day in the city, one more of those "safe places" where Lee could secretly slip a message off to George.

"What now?" Lee demanded. Everything he and George had planned extended from a single conception: a) The KGB had to learn everything about the U2; b) the CIA must make certain the Russians happened upon such information so its existence could serve as a deterrence to atomic war; c) American security could not be allowed to appear lax; d) an individual traitor could, owing to a 'coincidence' of his past military experience, offer the KGB such details; e) the Russians would detain such a person in the provinces until convinced of his sincerity; f) if this were decided in his favor, he would then be brought back from Minsk to Moscow, serving there as a secret agent.

Overnight, all that was ruined. The Soviets had in their possession an actual U2 jet, as well as the pilot. Listening to news reports about a wild card—the weak link in the plan that George, despite his genius at espionage, had somehow missed—now rendered Lee's function in Russia largely irrelevant.

"Change in legend," George replied. "L.H.O. disenchanted with Russia, longs to return home." With that, Lee had to now rewrite the fictional character who shared his actual name.

"If I should decide to return to the U.S.," he asked Ella, "would you consider coming along?"

That bitch! She never loved me ... If I could, I'd like to wring her pretty neck with my bare hands...

Trusting Lee implicitly to fill in the blanks as to details George left everything open except the grand finale: Home-word bound, where another assignment, Lee trusted, would be waiting.

The first thing to do was create a fake diary in which he re-imagined everything, viewing events he previously accepted as

236

positive in the most unflattering manner to provide a basis for his about-face. Here, Lee hesitated. One way to achieve this would be to express a growing distrust of Marxist ideals. That, he decided, was too simplistic; too likely to be questioned as suspicious when he filed papers requesting his release.

I'm too good at this spy game now to trap myself with such a feeble cover. This must be more complicated, more convincing.

Quickly, his nimble mind seized on another, more believable approach. The problem was not Marxism per se, which Lee actually did find impressive in its purest form. The problem: Lee (the 'real' Lee) found some of those ideas attractive, if as a CIA plant (a 'legend') he was supposed to reject the Red way.

Constantly, he told himself that he did. But another of those little voices inside questioned whether that remained true. The ideal of human equality, he could not deny, was most appealing. That poor people, like he and his mother back home, ought to be regarded as society's spine rather some ugly appendage, struck him as valid. Of course, that was not the way things worked around here. Pompous party officials lorded it over the working class.

Lee was, then, able to maintain his loyalty to his sworn cause —America and all it stood for—owing to his contemptuous feelings for the despicable realities in contemporary Russia.

That's it, then! My new legend will incorporate much of what I truly do believe. The problem here is not that Marx, or Lenin, or Engels were wrong. Only that the Soviet Union, living and breathing those values during its first decade of existence, tragically fell into Stalin's hands.

A country, any country, is only as good as its current leadership. Khrushchev is as bad as Stalin. The premise itself from Marx through Lenin was enlightened. Yet I despise the results once a lofty dream passes from the greatness of a libertarian like Vladimir into the hands of lesser, self-serving men.

Yet how will George react to all of this? I know he will take delight in reading my faux journal of a gradual defection from belief in contemporary Russia to disparagement. What might be the case, though, if he were to learn this is not very far from what I, the real me, have come to believe?

That communism, if and when fairly implemented, is not the natural enemy of democratic capitalism but a likely ally?

"I become increasingly conscious of just what sort of society I live in," Lee wrote that night. "Mass gymnastics, compulsory after work meeting; usually political information meeting. Compulsory attendance at lectures and the sending of the entire shop collective (except me) to pick potatoes on a Sunday." The communist Party secretary at the Factory, whom Lee had always found friendly, he now described as "a fat, forty-ish no-nonsense party regular" who forced Lee to attend "fifteen meetings a month ... always held after work time." Such insistent regimentation must "turn to stone all except the hard-faced communists with roving eyes looking for any bonus-making catch of inattentiveness on the party of any worker."

A week and a half later, he concluded: "The work is drab. The money I get has nowhere to be spent ... No places of recreation except the trade union dances." (That was patently absurd, as he attended the movies almost every night, and there were endless cultural events such as ballet, opera, also comic and dramatic theatre of a type that did not exist in comparably small-to-medium-sized cities in the U.S.) "I have had enough!"

While the entries themselves would be convincing for anyone who gave them a quick read-over, Lee made the mistake of mixing up dates in this creative recreation of the past. He jotted down events as if he had done so at that point in time. What he would later present as his "daily diary" constituted what might better be called a non-fiction novel, filled with specific errors.

*

There was but one sticky point to all of this, as he had truthfully become nostalgic for the U.S. and very much wanted to return. Incredible as it might seem, Lee even longed to see his mother again, despite any ill feelings as to their relationship in the past. After such a long absence, the negatives had grown fuzzy, Marguerite's strange sense of devotion to Lee what he now best recalled. At any rate, the one drawback to going home was Ella, whom Lee at this juncture still believed in love with him.

That would be quickly concluded by her rejection of Lee. He bridled at the realization that he had been an innocent sentimentalist about beautiful women. *Never again*! He swore.

To facilitate his return, if it proved warranted, Lee had followed George's explicit orders as to how he must operate once he arrived back in Moscow. Lee was to offer to give up his U.S. citizenship without ever actually getting around to doing so. Had he, any such reversal would have presented a labyrinth of complications, taking years to resolve. As is, the situation might have been simple. The U.S.S.R. no longer desired to pay large sums of money to someone rendered worthless in terms of valid information who all at once spoke negatively of their land.

Everything might have gone like clockwork had Lee not met Marina. Believing her a none-too-bright Bardot-like beauty, unaware that this constituted a character created specifically for him, Lee fell in love.

At, of course, first sight.

Despite what he had been told in the service by a wise sergeant, he proceeded to make precisely the same mistake as had before, of course expecting totally different results now.

"Marina, will you ...?

"Give me time, Lee. Please? A week ..."

"I'll wait forever if need be, darling."

Already under orders to say yes, having been instructed to manipulate Lee into asking, Marina insisted on time to think so that Lee, no fool, would not begin to wonder if she accepted too quickly to be believed. The character called Marina had to be consistent and that girl would not jump so fast. She would hesitate, and in so doing make her manipulations appear invisible.

"Lee? Where have you been? Yes, of course, I'll marry you."

Seemingly, Lee proposed to Marina from his hospital bed. That in actually had been Lee's twin, the real Lee off in Cuba, trying to kill Castro to facilitate the Bay of Pigs invasion by making it difficult for Cubans to respond without their leader.

Lee's mission and the greater scheme had failed miserably. In proposing, the twin had been following orders from George, who withheld this from Lee while Lee recuperated in Miami. Lee's surprise, upon confronting Marina after a return to Minsk, must ring entirely, precisely true.

George knew that women, with their remarkable sixth sense, can detect an act, particularly on the part of a man in their lives, immediately. This held true even if that woman is herself offering a performance. Anyway, Lee's response had to be real.

"Oh. *That!* Why, that's *wonderful*, Marina. Wonderful!"

Reports trickling in from agents in Moscow and Minsk did point to the possibility that Marina was actually working for the KGB. And that, unlike Ella, she had been assigned to marry Lee. He could not be told this, at least not yet, for fear that Lee would become suspicious of her every move. And she, being a perceptive woman, would spot this in his eyes and manner.

This, George could not allow; it would interfere with his learning what he and the CIA must know, what they could discern from observing her attempts to collect information. Also, the Company had grown concerned about a group of Russians living in the Dallas area, serendipitously near Fort Worth, where Robert lived. This allowed Lee a logical reason to settle there.

These were American citizens of Russian descent who claimed aristocratic blood dating back to the czar. Their forefathers fled the Russian Revolution of 1919 even as so many Cubans now settling in Miami had run away from Castro and his own communist take-over forty years later. All claimed to be proud of their Russian heritage but pro-democracy and fervently anti-communist.

The CIA wasn't so certain. As several recent circumstances suggested, they might be employing their status as a welcome minority as a "legend" of their own making, reporting back to the KGB. One way or the other, the CIA had to know.

What better means to learn than have Ozzie bring home a wife who might be working for the KGB? If Marina were such a plant, and if the Dallas/Fort Worth Russians were something other than what they claimed to be, they would contact a recent arrival under the auspices of helping a fellow country-person feel at home, deep in the heart of Texas. While, without her husband realizing it, put his bride to work within their cell.

On the other hand, if Lee turned out not to be such a fool but a CIA agent, so much the better. Marina could employ her feminine wiles to draw from her fool of a husband all sorts of information he believed spoken in a special sort of confidence.

*

"I am returning to America. Will you go with me?"

"Oh, yes," Marina exclaimed, slipping into a seemingly spontaneous dance of joy. "Anywhere, Lee, in the world!"

"Now, I know you are filled with childish dreams about streets paved with gold. This is not the way things are."

"Those are only stories. Still, I know that life will be better for me there than it is, or ever can be, here."

Lee took Marina in his arms and kissed her. "I will do all I can to make our lives wonderful once we arrive. I promise."

"I know that, Lee. Oh, but I can't wait. Just think! Me, little Marina: In the wonderful world that is the U.S.A."

When Richard Snyder in Moscow received word from Lee that he not only wanted to return home but bring a Soviet bride with him, the official Consul and secretive CIA agent made certain the process went as smoothly as possible from his end. The KGB, eager to have Marina overseas, contacted the passport office to speed things along.

The only possible problems might be the FBI. There, so far as anyone knew, Lee was indeed a traitor, perhaps coming home to spy on the U.S. for the Russians. Hoover ordered his agents to question Oswald on return, the CIA still insistent that the FBI must not be allowed to know what the Company was actually up to. Not only with Lee, but as to any of their secret operatives.

Previous to the Oswalds' arrival, the FBI set up a special file to monitor their travels: 327-925D. Agent John Fain was sent from D.C. to the Fort Worth office to study Lee's every move, then report back to J. Edgar. This necessitated that the CIA create a counter-network to throw Fain off course.

For Hoover to learn Lee was a government agent, working for "the other side" of information security, without his own branch having been alerted to this for fear that the fewer people in on a secret the better, would likely cause a blow-up. Which could further complicate the duel of wits being waged between the Bureau in D.C. and the Company not far away in Langley VA. The situation had already grown tense enough without *that.*

So even as Fain attempted to learn more about what was going on in northern Texas, interviewing Lee's relatives, various CIA operatives were dispatched to keep knowledge about Lee's actual status, which Marguerite and Robert knew nothing about, from surfacing. Fain's interviews with them were, then, superfluous. On the other hand, once the couple arrived, the Company had to continually watch over Lee and Marina, in order to maintain the secretive status of his "legend." And hers!

Meanwhile, Lee flew from Minsk to Moscow on July 8, 1961, checking in at Hotel Berlin, visiting Snyder in a considerably less irritated mood than Lee had been in, or performed, on their previous meeting. Several days later, Marina joined Lee and was interviewed by Snyder's co-worker John McVickar, who found her a pleasant young woman. McVickar stamped her papers as "acceptable without suspicions or hesitation."

Pregnant, Marina announced that while the process took its course, she would fly to Kharkov to bid farewell to an old aunt. In actuality, the woman calling herself 'Marina' met with KGB officials, planning out her long-term approach in America.

This left Lee to spend his 22nd birthday alone, less than pleased at this status. After all, the previous year he had two beautiful Russians with him. That now seemed a lifetime ago. Lee wondered about contacting Rima and Rosa but guessed that, like himself, they had gone through considerable life changes during the intervening months. Those women would be totally different people now, with little if anything to say to a man who had briefly figured prominently in their own lives.

So Lee lay in bed, naked, dreaming of Marina, and the child that soon would add so much to their now intertwined lives.

Also, trying, as always, to grasp who Lee Oswald really was. This was a question that would consume this man throughout his brief existence.

As I study, relentlessly study, and learn new words, or discover the true meaning of words I thought I knew, I come to the conclusion that I am either a stoic or a narcissist.

So ardently do I wish to see myself as a stoic, in the old Roman sense: Refusing to show any emotions, however deeply I may experience them. Even moreso, perhaps, than 'normals.'

Always, though, putting on a false front to conceal my pain when insulted or rejected, so often the case in my life.

Am I better off now? I believed myself to have come so far, achieved so much, transformed completely.

Yet here I am, alone my birthday. As alienated and isolated as I felt when, as a lost little boy ...

Also, I fear myself to be narcissist: Unable to love, truly love, anyone or anything other than myself. Is it possible that I might be both? Like a schizophrenic, which I sometimes fear I may be, roaring from one extreme to the other.

Both elements inside me, waging a constant war with one another, for my mind, my soul. If such a thing even exists.

*

Back home, when a blithe J. Edgar Hoover suggested to the State Department that it might not be in America's best interest to have Lee back, Robert I. Owens in the Soviet Affairs section, he very much in the know thanks to constant contact with Allan Dulles, filed a report stating: "it is in the interest of the United States to get Lee Harvey Oswald and his family out of the Soviet Union and into the United States as soon as possible."

To Hoover's disbelief and anger, the other agencies set his deep concerns aside, doing all they could to pave the way for Lee and his bride, Marina now seven months pregnant, to come to America. On February 15, 1962, she gave birth to a daughter whom they named June. This occurred while waiting for her exit visa which, inexplicably to Lee, took much longer to process than had been expected. The Russian government had decided to purposefully create a delay so that the child would be born there. They were planning ahead: should it ever be necessary for Marina to make a hurried return home, the baby, born a Soviet citizen, would not create a problem that might delay their hasty exit from the U.S.

"Oh, Lee," Marina wept, these of course crocodile tears, she fully aware of the reasons for a slow-down in the process. "What if we are not allowed to leave? What will we do?"

"They can't stop us. I won't let them." How strong he felt when speaking so to Marina, the stoic side of him dominant now. Lee projected a false sense of total security. The narcissist in him too loved to believe this little lie about his own powers to change fate, determine the outcome, and win in the end. Lee had continued reading Nietzsche. A seminal line, "That which does not kill us makes us stronger," leapt up at him from the page.

It all makes sense now. My disastrous childhood? Necessary to make me the powerful man I am today. Thank you, then, God, for putting me through all the torture I cursed you for, over so many years. Not random and unfair, as I once falsely assumed.

All part of your great master plan. Assuming, of course, that there is a higher being, which I doubt. But do not dismiss.

Who am I? Someday, when I come to know for certain if you are there or not, then I will also know who I am.

*

Husband, wife and child soon traveled through Poland, East Germany, West Germany and the Netherlands. One night they were obliged to share a dinner table with an American couple. When during a pleasant conversation the husband inquired as to what Lee did for a living, the response, accompanied by a sardonic grin, was: "I might just be a spy!" All laughed loudly.

Then followed a joyous four-day vacation in Amsterdam. Arm in arm, the happy couple and their adorable child wandered the quaint streets, enjoyed sausage-rolls on the docks, giggled at brazen prostitutes behind red glass windows, and visited the Van Gogh museum. Lee experienced one of his great epiphanies there, staring at the famed self-portrait of a misunderstood man, his sad, bitter eyes gazing out at the onlooker as the world around him, as he portrayed it, reflected the artist's tortured psyche.

The brain beneath that anguished face had to be wondering if he were the genius his heart and soul insisted or the non- talent fool everyone in his world apparently believed him to be.

Such anguish! He paints the way I feel ... I am not alone ... others have walked this path ... and, in the end, many reigned supreme, if only after passing through hell on earth . .

The Oswalds took the Moscow-Berlin express to Rotterdam, boarding SS *Maasdam,* sailing for America June 4. Lee delighted at what he considered an appealing circumstance or one more bit of evidence his life did follow some pre-ordained pattern, the ever-twisting trail inextricably linked to that of his favorite singer/star, Frank Sinatra: The boat would dock at Hoboken, New Jersey, the scene of Sinatra's humble birth and childhood.

Lee couldn't wait to see the town for himself, albeit briefly, hoping to track down the building where The Voice had been raised. Like the Italian kid from a northern Sicilian ghetto in the U.S., this Southern boy from an urban slum had crawled up and out. Sinatra was blessed with that remarkable tool, his talent. Lee's attributes? Considerably less obvious.

Still, he'd never forgotten something Sinatra once said in an interview when the TV host asked him to explain how he had defied the odds and hit the big-time: "I refused to fail!"

Lee had accepted that as his mantra. If it was good enough for Francis Albert Sinatra, then it would be good enough for Lee Harvey Oswald. At any rate, he was home.

However bad his experiences here may have been, Lee was an American, true blue to the core. Why his patriotism remained so strong and firm, Lee could not yet put into precise words.

What was the line from that movie ... ? Oh, of course: Just because you love something doesn't mean it has to love you back. Monty Clift, From Here to Eternity, *1953 ...*

There was another movie, a modern western called *Home From the Hill,* made just two years ago, starring Robert Mitchum. It had been set in Texas, Lee even now on his way back there. The title derived from a poem Lee read while in that seventh grade English class, with that teacher who made all the difference.

A poem by Robert Louis Stevenson. How did it go?

Home is the sailor, home from the sea, The hunter, home from the hill ...

That's might be me the poet wrote of, long before I was born. I am the sailor, here on this ship's deck, gazing at the Statue of Liberty, my beautiful bride and wonderful child beside me. Sea-spray splashes up on us, circling gulls squawk, people cheer at the site New York harbor. I am the hunter, as I have stalked my prey, righteously killed my enemy.

No one can now doubt my manhood. His blood flowed through my fingers; I delighted in watching him suffer. I have killed and, if necessary, for my good or my country, will kill again.

I know now that this is what I, Lee Oswald, was born for.

I was blessed, or cursed, with a talent for killing.

"Darling? You look so intense. Is anything wrong?"

"No, Marina. Actually, things have never been so right."

*

Marina's disillusionment with what was supposed to be her own American Dream-come-true began ten days before reaching the U.S. On George's suggestion, Lee had booked them into a Third Class cabin aboard the *Maasdam,* hopefully not attracting any unwanted attention: i.e., where did these supposedly simple folk get the money for a luxurious passage? The FBI would ask such questions upon their disembarking, blowing his cover.

Though the guise worked, a toll was taken as to Marina: she despised the cramped quarters, the inedibly bad food, the sense of having been reduced from a Beautiful Person a short while earlier to a virtual pauper, when this great sea-change that she had agreed to brought her down, not up, socially.

"I do not mind the bareness of it all. But this is *dirty*."

"Stay strong. In a week we will be home. This *will* end."

Aboard the ship, a Russian-speaking waiter named Pieter Didenko delighted Marina with his conversations about the Old Country. Delicately, he let her know that he would be her KGB contact while sailing. Any messages which needed to be conveyed to the KGB could be passed through his resources.

Also, wherever in the U.S. the couple settled, she would be contacted. A network of Russian agents would quietly follow the Oswalds' every move. She hinted that Lee had said something to her about wanting to join his family in the Fort Worth area.

"Fabulous. Our most reliable people live near there."

After disembarking, Lee was singled out from the other passengers and interrogated at length by Spas T. Raikin. He claimed to be a Russian speaking caseworker with Travelers Aid in New York City. From the barrage of pointed questions, Lee guessed Raikin to be an FBI plant or an operative for the Bureau assigned to learn as much as possible as to what was going on inside his mind. Lee stuck to the legend he had concocted and which George heartily approved of. This left Raikin confused as to how Lee Oswald ought to be summed up: More socialist than communist and, from what he said, more pro-American than ever following his discouraging experiences in the Soviet Union.

"Will being back in America make you happy?"

"Happiness," Lee responded, "can exist only in taking part in a struggle to achieve a state in which there is no borderline between one's personal world and the world in general."

What in the name of God is this guy even talking about? Is Lee Harvey Oswald an innocent, a Soviet agent, or a philosopher?

Following a one night stay at the Times Square Hotel, where Marina expressed some delight in the bright neon lights below and constant rush and flow of people, everyone in some great hurry to be somewhere other than where they currently were, Lee, Marina, and June flew from New York International Airport on Delta Flight 821 to Dallas' Love Field.

There they were greeted by Robert Oswald and his wife Vada. "Welcome home, little brother. Keep your nose clean?"

"Of course. I brought one of your handkerchiefs along."

During the ninety minute car trip back to Fort Worth, where husband, wife and daughter would temporarily stay with the warm couple, Robert and Vada attempted to strike up a friendly conversation with their new family member. They were surprised to learn Marina spoke not a word of English. She would merely smile sweetly in response to everything they said, nodding her head in a manner that suggested she had not a clue what they were talking about but desperately hoped to be liked, accepted.

"She's very beautiful, Lee."

"Thank you, Vada. Does she remind you of Brigitte Bardot?"

"A little, perhaps."

"I think so. Very much. I always dreamed of being married to a movie star. Or someone who looks like one."

"I only hope she can make you happy. As the old saying goes, looks aren't everything."

"But of course they are!" Lee laughed.

Oh, my dear, pathetic brother in law. Are you ever in for it! As I guess you will soon learn ...

In actuality, the woman playing Marina, whose name may well have been Alexandrovana Medvedeva, spoke fluent English, this one of the many reasons the KGB picked her for this position. But by pretending to be ignorant, as well as a near-idiot, the lovely, apparently shy secret agent could create a situation in which people spoke openly in front of her, just as she wished.

*

At 7313 Davenport Street in Fort Worth, Marina marveled at the everyday objects of suburban American culture: toasters, a TV, an extra bedroom, two bathrooms and, most charming of all, a garden in their small back yard, rich with multi-colored flowers.

Her mood improved. She asked Lee in Russian if they would soon be able to afford something like this. He was obliged to tell her Bob had worked his way up to an executive with Acme Brick, and that since Lee must begin at the bottom, wherever he might find a position, such comparative luxury would be some time coming.

"Oh! But a short while, yes?"

"I'll work hard, Marina. I'll do what I can?"

"Soon, though. Something like this. For us?"

"Understand, Robert is paid higher than some common worker. Vada brings in additional money as a beautician."

"But this is what I want, at least for a beginning."

"I can't promise anything. Only that I'll try."

Lee noted disappointment in her eyes. Marina at once fell into a depression. Lee did, too, if for an entirely oppositional reason Marina could not possibly guess.

When George had instructed Lee to recreate his Legend, the manner in which he did so had been left up to the agent in the field. As such, Lee arrived at a decision to attack Russia's cynical form of communism, no better than the supposed opposite pole of fascism. As an American, he believed this fully, had before he even arrived, his experiences offering excellent proof of such a belief.

On the other hand, his "legend" held that he remained a Marxist-idealist, believing a pure state of all-power-to-the-people could be achieved and that such a state would be the best place on earth.

So he rejected Russia as a failed experiment, accepting other situations in the world as potential success stories.

The problem, if there was one, had to do with a gradual but serious blending process between his assumed legend and his true self. Lee had attempted to put his current state into words in his debriefing by Raikin. That extremely ordinary man clearly had no idea what Lee attempted to express.

One aspect of his earlier "legend," first in the service, then after arriving in Russia, was to decry the U.S. owing to his own past life: though a hard-working woman, his mother had not been able to bring herself and her children up from poverty. The American Dream of eventual success via hard work was but a myth. Perhaps the Marxist ideal, if ever fully augmented, would provide a better way of life for the common working man.

Over time, Lee had begun to believe that this might be the case. Life in the Soviet Union only assured him that such a pure communist state did not exist. At least not yet. And not there.

But could it? Will it? Could I help make that happen?

For the first time since their initial meeting, Lee had experienced a thought-process he did not share with George in any of their constant secretive correspondences. To do so would likely cause Lee to be drummed out of CIA service, and he did not want that. How powerful, as well as patriotic, all this made him feel!

Also, he did want to aid the U.S. in its conflict with the Soviet Union, which he had never admired, now strongly disliked.

Still, he had to reconcile the Company's abiding attitude—all Communism, in any form, anyplace in the world, constituted a threat—with a gnawing, growing belief that pure Marxism, if it ever instituted, might be better than capitalistic democracy.

*

Lee considered writing a book on the subject. But the need to find work so as to feed his family, rather than rely on the good will of Robert (Lee feared an ugly scene like the earlier one in New York), demanded that any literary career be put off indefinitely. Lee applied for a job with the Texas Employment Commission as a possible translator of Russian, should anyone be in need of such services. While this did not immediately provide work, it put Lee in contact with an executive at that office, Peter Paul Gregory. A friendly man, he suggested that Lee soon contact members of the local Russian community.

Meanwhile, Marguerite had arrived from Crowell, TX. Within a week Lee, Marina, and baby June shared an apartment with Lee's mother on Seventh Street, a baker's dozen blocks away from Robert's.

Though Marguerite made a fuss over the young woman and their darling baby, her personality was no different than before, other than perhaps more advanced in such directions.

"Oh, Lee. Such a wonderful family you have now! I'm so proud of you. And so delighted that you came back."

"Yes, Momma. Please understand, though. As soon as I locate a decent job, Marina and I want a place of our own."

"What?" Marguerite, suddenly appearing faint, collapsed on the couch. "After all I've done, all I've suffered ..."

"We're a young couple, Momma. A young *family* now."

"And me?" she wept. "I'm not part of that family?"

"That's not what I meant. Momma, stop crying, please?"

Marguerite had not changed. If anything, Marguerite was more Marguerite than before. Her bouts of hysteria and overdone performances of gentility confused and irritated Marina, who missed the calm, easygoing company of Robert and his family, as well as their more appealing apartment.

"Hang on, darling. This will all change—"

"Yes, Lee? But that's what you said onboard the boat."

Lee did find work with the Leslie Welding Company at its louver-door factory where he labored as a humble metalworker. At least this allowed him, toward the end of July, to move out of his mother's apartment, over to their first "own place" at 2703 Mercedes Street. Even as Robert drove them there, Marguerite sobbing about being deserted once again by her baby boy, Lee experienced a sense of déjà vu.

What he'd hated most about his childhood was the constant dislocation, those frenzied moves from one place to another. Now supposedly in charge, the same thing was happening once again.

"Here, Lee? Here is where we'll stay?"

"For the time being, Marina. We'll have to see ..."

Meanwhile, Lee sent to George the documents he'd smuggled out of Russia: photographs of the emergent technology at the factory where he'd worked, images too of the adjacent military compounds he had taken while off on hunting trips with his .22.

Breaks in the monotony arrived in the form of a flurry of invites to homes of local 'White Russians.' In particular one senior citizen, George Bouhe, a successful accountant and ardent capitalist, accepted Lee and Marina with open arms.

At one party that took place in late summer at Bouhe's home, another guest, Anna Meller, noticed a sincere if terrible contradiction whenever Lee was asked to join a conversation. Years later, she would recall: "He's against the Soviet Union; he's against the United States. He made the impression that he didn't know what he likes."

In fact, Lee had finally come to understand precisely what as a unique individual he did and not like. "Each one of us," Lee explained to Meller, "ought to be always out and about, attempting to take the best of possible worlds we can imagine, and make that come to life around us."

"If you want to live in a dream world go visit Disneyland."

"That's just my point. What is that called? 'The Happiest Place on Earth?' Well, why not make the world more like *that*?"

"Because it's a fantasy. This? Reality!"

"Sometimes dreams do come true."

"Yes. I believe they're called nightmares."

Somewhere in-between the extremes of raw capitalism and corrupt communism, there might be a Utopia in which the people, actual people, true people, the workers, could at last become the center of interest. Could America, if we would only accept and adopt the best aspects of socialism, become that Shangri-La?

*

Lee was wondering about that one day when a sudden rapping came at the front screen door. Hurrying to see who it might be, Lee found himself face to face with a 6' 2," early fifties, immaculately coiffed, expensively suited gentleman; his hair silver-grey, the stranger spoke in an upper-class European manner that combined elements of the old Russian aristocracy with a seductive Austrian lilt.

Epicurian. That's the first word that come to mind upon meeting whoever this is. I don't mean that in a positive way.

"Hello," the jovial fellow announced with supreme self-confidence. "My name is De Mohrenschildt. My wife Jeanne and I live in Dallas. I heard from the Fort Worth Russians you and your family had recently arrived so I swung on down to say 'hi.'"

For reasons he could not fully comprehend, Lee hated this dapper intruder on first sight.

CHAPTER SIXTEEN:
DEEP IN THE HEART OF DALLAS

"In my opinion he had two lives, spending most
of his time in his own separate life."
—Marina Oswald, reflecting on Lee, 1977

Members of the Russian community in Dallas considered G. De Mohrenschildt their mystery man. The most obvious aspect of his identity concerned business dealings with Col. Lawrence Orlov, an oil speculator. But while people knew the precise nature of Orlov's company, De Mohrenschildt's role remained fuzzy. What exactly did he do to earn his salary? No one could say, not for certain.

However, wealth and its vestiges (expensive cars, imposing home, hand-tailored suits, rumors of affairs with lovely women) create a confederacy of silence around awesome individuals.

On that first visit to the Oswalds' home, De Mohrenschildt regaled Marina with glorious tales of his escape from the Russian revolution while still a child. According to this scenario, his father, a marshal of the old nobility, and mother were killed by crazed peasants. But not before passing their eight-year-old boy to a tribe of loyal gypsies. They smuggled the child out of the country and, in time, to France. Distant relatives there provided him with a first-class education.

What De Mohrenschildt did not confide to the Oswalds: In May 1938, he arrived in the United States aboard the *SS Manhattan*. A year later, authorities arrested him when 'Jerzy' (as he now called himself, claiming to be Polish) was caught sketching naval installations at Port Aransas, TX. Accusations that he might be a German spy were dismissed by the articulate European. He was a filmmaker, he said; these merely story-boards for a movie he would shortly produce. Yet no one in Hollywood, when contacted, had ever so much as heard of him.

During World War II, he initially appeared to prove his loyalty by offering to oversee all operations of the French underground in the United States. An FBI investigation rather suggested that he had infiltrated this organization to provide stateside Nazi agents with key information.

Ultimately, no one could decide if this man was an agent, a double agent, or triple agent; and, whichever he might be, if De Mohrenschildt ever owed any true loyalty to the Allies or the Axis, or if he were manipulating everyone for reasons known only to himself, probably for the sake of personal gain.

In the end, any evidence against De Mohrenschildt proved so self-contradictory that the authorities shook their heads with frustration and allowed him to walk free. Still, the FBI kept an open file on this man, as did, beginning in 1957, the CIA.

When the Cold War with Russia replaced the hot one against Germany, everything altered. Clearly, De Mohrenschildt had established contact with Soviet operatives who had entered our country. Yet he lived so lavishly as a capitalist that all his whispered asides—"I'm infiltrating, don't you see, to serve the U.S.?"—were, if not entirely believed, anxiously considered.

"And so I appear before you now, proud both of my Russian heritage of a type that is no longer recognized in my homeland and of my status as a U.S. citizen as well."

Lee smelled a rat. The way in which De Mohrenschildt spoke struck him as so many details picked up while watching old movies: Adolph Menjou by way of Maurice Chevalier crossed with Erich von Stroheim. As someone who had drawn his own identity from films, sniffing out a similar approach on the part of this different person did not prove difficult for Lee Oswald.

*

"Which would you care to hear first: the good news or the bad?" De Mohrenschildt asked early in October, 1962. He, his eighteen-year-old daughter Alexandra, and her husband Gary had driven down from Dallas, ostensibly to catch the Van Cliburn competition, they claiming to be musical sophisticates.

"Why don't you choose?"

"I will, then! The bad isn't, in truth, so bad at all. You must move to Dallas at once."

Just as Lee had suspected, the seemingly magnanimous man hoped to seize control of their lives. If De Mohrenschildt did turn out to be what Lee suspected——he had spoken to George, who confirmed this shady figure was on their dubious-persons-list— this move would be for political as well as personal reasons.

"We like it well enough here."

De Mohrenschildt glanced around the small, shabby apartment while rolling his eyes in contempt for the sad surroundings.

Oh, this guy is good! Very good. But I'm better.

"A close friend of mine in the Russian community has found a more rewarding job. And you will earn twice as much."

"Metal-working is an honest task for a working-man."

"Oh," Marina gasped, trippingly assuming center stage in the little scene. "Lee, that would be wonderful. At last we could have a place like your brother Robert's. You *did* promise."

During the next several days, Marina wrote to the Soviet Embassy in Washington, informing Vitaliy A. Gerasimov as to her current whereabouts. He operated in the U.S. much as Richard Snyder did in the Soviet Union. An embassy job served as cover for his secretive role as intelligence-gatherer for the KGB.

When Gerasimov responded, stating that her new status had been placed on file, he communicated through sub-textual implications his role as her key contact. In truth, Marina, like Lee, had begun to waver. She would gladly consider deserting the Soviet Union if she came to believe a more happy life might exist here.

What's best for me and June? I must decide and soon.

Considering her unattractive apartment, Marina had determined they must make the move to Dallas. Once there, if she so chose, she could prove more useful to the KGB in such a prestigious area. On the other, should she choose to abandon ship and join Lee in marriage for real, how better to relocate there, in an upscale development, her husband transformed into a white collar worker.

Once in Dallas, I'll discover what I ought to do.

Though sexual relations between wife and husband had been nil since moving into "the dump," that changed. As a result, Lee began to appear less dour and pallid, whistling on his way to work. At her insistence, he traveled to Dallas for the job interview.

After all, I did promise, as Marina said ...

Everything might have worked out precisely as Marina had planned were it not for something that occurred several nights later, even as they were preparing for the move. While Marina slept soundly, the phone rang. Lee answered.

"Lee!" George spoke in a hushed voice, calling from Miami, Langley, wherever he might happen to be at the moment. "You must listen, and listen carefully! Your wife is a KGB agent."

"Marina—"

"There *is* no Marina. The actual name of the woman living with you is believed to be Alexandrovna Medvedeva. Marina is her 'legend.' She married you so as to come to America as a spy."

Lee felt dizzy. "But ... we have a baby ..."

"All part of the KGB's master plan. I know this must hurt. Hurt terribly! That's not why I'm telling you. From now on, be ultra-careful what you say in front of her. Understand?"

"I understand," Lee gasped, "that my marriage is a sham."

I'm her … patsy!

"Continue as if nothing has changed. She must not know that you know. Keep a close eye on her, watch for anything suspicious she may say or do. But act as if everything is just as it was."

Lee hung up. He sat on a dilapidated wicker chair on the porch for several hours, staring into space. Then he heard the baby crying inside. Marina would give the child a bottle and that would shut June up. Moments later, the sobbing halted.

"Lee?" Marina called. "Where are you?"

"Here," he said softly, re-entering. Marina, smiling, moved toward her husband, expecting an embrace. Instead, he fell into a rage and beat her. She screamed for mercy, but when Marina fell to the floor Lee came over on top of the terrified woman and kicked her twice. Hard.

I won't be your fall-guy. I won't! Or anyone's …

Then he strolled to the refrigerator, took a can of beer, and sat down on a stuffed chair. Lee guzzled the brew, muttering to himself while she attempted to rise up from the floor.

*

Several days later, De Mohrenschildt and his wife Jeanne, having learned of the incident via a frantic phone call from Marina, drove to the Oswalds' in their chic convertible, doing so during the day, while Lee remained at work. De Mohrenschildt told Marina to pack her clothes, take hold of baby June, and come with them at once.

Twenty minutes later they arrived at a pleasant, spacious home in Farmers Branch, an upper-middle class Dallas suburb. Here lived Henry C. Bruton, with whom De Mohrenschildt had cultivated a friendship half a year earlier. He had managed this by charming the serious-minded, level-headed retired admiral's giddy wife, impressed as so many upper-middle-class Americans are with aristocratic Europeans. He now begged Mrs. Bruton (her husband was away on business) to allow this beaten woman and her child to remain there for the time being.

The well-intentioned lady took one look at this child-woman and the poor baby resting in Marina's arms and readily agreed.

Perfect! I'll be in their home, the home of former director of Naval Communications; the man who not long ago reorganized the global system which the U.S. Navy employs to choreograph the movements of submarines, battleships, aircraft carriers, jets, even nuclear missile bases. Information the KGB hungers for!

"When your husband returns," Marina said, having picked up some everyday usage of English, "I hope he won't mind—"

So I will play the dear, abused 'adopted-daughter' figure, with access to this home while the admiral is off in Richardson. I will discover Bruton's copy of the codes and relay them to the embassy in Washington, the information then going from there to Moscow. I will alter the course of history, thanks to my natural gifts: my beautiful face, this perfect body, and a brilliant brain.

"You let me take care of him. Make yourself at home."

If all of this works out as I believe it will, Lee Harvey Oswald can crawl off and fuck himself for all I care. And if not then I can always take him back for the sake of our baby.

"I hardly knew my own mother. Oh, can I consider you my mother? That would be so wonderful."

Either way ... I win! Me. 'Marina' ...

"What the name of God do you think you're doing?"

The small group in the Brutons' living room had become so intense in their discussion they did not realize someone stood at the screen door. Lee: unshaven, his hair slicked back in a retro-1950s greaser style, wearing a dirty T-shirt, jeans, and cowboy boots. He slammed the door open and entered, like an angry beast. A skinny real-life incarnation of Stanley Kowalski, Tennessee Williams' brute likewise hailing from New Orleans.

A Streetcar Named Desire one more film Lee had loved.

"We thought it best for Marina if we—"

De Mohrenschildt didn't have an opportunity to finish before Lee grabbed Marina's left arm and pulled the woman, her baby cradled in the right, out onto the street.

"I know what's best for my wife! You all stay out of it."

Shit! My idiot of a husband had to show up and ruin all these carefully laid plans. In only a few days I'd have—

*

Back to the apartment on Mercedes Street in Fort Worth. But if De Mohrenschildt had failed to slip his new protégée into the home of a recently retired Naval officer, he had but begun his mission to bring the Oswalds to Dallas, What De Mohrenschildt didn't know was that the CIA understood what he was up to, planning to manipulate his manipulation for their own good.

George had contacted J. Walter Moore, top CIA operative in the Dallas area. George instructed him to approach Lee directly about this upcoming attempted abduction. As the Company hoped to set a trap and snare both De Mohrenschildt and Marina, such a move was as imperative to "our side" as to "theirs." Moore's message was clear. When De Mohrenschildt visited the Oswalds a few days later, acting as if the incident at the Bruton's home never occurred, again encouraging Lee to take a better job and relocate, Lee played his role and agreed, saying it was all for Marina's sake. Still bruised and battered, she came alongside her husband and kissed him gently.

"It's set, then? Wonderful. I'll make the arrangements."

Asshole! While Marina is spying on me, I'll be spying on her. In Japan, I learned the oldest of Asian curses: May you get your heart's deepest desire. That's about to happen to you, my phony-aristocratic 'friend.' And you will pay dearly for it!

The Oswalds would live at the home of De Mohrenschildt's daughter and her husband for the time being. This would allow him to keep them under constant surveillance. Only it didn't work out that way. While Marina did move in with the Taylors, Lee insisted, for reasons he would not explain, on taking an apartment of his own. Also, he set up a post office box so that his mail would not have to pass through others' hands.

Lee did, however, allow De Mohrenschildt's influential friends to arrange for a job at Jaggers Chiles-Stovall, one of Dallas' largest typesetting firms, located downtown. There Lee used his photographic skills to create layouts for varied advertising displays.

"Hey, Lee. Very good work. We're lucky to have found you."

Shortly, however, Lee noticed that Jaggers did other jobs, too, including projects for the U.S. military. Here, those raw pictures taken by U2 surveillance planes of the Russian terrain were transformed into accurate maps that could then be used to pinpoint Soviet military and industrial locations. Though these were supposed to be kept Top Secret, Jaggers contracted for this work only if they guaranteed the military brass such stuff would be considered Confidential, clearly that wasn't the case.

Important papers were left out in the open, spread across desks, the company clearly lax. Their attitude must have been: Come on, we're all good Americans here. Right?

Okay, I'm beginning to get it. De Mohrenschildt is a Soviet spy. So far as he knows, I'm still on their side, having never renounced my Marxist beliefs. He will ask me to photograph those maps and turn the pictures over to him so he can relay them to the U.S.S.R. Then they will know how much the U.S. knows.

My guess is, George will want me to go along with this.

"So that's why De Mohrenschildt wanted you in Dallas so badly. Strong 'check' move on his part. Here's how we'll 'check-mate' him. Alter the 'legend' again. Start expressing second thoughts about Russia. Maybe you were too hard on the system. You're thinking maybe it's time to reconsider, arrange for you, Marina, and June to go back. Make sure De Mohrenschildt hears this."

"Listen, before you hang up, one other thing. While in the darkroom, and using the film drying machine, I noticed something else. In addition to the Soviet Union, a large number of the U2 photos appearing daily now feature images of Cuba."

"Huh! The military didn't tell us about *that.* Maybe they think there are secrets too secret even to share with the CIA."

"Well, I thought you ought to know. Lots of Cuban place-names. It appears they're constructing concrete bunkers in hidden enclaves. My take? They're installing some sort of electronic equipment in the eastern area near San Cristobal."

A long pause at the other end. Then: "The Cubans aren't sophisticated enough for that. My guess? The Russians are in this up to their necks. What we feared most: Soviets in Cuba."

"Creating observation posts to detect our U2 flights?"

"Could be even worse than that. Missile launchers, atomic warheads pointed directly at the U.S."

"Oh, shit. Just a hop, skip and a jump south of Florida? What a terrible advantage that would give them if war—"

"Can you re-photograph all the Cuban stuff, send it on directly to me? We'll then get it to the president."

"Of course. Maybe that'll repair things between Kennedy and the Company after that ugly mess at Bay of Pigs."

"Maybe. I don't know. I don't trust him, ever since he laid the blame for that fiasco on us. I gotta say, though, Lee, who I do trust. You! You've proven yourself our very best operative."

This time, a pause at Lee's end. "Thank you!"

"One last thing. It would be opportune for us to know what sort of information De Mohrenschildt already possesses. You ready to put some of your expert marine training into effect?"

A week later, De Mohrenschildt left Dallas for a three-day business trip. As always, he remained mum about precisely where he was headed, even to his wife Jeanne. To keep her mind off any growing concerns, repressing her fear that she might be married to a traitor, Jeanne flew off to New York for upscale shopping.

When De Mohrenschildt returned, he knew at once that the papers in his office were not in the same arrangements he had left them. Reports about his expedition to Mexico and Central America had clearly been marked in pencil. This had to mean that someone slipped in, photographed everything, those half-erased pencil marks employed to focus a camera.

The CIA did this! Lee Harvey Oswald can't be ruled out. These are the very kinds of skills I was going to ask him to employ in copying maps at Jaggers for us. Might he be a triple threat? If so, he and I have more in common than I realized.

*

Lee broke and entered De Mohrenschildt's home under orders from George. Shortly, he would attempt a more serious crime on his own. To a degree Lee's appetite for blood had been whetted by the killing of that taunting marine in the South Pacific. Then he had been involved in personal revenge on a bully.

Now, another plan took form, one he knew George would not approve of. Lee devised a plan to assassinate an American military officer. Slowly, the idea developed in his unique mind.

"Lee? What's wrong?" In the wee small hours of the morning, Marina emerged from a deep sleep, filled with nightmares.

She had been drawn to consciousness by a realization that her husband sat, rather than laying beside her. She could feel his intensity, smell his cold sweat, sense the wild emotions now possessing him. On some level she realized that, for at least a moment, performance was no longer the order of the day.

"Nothing's wrong," Lee whispered. "Everything's right. I understand now what I was born to achieve."

"What?" she asked, rising up naked from beneath the sheets. Marina seized the shivering youth in her arms.

Whoever she is, whatever her name may be ... at this moment, I so want to believe her love for me is sincere ...

"I must assassinate an enemy of the people," Lee confided.

He felt as she did. George's words of warning about her true status, their marriage a charade, mattered not a whit, to him or to her. They were man and woman in the most primal sense.

Come morning, all of that might be lost, dawn's light bringing reality back into play. At this moment, they existed in near-darkness, the black enormity cut by moonlight, sneaking through the window, carrying lunacy into their shadow-world.

"What?" Marina gasped, cradling Lee like a child, he as much a baby for the moment as June. "Have you gone mad?"

They were in Dallas now, together again, at the apartment in an old house on Elsbeth Street in Oakcliff, a Tudor-style building with handsome brick which Lee rented for $68 a month.

A month later, they would move to yet another apartment, a mere two blocks away, on Neely Street, a considerably downscale piece of property with shingles falling off its façade and a strange smell in the hallways. This would mark their eleventh residence in less than half a year.

She sensed that her husband, for reasons unclear to her, perhaps even to him, now repeated the pattern of his youth.

"How can I tell you anything?" he sobbed. "I know you are not who you claim to be. Marina is only a myth."

She drew Lee down on the bed, crawling over on top.

"Forgive me," she cried, her words emanating from some deep space inside her, from the heart, not the head, as she had no control over their flow. "It's true. Can you forgive me, Lee?"

"Yes, and I'm truly sorry I hit you. I was so shocked—"

"I understand. The sense of betrayal you must have felt—"

"But I betrayed you, too. Pretending to be what I was not."

Her mouth shushed him with kisses. "Listen to me. None of that matters now. Not who you were, or are. Me neither. At this moment, we are man and woman, husband and wife. Nothing matters but the two of us. Not country, not values, not politics—"

"How I wish I could believe that."

"Believe it!" She then proceeded to fuck him in a way that Lee had never been fucked before. This was not pleasure-fucking or power-fucking; not ego-fucking, fantasy-fucking, manipulative fucking, mercy-fucking, or procreation-fucking. Not any kind of fucking other than the purest fucking that exists, fucking which is instinctual rather than conscious. Their fucking alternately gentle and crude. Fucking that felt creative, fucking as the world's original art form, long before humankind diverted such passion into philosophy, painting, poetry. They fucked as if their lives depended on how hard each could fuck the other.

Neither fucked for him or herself, only for the mate. They fucked their brains out. Their hearts, souls, and bodies, too. They fucked until they couldn't fuck anymore. Then they fucked some more. They fucked until the sensuality of fucking gave way to something far more profound. Spiritual, even.

They fucked as ancient Celts fucked, in the moonlight. Fucking as a form of worship to some dark pre-Judeo-Christian goddess. Fucking not as civilized religions perceive fucking, as original sin; rather, as a form of prayer, a full surrender to nature within the self as a means of absolutely surrendering to the greater, outer nature around them. They said nothing to one another the entire time, for that would have broken the spell.

They fucked as a means of communication that eons earlier preceded language; a primitive, pure means of revealing all to another person. And when, finally, they finished fucking, each felt born again. Their lives would start over; a clean slate.

259

"From now on," Marina whispered into Lee's ear, "it's you and me against the world."

"I knew that before you told me."

"Of course you did."

"This is real, then?"

"As real as it gets. As real as it can ever be."

"They can't beat us. Not now that we have each other."

"We do, don't we? We didn't. Until tonight."

"Now, tell me what consumes you so. Your secret is safe with me. That was not true before. It is now. You must believe."

"I do! Marina ...if that is indeed your name ..."

"Shakespeare said: 'What's in a name? That which we call a rose by any other name would smell as sweet.'"

"So you're smart. And educated."

"Yes. From now on, I will always be the real me with you, whatever you choose to call me. Now, share the real *you*."

"Since I was little, I believed I had a special purpose in life. Never once did I feel normal, another ordinary person. I was an invisible man, worthless; or I had some higher function to perform. For me, there could be no in-between. Either Lee Harvey Oswald was nothing at all or a truly great man."

Marina gasped, sincerely weeping, "You are frightening me!" She held him tighter than before, as if his life, and her own, depended on her assuming the strength of an Earth Mother.

"I'm frightening myself," he answered, kissing her hair, cheeks, mouth. "I was born to take another man's life—"

"You'll go to jail," she cried. "Maybe be executed—"

"Not," he insisted, recalling Nietzsche, "if I truly am what I believe myself to be: beyond good and evil."

The Superman. A supreme being. Unrestricted by morality.

Not that I can't be wounded, even killed. Only that such a thing would not mark the end of Lee Oswald. Only the beginning.

*

If Dwight D. Eisenhower was the kindly Dr. Jekyll of those generals who commanded our military during World War II, then Edwin 'Ted' Walker provided his dark *doppelgonger,* an evil Mr. Hyde. Ike, according to those who worked with him, performed a spontaneous victory dance after learning that President Harry Truman would follow through on the late Franklin Delano Roosevelt's decision to integrate the military and begin the end of racism in society; Ted, as members of his command recall, spat.

He complied, only because as a general he could not disobey orders. A dozen years later, President Eisenhower put Walker in charge of the forced de-segregation of public schools in Little Rock, Arkansas. Again, the general followed his commands.

Eventually, Walker retired from the military in protest. As a civilian, and by entering politics, he could defend everything he held most dear: a white Protestant ruling class, lording it over what he referred to as "the mongrel races": blacks, Jews, Italians, Spanish, Asians, the Irish. Catholics constituted in his mind an "impure" breed of Christians.

"Hitler had the right idea," he told his supporters. "We can't put the ethnics in camps, this being America. But we sure ought to go back to the good ol' days when we didn't let them sit next to us on buses or use public toilets."

For Walker, the breaking point came when an Irish-Catholic was elected president of the United States. Ted could no longer take pride in saluting the flag. His anger turned to rage.

"We have to take our country back before it's too late," he howled. A small minority of Americans agreed with him.

When JFK announced that the army would be deployed to Mississippi in September, 1962, to assure an African-American, James Meredith, be admitted as student at the state university, Walker decried JFK represented an even more clear and present danger than Ike. This, despite JFK's secretive leadership in the attempt to overthrow Castro during the CIA led Bay of Pigs, and the president's upcoming face-off with Khrushchev over Russia's deployment of missiles in Cuba. Working from classified data referred to him by the CIA, these military secrets had been uncovered by a top agent working out of Dallas, Texas.

What did George say so long ago now? 'Keep this in mind, Lee: John Fitzgerald Kennedy will become the most important person in your life ...'

To a moral monster like Walker, none of this mattered. A common belief that all Americans ought to be equal, regardless of skin color, qualified Ike and JFK as part of the problem in Walker's patently racist mind.

"I only wish someone would shoot him," Walker confided to his closest friends about JFK. He dare not say something like this in public for fear of being branded a traitor ...

To Lee Harvey Oswald, a fervent supporter of Eisenhower's 1957 effort at desegregation and JFK's 1962 follow-up, such statements qualified Gen. Walker as an enemy of the people. If America were ever to move forward, become the great land it had the potential to be, such a fascist must be silenced.

Gradually, Lee had come to believe that this was the job he had been born for. Save JFK; save America. Kill Walker.

Without George or the CIA knowing anything. They likely wrote Walker off as a nut-case appealing only to extremists.

But that's how Hitler got started. Early on, no one took him *seriously. Then, when they finally did, it was too late. All those innocent lives lost! I know what people say: 'It can't happen here.' Well, I know better. It can, unless we stop it.*

Or, more correctly, unless I *stop it!*

*

On January 28, Lee—employing the alias 'A.J. Hidell'-—put in an order with Seaport Traders, in Los Angeles, for a .38-caliber Smith and Wesson revolver, the cost $29.95 plus postage and handling. Nine days later, the gun was delivered to his Elsbeth Street apartment.

In mid-March, a Mannlicher-Carcano rifle, complete with state of the art telescopic sight, arrived for Lee, now living on West Neely, addressed to his alias.

"Lee? Are you going to take up hunting again?"

"In a manner of speaking, Marina."

Lee took to slipping out of the house late at night with his Imperial Reflex camera. When he arrived for work at the photographic lab the following day he carried along with him undeveloped rolls of film. In the evening, he returned with blow-ups of an alley behind some stately house in the Turtle Creek section of Dallas.

Marina begged to know what was going on. Lee insisted that he trusted her completely now. They truly were man and wife. Now and forever. But she was safer not knowing.

"If what you say is true, I ought to know everything."

"I can't and won't endanger you."

On March 31 Lee, dressed entirely in black. He cradled his new rifle, the pistol worn on his hip as a Western cowboy might position it, holding in his free hand copies of Red newspapers, *The Worker* and *Militant*. Lee instructed Marina to take his camera from the kitchen table and requested that she accompany him into their narrow back-yard. There, Lee raised the rifle and, offering his signature sneer, insisted that Marina snap pictures.

"What for?" she dared ask.

"Posterity."

On April 5, while General Walker traveled on a fund-raising tour to fund his anti-equality-for-ethnics political campaigns, Lee took his rifle, positioned himself in the alley behind the general's mansion-like home, and stared through the telescopic sight into Walker's office. There he general often sat alone.

"Where are you going?" Marina whispered as he left.

262

"Target practice," Lee laughingly replied.

When he returned, the gun was gone. Marina so wanted to believe Lee had abandoned it. More likely, he hid the piece for future use. She couldn't sleep, thought about calling the police for Lee's own good. If she did that, he would never forgive her.

He demands total loyalty. I cannot deny him this.

On April 10, Marina headed over to the home of one Ruth Paine, another Russian émigrés, living in Irving, for a visit. As the two conversed, Marina burst into tears and threw herself into the stunned woman's arms. When Ruth asked if Lee were abusing her again, Marina offered a surprising retort: "I only wish it were that!" When Ruth attempted to learn more, Marina refused to continue, though she wept uncontrollably.

When at last the tears subsided, Ruth suggested that Marina leave Lee and move in with her. Marina agreed to consider that. She also mentioned that she had been thinking about a return to Russia for herself and baby June.

"And ... Lee?"

"That is yet to be determined."

Marina truly did love Lee now. But she had to put her baby first, all dreams of romantic adventures in espionage long gone. As an acceptable holding pattern she'd remain in Irving, thereby removing herself from Lee's immediate presence without actually deserting him. That was the best Marina could do for now.

"Yes, Ruth. June and I will move in with you at once."

This explains why Marina was not at home when Lee returned from work Wednesday, April 10. Confused, he scrawled:

> If I am apprehended by the police tonight, or killed by them, or am forced to flee without seeing you and the baby one last time, send any information as to what happens to me to the Soviet embassy in Washington. Newspaper clippings, any hard-copy that you can locate. As you know, The Red Cross in Russia serves the secret police. They can help you!

At nine p.m. precisely, General Walker, having returned home the previous day, sat at his desk before the half-open window, preparing his income taxes. A bullet tore through the glass, past his left ear, into the rear wall. The plaster there exploded, shards flying over Walker, leaving the general white-washed. He, utterly unaware of the irony here, sat motionless, not believing this had happened.

Seconds later, he regrouped, leaped up, and called the police. They arrived shortly and thoroughly searched the area but the would-be assassin was long gone, and without a trace.

I had him in my sights. Even a lousy shot such as I could not miss at that range, not with a telescopic site. So how did it happen? Blame Dostoevsky, the existential issues he raised in Crime and Punishment. *Does any person have the right to take another man's life, even for the good of humanity?*

While I don't necessarily accept that such a thing is wrong I'm not altogether certain I can live with it. Something in my subterranean self rose in opposition against my conscious intent and caused me to blink. Alright, that's over and done with.

I can't change the past. But if push ever comes to shove again— if I ever have to kill a man I consider evil to do good for humanity— then Dostoevsky be damned, I will shoot true!

One of the many films Lee had watched on TV in his youth was titled *Man Hunt*. Released to theatres in 1941, after America entered the war, it was written and filmed before that occurred. The story concerned a rogue male, played by Walter Pidgeon, who sets out alone with his rifle, planning to assassinate Hitler.

Tripped up in his effort by unforeseen circumstances, he fails to accomplish his task. There are no regrets as to the attempt. "Millions of lives would be saved!" he insists.

"Millions of lives would be saved!" Lee told Marina when she returned home to pick up clothing and bid him farewell. He shivered with fear, answering her hesitant question about what he'd been up to by admitting that only a little more than an hour earlier he had attempted to assassinate General Walker.

Unable to respond, she packed her bags, grabbed the baby, called a taxi and headed off the home of Ruth Paine.

"It is not that I love you less, Lee," she said while on her way out the door. "Only that I love our child more."

*

"Lee," De Mohrenschildt asked when he came to visit the following day, after the news reported an anonymous person had attempted to take Walker's life. "How did you miss?"

"First, how did you know it was me?"

"Who else?" De Mohrenschildt asked, extending his arms.

"In truth," Lee laughed, "I'm trying to understand that."

Lee never saw or spoke to De Mohrenschildt again. Nor did Lee have an opportunity to take a second shot at Walker. That night, George called him at home, obviously considering the situation too important to wait for the secret phone contact.

"Have you gone freakin' *crazy?*"

264

"Maybe I've finally come to my senses."

A long pause. "Do you want to continue as an agent?"

"More than anything in the world."

"Alright, then. I cannot allow you to remain in Dallas if I believe you may be planning another attempt. Tomorrow, board a bus to New Orleans. There's work that needs to be done there."

"Is that an order?"

"Yes. Listen, Lee. I hate racism, too. We all of us do. But that's not our primary concern at the moment."

"It's *every* decent man's primary concern. *Always!*"

"Yes, yes. But we have another big job coming up and you are the one to handle it. See you in the Big Easy."

Alone, missing his wife and baby daughter, Lee spent his last night in Dallas sipping beer and crying over old Sinatra records. One song, called "The House I Live In," referred to the U.S. itself, those many wonderful 'rooms' open to its citizens, each some aspect of our abundance of riches. Lee appreciated the final line: "Most of all, *the people*, that's America to me!"

Me, too! As always, you speak directly to me.

In its purest form, that's what Marxism is all about. Trying to achieve the most good for the largest amount of ordinary, everyday people. I hear you, Frankie. I get it.

This led Lee to reconsider the current president, John Fitzgerald Kennedy, if for no other reason than that Sinatra had campaigned for JFK. For the longest time, Lee had taken George's word on anything and everything at face value. That included JFK. Up until Bay of Pigs, JFK was considered to be a wild card; no one in the CIA seemed certain as to what this new president might do next. Initially they supported him, as JFK did appear to clearly favor them over the FBI.

Then came the Bay of Pigs, a turning point in the relationship between the president and the Company.

That's when everything swiftly headed south, for JFK and the CIA figuratively. Now, for Lee Harvey Oswald. Literally.

CHAPTER SEVENTEEN:
LONG NIGHT'S JOURNEY INTO DAY

"No good deed ever goes unpunished."
—Clare Booth Luce

A man of quiet confidence, yet one who well understood that things can always go wrong, Richard M. Bissell, Jr. spent most of that mid-April weekend in 1961 seated in his office, waiting for the phone to ring. Knowing that when it did and he received reports from the front line of combat in an undeclared (and, if Bissell's plan worked, invisible) war he'd ring up JFK and share the news, good or bad. Considering Dick Bissell's mixed feelings about JFK, he hoped and prayed all had gone well.

Also, Bissell would stay in touch with Adlai Stevenson in New York. Our ambassador to the United Nations had in Bissell's mind been one of the thornier elements in this affair. From day one Bissell, feared that what he condescendingly referred to as The Egghead Factor could prove the loose screw in an otherwise perfectly functioning machine that he had carefully constructed.

In anticipation of this, and following full authorization from his boss, CIA director Allen W. Dulles, who had spoken of this briefly with JFK, Bissell sent a top Outfit representative, Tracy Barnes, flying off for an unannounced visit to Stevenson's office along Manhattan's East River. This occurred a week and a half before the Bay of Pigs invasion began. Barnes knew what Bissell had told him, which was what Dulles had said to Bissell; JFK, to Dulles: Get Stevenson behind this. We need him!

"Make certain Stevenson grasps that what he says or does not say will likely determine the manner in which the world perceives America for the remainder of the 20th century."

However much of a liberal, however huge Stevenson's moral conscience, however sincere his desire to be the most honest man in politics since Abe Lincoln, this came down to what was best not for Adlai but his country. Would he swallow hard and agree?

"He's a Democrat. He ought to be loyal to his party and the sitting president."

"Stevenson is loyal to America first, to his own sense of democracy second, and to his integrity third. Here's what you need to consider to understand him. Adlai once claimed that communism is a corruption of our human dream for justice. He understands that democracy, American style, with all its flaws, offers our best hope. He's a realist, not an idealist."

"That quote will serve as a key to my unlocking him."

"Yes? Well here's another. Though Adlai may be a registered Democrat, deep down he wishes that he could have remained as an independent. As he has claimed, that's someone who wants to take the politics out of politics."

"If JFK is the career politician personified, then Adlai rates as a true statesman."

"'A politician is a statesman who approaches every question with an open mouth,' according to Stevenson."

"Explaining why Jack won the presidency and Adlai lost."

"Twice."

"And why he would've lost a third time, even to a sleaze like Nixon, had he chosen to run again the last time around."

"Ask the public what they most want in a president and they say 'sincerity.' Yet the moment a candidate reveals himself to be unbendingly sincere, his candidacy is dead in the water."

"That defines the distinction between devout political ideals and the realities of politics?"

"The distinction and also the irony. The terrible reason why cynics win elections."

"Which, as any professional pol will tell you, is what the people most complain about: abject cynicism."

"It is in the American character to claim to hate that."

"Yes. And in our character to vote for it every time."

*

The official line had long held that Stevenson knew nothing about the recruitment and training of Cuban exiles down south in Miami. Then again, only a blind, deaf oaf could possibly have remained oblivious to much of what took place in broad daylight. Deeply concerned about the emergence of what he'd been the first to negatively dismiss as 'cowboy diplomacy,' Stevenson months earlier called the White House in a panic to set up a meeting.

"I know how busy Mr. Kennedy is. But I must see him!"

"Very well, Mr. Ambassador. I'll try my best."

A year and a half following Eisenhower's '56 re-election, Ike's second victory over Democratic candidate Adlai Stevenson, things no longer ran quite so evenly in the country. The economy faltered; experts began employing the dreaded 'r' word, fearing a deep recession. As a result, mainstream people were no longer happy. This could only benefit the next democratic presidential nominee. He would run against what could now be posited as a disappointing Republican administration. If, as most everyone assumed, Richard Nixon, Ike's V.P. for eight years, became that party's standard bearer, the man's unpleasantness could aid the Democrats. Do you really want eight more years of the same? And with a man you would not want to buy a used car from?

We can offer you a New Frontier!

From the moment JFK appeared on the scene, young people embraced the possibility that Stevenson's values might at last be actualized by this charismatic newcomer. Many loyal Dems hoped, trusted, requested that following the election, JFK appoint Stevenson as Secretary of State. That didn't happen. A younger man, Dean Rusk, won that spot. Now an elder statesman, Adlai instead received the honor of being named our ambassador to the United Nations, headquartered in York City.

Those rock-ribbed Republicans and right wing extremists, desperate to return to the old Fortress America attitudes that dated back to before the World War I, would quote our first president out of context: "Our country should avoid all foreign entanglements!" The most extreme among these were residents of the rural south and far west. There, a logo appeared not only on lapel buttons and bumper stickers but painted across the solid rock of high-reaching cliffs: "U.S. OUT of U.N.!"

Somehow, such citizens must be persuaded to accept that America could no longer exist as an island of democracy when political seas had grown turbulent and complex. Such waves splashed Third World problems up against America's shores.

Who better for that job than honest Adlai?

Part of the reason JFK had been elected, despite a rigid Catholic background which made some heartland types nervous, was that he'd cultivated a Teddy Roosevelt image: intellectual Rough Rider, a man not only of articulate words but also bold deeds.

"You know," the President said as they sat across from each other in the Oval Office, sipping coffee, "when he couldn't slip off to golf, Ike used to take his mind off The Cold War by coming in here and reading Zane Grey novels."

"I'm aware, Mr. President, that Ike liked cowboy stories."

"I do, too. Except I find those books awfully dated."

"In all honesty? I don't read them."

JFK grinned, knowing how much Stevenson enjoyed the serious novels of John Updike and John Cheever, as well as other acute observers of everyday upscale American life.

"No, I didn't imagine you would. Personally, I like light reading. The frontier spirit, that sort of thing."

"In truth, Mr. President, isn't that more myth than reality? As someone who enjoys books on history, I know—"

"Yes, yes. I'm sure you can rattle off all the facts, Adlai. I read history, too, you know. But I'm also a man of the people. And do you know where the masses get their ideas?"

Stevenson swallowed hard. "On the six o'clock news?"

JFK smiled while shaking his head 'no.' "At the movies. And from popular fiction, which more often than not gets turned into movies. Have you seen any good movies lately, Adlai?"

Why are we talking about trashy books and Hollywood films? I came here to ... oh, I get it. He's tooling me. Of course. I can feel it. The Kennedy charm. He's as charismatic as a movie star and knows it. And he uses it to his own purpose.

"Truthfully, Mr. President, I'd rather talk about—"

"We will, Adlai." About to close in for the kill, JFK smiled sweetly. "And, please, call me Jack. My friends do."

Adlai found himself capitulating. "I appreciate that."

"As do I! I want to thank you for being a loyal friend, a loyal Democrat. And, most of all, a loyal American."

"I do try, sir."

"You do more than try. You get the job done. Now, you see, I have an extremely important job that must shortly be done."

Please, God, let me be strong!

"I know. That's why I so needed to come here today."

"Of course. So now let's discuss whatever you wish."

*

That conversation took place three months prior to the attack, first by air and then sea to land, on Cuba. One week before what those in the know referred to as D-Day II, Tracy Barnes arrived in New York City to confer with Stevenson. His mission: Seal the deal JFK had initiated. Barnes was what all in D.C. circles referred to as 'a good soldier': entirely committed, earnest, dependable.

On April 13, radio announcers reported Manhattan's weather as 'overcast'; dark gray skies above, a slight hint of sunshine occasionally cutting through, hinting at spring. Stevenson stood by his window at the United Nations building in Manhattan's Turtle Bay area, peering down at pedestrians strolling East 42nd Street. Most were at best only vaguely aware of international

269

problems raised within this stately building, constructed some thirteen years earlier. How deeply he cared about such people!

And how fiercely he wanted to believe the current president felt for those ordinary, naïve, decent folks as he did.

"We in Washington have an inkling," Barnes stated, seated and gazing at Stevenson's back, "that a considerable number of Cuban democrats will attempt to retake their country. Some reports suggest it could occur in days. We don't know that for certain. Some of us, myself included, believe it will. If so, my guess is, this will begin late Friday or early Saturday and be all over by Monday. At that time, Castro will be dead."

Momentarily, Stevenson stood as still as the proverbial statue. Barnes worried this man he had patently lied to—lied by omitting that CIA agents would direct the mission while the sea-to-land invasion would be launched from U.S. Naval vessels—might suffer a major stroke. Barnes was about to hurry over, sincerely concerned, when the silver-haired ambassador suddenly spun around.

To Barnes' shock, Stevenson looked to have been crying. "Tell me precisely what it is you want of me," he gasped.

"Mr. Stevenson, please." Not incapable of empathy, Barnes' heart went out, touched by this man's vulnerable appearance and his threatened tone of voice. "You sound as if I'm Old Scratch himself, here to steal away your immortal soul."

"Ha!" Not the sort to laugh out loud, Adlai shocked Barnes with his unexpected outburst. "You nailed that one."

"Oh, Mr. Ambassador. Please ..."

Barnes cautiously rose and stepped forward. He'd had some brief contacts with this man in the past and respected him.

"Please, what?"

"Mr. Ambassador, please keep in mind that, though there will be blood, all of this—if in fact it does happen—will absolutely lead to a greater good for everyone."

"Sir, I do not doubt the nobility of your intentions."

"Thank you! So—"

"Who claimed that the road to hell is lined with them?"

"I ... can't recall."

"No matter, only that it was said."

"Sir. We must do what we think is right—"

"Don't tell me!" Incredible, but Adlai actually appeared angry, an emotion he had not seemed capable of. "I know. Because you ... me ... *we* ... are 'the good guys.'"

Without hesitation, Barnes replied: "Precisely."

"But you see," Stevenson continued, abruptly turning away, "I'm not certain I believe in good guys anymore. Or bad-guys. I did once. Back during the war. Surely, Hitler was the monster. We, in ending his reign of terror, qualified as dragon-slayer."

"Even as Castro is now. White Knights are needed again."

Stevenson's eyebrows rose high, his mouth pursing. "Do you think so? Make no mistake about it, I'd love to believe what you say. And that by opposing the bad qualifies us as good. But ... let me be honest here ... lately, I do have my doubts."

What pitiable eyes this man has, Barnes thought. *The opposite of JFK's. JFK reduces you to rubble with a glance. This poor bastard? His eyes offer a wide-open window into the world of his soul.*

Barnes honestly regretted what he had to do next. Still, he did his job. "No question Castro spells bad news for the U.S."

"Perhaps because we made him that way?"

"I can't answer that, Mr. Ambassador. In all honesty, I really don't know that you're wrong there."

"So ..."

"What I *do* know: What's past, right or wrong, is past—"

"Don't tell me," Adlai interrupted. "That was then; this, now. God, how I *hate* that expression."

"People use it all the time these days."

"I wish they wouldn't. It sets aside any commitment to authentic, meaningful, ongoing standards."

"Still, we live in the present tense. We are Americans. Like any nation, we must put our own survival first."

"Which means bringing down Castro?"

"That's a bit harsh. Let's say, rather, we will stand aside and allow our Cuban allies, those who love us and hate him, to accomplish that task for us. Do you have a problem with *that?*"

What followed marked the longest pause in the conversation. "I ... do not. I know people will die. But that's the way of the world. If the Cubans can accomplish this by themselves—"

"Wonderful! That's all I need to—"

"I wasn't finished! Will you give me your assurance, your absolute word of honor, that the United States will not, through either military or para-military units, assume any active role?"

"I absolutely promise you we will not," Barnes lied.

Fuck! This is one rough job. But somebody has to do it.

Stevenson stared hard into Barnes's eyes, trying to grasp whether the man were telling the truth. "You are here, I assume, as a representative of the president, the State Department, and the CIA?" he asked.

"That is correct."

"As a member of that organization, can you swear to me, and in so doing imply the honor of Dulles—John and Allen, for that matter—and the president, that this 'operation' as you call it will be entirely managed and carried out by anti-Castro Cubans?"

Barnes was too savvy to hesitate: "I can tell you that is absolutely the case," he lied. Not wanting any slack in the exchange to allow Stevenson a moment to reconsider, Barnes continued his barrage. Cubans would fly from abandoned airfields. No U.S. representatives would be involved. We would do nothing but wish them luck. If they fail. Too bad. But if they should win, so much the better.

Stevenson had to curb a desire to snicker, though cynicism was not a natural emotion for such a man of integrity. "What's a man to do?" he suddenly asked, shaking.

"The right thing."

"Ah. But how do we know what that is?"

Out of respect for Stevenson, Barnes could manipulate him no more. He replied: "That, as they say on TV, Mr. Ambassador, is the 64,000 dollar question."

A minute later Barnes was gone, leaving Adlai alone in his office, sobbing. The ambassador prayed he'd been told the truth.

If he gained any inkling that was not the case, he'd remain loyal to his basic values despite whatever the next days might bring. He rolled this whole thing over in his mind, returning to the conversation he'd had with Kennedy three months earlier.

*

JFK had segued back to where their discussion began; Ike and his beloved Zane Grey novels, those potboiler Westerns lowbrows read. Mostly, as JFK had mentioned offhand, these centered around a cowboy named 'Lassiter.' The man with one name. A foreboding stranger who rides into town and cleans it up, then drifts on to his next bold act.

"Funny, how heroes come and go. Today, I'd imagine only older people, from Ike's generation, reach for those books." JFK opened his desk drawer and pulled out a paperback, tossing it to his guest. "Have you read this?"

Confused, Adlai perused the cover. *Casino Royale*, its title announced. Below that, the image of a menacing looking man—suave, surly, self-possessed—cradled a Baretta. This threatening character wore a perfectly tailored suit. On either side stood a beautiful woman, both in skimpy bikinis. One blonde, the other brunette. Each leggy lady assumed a stance at once regal and servile, a pair of queens conquered.

272

All three were situated on a beach in Bermuda or perhaps the Cayman Islands. On the cover's bottom, the author's name appeared in blood red type: Ian Fleming. Adlai flipped to the first page, where the headline read: "licensed to kill!"

JFK chuckled. "No, I don't imagine you have. Anyway, I enjoy them. I believe this, or maybe one of the others in the series—they've become extremely popular during the last year, though written some time ago—will soon become a major film."

"From what I can see it looks a bit risqué for Hollywood."

"My guess? What they can and can't do in movies is about to change. The thing is: this James Bond chap, in my mind, rates as the contemporary equivalent of the old-timers like Lassiter. Instead of plodding along through sagebrush on a horse, he zips across the continent in an Aston Martin. Kills not in a fair gunfight but without compunction. Or mercy. Enjoys lovely women, without feeling any need to make a serious commitment."

My God, the president is describing himself. *JFK gets his notion of who he is from such books. Or already had a vision of a* Playboy *President and, when he came in contact with this Fleming fellow's novels, crystallized his own self-image.*

Either way, James Bond and Jack Kennedy are one and the same. And he's the most powerful man in the world ...

"Take the book with you. Read it. Tell me what you think."

*

They had not spoken since, either in person or over the phone. But Stevenson had read the novel while waiting at the airport for his shuttle. What he encountered horrified him even as it must have earlier enthralled the president. Here was an entirely amoral saga about a nasty sadist, not only willing but eager to inflict death. And, before death, considerable pain on any enemies. These included many of the women he bedded.

"Oh, I've been meaning to read that!"

Stevenson had been drawn out of his cerebral reverie by a young stewardesses standing nearby. Pert and pretty in a fresh new uniform, the girl embodied her profession as presented in TV advertisements: "Come fly with me!" a fresh blonde sky-girl suggestively beckoned to viewers in airline commercials.

"You look too sweet," Stevenson mumbled, knowing she had no idea who he was, "to indulge in such trash."

"Oh, I don't know," she winked. "I like to be a little daring, at least when I'm at home reading. Or at the movies."

A beautiful woman is one you notice. A charmer is one who notices you. This girl is a charmer.

Doubtless she'd go see that film JFK had mentioned when released. She and millions like her. And, as movies always do to the masses, the James Bond film would condition this girl, and others in the audience, to think that operating as a reckless airborne cowboy, utterly amoral, in the early Sixties, has recently become acceptable.

"Here, you're welcome to this copy."

He handed her the book. Might as well save her thirty-five cents. What would she say if he told her this was the very copy that our sexy young president read? Doubtless she voted for him, whatever her political allegiances. Because JFK rated as *cool.*

Suddenly, Adlai Stevenson felt very old and very tired.

*

In New York City, Dr. Jose Miro Cardona, head of the Cuban Revolutionary Council (despite its title, a fervently *pro*-U.S. group) called a press conference to offer a statement. In exalted language, Cardona praised what had been referred to as a three-man-defection, the words that the Cuban who had flown from Nicaragua to Miami had employed, as a "heroic blow for Cuban freedom." He explained that he'd known about the scheme for some time.

"The Council has been in contact with these brave pilots" daily, offering advice as to the upcoming event, he insisted.

Further, Cardona claimed, he had days earlier suggested to the flyers that if anything untoward occurred, they ought to consider Miami as their alternative destination.

This address was carried over the radio, allowing Bissell to breathe a sigh of relief and, momentarily, relax in his D.C. office, feet up on the desk, praying for more good news.

Instead, the voice on his radio reported that, shortly after the bombing of Havana subsided, Castro summoned Sergei M. Kudryavstsev, Soviet ambassador to Cuba, to his offices. Two armed Cuban guards arrived at Kudryavstev's residence, escorting him to a waiting military car. Once Kudryavstev, known to be a KGB member, arrived at headquarters, he and Castro jumped on the hot-line to Moscow to learn what information might already be available from that world capital. Once they listened to the Russians' report, the Beard contacted his Foreign Ministry.

Officials sent word to members of the foreign press corps stationed in Havana, as well as a handful of international reporters, to assemble. A spokesman announced that Cuba now had proof positive that, while members of the United States air force hadn't been aboard the planes which carried out those bombings, the strikes had been planned, orchestrated, "directed" (Castro's term) by the U.S. as if this were an action movie.

As millions of Americans listened, Stevenson included from his office, the radio reported Castro had as a result ordered Cuba's delegation to the United Nations to "directly accuse the U.S. government of aggression." A sudden sickening sensation, worse than an attack of flu, overcome Adlai as he heard the words from Havana, ricocheting and echoing all over the world.

Castro insisted that his "country, on a war basis, will resist" the ongoing attempt at American imperialism.

Desperate as to what he should do and say when his turn came to speak, Adlai reached for the phone and rang the Naval Air Station at Boca Chica. An operator answered. Grasping for some means of handling this in the minutes left to him, Adlai introduced himself as a 'reporter from a daily newspaper.' That was easy to pull off; in his youth, he had worked as one.

A five minute delay. Then, a gruff, hurried male voice answered: "Rear Admiral Rhodam Y. McElroy here."

"Hello, Admiral. I'm calling about what took place there earlier. Of course, we also wish to know more about the flyer who landed in Miami—"

"We're playing host to a passle of pro-American Cubans today!" Admiral McElroy chuckled. "Well, God love 'em."

"Yes, sir. Anyway, I was hoping you'd make a definitive statement about precisely what happened in Boca Chica."

"You can quote me: 'One of the stolen B-26s involved in those blasts against Havana this morning landed here.'"

"You are absolutely certain, sir, the plane took off from Cuba? And, after being hit, proceeded to your post?"

A long pause, the Admiral apparently mulling Adlai's words over and over again. Then: "I don't get your drift."

"I wanted to confirm: Are you *certain*?"

A longer pause. "Why shouldn't I be?"

"Well, with all due respect, why should you?"

Another pause, longer still, more awkward. "Because he told me so," McElroy snarled at the faux journalist.

"That's what I was driving at, Admiral. All we have to go on is that the man said so? No collaborating evidence?"

"No, *what?*" A string of raw expletives followed. "Let's just say, this guy strikes me as a good egg. How's that?"

"Well, I was listening to Fidel Castro's speech on Radio Havana. He claims that in actuality all the planes flew in from Nicaragua, departing there with full American cooperation."

Admiral McElroy's voice took on the quality of an angry John Wayne in some old World War II film. "Let me ask *you* a question: Who would you believe? Me, or Fidel Castro?"

With that, McElroy slammed down his phone.

*

An ugly debate, initiated by Ron Roa's spirited speech, raged throughout the United Nations that afternoon. An hour earlier, Roa had attempted to interrupt a General Assembly meeting to decry America's purported involvement. He'd been cut off by the man in charge, Ireland's Frederick H. Boland, who insisted that such a discussion couldn't proceed. The incident in Cuba did not appear on the morning's official printed agenda. Roa had to be quieted, removed if necessary by guards, so that the proper order of scheduled business might proceed.

At that point, Valerian Zorin of the Soviet Union rose, requesting a special meeting on the issue this very afternoon. Though Boland argued against this, the assembled body flipped out of control. Delegates howled that such a crisis was precisely why the U.N. had been created and that it ought to take precedence over the minutiae of everyday affairs, that Boland, visibly intimidated by the extreme response, had to agree.

All but shrieking, Roa called what had happened a "cowardly surprise attack" on his homeland, carried out by Cuban-born "mercenaries," assembled by the American government, trained in Miami "and Guatemala by experts working at the Pentagon and by members of the Central Intelligence Agency." Though Roa had to be considered an enemy of the United States, Adlai, listening in, sensed the absolute sincerity in this man's voice.

Roa then explained that the U.S. had added insult to injury by not only launching an attack but "cynically" offering a bold-faced lie that those bombs had been dropped by defectors. Roa tore into a fury about Dr. Cardona, insisting that he knowingly dissembled when claiming to have earlier been in contact with the defectors by phone. Roa added that even if Cardona told the truth here, his very speech violated U.S. neutrality laws.

At that moment, a brief recess was called to allow Adlai Stevenson time to reach the meeting hall. His long legs nearly failing him, the U.N. ambassador nervously headed down the corridor.

My moment of truth has arrived. And I still don't know what I will say, or not say. I won't, until I begin speaking ...

Honest Adlai. Even Republicans who opposed all the liberal values Stevenson and Kennedy stood for agreed that there was no question the former always spoke the truth as he saw it.

Do I serve the good of the country or my own reputation?

Listening intently in his own D.C. office, Bissell noted a hesitancy in Stevenson's voice he'd never noticed there before. Yes, two aircraft did land at Florida airports earlier, Adlai began, his phrasing uncharacteristically awkward.

"These pilots, and other crew members, have apparently defected from Cuba in defiance of Fidel Castro."

Damn it! Why stick 'apparently' in there? Either they did or they didn't. Come on, Adlai. You promised!

Hands waved all across the hall. Ambassadors shouted out questions until hoarse. Stevenson addressed them one by one.

"No United States personnel participated. No United States Government airplanes of any kind participated."

Better. 'No' means no, at least when Stevenson says so. Whatever, of course, the truth may be. But if people believe that Adlai speaks only the truth, now this is 'true.'

Even if happens to be the opposite of what had actually occurred.

"These two planes, to the best of our knowledge, were Castro's own air force planes. According to the pilots, they took off from Castro's own air-force fields."

'To the best of our knowledge?' But that leaves room for doubt. 'According to the pilots'? You're giving them just what we did not want them to hear—that we still only have their word to go on as to the escalating situation ... Fuck it, Adlai!

Apparently, as all listening gathered close to see, Adlai raised a photograph high for members of the Assembly. "I have here a picture of one of these planes. It has the markings of the Castro air force on its tail, which everyone can see for himself. The Cuban star and initials FAR are clearly visible."

Proof positive; seeing is believing. Okay, okay. We might just survive this God-forsaken ordeal. Stick to your guns ...

"Steps have been taken to impound the Cuban planes and they will not be permitted to take off."

With that, Stevenson waved off all further questions and, appearing faint, retired from the podium.

*

By the end of the third week in April, 1961, everyone in the world who followed the news was well aware not only that Honest Adlai had lied bold-faced but that everything Fidel Castro claimed was absolutely true. There had been no organic, spontaneous attempt at revolution in Cuba. All that occurred—the bombing of the country's airports, the invasion from sea—had been carried out, as Rosa had announced in the U.N., by the United States.

The most observant journalists, including some in the U.S., pointed out that the nine planes which had composed the squadron were not precisely the same model and make as those currently owned and operated by Cubans. Small details such as windshield shape and tail-size attested that these were similar but not identical. No question, the CIA had overseen everything.

The big issue now: *How high up did all of this reach?*

Previous to the pro-American Cubans landing, only to be massacred on the beaches before they could move up off the sand and into bushes on the rim, a new organization had been formed in the most clandestine quarters of Washington by men who knew they would shortly be held responsible for this fiasco. It would be known, in secret, as 'The 54/12 Group.' The 'club' cut across all pre-existing lines and venues; they hailed from the key information gathering communities, the military, and politics.

From day one, they believed that John Fitzgerald Kennedy, initially a wild card, now qualified as something more dangerous still: a loose cannon. That he could and likely would destroy all their careers was not, to men holding such values, the most horrific part. Far worse was his power, as president, to cripple the work they did, through strategy backed by force, to maintain world peace. Ultimately, though, what most motivated each was a commonly held belief that JFK posed a far greater danger to the country and the world than either Castro or Khrushchev.

JFK would do anything, they were now certain, say anything to further his own cause: The Kennedy Legacy. Which meant that not only they and their work were expendable. So too were the best interests of the U.S. That, they could not accept. This, for members of The 54/12 Group, constituted the final straw.

They knew J. Edgar gloated when JFK self-servingly went on TV and radio to damn the CIA for daring to try and pull off such an absurd mission without his say-so. And that, as a result, the president must now re-evaluate his support of The Company, decide whether it ought to be shut down. The FBI's old bulldog might, in the end, yet have the last laugh.

History provided JFK with his opportunity to redeem America's reputation and cement his own living-legend status a year and a half later, between October 8 and 14, 1962. Castro, nobody's fool, assumed that Bay of Pigs had merely been wave one; next time, the entire American military would come at him.

Until then Castro had been wary about accepting Russia as an ally, fearing they were no better than the U.S. He continued to accept weapons and rubles. Still: Let them, as Khrushchev tried to persuade Castro, move men and machinery onto Cuban soil?

Before you know it the Soviets will run the place! Castro turned down one offer after another from the Soviet Premiere.

That was then; this, now. After Bay of Pigs, that request took on new merit in terms of Castro's own survival. The fiasco of mid-April 1961, carried out as a means to keep any Russian nuclear warheads out of Cuba, proved a self-fulfilling prophecy.

Before that, Castro mis-trusted the Americans. Now? He came to openly loathe and secretly fear them. As for the Soviets? Fidel Castro expressed the same basic political philosophy as so many of his opponents: any enemy of my enemy is my friend.

Hey, Nikita: Come on down! With nuclear weapons for a deterrence, there will be no further attempts at invasion.

Only Castro underestimated JFK. Or, more correctly, failed to grasp how delicate JFK's position had become following the previous year's debacle. If the president hoped to regain his image as an intellectual warrior prince and win re-election in 1964, he had to talk tough. Stand firm. Be strong.

This time around he did just that. Dismissing the CIA, in his mind responsible for his current problems, JFK decided that now he would handle things himself, brother Bobby his only back-up.

If the missiles were not removed immediately JFK would, under auspices of the old but abiding Monroe Doctrine, assume Khrushchev declared war. Someone had to give; Nikita blinked.

The missiles were removed. JFK renewed his image as our young hero-president. Also redeemed, at least somewhat, was Adlai Stevenson. Armed with evidence of the missiles that the U.S.S.R. hoped to deny, he faced off with Valerian Zorin in what became one of the most memorable of all U.N. confrontations.

First, the supremely logical Adlai: "You, the Soviet Union, has sent these weapons to Cuba. You, the Soviet Union, has upset the balance of power in the world. You, the Soviet Union, has created this new danger ..."

Then, after Zorin attempted to imply that the U.S. hoped to manufacture a false crisis, an emotional Adlai expressed anger: "Do you deny that the U.S.S.R. has placed, and is placing, medium to intermediate range missiles at sites in Cuba? Yes or no? Don't wait for the translation. *Yes or no?*"

Nobody had ever seen Stevenson like this before! Finally, when Zorin, rather than lie, tried to remain mum: "I am prepared to wait for the answer until hell freezes over."

"God, almighty," JFK said to Bobby as they watched the confrontation on TV, loving every minute of it. "If only he had shown such spark while running for president, he would've won!"

*

No sooner was the crisis over than JFK and Bobby, basking in their success, asked each other: What the hell do we need the CIA for? Besides, now that we've shown Castro who's boss, maybe we can normalize relations. Obviously he's there to stay.

Why cut off our nose to spite our face? Let's learn to live with the guy, open a discussion. He sure isn't going to rely on the Russians wholeheartedly, as before, now that Nikita blinked and pulled out his technology.

Jack, I think you're right. Things change. This could be the beginning of a new era. Now, if we can only convince Castro it was the CIA, working on their own, that tried to assassinate him, and not the two of us, there's no reason why ...

The Company, to put it mildly, did not appreciate that.

Angrier still were the anti-Castro Cubans in Florida. Until then, JFK had been perceived as their savior. Overnight he transformed into Satan on earth.

Not the CIA. The Cubans in Miami were aware that Kennedy's decision to not only abort Bay of Pigs but allow their friends and relatives to unnecessarily die has been his, not theirs.

Throughout the Cuban community in the southeastern U.S., the word spread: though we love the United States dearly and consider the CIA our friends, we have been betrayed by the man we trusted most of all. This cannot go unpunished.

They did not stand alone as to this strong sentiment.

CHAPTER EIGHTEEN:
DEJA VU

"CIA, FBI? We're all swimming around in the
same alphabet soup these days."
—Leo G. Carroll as "Head of Security" in
Alfred Hitchcock's *North by Northwest* (1959)

Eclectic, Frank Sturgis, aka 'George', decided while considering the dozen people seated around an ovular oak table. When was the last time he had come to such a conclusion ...?

Oh, of course. Cuba; November 30, 1960. My God! Was that less than three years ago? Seems like centuries.

Everything is so different. The thought that these people could come together then would have seemed madness. Now? Common sense. For here I am, representing the CIA, while ...

To George's immediate right sat a middle-aged man who, only a few years previous, had been a member of the FBI. After that, he'd gone into business for himself, occasionally employed by the Company, today representing the Bureau. Just beyond him, a State Department official: gray hair and matching suit, deeply concerned, profoundly quiet.

Continuing on and around: a beautiful brunette, the sort that you expected to see as window-dressing in Hollywood movies though she'd never appeared in one; the Russian consul, known to be a KGB operative; a member of the Miami anti-Castro Cubans; a representative from Castro; the best-looking man in the Mob; a former vice-president; a slender blonde; an admiral, a five-star general. And, finally, a much revered show-biz celebrity.

"So here we all are," George sighed. The others laughed uneasily in this safe-house, the one room in Washington, D.C. absolutely guaranteed to be 100 % free of internal wiretaps.

"Where's Lee?" the FBI representative asked.

"That's our first point of business. Two days ago, I approached him with our proposal."

"Did he turn you down?" the anti-Castro representative wanted to know. "But you said that—"

"I know what I said. He did not turn me down. Not yet."

"What precisely did he do?" the FBI man wanted to know.

"He visibly recoiled in horror."

"Lee's been so loyal—" the Mafioso mused.

"Lee was loyal to an idea he has in his head. His notion of patriotism turns out to be different from our own. At any rate, he's supposed to call me today with his final decision."

"If not Lee, who will ..." The State Department man couldn't finish his question so George performed that function.

"Get the job done? Deciding that is our major concern. But I must say, I don't anticipate it will be Lee Harvey Oswald."

*

One day before the original 54/12 Group met, the subject of their current discussion strolled along Bourbon Street. Like his mentor, Lee experienced a sense of déjà vu. The last time he'd taken this route had been in late April, 1954.

I was fifteen years old then. I arrived feeling like a sick bird, pirouetting to the ground. Only to soar Phoenix-like back up into fresh skies after watching Suddenly.

A warm drizzle descended, even as it had that now long ago day. Lee glanced around at the drops landing on neon between Canal Street and Esplanade Avenue, the fabled eight blocks which constituted upper Bourbon. He passed Jean Lafitte's Blacksmith Shop, a vestige of that noble pirate who, at a crucial moment in our history, chose to do the right thing and help Andrew Jackson defeat the British. Nearby stood the Old Absinthe House, once a place of shame for those not strong enough to resist its lurid temptations, today a tourist-trap like most other artifacts.

Even the streetcar named Desire awaited world-travelers anxious to pose on its façade for the cameras of friends.

Not everything appeared the same. The recently elected District Attorney Jim Garrison had, on paper at least, closed down houses of prostitution, hoping to create a family-friendly atmosphere. Still, at hot-spots like Beyond the Green Door and Nightmare Alley, a visitor could still seek out girls of the night.

Even in broad daylight, no pun intended.

Not Lee. For one thing, he loved—sincerely, truly, even devotedly loved—his wife, now that they had come to terms with each other's true identities. Besides, pleasure of any sort—drinking, gambling, whatever—was not now a preoccupation.

The time to decide had come. He must reach a conclusion today that would determine the rest of his life. And far more. The fate of his country—*the world!*—was at stake here.

"Your next assignment," George had whispered when they met two days earlier in the safest of all the Big Easy safe-houses, "will

282

be the most important of your life." This occurred in the office of Guy Bansila, an FBI agent and private-eye. Located in the Newman Building, this enclave featured an entrance on 531 Lafayette Street and, around the corner, another at 544 Camp.

George employed the former. Lee, following instructions from eccentric airline pilot George Ferrie, opted for the latter.

"Stop talking in circles and—"

"Brace yourself. On November 22, President Kennedy is scheduled to arrive in Dallas. A motorcade will whisk him through the downtown area, on his way to deliver several speeches. He will never arrive at those destinations."

"Why?" Lee, growing anxious, asked.

"Because," George continued, eyeballing Lee, "before he can, you will assassinate the president of the United States."

*

Lee had arrived in New Orleans by bus from Dallas on April 25, carrying precious little along with him: a few clothes and books he'd hastily shoved into a pair of duffel bags, his secret papers, and the dismantled Mannlicher-Carcano rifle, along with its telescopic sight. The moment he disembarked, Lee headed for a pay phone and called Lillian Murret, she happily surprised to hear from her relative.

"My God. Lee? I'd know that voice anywhere!"

Lee had not contacted his aunt since mid-October, 1956, when he called to say he'd joined the Marines and would stay in touch though he failed to do so. Recovering from her surprise, Lillian inquired as to whether Lee had a place to stay. When he admitted he did not, and was likely headed for the Y.M.C.A, she invited Lee to her home over on French Street. Each morning, he rose early and, after a breakfast prepared by Lillian or her daughter Marilyn Dorothea Murret, a schoolteacher, headed off job-hunting.

"It's so wonderful for me to rediscover my family."

Both women were fascinated that after returning from a long day's fruitless search, he would not, like any ordinary person, plop down in front of the TV after supper. Instead, Lee hurried up to his room, where he read late into the late night. "I didn't have the benefit of higher education," Lee told them. "I hope that, after the Revolution comes, all Americans, no matter how humble their origins, will be able to attend college..."

"What revolution?" Lillian, confused, asked.

"Why, the world-wide revolution, of course."

Lee had spent a great deal of time thinking during his bus trip eastward, alternating quiet meditation with reading. *The Brothers*

283

Karamazov, Dostoevsky's final work, struck Lee as greater even than *Crime and Punishment*. How artfully the master spun what initially seemed little more than a domestic squabble in Staraya, Russia, as an absent father left his lonely sons to fend for themselves, into tragedy worthy of the Bard.

An absent father? Domestic squabbles? I can relate to that!

As one after another of the brothers were introduced, Lee related in turn to each: Dimitri, the hedonist, who wallowed in diversions of female flesh; Vanya, the man of logic, observing human suffering and as a result questioning the concept of a benign God; Aloysha, the boy whose faith could not be shaken by anything worldly, offering Vanya one extreme pole, if only his Existential questions could be set aside; and Smerdyakov, a dark nihilist who had given up not only faith but even the ability to care for humanity, the other extreme that also drew Vanya.

Ultimately, Vanya served as Doestoevsky's central figure. For it was he who must decide whether to abandon all hope and enter the abyss from which there was no return, or be born-again, somehow accepting that life still had meaning.

Alternately, Lee read, transported into this land of long ago and far away, and slept. When he did, Lee dreamed, fiction by Dostoevsky mingling with facts of the contemporary world. His unconscious mind returned to "The Grand Inquisitor": a Spanish nobleman who embodied Satan on earth, rejecting Jesus on his Second Coming, yet embraced, even kissed, by the innocent one.

What did this metaphoric episode finally mean? Should Lee too strive to love rather hate? If so, then he must reject the words George had passed on to him as a mantra, replaced by a code of his own: *Any enemy of my friend is my brother.*

This is the person who had met with George, he unaware of the sea-change within Lee, shortly after arrival. Yesterday, Lee had been told he would have the honor of killing Kennedy.

This appears vaguely familiar ... I feel as if I've been here before ... Oh, wow! ... Yes, I do remember ...

Lee found himself on a side-street, standing in front of the same run-down theatre he'd entered in 1954. Could history repeat itself? Might he once more find himself at the movies?

Lee glanced up at the marquee, which read: THE MANCHURIAN CANDIDATE starring Frank Sinatra. *Holy! Accident or destiny?*

*

From the moment this film began, Lee sensed that he was watching something other than a conventional Hollywood movie, despite Sinatra's star-power and big-scale production values. For one thing, there were no opening credits, not even a logo to identify the studio.

"Korea 1952," appeared over the shot of Sinatra, playing Major Ben Marco, seated in the passenger seat of a military convoy truck beside Laurence Harvey. The cultivated English actor had been cast as Sgt. Raymond Shaw. Together, they pulled up to a brothel where troops partied inside. Looking dour—*isn't that the word so many people use to describe me?*—Shaw left the vehicle and entered, assembling his squad for a combat mission.

Clearly, these soldiers had one thing in common: To a man, they hated Raymond, considered him pompous. As to their insults, Raymond answered with a sneer.

That's me! Not educated and refined like him. Still ...

Shortly, they were taken captive, subject to brainwashing. An ever-circling camera alternated between an image of the Reds observing these captives as this scene realistically played out, and the manner in which the Americans saw, in their minds, what took place: they guests as some American garden-club.

I read an article somewhere, I think Saturday Review, *that claimed movies will be different in the Sixties ... the old clichés will fall away. In their place, more 'daring' films.*

What alternately appeared as a normal American lady and a cruel communist agent approached Raymond, instructing that he pick out a squad member he disliked the least and strangle him. Without hesitation, Raymond did. Later, Raymond was instructed to approach his friend Marco, borrow that man's pistol, then shoot a boyish trooper between the eyes. Raymond did as told.

As the Red leader explained, the notion that a man who has been brainwashed cannot be forced to commit an act that he finds morally repulsive is but a myth. Here was evidence. Two corpses lay on the stage, victims of Raymond's brainwashing, proof that the process worked.

All this has something to do with me! Let's wait and see.

After the surviving soldiers returned home, they shared a single opinion of their sergeant: "Raymond Shaw is the kindest, bravest, warmest, most wonderful human being I've ever known in my life." Whenever Raymond's name came up, diverse characters would repeat that precise phrase as if by rote.

My God! Could that be true of me? Like Sinatra and the others, without even knowing it? Perhaps I've been listening to George for so long, without argument, I've lost any ability to think for myself. Accepting point blank my "legend."

If so, is there anything left of Lee Harvey Oswald, the person I once was as compared to the persona that I play?

*

Initially, things went smoothly in New Orleans. When not out looking for work, Lee felt a compunction to make contact with his roots, as if aware on some level that the final chapter in the brief drama constituting his life had begun to unfold. On the final Sunday in April, four days after arriving, he headed out to Lakeview Cemetery. Here, his biological father lay buried.

In all these years, Lee had never once visited the site. Marguerite hadn't brought him here, claiming "let sleeping dogs lie." As always, Mama spoke in annoyingly time-worn clichés.

Had you lived, might everything have turned out different? I guess that's one of those things I never will know ...

The following Monday, Lee borrowed Lillian's phone book and poured over the listings for everyone in New Orleans with the last name of 'Oswald.' One by one, he called each, politely introducing himself, asking if they might possibly be related.

A few hung up; most were pleasant but said 'no.' A lady named Hazel answered: yes, indeed, she was the widow of his father's brother. Lee took a bus to the outskirts of town and visited her. A simple, gentle woman, Hazel offered Lee tea and cookies, which he accepted in his most humble guise.

"To think, after all these years, you would show up."

They spoke for hours about her memories of Lee's dad, who came to life at last as a decent, hardworking fellow. As Lee was about to leave, Hazel recalled a framed photograph up in the attic.

"I want you to have it, Lee. After all, it's been sitting there gathering dust. Hopefully it'll mean something to you."

Lee thanked her profusely. In the faded portrait, Lee's father smiled pleasantly. Lee set the framed image on the desk in his room. He fell asleep considering what might have been as compared to what was.

A week and a half later, Lee found a perfunctory job. He would lubricate machines used to process coffee at the William B. Reily Company on Magazine Street. He took a furnished apartment several doors down, so there would be no need to waste money on bus fare. Though paid a mere $1.50 an hour, Lee gleefully phoned Marina at Ruth Paine's house in Dallas.

"It's me. I've got a job and a room. Come, please?"

"*Papa nus lubet!*" Marina cried, cradling baby June. Lee knew enough Russian to understand this meant "papa loves us!"

For all he knew, Marina might still be in touch with the KGB. He, certainly, kept in daily touch with George. None of that mattered. No matter what happened in the world, it could not touch them now. Not after that sublime night in Dallas

"Come quickly, Marina? I so ache to hold you and June."

Lee was to be disappointed. Though he offered to send Marina bus-fare, she allowed Ruth to drive them down and remain for several days. Lee tried to make the best of it, showing the women around his beloved Quarter, pointing out quirky facts as to the saints and sinners whose intrigues caused this town to be called The Big Easy. He could tell that Marina, at least while under Ruth's influence, grew ever more uneasy.

Yes, she appreciated the rich atmosphere. But the apartment was shabbier even than the worst they'd occupied in Dallas-Fort Worth. Here, there were cockroaches, something new to her.

"Oh, God, Lee. When I stepped on one, it *crunched*."

Things improved slightly after Ruth headed home. Then Lee could take Marina out to enjoy the few delights he had known as a boy. Along Lake Pontchartrain, anybody could roll up their pants nearly to the knees, step into the shallows, and go crabbing. She, five months pregnant with their second child, laughed out loud as the green-backed creatures desperately tried to slip away sideways.

"You did this as a child? With your friends?"

She sensed at once that the question, however innocent, saddened him. "I didn't have friends. I went with my mother."

At that moment, Lee noticed something that had eluded him. When Marina turned, her manner of movement recalled Marguerite, as she had appeared when they two crabbed here together.

*

As Raymond Shaw stepped off the plane from Korea, reporters anxious to speak with him instead found themselves interviewing his mother. Eleanor, played by Angela Lansbury, darted into the midst of the hero's homecoming, turning these proceedings, in Raymond's words, into "a three ring circus." Also, she affected an accent meant to suggest Southern gentility, coming across rather as vulgar.

Marguerite. She might as well be playing Marguerite!

Accompanying Eleanor was her second husband, Raymond's step-father, a right-wing senator from some unspecified state. "My two little boys," Eleanor cackled, embracing them both.

Perhaps this is why Raymond is so dislikeable, an upper-class version of myself. Marguerite was the one who made me the way I was then. Why? It played into her deep, desperate needs.

"It's a terrible thing to hate your mother," Raymond Shaw confessed to Ben Marco. "But I didn't always hate her. When I was a child, I only kind of disliked her."

287

Does everyone in the world experience what I do at the movies? Believe the words and images are personal?

When Raymond mentioned that he was going to work for a liberal newspaper editor, mother screeched: "That communist?" Later, a moderate senator played by John McGiver says of Eleanor to Raymond: "One of your mother's least endearing traits is to refer to anyone who doesn't agree with her as 'a communist.'" As for 'Johnny,' Eleanor's right-wing spouse, he raises a worthless piece of paper in the air and absurdly announces: "I have here a list of 200 known communists working in the Defense Department."

He's supposed to be McCarthy! This isn't just one more thriller. This film's about politics. And they're making a clown out of the man who terrified everyone so back in the Fifties as today the fear of anything Red diminishes. That's the way I've been thinking. Castro might have leaned toward democracy if we hadn't out of mindless horror at the thought of 'revolution' pushed him into the enemy camp by trying to kill him.

Who knows? With all the indignities we've heaped on the Beard, maybe it's possible to win him back? If someone took it upon himself to head on down there, talk sense with the guy, maybe he'd be willing to let bygones be bygones ...

All it takes is one man daring enough to give it a try.

Raymond was trained to kill, the big Chinese guy with the huge mustache laughed, and not remember that he'd killed. Sent back to the U.S. to do the bidding of Manchuria and Moscow. All one of their agents need do was place a phone call, instruct the brainwashed youth to play solitaire; once Raymond turned over the Queen of Diamonds, his own self disappeared.

The enemy agents had Raymond kill his old mentor at the paper so he, the bright assistant, could assume the duties.

"There's something phony going on," Ben Marco, sweating at night with terrible dreams, told his military superiors. "With me, and Raymond Shaw, and the whole Medal of Honor."

Marco had seen to it that Raymond received the decoration for wiping out an entire enemy brigade. He had wiped out an entire enemy brigade. That never happened. Marco too was brainwashed. Other soldiers also experienced the nightmares in which the truth, as they knew it to be, attempted to work its way up from repression to a conscious level.

I don't necessarily believe George set out to brainwash me. All the same, he did create an identity I assumed. Until lately, when I've begun to harbor second thoughts. Just like Sinatra in his latest film.

Unlike George, I now believe that a balance between the extremes of far right and far left allows for individual initiative while insuring community survival. This has existed since Franklin Delano Roosevelt and The New Deal.

Kennedy? He stands for the same thing. The New Frontier: Ask not you're your country can do for you; ask what you can do for your country. Best of all, his civil rights initiatives attempt to extend that "you" to black people at last.

My kind of president. And they want me to shoot him?

*

George had remained in daily contact with Lee during those hot spring months leading up to this crisis. And, unwittingly, George set Lee's then-vague attitudes in place with another of his tactics. George instructed Lee to write a letter, dated May 26, to Fair Play for Cuba Committee, headquartered in New York.

This organization called for the U.S. to recognize Cuba and commence with a normalization of relations. Lee's instructions were to request he be allowed to open a F.P.C.C. branch in New Orleans. George's strategy: this would allow Lee to infiltrate the group and then help the CIA keep tabs on its members.

From the start, however, when he began reading materials mailed to him, Lee sensed that their approach was more or less identical to the one developing in his mind. Again, he dared not mention this to George. For the time being following orders, Lee rented a small room in an office building at 544 Camp Street. This would allow him to initiate such an infiltration.

Hardly by accident, this happened to be adjacent to where FBI agent Guy Bansila, along with George Ferrie and a local businessman, the ardent anti-communist Clay Shaw, orchestrated local anti-Castro activities. 'George' created this arrangement so Lee, upon receiving information, could walk across the way and turn it over to his confederates.

But do I really want to do that? And since when is the CIA comfortable working with the FBI? Are they coming together now?

*

Marina experienced déjà vu as she woke in the night at the realization that Lee was sitting, rather than lying, beside her. For a moment she believed they were back in Dallas. Then she realized where she was, Lee lost in the throes of yet another of his nocturnal epiphanies. As in Texas, she rose up beside him.

"What is it?" She kissed his cheek. "Tell me."

"I now know what I must do next. In a word? Cuba."

"You've been assigned to try and kill Castro again?"

He gasped. "How did you know I once attempted to do that?"

"I know everything. That's not important now."

"You're right. All that's important—other than you and me and baby June—is what I've got to do. And it isn't kill him. Marina, I must be the one who makes Fidel see that now there's an opportunity to put the terrible past behind us ..."

Lee had been considering several things JFK said in recent weeks. Clearly, Kennedy had turned against the CIA: "I don't think the intelligence reports are all that hot. I get more out of the New York *Times*." Several days later he also announced: "Communism has never come to power in a country that was not disrupted by war, or corruption, or both."

The president must be referring to Cuba. Castro turned left as a reaction to Batista's right-wing regime and the unannounced war the U.S. had unofficially declared. If such belligerence were to cease, might not Castro come around to a more democratic approach to government?

"But, Lee," she wept. "You have no official power—"

"All the better. Any power I have comes from my will to do the right thing. This is about the great good a single person can achieve if only he believes in his own abilities to—"

"You heard that in some old film. John Wayne or Errol Flynn said something like that, and it got stuck in your mind. Yes?"

"Well? Shouldn't we strive to be like those heroes? Robin Hood, Davy Crockett. Righting the world's wrongs—"

"Lee, darling. Don't you understand? That's *only* a *movie!*"

"Shouldn't life be more like the movies?"

"Yes, But it isn't! That's the whole point. Why we go to movies. There, everything can work out wonderfully at the fade-out. This is reality. There are no happy endings."

"I can't accept that."

"But how would you even get there? It's illegal to travel from the U.S. to Cuba now."

He cradled her in his arms. "I've thought that through. Mexico! If I travel down there, I can pick up a Visa—"

"What makes you believe the Cubans will approve it?"

Now, Lee grew excited. "I've figured that out, too. George ordered me to create a new 'legend' in which I appear to be a pro-Castro activist so as to betray that cause? Well, I'm already 'in.' Only I won't betray them. I'll betray George."

"Lee," Marina gasped. "He'd have you killed—"

"Not if I outsmart him."

Thanks to a paper-thin beam of moonlight seeping in the window, Marina could see that Lee now grinned from ear to ear. As he did whenever he'd convinced himself he was the master.

"Don't under-estimate George, Lee. He'll—"

He hadn't even heard her warning. "As he wants me to do, I'll attract as much attention as I can to myself with Fair Play, allowing George to believe this is all being done to bring them down. Instead, I'll head to Mexico, bringing evidence of my work for pro-Cuban forces with me. Once the people at Castro's embassy see that, they'll let me into the country. I can argue for a pro-American, pro-Democracy, pro-Kennedy and anti-Russian, anti-communist, anti-Khrushchev Cuba."

"And you believe, you honestly believe, that you, acting on your own, with no back-up whatsoever, can achieve this?"

He turned to face her, out of his private zone, back in the world of one man and one woman, together in one bed. "I don't believe—I *know!* Marina, from when I was a child, I sensed there had to be a purpose to my life. I've found it! Show the world that democracy and socialism can co-exist in a new order."

"Who do you think you are: Jesus Christ?"

That was a difficult one to answer, but Lee did. "Yes. I guess I do. On some level, I always have."

"Well, they'll crucify you, too, if you attempt this."

"If that's the only way to bring The Word, so be it."

Marina sobbed. "And, me? June? The baby yet to come?"

Lee kissed her head gently. "You must know I love you and our family more than anything else. But what I speak of reaches beyond that. A man must do what he must do."

"So be it, then," she said, capitulating. "But I won't watch you die. Tomorrow, I'll pack and return to Dallas."

"Like me, you have to do what you consider best."

"I'll always be waiting for you, Lee. I love you."

"How can you? I'm not lovable. I never have been."

*

In *The Manchurian Candidate,* Raymond Shaw also discovered his one true love. Like Marina, a beautiful child-woman, half naive fawn, half Earth Mother. *Joslyn.* She was played by Leslie Parrish, a young blonde who looked amazingly like Marilyn Monroe back in the early 1950s, still fresh and giddy, with that open smile which in time gave way to hard, cynical laughter.

"I'm not lovable," Raymond wailed. "Yes, but I love you," the blonde, insisted. At once innocent and experienced, however improbable that may sound, Joslyn reminded Lee of Marina.

Joslyn's father, a milk-toast liberal senator, finally found the courage to face off with Eleanor at a costume ball. She asked him to support her Johnny for the vice-presidential nomination; he railed at the terrible mischief these two caused for America in the name of right-wing causes.

"I think if Johnny were a paid Soviet agent," the senator concluded, "he could not do more harm to this nation than he is now!" What irony, Lee thought. This arch Right Winger achieves precisely what the communists most desire: Americans turning against each other as during the McCarthy era of the early 1950s.

"The Queen of Diamonds," a psychiatrist told Marco about the symbol employed to set the brainwashed Shaw off on one of his missions, "is reminiscent of Raymond's mother."

A couple had entered and sat behind Lee. The man clearly was familiar with the Richard Connell novel on which this movie was based. He whispered to the woman beside him: "In the book the relationship between Raymond and mother is more extreme. The reason he's the way he is? They slept in the same bed until he was sixteen. That's what made him such an intense nut case."

Until the age of sixteen? Longer even than Marguerite and me. It seemed so nourishing then. My mother consumed me in ways that I can't even begin to comprehend. Just like Raymond.

Both of us tragic figures, like Oedipus of old. What would I have done in life without that seventh grade English teacher?

During the party, Joslyn arrives wearing a Queen of Diamonds costume. Raymond crumbles into her arms, unable to resist her. As if he had found a socially acceptable way to sleep with Eleanor, the two women inseparable in his mind.

Is that true of me as well? Marguerite, Marina ...

Then, at his mother's command, Raymond Shaw, not realizing what he's doing, calmly kills Joslyn and her gentle father.

Now, the deceased liberal senator's words make sense, as does the film's title. Johnny, the right-wing crazy, is a plant by the communists. How better to destroy the U.S. than from the inside out, the McCarthy figure a tool of the Reds? They believe if such a man is elected president, after assuming the murdered nominee's place, the country will grow so dissatisfied with him, far to the right of, say, Batista, that America must experience a revolution in response, even as in Cuba. Then, communism wins.

"They can't make me doing *anything,* Ben. Can't they? Anything!?" Meaning that which is repellant to his human nature.

"We'll see, kid. We'll see what they can do and what they can't do." Marco knows what Raymond does not; Eleanor and Johnny want Raymond to kill the presidential nominee when he addresses the convention in New York's Madison Square Garden. Precisely as this middle-of-the-road hopeful delivers his key line: "Nor would I ask my fellow Americans, in defense of our freedom, that which I would not gladly give myself—my life. My very life."

A great statement. A Kennedy kind of statement.

Raymond is to hide above, shoot down with a rifle fitted with a telescopic sight. He became a marksman in the service.

Just like me! How complex the political game of chess can be. Only by supporting one's arch enemy can the check-mate move occur. I ought to know; I'm in this up to my neck.

Spotting the streak of light from his place in the vast auditorium, Marco rushed through the building's inner workings, hoping to arrive in time to stop Raymond.

What do I do now? Watch the rest of the film and find out.

When the major yanks open the door to that small booth, out of breath, Raymond brings the presidential candidate into his sights ... then swerves to the right, shooting his mother and father-in-law. Clearly, the Red Chinese agent was wrong. Raymond broke beyond bounds of brainwashing, turning the gun on them.

Yes. Now I understand what I must do ...

"You couldn't have stopped them," Raymond wept to Marco before taking his life. "The army couldn't have stopped her. I had to!"

Suicide; which I have so often considered. Perhaps I'll do that as well, take my own life, once my purpose in life is, like Raymond's, fulfilled ...

*

Minutes later, Lee stumbled out of the louse-ridden movie house. *This can only be fate, bringing me around to where it all began. Sinatra again instructing me, reversing the message of* Suddenly. *If that were one bookend, this is its opposite.*

I feel like all four Karamazov brothers rolled up into one. So lost was I after George's call. Do I still have any semblance left of free will? Am I fated to follow his command or might I, like Raymond, do precisely the opposite?

This wasn't only a movie. Like Raymond, I'll agree to go through with it, as George requested. Then, at the last minute, I'll take out the true enemies of the people.

Half an hour later, Lee called George and apologized for his earlier hesitancy, agreeing to kill JFK on 11/22/63.

*

"Lee called me," George informed the committee members. "He apologized for his hesitation and has now accepted."

"So?" the FBI man said, shrugging. "It's settled."

"Not if I know Lee. Remember, I mentored him. Beyond that, you might even say ... I created him."

"Like Frankenstein with his monster?" the blonde suggested.

"As you'll recall from that old story, the creature was supposed to carry out the doctor's orders. Instead, he turned on the man who had created him and destroyed Dr. Frankenstein."

"As you now believe Oswald will?" The pro-Castro Cuban asked, his voice riddled with concern.

"I know him better than anyone else. Better than his wife, his mother. Perhaps I know Lee Harvey Oswald better even than Lee Harvey Oswald knows himself."

"What's your concern?" the brunette chimed in. "Do you think he'll get cold feet at the last minute?"

"That's not Lee. The problem is more serious. Lately, He's been talking a lot about Kennedy, particularly the Civil Rights initiatives. Lee has always considered himself ... I think the term he employs is 'a white Negro.' Any friend of the colored people is, therefore, ipso facto Lee's friend as well."

"And any enemy ..." the anti-Castro Cuban added.

"... his enemy," the State Department man concluded.

"My worry is that Lee agreed to carry out the assassination only after deciding against doing so."

"Meaning," the Mafioso in turn responded, "he's taking the job to make certain it doesn't get accomplished."

"Lee once told me that, as a kid, his favorite TV show was called *I Led Three Lives*. I believe that's what he's doing now. Or at least attempting to achieve."

"Meaning he'll double cross us?" the general asked.

"Not as Lee sees it. He'll do anything, including sacrifice himself if need be, to stop what he believes is wrong. It's more on the order of, I'd say, a triple-cross."

"But we're not wrong," the former vice-president insisted.

"In our minds. Just as Lee, in his, is absolutely right. The point is, Lee is playing a kind of chess game. Well, I've played with him on occasion. Good as he is, I'm better. I know the strategies he always relies on to create a check, allowing me to check-mate him. I've come up with a way this can further benefit us."

George then explained his plan. They would take Lee up on his offer while also assigning several other shooters to take down Kennedy. If George's guess as to Lee's reasoning proved inaccurate, no problem: with three marksmen firing from three different positions, chances of success were that much better. If Lee came through, he'd escape with the rest of the team.

If Lee refused to take a shot, likely one of the others would bring the president down. Then, when the moment of truth came around, George had a plan to pin the assassination on Lee.

"If Lee betrays us," George concluded, "then he'll be our fall guy, making it easier for the team to escape."

Everyone agreed on this course of action. They mapped out plans. Lee should be told that he was now one of three separate shooters. That would insure he arrived at the scene, to aid or try and avoid the assassination. When push came to shove, Lee revealing his true colors, George would take it from there.

"Is everyone agreed on this course of action?"

"Agreed," the others chanted in unison.

*

It was late evening when the meeting let out. George bid his fellow conspirators good-night and stepped into darkness. He needed to wind down. Most men would head for a bar but he didn't drink while on a major operation. A film was better. That was one of the things he and Lee did have in common: both loved to escape from reality by taking in a movie. The difference was, at least in George's mind, George knew Hollywood films to only be fantasies. Lee foolishly took them far too seriously.

Perhaps that's what distinguishes Lee the most in my mind. I've never met a man who can be so deeply touched by a film!

Still, when George walked three blocks northward to the nearest theatre, he couldn't control himself from laughing at the irony. Playing there was *PT-109,* starring Cliff Robertson as a heroic, lionized, larger-than-life John Fitzgerald Kennedy.

CHAPTER NINETEEN:
HE DID IT HIS WAY

"America's politics will now also be America's favorite movie."

—Norman Mailer, commenting on the election
of John Fitzgerald Kennedy, 1960

On July 6, 1963, James Stewart received a phone call in his Miami office from Santo Trafficante, Jr. in Tampa. As 'Jimmy' happened to be alone at the time, he shifted to the name Santo had previously addressed him by: Johnny Rosselli.

Ordinarily, they'd make a date to meet somewhere between their two Florida cities to talk business in the privacy of some mob-owned club. This time, Santo mentioned that he had preview tickets for a movie to be screened in Tampa the following week. He wanted Johnny to drive up and join him for the event.

Nobody's fool, Rosselli sensed this had to be something big. From the neutral quality of Santo's tone, Rosselli couldn't guess if he'd landed in trouble or if his unique talents were about to be called into play once more for The Organization.

According to the rules of the game, Johnny Handsome knew he was not allowed to ask questions. Cordially, seemingly calm, he accepted. They met in a Tampa theatre lobby, Santo looking as always like a city-clerk in his thick glasses and rumpled suit.

They entered the auditorium and took seats midway down the main aisle. The house was packed. Theatre lights dimmed, a projector's bulb blasted on behind them, and Rosselli watched as the title appeared: *P.T. 109.*

Johnny sighed with relief, knowing it was not he who had landed in hot water but the film's subject. JFK was played, at the president's request, by a handsome leading man, Cliff Robertson. He didn't resemble JFK at all. This, rather, was how JFK saw himself and wanted the world to perceive him, now and forever.

Young JFK, or his fictionalized persona, turned disaster into the stuff of legend, leading his crew on a swim to safety. When one sailor couldn't keep up, JFK, refusing to let a single man die, grabbed the fellow by the collar and dragged him along.

How exciting for an audience to see their current president depicted as a man of action worthy of their current fictional favorite, James Bond. No matter that JFK might well have been court marshaled for allowing his P.T. boat to be rammed by an enemy sub, something no officer had ever before let happen.

Santo and Johnny exchanged glances, each aware that it had been incompetence on JFK's part that caused the P.T. 109 to unnecessarily sink; those reports of courage under fire were drastically overstated.

At one point JFK swam away from his men, marooned on an island; Robertson made this seem a courageous gesture in the Hollywood version. Anyone with knowledge of military process understood that this was dereliction of an officer's duty.

"He fucked up, Johnny. And they're cheering him for it."

"He's the hero of a Hollywood movie now. People always cheer for whatever that kind of guy does, right or wrong."

From now on, no one in the world would believe that JFK had screwed up royally. For they'd seen the truth, if only in the sense that seeing is believing. Powerfully depicted in a film that put an official seal on the past. Whether what they witnessed had any bearing on reality no longer mattered.

This version of events was the one that had now been immortalized on celluloid. It would be seen everywhere and for years, decades even, be repeated on TV.

An hour later, the Mafiosos sat opposite one another in a quiet corner of a spaghetti house owned by Trafficante. Clams and linguini, the rich smell of choice garlic rising from two steaming plates, lay untouched. After what they'd experienced, neither man had an appetite. Thanks to them and their contacts, JFK had been elected to the presidency of the United States. As an Irish Catholic, he could not have reached that top plateau without such help. A deal had been cut. Now? With Jack's go-ahead, Attorney General Bobby had declared war on The Mob.

"When 'the brothers' wanted to fuck Marilyn Monroe, we went an' arranged that for 'em," Santo muttered bitterly.

"Then they wanted her shut up. We fixed that, too."

"It's time to start seriously talking about fixing them."

They tried to relax. As always, this meant Sinatra on the juke-box, one classic cut after another.

*

Following his big comeback in the mid-1950s, Sinatra soared up the entertainment-biz ladder from star to superstar. If at that point there seemed nowhere higher to go, an even greater status awaited. Until Humphrey Bogart's death in 1957, that actor reigned as uncrowned king of what was known as The Rat Pack, insiders even among Hollywood A listers. Following Bogie's passing, the clique might have floundered had not Sinatra stepped up to accept the mantle.

Immediately, his best buddies became the new power elite: fellow saloon singer/actor Dean Martin, British-born leading man Peter Lawford, the multi-talented African-American singer/dancer/actor Sammy Davis Jr., and the wry/dry Jewish comic Joey Bishop. By the early 1960s they were co-starring by day in the Vegas-shot movie *Ocean's 11*, headlining together at a casino by night.

"Ring-a-ding-ding," they chimed. The crowds went wild.

Sinatra garnered a reputation as a man with two distinct personalities. He could be mean-spirited beyond all conception if the liquor rushed too swiftly through his system. Feeling guilty the morning after he'd become a sentimentalist, over-tipping valets who happened to smile brightly at him.

Vegas became a new wild west, they a gang terrorizing the town, no one willing to try and stop them. Women were broads to be bedded. The more out of control they became, the more extreme the public's fascination with it all. Yet, despite shallowness and insensitivity, there was another side to Frank, who fiercely dedicated himself to the then-burgeoning Civil Rights movement.

"It's time to turn this thing around. Let's do it!"

Among the Rat Packers, Davis had grown closest with Peter Lawford, a mediocre contract-player at MGM who owed his sudden stardom to Sinatra's friendship. As it happened, Lawford was married to Patricia Kennedy, JFK's sister. During a fund-raiser for the senator, Lawford introduced Sammy to JFK.

When these two enthusiastically explained JFK's position on civil rights to Frank, the leader of the pack expressed interest in meeting the man and possibly campaigning for him.

This, despite enmities between the Italian-Sicilian crime organization and the Irish, so often in the past cast in the life-theatre of crime as their police antagonists.

"You *gotta* meet Jack, Frank. You just gotta!"

"Alright, Sammy. If you're so enthused, I will be too."

The young politician and the suave singer were already emerging as key icons for the upcoming decade. Why shouldn't they team up? Sinatra had "High Hopes" rewritten as the JFK theme song during his 1960 presidential face-off with Richard Nixon. JFK introduced Frankie to the fashionable set, people with power and prestige in the political arena. Sinatra helped Kennedy slip off for his secret walks on the wild side.

"You actually know Marilyn Monroe, Frankie?"

"Do I know her? That's putting it mildly, kid."

"Well ... I'd love to 'know' her, too."

There were those in the Rat Pack, particularly Dean Martin, who didn't approve. To Dino's way of thinking JFK seduced Sinatra into becoming the Bostonian's pimp. When he attempted, treading with caution, to broach the subject, Frank waved Dean away.

"I trust him like a brother. Once he's in the White House, we'll all be invited. Now, ain't *that* a kick in the head?"

*

Meanwhile, things were changing in the Mob. Charles Luciano had long since been deported from Cuba to Italy. Certain that drugs would be the next big thing, he set up a Sicilian-U.S. connection, hoping to flood America with heroin, providing a similar source of illegal funds as whiskey and beer had during Prohibition. Charley would follow this up with cocaine.

This 'connection' would be headquartered in Palermo, where Luciano, his health rapidly fading, lived out his final years. Meyer Lansky, who had retired to Miami Beach to play the role of a kindly grandfather, had to hurry off to Israel when the T-Men came after him once again. This left a new set of young turks fighting for Mob dominance. Vito Genovese and his crime family made a major power grab one month later. Several of his boys whacked Frank Costello, Lucky's last significant representative. This eliminated the final stateside representative of the old days.

At Vito's invitation, sixty-six mobsters descended on the small-town of Apalachin, New York for a summit meeting in which Genovese planned to stake out his dominance over all organized crime. Things went south when the isolated farmhouse was raided by police, sending mobsters running off in all directions. This November disaster allowed Sam Giancana to make his own influence felt. Having reached the top of the ladder in Chicago, he made the point that if that big meeting had taken place in the Windy City, no such travesty would have occurred.

As Mob members were dragged before grand juries, Gold's words echoed in their ears. By 1959, he had become The Man. Gold was God, to Mafiosos and their small circle of friends.

Among those accepted into his sphere of influence was Frank Sinatra. However warmly Frank felt about Charley, who would pass away at age sixty-two in 1962, no question Frankie's immediate loyalty shifted during this period. Before long, Frank would broach a subject of great seriousness and much controversy.

"Sam, can we set up a conference? This could be a biggie!"

Word had reached Sinatra, indirectly through JFK's aged father Joseph, that his son needed a favor. Frankie's support had been appreciated. That might not be enough to put Jack over the top. The final decision would come down to two states and, more specifically, two areas within those states. In Illinois, key districts of Chicago. Likewise, West Virginia territories.

Was it possible that Mr. Sinatra might speak of this with Mr. Giancana? The Syndicate had always operated out of Chicago; West Virginia served as yet another Mob headquarters. The situation certainly seemed serendipitous.

"Wow, that's a biggie. But, yeah, I can try."

Still a naïve kid at heart despite that cruel façade, Sinatra all but danced with delight. To be the go-between, the key link connecting the next president and The Mob.

Ring-a-ding-ding! The thrill of it all ...

*

Tenuously, Old Sam listened. "But can we trust them?"

"I'd stake my life on it."

"That may be the case!" Giancana's dark eyes darted about mirthlessly as he spoke in cautious terms.

"This guy's become like a brother to me."

"I don't know, Frankie. I mean, he's *Irish*. Not that I give a fuck about race. Like, what would we do without the Jews? Charlie always had Meyer. Today, Willie Moretti's in bed with Longy Zwillman. But The Micks? Jesus! I just don't know."

"Maybe that was then; this, now. Things change."

"Do they? Maybe. But you know what some people say? The more things change, the more they stay the same."

"So you won't—"

Behind a sprawling mahogany desk, Sam shifted in his seat. "Yeah, I will. We'll bring in both districts in Chicago. Down south, too. Put your guy in the White House. When Frankie asks for a favor, he gets it. With me, as with Charley."

Sinatra moved forward, warmly grasped Sam Giancana's hand, and kissed his ring finger in deference. "Thank you."

"I want you to listen, now. If this works out like you say, we'll be thanking you. Because once he's in the cat seat, he'll have to remember every single day who put him in that position."

"Capiche!" Sinatra firmly shook Giancana's aging hand. He perceived no problem. JFK was hardly a fool.

Surely, he'd get the big picture ...

One week later, Sam Giancana met with Joseph Kennedy, Sr. Apart from their ethnicities the two had a great deal in common. Both were known to be shrewd, unsparing, and hard as nails when it came to business. Just as the Mob had always relied on movies and alcohol as fundamentals in building wealth, so had Kennedy. In a shadowy room, during one of the most secretive meetings ever held in the history of America, the two came together.

"So: You really think your kid's tough enough for this?"

"Sure. He hates the same as I do."

"Well," Giancana sighed, grinning. "This whole thing can be arranged. But it's gonna cost."

Relaxing somewhat, the elder Kennedy smiled back. "Don't buy a single vote more than necessary. I mean, I'll be damned if I'm gonna pay for a landslide."

*

Shortly thereafter, JFK won the election by one of the tightest margins in presidential politics. No sooner had the Kennedy era begun than Frankie was wined and dined in the White House. JFK's wife didn't care much for him so Sinatra came to think of Jacqueline as a snob, turned off by him being Italian.

Jacqueline Bouvier Kennedy cared not a whit as for anyone's ethnicity. Her problem was not prejudice but personality; from day one, Jackie pegged Sinatra as a pimp at heart.

The snapping point came when he let slip a statement that revealed he was the one who orchestrated her husband's wild carousing with Hollywood's glamour girls.

"Well, as Jack told Marilyn ... Ooops! I mean, Jack said *about* Marilyn, to *me* ... in confidence, of course ..."

What kind of a man is this? And, according to the birds of a feather adage, what kind of a man does that make my husband?

Once the election was a done deal, Giancana planned to make use of Frank's position in JFK's unofficial cabinet.

Frank's happy. Jack's happy. Joe's happy. But most of all, I'm happy. And it better damn well friggin' stay that way ...

First, they'd hooked JFK up with Marilyn. She, like Sinatra, dreamed of class and thought that banging a president, instead of movie executives, would provide her with that. As to JFK, he wanted to fuck a fantasy. Neither was fully satisfied, but then again, who is when a dream becomes reality? The actuality, however good, can't possibly live up to the perfection that exists only in one's imagination.

At any rate, Marilyn got JFK talking before and after and sometimes even during. She dutifully passed all he said along to

301

Frankie, who in turn delivered the messages to Sam. A romantic at heart, Marilyn made the mistake of falling in love with JFK.

"Jack. Do you, in your fantasies, ever wonder what it might be like if the two of us were ... *married*?"

Immediately, he recoiled, as if in abject horror, made some silly excuse to get out of bed as swiftly as he could, then refused to take her ever more frenzied calls to the White House.

When Bobby mentioned he'd always been jealous of his big brother's conquest, JFK gave him the go-ahead to make a move. Shortly, he and Marilyn were involved. Marilyn, being Marilyn, quickly decided Bobby was the great love of her life.

Bobby? He'd fucked her. Now he would like to forget her.

The shit finally hit the fan on the night of May 19, 1962. A gala had been planned at Madison Square Garden in New York to honor JFK's 45th birthday, officially still ten days off. Marilyn talked her way into a seemingly innocuous star-turn, singing "Happy Birthday, Mr. President" before the audience of 15,000 high level celebrities, from politicians to the *literati*.

"Happy birthday to you; happy ..."

Even as she stepped up to the microphone, JFK sensed an absolute disaster in the making. Still, though, he managed to smile from ear to ear throughout the proceedings, Marilyn for that brief, intense moment completely in charge of everything; she, shimmering in the lights, queen of the whole wide world.

The proverbial woman scorned, Marilyn now appeared like a light bulb someone has snapped on. She was out for blood-vengeance as only a beautiful woman can administer such punishment.

Marilyn had been sewn—literally!—into a form-fitting Jean Louis gown. Fashioned from flesh-colored marquisette material, her costume studded with 2,5000 sparkling rhinestones.

"... happy birthday to *you!*"

As the lights dimmed low and she delivered her sultry, vulgar, finally lewd variation, the crowd sighed, gasped, then groaned. An illusion was created in which M.M. appeared nude other than the faux diamond sparkles adorning her lush figure.

Leering at JFK, she concluded the number and marched off.

"The bitch has gone too far," JFK told Frankie. He nodded glumly. Marilyn Monroe rated as a clear and present danger. No big problem when you had friends to take care of such things.

On August 5, the body of 36-year-old Marilyn Monroe was discovered on the floor of her Brentwood apartment. The first L.A. police officer on the scene, Sgt. Jack Clemmons, claimed the arrangement of her arms and legs, as well as the suspicious manner in which bottles of pills were aligned near the corpse, caused him to consider this "the most obviously staged death-scene" he'd ever encountered.

His insistence that Marilyn was murdered fell on deaf ears. Dr. Thomas Noguchi, of the L.A. County Coroner's Office, ruled that "acute Barbiturate poisoning" led to the star's passing, a "probable suicide" though possibly an accident.

According to gangland legend, a coalition of mobsters and CIA agents took care of that nasty business, believing that in so doing they cemented relations with the White House. Not taken into account was JFK's Machiavellian inclinations. The idea that such help would earn future loyalty never occurs to someone who believes primarily in his own self, everyone else a potential sacrificial lamb, no matter how loyal in any previous crisis.

Giancana was a Machiavellian, too. With his plant in the president's bed gone, he required another. One choice seemed made to order, a dazzling brunette named Judith Inmoor. Movie-star gorgeous, she had never stepped in front of a Hollywood camera though her sister, 'Susan Morrow,' performed in several films, most memorably *Cat Women of the Moon,* 1953.

Judith had married a supposed rising star, William Campbell, in 1952. His alcoholism and arrogance caused him to be dumped by the major studios. By 1958 Campbell could win roles only in B junk movies. Judith divorced him. Soon she was hanging-loose with Sinatra in Vegas. Frankie introduced the beauty to his pal JFK, soon to be president. They slept together that night.

"Thanks, Jack. When you're president, I'll remember."

"This is our first night together, Judith. Not the last."

Sinatra had also introduced Judy to Johnny Roselli, who brought the girl around to Giancana. On the outs at that moment with Phyllis McGuire, Old Sam took up with Judy. When Phyllis returned, Gold needed to farm Judy out. With Monroe eliminated, Judy Inmoor filled the bill. Shortly, she was a regular guest in JFK's bed, as he had promised some time ago.

"Me, the president's mistress! Amazing. Just *amazing.*"

Judy thrilled at the danger. She carried missives back and forth between JFK and Giancana, detailing the plots to kill Castro. Judy would hand them to Frank, who would pass them over to Johnny Handsome, he in turn delivering them to Sam Gold.

"Did you ever notice, Jack, that your wife ... Jacqueline ... and I ... look a lot like each other?"

"The resemblance is striking. You could be twins."

"How do you tell us apart?"

"Simple. You're great in bed."

*

Things became hairy when Jacqueline found a pair of pink panties in her pillow case. That night, as she and JFK slipped under the sheets, Jackie smiled sweetly, then slapped him across the face with the lingerie, hissing: "Would you please find out who these belong to, darling? Because they aren't my size."

JFK raged at Judy when next together, claiming that she'd left the panties around on purpose, to break up JFK's marriage. She was out: just like that. *Bye, bye, bitch!*

Hell hath no fury like ... Judy Inmoor Campbell snapped. "Yeah? Well, maybe *Sam* will have something to say about *that!*"

JFK was not known for going pale in the face but at that moment he did. A light went off in his head: Judy was a plant. Anything and everything he said during pillow talk made its way to Giancana, through Sinatra.

"That's it, isn't it? That's what you were here for?"

"At first, perhaps. But Jack, I really did fall in love—"

When Sinatra paid a surprise visit one week later, JFK accepted him into his private lounge but remained cool, remote, distanced throughout the visit. Frank left after an hour feeling dejected. It didn't take him long to put two and two together. When he confronted Judy she admitted JFK now knew that their arrangement had been uncovered.

Sinatra grasped that his own golden age in Camelot was over. Sir Lancelot was banished from the castle, doomed to wander the wastelands so long as JFK remained king.

That bastard. After all I did for him ...

That was his problem. If JFK merely forced Frank out of his D.C. inner circle, nothing would have been hurt other than Sinatra's feelings. Only that was not JFK's way.

That little shit. After all I did for him ...

JFK was mad, damn mad, and he wanted revenge. On Frank Sinatra, but also Giancana. On the whole rotten bunch of them.

Shortly, he came up with a strategy.

As Attorney General, Robert Kennedy had launched a full throttle attack on the Ku Klux Klan. JFK suggested that Bobby now employ the Justice Department to launch war on organized crime.

Meanwhile, JFK announced he would shortly take a vacation (sans wife and family) in California. Guessing his former buddy meant this as a sign that he was about to be let back 'in,' Sinatra assumed JFK would be staying with him and spent a fortune on having his home refurnished for this great occasion. Then word reached him that JFK had accepted an invite from Bing Crosby.

Here was a double-edged sword of an insult if ever one did exist. First, Crosby had been Sinatra's only competition as the greatest pop-jazz singer of the century.

Second, he was ... a Republican! And, by the way, Irish.

Old Sam was right, after all, about them.

In a snit, Sinatra tossed Lawford out of the rat pack. Bobby meanwhile approached J. Edgar Hoover, requesting that the FBI join his new crusade. The old bulldog would have none of it, knowing that ancient, embarrassing photograph still sat in a Chicago Mob office file. Furious, Bobby considered the Bureau's head hancho, and his entire organization, to be irrelevant.

We'll do it without you, J. Edgar. The less involved in bringing the Mob down, the greater glory for those who served.

Terrified of the Kennedys, Hoover had agents tail both brothers. Once aware of JFK's affair with Judith, the FBI head put pressure on the president, applying political blackmail. The Bureau demanded JFK's assurance that the FBI would not be phased out, and that Hoover would remain its head.

Shortly, JFK backed away from the FBI's competition, the CIA, to the chagrin of The Company's men. Not that this in any way satisfied Hoover. If JFK could so quickly turn on his pals, what would he do about an old enemy like himself?

All this while, Bobby had been working on his own plan to 'get' the mobsters. He increased the number of legal indictments against crime figures by 800 %. To the Kennedys, this seemed a fitting retribution for Giancana's putting plants in JFK's bed.

That, however, was not how Giancana saw it. He was the one who had been betrayed. And now? Look at this mess!

"You swore he could be trusted."

"I'm so ashamed!" Frankie wept like a child. Sam calmed him down, patting Sinatra on the hand, like a father with his son.

"Relax, Frank. Everything will be alright."

"Whatever you do to me, I accept, understand—"

"Not you, Frankie. You were taken in, even as I was."

"You're going to whack Bobby? The Attorney General?"

"Who said a frickin' word about him?"

Sinatra gasped. "The President of the United States?"

"His little rat of a brother wouldn't be doing this if he didn't have the top man's full backing."

"But ... kill the *President* ... couldn't we just—"

"Have you forgotten the old Sicilian saying? 'When you set out to finish a snake, you cut off not the tail but its head.'"

Never had the Mob whacked an honest opponent. Like Sam Giancana, Sinatra well knew that the popular TV series *The*

Untouchables was but a piece of violent fiction, despite real names employed for characters. On the show, mobsters constantly tried to rub out Eliot Ness, non-corruptible Fed.

In actuality, nothing like that ever occurred. However crude and brutal the game might be, there were rules. Numero uno: You didn't shoot an honest cop. You battled in court. If you lost, you went to prison, as Chicago's Al Capone had.

In the 1940s, that scenario had been replayed in New York. The Syndicate was scared shitless that Thomas Dewey might shut them down. But when Louis Lepke, one of their own, became frustrated with the pressure and confided to some colleagues that he was considering a hit on Dewey, word swiftly reached the top. The big bosses then, Luciano and Lansky, at once agreed that Lepke had to go. Not Dewey; Lepke. Not your enemy, not if honest.

But when one of their ilk came to you with a deal? Then, the ultimate rule applied: Nobody betrayed the Mob and lived. It didn't matter how high up the guy may be. No exceptions.

"Still, Sam. He's the number one man in the country."

"The world, actually! Any objections, Frank?"

"It's not for me to say, Sam. Which of the boys will—"

"You gotta be kidding. The trail would lead back to my own doorstep. That ain't gonna happen."

"Who, then?"

"We've got a new partner, the CIA. Plus the Cubans in Florida will help out. Kennedy betrayed both those organizations. And Castro hates him for all the assassination attempts. Actually, a whole lot of people want JFK dead."

"How could he possibly believe he'd get away with it?"

"Ah, what's the Greek word, Frankie? Hubris! Yeah, that's it. A guy gets powerful, real powerful, sooner or later he comes to think he's *all* powerful. Forgets that there's always someone, or something, way more powerful than him."

"It's like he loses sight of his place in the universe. And ... Bobby?"

"Once Jack is gone, he means nothing to us. Unless he ever decides to run for president. Then, of course, we'll ..."

Frank laughed sardonically. Giancana wanted to know what he found so funny. "I'll tell you, Sam. Kennedy's bitch of a wife? She'll make one gorgeous widow."

"Yes. Jacqueline Kennedy will look beautiful in black."

*

On November 22, 1963, at 4:20 in the afternoon (Central Time), a young female FBI agent placed a call to headquarters in D.C. When a secretary answered, she asked to speak with the

306

director. Told that he could only be reached in an emergency, she then explained she held in her hand an information packet that had been dropped off several days earlier by Lee Harvey Oswald, the man who only a few hours before presumably shot the president. The envelope was marked "private and confidential" and "to be opened immediately in the event of my death."

The secretary told the young woman to hold on momentarily. Less than a minute later the director's immediately recognizable voice boomed on the other end. He wanted to know if agent James Hosty happened to be in the building and was informed that Hosty had hurried to police headquarters to oversee questioning of the key suspect. The director told the young woman to get Hosty back at once. When she asked if she ought to open the envelope the director gasped and told her no. Upon return, Hosty's orders were to shred the unopened document and destroy the remains.

Hosty hurried back and was met by Shanklin, his superior, who relayed to Hosty what the secretary had told him. Shanklin wanted to know if there might be anything else that connected the FBI office to this doomed missive. In reply Hosty said that he had written a memorandum about the reception of Oswald's manuscript. Shanklin ordered Hosty to destroy that, along with any other evidence linking Oswald with this office. Hosty did as told, flushing the remants down a toilet.

*

On November 23, 1963, Lyndon Johnson arrived at the White House for his first full day in office as president. Before he could settle down to business Johnson found McGeorge Bundy, JFK's Assistant to the President for all National Security Affairs, awaiting him. Johnson sensed that Bundy appeared more fidgety than usual. Without a word, Bundy nodded, indicating that the president should follow him down a corridor.

Minutes later, the pair passed by two armed guards, through a steel doorway with 54/12 emblazoned on it. The situation room, as it was called, had been created in a cellar-like compound far beneath the White House basement, existing as an unknown cellar beneath the known one. Johnson gasped at the sight: immense wall maps, ticker tape machines, state of the art radar equipment, TV monitors, all these interconnected with brightly colored wires, abetted by a complex telephone system beyond that in his White House suite. This would be the only occasion on which he'd be invited—it felt like an order—to enter this sacrosanct place.

For the remainder of his current term and after winning re-election, LBJ's contact with 54/12 would be Bundy, abetted only by occasions on which LBJ was visited by John Alex McCone, then-director of the CIA, the person for whom this secret enclave had been built. For a wide-eyed, slack-jawed LBJ, the vast bunker recalled the Bat-cave in D.C. comics he'd read as a kid, combined with elements from the title villain's deep-in-the-earth hideaway in *Dr. No*, the first James Bond film. He and Ladybird had seen that following a high recommendation by JFK.

"We'll make this brief, Lyndon," McCone stated in a flat, business-like tone. "I take it that you look forward to a long and happy run in the White House?"

"That's what I'm hopin' for."

"I have no doubt that can be arranged, so long as you understand the one absolute rule now in existence."

"I'm listening."

"From this room, I make all decisions concerning America's involvement in international affairs. I will convey necessary information to you through McGeorge. He'll report to you daily so it won't be necessary for you to meet with us often."

"Us?"

McCone indicated the numbers on the wall. "54/12. Lyndon, understand: the CIA and aligned organizations will operate covertly throughout the world, in the best interests of the United States. You will be informed of our activities."

"But ... I'm the president!"

"Yes, that's true. And, Mr. President, do you know what George Clemenceau said way back in 1919?"

"'War is now too important to be left to the generals.'"

"Precisely. Today? Politics is too important to be left to the presidents. We—the 54/12 Group—learned that the hard way."

"But what will I do ... say ..."

"As to the public, we don't care, so long as you keep any mention of us out of it. Tell them the truth or tell them lies. As to social issues, you're the boss. But when re-election time comes around again, if things in Southeast Asia are going well, tell the people you'll wrap it up in Vietnam quick as possible. If things get sticky over there, tell them that if they vote you back into office, you'll make certain American boys don't die doing the job South Vietnamese boys should be doing. If we ascertain that the war can be scaled down, it will be. You can claim it was your doing. They'll love you for it. If we see fit to escalate, you tell the public that you meant what you said when you said it, but that was then, this now. Circumstances altered. Things change. We will make such decisions."

"In Vietnam."

"Yes. Also, everywhere else in the world."

"And I have no alternative but to follow your orders?"

"Sure," McCone laughed. "You can end up like Kennedy."

*

On November 24, at approximately ten a.m., Capt. John Will Fritz of the Dallas Police department's homicide office gave up in his attempts over the past twelve hours to wring a confession out of Lee Harvey Oswald. During this procedure he'd been joined by Hosty and another FBI agent, James Bookhout. Despite their combined talents at drawing the truth out of a suspect, Oswald refused to say anything other than that when JFK was killed he'd been taking his lunch on the first floor of the Dallas Book Depository. Other employees who had been there at that time insisted that they couldn't recall Oswald's presence.

"If that were so, why did you slip away moments later?"

"I didn't think there would be any work done that afternoon so I just left."

"Where did you go?"

"Home. Having heard what happened to the president caused me to sweat like a pig. I showered, changed clothes, went out."

"Where did you go?"

"To the movies."

"Isn't that odd?"

"What do you mean?"

"I don't believe that's what most people would have done."

"Well, try and understand this: I'm not most people. I'm me. I do what I do, not what I think others would. How's that?"

"Why would you carry a pistol into the theatre?"

"Self-defense. There was a killer running around loose!"

Oswald was asked if he'd like a lawyer and he mentioned a top New York attorney. Oswald appeared in a line-up. When the police found three cartridges from Oswald's pistol near the body of a policeman named Tippit, who had been murdered shortly after the shooting of the president (it was this crime Oswald had been arrested for), as well as three bullets near the window that Oswald might have occupied, holding his rifle, as JFK drove by, he was now arraigned before Judge David Johnson for "the murder with malice of the president." Hours earlier Lee had been accused of killing Tippet in a different area of Dallas.

Fritz, following direct orders, began to prepare Oswald for a transfer from police headquarters to county jail.

309

"My name is Thomas J. Keller," a tall, rugged fellow said to Oswald just before Fritz's men moved the suspect down to the basement for his car ride from one incarceration to what was supposed to be the next. "I'm with the Secret Service. You claim not to be guilty of killing the president."

"That is absolutely correct."

"I'd be very anxious to talk with you to make sure that the correct story, as you believe it to have gone down, developed."

"I'll be glad to. Just as soon as I meet with my lawyer."

Nodding, Keller stood back and watched as the handcuffed Oswald was accompanied to the basement, where an unmarked car awaited him for the move. Once below, in the bowels of the building, Lee was stunned at what awaited him.

Flood-lights were turned on and bathed him to the point of blindness in an eerie white light of the order some movie star might experience while arriving for a premiere. Photographers snapped pictures while journalists called out for a statement.

This is it. The moment I've waited all in my life for!

"Here he comes," someone shouted.

What was it Cagney said in some old gangster film, just before they blew him away? 'Made it, Ma. Top of the world!'

"Mr. Oswald, did you kill President Kennedy?"

Marguerite? Are you watching TV? Just like in the movies. Top of the world ...

"Did you act alone or were you part of a conspiracy?"

What did Gloria Swanson say in Sunset Boulevard*? 'I'm ready for my close-up, Mr. DeMille ...'*

"Mr. Oswald, please. Make a statement."

What did a world-famous author claim to want most in a French film? To become immortal ... and then die.

"I'm a *patsy*," Lee cried out into the camera. "A patsy!"

CHAPTER TWENTY:
THE LAST PICTURE SHOW

"He who has taken wife and child has
given hostages to fortune."
—Henry David Thoreau, 1841

"Mr. Brewer? Come look at this, will you?"

John Calvin Brewer, the youthful manager of a prominent shoe store on Jefferson Street, hurried over to the twin front windows. He had, like most everyone else in Dallas, been riveted to the radio all day. During the noon hour gleeful broadcasts of the presidential motorcade kept his staff and their clients spellbound. Then, horror intruded. Shots were fired. The president, wounded in the head, had been rushed to Parkland hospital.

Some people in the store screamed. Others wept. A few fell silent, unable to digest such inconceivable information.

"What is it, Alice?"

Sirens whirred as police cars tore by, headed for the spot where Tenth intersected with Dalton. From there, a few blocks down from the shoe store, more gunfire had been heard. Rumors from people stepping in from the street had it that a policeman, apprehending a suspect, lay dying on the concrete.

"Look!"

The alert sales-person had noticed a slender young man, appearing anxious for himself rather than concerned for others, hurrying west on Jefferson. As the two police cars whizzed past, the young man, acting differently than anyone else, darted into the extended entry-way to the shoe-store, turning his face away.

"Something's not right here."

"Mr. Brewer, what should we do?"

Some of the other horrified people in the store had come up behind them to get a look at whatever suspicious actions were taking place. Suddenly a makeshift community, they watched as this man, brow furrowed with anxiety, continued along the street, twisting and turning his way through waves of zombie-like citizens.

Brewer observed as the man approached the Texas Theatre. He did not buy a ticket, slipping in alongside other patrons.

"You're in charge, Alice, until I return."

"Mr. Brewer, where are you going?"

"Stay calm." With that, he left the building, following the route Oswald had taken. Moments later Brewer stood in front of the theatre, explaining to a stunned cashier in the glass booth what had occurred. Without hesitation, the girl reached for her phone and called the police. While waiting for their arrival, Brewer glanced up at the marquee. A pair of World War II action films, *Cry of Battle* and *War is Hell!*, were double-billed.

"Of course, it may turn out to be nothing, Miss."

"Let's hope so. But you were right to let me know."

Then one patrol car after another came tearing around the corner, screeching to a halt. More than a dozen men in blue poured out. People on the street gathered, sensing something big about to happen. The policemen quickly closed off every exit.

"Mr. Brewer? I'm patrolman McDonald. Would you be able to identify the suspect?"

"Absolutely."

"Alright, then. Come with me."

They proceeded down an alleyway adjacent to the theatre and approached the rear exit. As they entered, the theatre lights brightened. Detective Paul L. Bentley had rushed up into the balcony and instructed the projectionist to do this. Moviegoers couldn't grasp what might be going on.

The film continued to roll as Brewer and MacDonald stepped onstage, dwarfed by the larger than life image of Van Heflin and James MacArthur battling over Rita Moreno. For a moment, viewers couldn't tell where the show left off and reality began.

"That's him," Brewer affirmed, indicating a man off to his left, seated a few rows down from the lobby. "He's the one."

From all directions, uniformed and undercover policemen swarmed over Oswald. They awaited McDonald who, followed by Brewer, swiftly proceeded from the stage to this man's spot.

"Hey, fellas," Lee said, sneering. "Will you please back off and leave me alone? At least until the film finishes up?"

*

On October 15, Lee stepped off the bus that had carried him back from Mexico City to Laredo, Texas, at the Customs Shed. There all would be subject to search before proceeding over the border. This was a notably different person than the one who had crossed southward on September 26. Quiet, sober and humbled, he hurried to a pay phone and called the home of Ruth Paine.

"Marina doesn't want to speak with you, Lee."

"Ruth, this is important. Everything will be different—"

"How many times have you told the poor girl that?"

"This time, I mean it. *Forever.*"

A long silence. Then: "I'll check with her. That's all I can do." Lee thanked Ruth profusely and waited. Five minutes later, she came back. "I tried. Marina can't take any more."

"Tell her Lee said 'everything will be the way she wants it. Not the way I think she wants it. I'm a changed man.'"

Yet when he arrived in Dallas, Lee did not immediately make the trip to Irving. Though he would have been welcome to stay overnight at the Paines' house, Lee checked in to a YMCA. The following morning he searched for an apartment, locating a room at a house on North Marsalis, in Oak Cliff. That afternoon he lined up at the Texas Employment Commission in hopes of scoring a job. Lee applied for a position as a typesetter, failing to mention his dyslexia, which might well have disqualified him.

Then he stepped alongside the highway, stuck out a thumb, and hitched up to Irving. When he appeared at the screen door Marina happened to be passing by. Lee's presence, so unexpected, this coupled with her even then thinking about him, caused Marina to gasp. Ruth and her estranged husband Michael, hearing voices, approached, saw them together, then made some flimsy excuse to go out for an evening drive. Marina hesitantly let Lee in.

"First, I want to see June."

"Later. She's sleeping."

"Alright, then. Let's you and I have it out."

"We said it all in New Orleans."

"Everything's different now. This is 'the new Lee.'"

"Oh? What happened to Jesus Christ, off to save the world?"

"Never again. I have only one mission, now and forever."

"And what, may I ask, is that?"

"To be the best husband I can to you. The best father to baby June. And our child yet to be born."

"From the Second Coming, then, to Norman Normal?"

"Marina, I think that deep down that's what I've always wanted most. Now, I truly believe I can have it."

Lee then proceeded to explain. He had left her believing he'd found his great purpose in life and traveled to Mexico City, despite Marina's objections, to achieve his mission. While there, and on the bus trip back, he came to understand that all he'd ever believed to be frivolous turned out to be what really mattered. Conversely, all Lee had held important? Utterly worthless.

"Make me believe you. Lee, I so want to."

*

"United States leaders should think that if they are aiding terrorist plans to eliminate Cuban leaders," Castro said, "they themselves will not be safe." Lee gasped at the words, spoken over a world-wide radio connection from Havana. When asked what might be his response, Castro growled: any such attempts would be "answered in kind." Still in New Orleans, already convinced he must personally do something to diffuse the heightening tension in the world, Lee took this as Castro's direct threat to JFK.

Not the CIA, who had for years employed operatives like Lee himself to try and debilitate, then murder Castro. Kennedy!

I must get down there at once. Somehow reach Fidel. Explain that Kennedy and the Company are now entirely at odds.

Me! I'll help Kennedy and Castro set the past aside.

Castro's ultimatum hadn't received a direct response from the White House, JFK not wishing to dignify it. Nonetheless, JFK had Bobby and Gen. Maxwell Taylor call together a committee of a special group within the National Security Council. They convened at the Department of State on September 12, at 2:30 P.M., to initiate future positions on Cuba and the Company.

"We must reach a conclusion and do so today," Bobby began.

Were the CIA to attempt even once more to take Castro's life, there existed "a strong likelihood that Castro would retaliate in some way." Most likely this would constitute only a "low level" response. Still, it would be unwise to assume that something considerably bigger couldn't possibly occur.

"So what do we do?" Taylor asked. "I for one don't believe that we can simply sit back and let events take their course."

"Most certainly not," Bobby answered. "Here's one thought. Some time ago in Florida, I met an extremely dedicated agent. He was with the CIA at the time, but appears, from our sources, to have experienced an alteration of position not unlike the one we here today are mutually expressing."

"Might he make the connection with Castro for us?"

"Possibly. Though we can't sneak him into Cuba without arousing suspicions. The man would have to, if this were to work, proceed to Mexico, there to legally enter Cuba."

"At every turn, the CIA would create resistance."

"Yes. While, I'd guess, trying to convince this agent that they are doing all they could to help him."

"Do you believe such an approach could succeed?"

"I believe the odds are against it. Formidably! Also, that we have absolutely nothing to lose in trying."

314

"Except, possibly, the agent's life."

*

On September 25 Lee had boarded a Continental Trailways bus at Nuevo Laredo, crossing over into Mexico. He happened to be seated next to a surgeon from England, John Bryan McFarland. That man innocently asked Oswald why he was heading south.

"Actually, to try and arrange travel to Cuba."

"Oh," McFarland responded. "Why go there?"

"To see Castro," Oswald said, flashing his signature sneer.

Lee disembarked at the main Mexico City bus terminal at ten a.m., September 27. He walked to the nearby Hotel Comercial, a dump at which he could pick up a room for slightly more than a dollar a day. After washing and shaving, he hurried over to the Cuban Embassy. There Lee explained his desire to visit Cuba (if not his specific plan) to a hostess. She arranged a meeting with the consul, Silvia Tirado de Duran. Lee presented that surprised official with a brochure of newspaper clippings about his heady involvement with Fair Play, introducing himself as one of those "righteous" and "enlightened" U.S. citizens.

Nobody's fool, de Duran put two and two together, guessing that this grinning character had some sort of a hidden agenda.

"I will try and hurry this through at once," she lied.

"Thank you for that," Lee sincerely replied.

As he supposedly hoped to travel to Cuba so that there he could make plans to relocate himself and his wife and children in Russia, she told Lee to have photographs of himself taken.

"When you return with them, the process can begin."

Lee shuffled off whistling, assuming things were going his way. Senora Duran reached for her phone and began placing high level phone calls, the first to her contact at the Mexico City Soviet consulate, explaining the situation. That consul in turn placed calls to Russia while she did the same to Cuba.

An hour later they spoke again.

"It is possible that Oswald is what he claims to be," the Soviet consul said. "More likely, he's a double or even triple agent, with an agenda so complex it defies description."

"In that case, my strategy will be: stall, stall, stall."

Everyone treated Lee with the utmost politeness. But other than extending sweetly insincere smiles and offering their best wishes, Lee quickly realized he had run into a brick wall that he could not crash through. When he returned, in great spirits, at the Cuban Embassy with the photos, de Duran explained she had contacted the local Soviets in hopes of speeding things along.

The embassy there had informed her that as Lee didn't already have an entry visa to Russia, achieving one that would allow him to travel from Cuba to that country might take months.

"That's alright," he, gathering his wits, replied. "I'll go to Cuba and wait there." That was, after all, his chief plan. Returning to Minsk was back-up for him, Marina, and the children.

"But, as it turns out," she continued, pursing her lips, "that too will be more involved than I originally believed."

She then began to list a series of small, ridiculous issues that the woman spoke as if by rote. As she did, Lee felt one of his rages overcoming mind and body. He insisted that she stop talking and bring him to her superior. She led Lee down one more of those lengthy couriers he had spent so many minutes of his life passing through on his way to confront people of importance.

The chief consul, Eusebio Azque, formally accepted Lee into his office. Despite (perhaps because of) the tirade to follow, he insisted that while Lee certainly had the right to request a visa, and that he and Senora Duran would be "willing" (he did not say "happy," Lee noted) to initiate the process, nothing in the New Orleans portfolio warranted any "special consideration" for a speeded-up visa. Nor could he assure this panicky-looking man that he would receive a visa to Cuba, much less Russia.

"In addition to your own portfolio," E. Azque concluded, retrieving a manila folder from his drawer and shoving it across the desk toward Oswald, "we have to consider these."

Knowing what was coming, Lee inspected the contents. Here he found one after another report about his activities in the anti-Castro movement, including evidence that Oswald had been one of three CIA agents who in 1961 attempted to kill Castro.

"Yes, yes," Lee sighed, pushing them back across the desk. "But I've undergone a radical change. Now—"

"Perhaps, Mr. Oswald, you like a pendulum shift back and forth so often that no one can ever know your true position?"

Unable to form coherent words, Lee shouted something about Azque being a narrow-minded fool. He roared out of the building, hurrying back to his sordid hotel room, collapsing in confusion on the stale-smelling bed.

On a visit to the Soviet Embassy Lee fared no better. For three days he lay on the rumpled sheets of his cot-like bed, sweating, waiting, thinking. He'd brought a book along, Kafka's *The Trial*, which he'd attempted to read when Johnny Rosselli had handed him a James Bond book at the resort-like 'hospital.'

That feels like a lifetime ago now! How appropriate Ian Fleming had been for reading material there. Apparently I've come full circle. Kafka's right on target today, particularly the tale of poor K., put on trial in some surreal version of our world for a supposed crime no one will even reveal to him.

That's me. Not James Bond. I'm the underground man. I started that way. I'll end that way. A face in the crowd.

Still, the phone did not ring. On the fourth day, at his wits end, Lee barged back into the Cuban embassy. He confronted Duran again, with no success. At her suggestion he ran back across the way to the Soviet embassy where he fared no better.

I'm trying to save the world and no one will help. George would of course know my every move. He may be working against me. Putting up road-blocks at every corner I reach. Forcing me back to Dallas to do his dirty work: kill Kennedy.

Alright, then. Two can play that game. But I'll check-mate him. Go to Dallas but not see the assassination through.

*

Having finished *The Trial*, and with no time to pick up anything else to read, Lee spent the return bus trip rolling over the situation in his mind. He was certainly not going to kill JFK for the CIA, the Mob, whoever else might be in on that deal now. Nor had he been able to create the Kennedy-Castro link he had a week earlier believed himself born for.

What now, then?

Marina. I see her face so clearly. Recall the things she said when I let her leave New Orleans. All she wanted was a normal life. With me! Our little girl and the child to be.

Let's follow that trail. Go back, back, back to time long before I ever came to believe I might be worthy of greatness.

What was it I most wanted then?

To be ... normal. The very thing I'd been denied. They didn't let me in the scouts. I didn't have a girl-friend in junior high, not even a homely one, much less a pretty girl.

Now? I've got everything I want. The package. How could I not have seen it? Perhaps as it was so close before my eyes.

"One more chance," Lee begged Marina.

"The little boy no longer wants to play hero?"

"Please don't be sarcastic."

"How else can I respond? All your grandiose dreams—"

"Turned to dust."

"So now you are a man without a purpose in life?"

Weeping, Lee approached her. "But I do have a purpose. You and the babies. Being the best husband and father I can be."

She allowed him to gently press his hand against her tummy, feeling the life readying to burst forth. "Someday the call will come again from George. When it does, you will—"

"No! I swear. George seems a great Satan to me now."

Now it was Marina's turn to cry. "I wish I could believe you." She gripped him tightly, both her hands clawing at Lee's shoulders. "I want so little today, as compared to the brat who was too beautiful for her own good."

He cradled her, firmly but gently. "You, me, and the kids. That's all. But ... That's everything! When you've been denied normalcy all your life, it turns out to be what you want the most. We can have that. One more chance, Marina?"

"Of course, Alik. I cannot say no."

He breathed in deeply. "Not Alik, though. Ozzie."

"Your Marine nickname?"

"Yes. But also 'Ozzie' on TV. You've seen *The Adventures of Ozzie and Harriet* since living in America?"

"Yes, of course. Everyone watches it."

"When I was a child, I hated it. Because I thought that was only an absurd dream of the way things are supposed to be."

"And now?"

"I know better. From now on, we'll enjoy *The Adventures of Ozzie and Marina*. With our own two children to raise."

"You used to want to be James Bond in a spy movie."

He laughed. "Now? The guy next door on a TV show."

They left the living room, proceeded along to her bedroom. Alternately weeping, laughing and kissing, they spent the night in each other's arms. Owing to her condition they did not engage in sex. Still, Lee and Marina made love, if in a spiritual sense.

*

All that Ozzie needed now to complete his transition to domestic normality was a decent job. Magically, one appeared.

Lee hadn't received that typesetting position. The employers, running a routine check, became aware of his previous communist ties. Any bitterness dissipated when what certainly seemed like serendipity occurred. Through a friend of a friend of a friend, Ruth Paine learned that a Mr. Truly, manager of the book depository, needed to fill a slot. She passed this on to Lee during one of his weekend visits. Continuing the pattern of his youth, Lee had changed addresses, now living at a rooming house temporarily managed by Earlene Roberts on North Beckley. Ruth offered to let Lee move in now that things were normalized between him and Marina. But Lee insisted this would be too much of an imposition.

As soon as he found work and put a little money aside, he'd rent a place where his family could truly become a family, creating the beginning of an American Dream come true.

"You're a former marine? I do like to support servicemen."

"Thank you, sir. I'm a family man; my wife is about to have our second child. I can guarantee you an honest day's work."

"Do understand, essentially you'll be a shipping clerk."

"Sir, just give a chance. You won't be disappointed."

Truly rose from behind his desk even as Lee, sensing that the interview was concluded, did so as well. "Can you start at eight a.m. sharp next Monday morning?"

Lee excitedly called Marina with the good news. She wept. Everything appeared to be falling into place, as Truly mentioned one of Lee's co-workers often drove over to Irving after work.

"He's offered to give me a lift on Fridays, bring me back early Monday morning. I won't even have to hitch-hike."

"Everything's turning out ... perfect."

But the world, as I've learned, abhors perfection even as space does a vacuum. There's got to be a catch somewhere...

Yet things kept getting better. When he arrived at the Paines' house on Friday, October 18, with three days work behind him, he—wondering if in all the confusion anyone would recall this was his 24th birthday—knocked on the Paine's door at seven p.m.

"Surprise!" Marina, cradling June in her arms, appearing ready to burst with child, cried out. She, the Paines and their children had readied a birthday celebration. They wore silly paper hats, threw confetti in the air, blew on plastic whistles and proffered inexpensive, wonderful little presents: a cheap tie, a plastic shoe-horn, a bottle of Old Spice shave lotion.

"I've never had such a fabulous birthday. Not ever!"

Maybe it's going to be alright now. He seems so sincere in his desire to conform. That's what every non-conformist most wants. He took the other route only because no one gave him the chance to fit in. Now, he's finally been allowed that ...

As if for a final gift, Marina felt her first pangs of labor on mid-afternoon, Sunday. As Lee still could not drive, Ruth took Marina to Parkland Hospital while Lee remained behind, watching over her two children and June. On Monday morning at six, minutes before Wesley Frazier swung by to pick Lee up, Ruth called to say that Marina had given birth to another girl.

"Oh, Mama. You're wonderful!" Lee cooed later that day, visiting his wife and new child in the hospital.

"Lee," Marina giggled. "You never called me that before."

"Well, that's who you are from now on. Mama!"

319

Oh, God! Please don't let him confuse me with Marguerite.

They decided to name the baby Audrey Marina Rachel, but always they called her 'Rachel.' People at the book depository noticed that their fellow worker not only did his job diligently but excelled as if hoping for an eventual promotion. Mr. Truly held Lee up as a model of responsibility.

He's good. So very good. Which is fine. Still, something's not quite right. He's better than good. It's as if the perfect worker showed up. Could he be too good to be true?

Lee arrived early for work and left late, though no extra pay compensated him for that beyond the rigid $1.25 an hour for filling textbook orders. Arriving at the Paines' each Friday, he would hug his wife, cuddle June and Rachel, then get down on the floor and play with little plastic cowboys and Indians beside the Paines' boy Chris, in a way Michael failed to do. If Michael Paine felt uncomfortable with domestic duties, Lee reveled in them.

On Sunday afternoons, Lee stretched out on the carpet of the Paines' living room and watched football. Michael Paine, visiting his estranged wife, had to literally step over Lee.

"I never thought I'd see a radical spend a full day in front of the TV grooving on sports," he said sarcastically.

Momentarily, Lee grew sullen. "That side of me is gone."

One Saturday evening, Lee said to Marina: "Let's take in a movie." They headed for the drive in, the children in the car with them. There, they feasted on fresh popcorn and stale hot dogs, watching a ridiculous piece of junk called *Cuban Rebel Girls,* enjoying every minute of their time together.

Lee seems quite taken with the blonde girl playing the lead. She is very pretty. He has always been fascinated, obsessed even, by beautiful women. Particularly blondes.

Now, though, he's riveted by her in a way I've never seen before. As if there's a personal connection ...

How like a man! We women notice everything. Particularly when it concerns our husbands and other women ...

"That girl, Marina? She almost got to play 'Lolita.'"

"Really? But, Lee. How would *you* know that?"

"Oh! Uh ... I ... read it in a magazine."

By the time they reached the Paines' home, whatever had consumed her husband had passed, he 'the new Lee' again.

*

"Hello, Lee."

"Hello, yourself. Who's this?"

A stunned silence at the other end, followed by: "George."

Shit! I had willed him out of my mind, so completely and intensely wanting him gone that I allowed myself to forget that he even exists.

I pretended that if I forgot him, then he would forget me too. But it doesn't work that way. Except in a mind as strange in its strategies as my own. Now, reality again intrudes ...

"Oh!"

"Lee? Are you alright?"

"Yes, yes. Of course. Forgive me. I ... got confused."

"That's understandable. How many times have we shifted your 'legend' in the past two years? Anyone would."

"Something must be important or you wouldn't call me here."

Lee was at his rooming house. He'd finished work, eaten dinner at a simple cafeteria, and was preparing to call Marina, as he did every evening at around seven. L.H.O.: Norman Normal.

"Lee! 11/22/63. Right?"

"Oh, yeah. Right, right."

"Man! I can't believe how easy it was to get you set up at the Book Depository. The motorcade will have to come close to stopping in front of your building. Should be an easy shot."

Everything is clear to me now. I'm working at the book depository not because I made it happen, or destiny did the job. I'm there because George moved his pawn across the chess-board.

In my idiotic way—what did Marina call it once, my inconceivable innocence?—I believed if I simply failed to show up and do the killing that day, then it wouldn't happen.

"Of course," Lee mumbled, barely aware he still spoke to George, half-believing he was only thinking out loud. "The president's motorcade will approach the building as it comes down Houston. Then there's that sharp left onto Elm."

"It's important you do the job from the sixth floor."

"I work on the second and third. Take lunch on the first."

"The sixth, Lee. That's imperative."

"Whatever you say."

"Lee, it sounds as if you'd forgotten all about this."

"No. Not really. I just had another baby. Or Marina did—"

"I'm very much aware of that. Congratulations."

"A little disoriented, that's all."

"From this moment, you must focus on the shooting. Nothing else can matter. *Nothing.* Do you understand?"

"Absolutely."

"Good boy. Be assured, we've got you covered. It's best if we don't talk again until that day. There will be a support system to spirit you out of town moments after the shots are fired. Don't worry. All will go like clockwork."

They hung up. Lee, shivering and sweating worse than ever in his life, could not bring himself to call Marina. Nor did he go into the lounge and watch television. He lay still as he could on his bed, staring up at the ceiling as he'd done many times before.

Everything will be alright. I'll simply not show up. The motorcade will pass as it's supposed to. The shot will not be fired. It's possible that George may haunt me for the rest of my life after I fail to pull the trigger. What do I do about that?

I've got it! I'll write a tell-all journal, drop it off at some safe place. The FBI! That'll be perfect, as they hate the CIA. I'll label it 'to be opened only in the case of my death.'

Then, immediately after the Motorcade passes by without incident, I'll call George, tell him I'm out. But that he had better not go after me in any way, or ever try to harm JFK again, as that journal is in FBI hands now.

I'll swear to keep my mouth shut, so long as the Company leaves me and my family alone ... What can he do about that?

The President will not die by my hand. He'll live by it.

A normal life for me at last. God knows, I've earned it!

*

In the wee small hours of the morning, Lee woke with a start. The nightmares had returned, even as they did to Sinatra in *The Manchurian Candidate*. He sat up in bed, panicky.

Wait a minute. What did George say earlier? 'We'll have you covered.' As with the team when I flew down to kill Castro.

Not just me. Two other gunmen as well.

That's George's 'way': The triple-shot. Then and now.

'Shots fired.' That's what he said. Not 'shot.' 'Shots'!

What else? 'The entire team' will be rescued before anyone can get their hands on us. Of course. I was to be his pawn, but not George's only one. There will be many.

Part of his great game-plan. Or so George thinks ...

*

On Thursday, November 21, Lee Harvey Oswald left work and met Wesley Frazier at five after five on Elm Street where that co-worker parked his car. Earlier, Lee had asked if he might drive up to Irving with him that evening. Frazier said 'sure.' That blue-collar worker had been surprised, however, as Lee never made the trip on a week-day. Only weekends. Except for the past one, when Lee mentioned he'd stay in Dallas, get stuff done.

"Anything special going on tonight, Lee?"

"Every time I see Marina is special."

322

"That's nice. I meant—"

"I *know* what you *meant*." Lee's voice sounded so harsh Wes did not pursue the issue further. To his surprise, Lee, so eager to listen to hot hits on the radio and talk, talk, talk about work, sports, and TV shows and such, remained stonily silent.

"Hello, stranger," Marina said caustically as Lee stepped out of the car, Frazier driving off. His wife had been watering the grass in front of the Paine home. She wore cut-off blue-jeans and a red shirt, knotted at the waist. Her hair was set in pigtails. Marina looked like the girl next door. No one would guess she'd recently given birth. Her trim figure had returned.

Everything I ever wanted, though of course, I did not realize I wanted that ...

"Hello, yourself." He knew why Marina appeared disturbed. Up until a week earlier he had called her twice a day, during his lunch break from the pay phone, again in the evening after he returned to the rooming house. For ten days, she had not heard from him. Nor had he arrived the past Friday as usual.

"So, on Sunday night, I saw baby June playing with the phone. That gave me an idea. 'Let's call Daddy!' I said. June giggled, seeming to understand. When the landlady answered I asked for you. She said 'no one lives here by that name.'"

Cautiously, Lee stepped closer. "I'm sorry. I forgot to tell you. I'm registered there under my old alias, O.H. Lee."

"So it's as I feared? Starting your old foolishness again. The little boy who wants to play at being James Bond?"

"This isn't what you think, Marina." Desperately, Lee tried to approach her, hold his wife close. She turned, though not before he witnessed an ugly expression cross her face as Marina stepped inside. "Please believe me," he called out, following.

"I made the mistake of believing you when you returned from Mexico. Remember? 'It'll never happen again, Marina. I swear!'"

Though she slammed the screen door behind her with terrible finality, Lee opened it and followed doggedly in her path. "I meant what I said then, and I mean it now."

Scooping Rachel up from her crib, even as June came rushing out with a goofy ear to ear grin smeared across her little face, Marina swiveled around, eyes dark, unforgiving. "What movie are we living in now? Don't expect me to guess. Tell me for once."

"I told you: no more movies."

"Yes, you did. You also said: *Ozzie and Harriet* now."

"Yes! Exactly."

She laughed to keep from crying. "Movies. TV. Lee, listen! Just once, couldn't we live in the real world? As others do?"

"Yes. After tomorrow. And forever. If ..." His voice trailed off. His eyes fell to the floor.

"If," Marina gasped, all at once sensing that something huge was happening here, "what?"

"If," he continued with difficulty, "I'm still alive."

*

"I'm afraid you won't be able to watch the rest of the show," Officer McDonald told Lee, still seated.

"What kind of a country do I live in, when a man can't mind his own business and catch a movie?"

"I'll need to have you stand, sir, while I search you."

Suddenly, Lee threw a punch, sending the police officer down hard. Other officers rushed to reinforce their fallen colleague. McDonald leaped up, returning the punch.

"Oooooooh!" Oswald screeched, reaching into his pants and belt for the pistol he'd shoved there, bringing it up quickly.

"He's got a gun!" someone shouted. People screamed. Some felt frozen in their seats. Others leaped up and ran. As they did, up there onscreen—though the house-lights were turned up, the film continued to run—Van Heflin and James MacArthur fired round after round at invading Japanese soldiers.

Moviegoers weren't sure if the shots were real or pretend.

Kill 'em all, guys. Mow 'em down. Just like John Wayne in Back to Bataan. *And, back in 1941, some real-life Americans taking on whoever was the enemy then. The faces change, the nationalities.*

Always, though, there's 'The Enemy.'

If, today, for the first time, it comes from inside.

This is too much! So it ends, as it began, with a movie?

"Well, it's all over now," Lee cursed as they took him away.

324

EPILOGUE: AS I LAY DYING
(PART TWO)

"In his own mind, every man is great."
—Sigmund Freud, 1921

"Doctor? We're losing him. Fast!"

I hear the voice, as if from beyond some unimaginable object ... part wall ... part veil ... part mist ...a woman's voice ... Not Marina, though ...

How I would love to hear Marina speak once more before—

... before I die. Of course, that's what's happening. Why didn't I realize that at once? A few minutes ago, pain in my gut beyond comprehension. Now, that's disappearing, bit by bit.

I thought maybe that meant they were saving me. It's the opposite though, isn't it?

I mean, this is it!

So what does it all add up to? Did I achieve anything?

Like that man in the French movie I saw several years ago ... my life's desire ... to become immortal, then die.'

Well, I've achieved the latter part. Obviously! But ... as to the former ... will anyone remember me?

Or will dust be my destiny ... my final fate oblivion?

*

"If you leave this house tomorrow morning, Alik ... Ozzie ... Lee ... I know I will never see you again."

In the darkness, between the sheets, Marina Oswald held her husband close. They'd just made love, total love, as they had that marvelous time when the two broke through all facades.

The night they became people rather than personas to one another. The most real experience either had ever known.

In or out of bed.

"Marina," Lee said, kissing her gently, thrilled that last night they had achieved such a level of intimacy once more, "I can't deny there is that possibility."

"But your promise—"

"Try and understand. I meant what I said—"

"'That was then, this now.'"

"No, no, no. I said 'forever.' I did mean it."

325

"So how can you—"

"I told you my dreams of greatness were gone. Any belief that there could be a political solution to the world's problems? Over. That I might achieve it, with greater glory going to *me*? None of that interests me. As I said: You, June, Rachel."

The first hint of dawn cracked through that spot where the window-shade almost touched down on the wood panel below it. "Yet in a matter of minutes, you'll walk out on me."

"It's a matter of principle. Not politics, not personal ambition. Those? Gone with the wind, as Marguerite would say."

"You told me nothing was more important than 'us.'"

Lee sat upright, like a coiled spring suddenly released. "I never said that. Never."

"Something like it ..."

"In your mind! Yes, 'Mama,' I said that all the superficial things I hoped to achieve appear ridiculous to me now. But this is not one of those things. Can't I make you see—"

"You have. You've made me see that, in the end, there is something more important than our marriage."

Realizing that to continue was hopeless, Lee rose from the bed and began dressing. "That's right. There is."

"Fine," she said anxiously. "Perhaps I can even accept that. Only you have to tell me what it *is*!"

"I can't," he replied, turning in the semi-darkness, the sun now steadily journeying upward in the sky outside.

"If I'm your wife, and I do mean what you say I do to you, you can tell me anything. Absolutely—"

"Anything but this."

Lee stepped close, bringing his lips to Marina's.

"And yet you must go."

How to answer? There must be a line from a movie that would suffice. He tried so hard to recall ...

"A man's gotta do what a man's gotta do."

"Didn't John Wayne once say that once?"

"Oh, yes. In *Hondo*!"

Now, finally, it was my turn to say it. God, for one single moment in my life, it's as if the Duke and I are one.

"Well, two can play that game, Alik. Lee. Ozzie. Whoever you are. So: 'Kiss me once, as if it had to last forever.'"

Lee recognized the words but couldn't place the film. Some chick-flick with Deborah Kerr, maybe. Still, he kissed her.

"Just like in the movies," Marina sardonically commented as Lee completed that gesture and stepped back to the dresser. She heard a little clink but couldn't guess what it might be.

"Yes," Lee said, heading for the door. "Always remember: you were the great love of my life."

My big exit scene ... and I played it brilliantly ...

The Paines hadn't risen yet. Good! Pausing briefly in the kitchen, Lee helped himself to a stale cup of coffee left over from last night. Then he left the house proper, entering the garage through a side door. There, objects belonging to him and Marina were stored. Lee snapped on the light and glanced around.

Lee carried with him a long brown bag he had fitted together from packing papers at the Book Depository, stapling, gluing, taping them together into a single holster-shaped sack. He had brought this with him when he entered the previous night and, as conspicuous as this might have been, Lee's intensity caused all present to overlook it. While Marina and Ruth fixed dinner, Lee had shoved his makeshift sack into the hall closet.

Now he brought this flimsy contraption alongside a large wooden box. In it were his rifle and telescopic sight. With the precision only a marine can administer, Lee swiftly broke the piece down, wrapping it in the paper shroud.

He left the building as Wes drove up. Lee slipped in beside the driver, simultaneously shoving his package into the back.

"What's that?" Wes asked.

"Curtain rods," Lee responded. "I'll spend my weekend putting them up in my apartment. Give the place some color."

"Good thinking." Wes gunned the gas and they were off.

Unable to fall back to sleep, Marina pulled herself up out of bed and switched on the light. Immediately, she noticed Lee had dropped his wedding ring down in a cup on the dresser.

So this is how it ends, Marina later recalled thinking, *the words not her own but that of a poet she once read and admired, not with a bang but a whimper.*

T.S. Eliot had, of course, been talking about the world. She, her relationship with her family. Their own little world.

Vaguely depressed, Marina wandered into the living room and switched on the TV, keeping the volume low so as not to bother anyone. It didn't matter which channel she turned to. Each would be covering the arrival of the Kennedys all day long.

Here, at least, was something pleasant Marina could focus on to get Lee, and whatever it was he might be up to now, out of her mind. What a wonderful alternative: Camelot comes to Dallas.

What better way to escape her troubles than by watching a fantasy come true?

*

Wes Frazier parked two blocks away from the Book Depository in his regular spot. Somehow, though, things felt different. On most days when they shared the trip, he and Lee would walk over to the building together, chatting about anything at all, from what football team was on top to who would win the next election.

Not today. As Wes locked his car door, he glanced up to see Lee scurrying on ahead, carrying his oblong package, alone.

Maybe he had a fight with his wife? Sure, that's it. No big deal or anything. Hey, that happens all the time …

At eight sharp, when Roy Truly arrived, the boss man noticed Lee already hard at work. Truly's top man darted about on the first floor from one huge cardboard carton to the next, marking off future shipments on his clipboard.

What a worker! Quite a guy, this Lee Oswald …

The morning passed uneventfully, though for this special occasion Truly had set up an old black and white TV in the first-floor lunchroom. That way, during their breaks, employees could catch a glimpse of Air Force One whizzing in from Fort Worth, the First Couple disembarking, Governor Connolly and his wife greeting them, then the foursome stepping into the sleek Lincoln limousine, on their way to a gala lunch at the Trade Mart.

Lee joined three black workers, Bonnie Ray Williams, Harold 'Hank' Norman, and James Earl Jarman, Jr., for a cup of coffee and a look-see at history in the making at 10:34.

This is the way it should be … black and white together … color doesn't mean a thing. We're just people, Americans all. That's the way I want it and the way Kennedy does, too.

No one will stop him from achieving what Dr. Martin Luther King addressed when he announced: 'I have a dream.' Some dreams do come true. This one will.

JFK won't die, at least not on my watch, though forces of immense power are gathering to achieve precisely that.

For my last public duty, I will save the day. Didn't George once tell me Jack Kennedy would become the most important person in my life? Well, he was sure right about that!

If not, at least from our current perspective, in quite the way that he intended his statement …

"There is nothing more stupid, Lee, then doing the same thing, time after time, always expecting a different result."

Yes, Sergeant. You were right about that. Only now I'm doing the opposite of what I've always done before.

My own thing. The right thing. The final 'thing' …

Then, back to Marina and the kids.

Or ... If God wills it ... I too will become immortal, then die. But what an honor that will be ...

To be recalled, down through the ages, as the man who gave his life to save Kennedy.

'Finally made it, Ma! Top of the world!'

*

By 11:10 A.M. Lee had slipped off from the others, up to the sixth floor. Earlier that morning he had hidden his rifle among myriad cardboard cartons and similarly colored wrapping paper scattered all about. The entire area presented a terrible mess, one people would avoid. In addition to such usual storage materials, as well as books stacked high in gigantic piles, most of the floor had been torn up for repairs and restoration.

Five men had spent the morning laying down fresh plywood. They arrived shortly after Lee slipped in to conceal his weapon in a back area where they would not likely go.

Now, those workers broke for what Lee knew was going to be an early and long lunch. They'd watch the motorcade on the first floor, until the procession arrived out front. Then everyone would hurry to the windows or out the door to actually catch a glimpse of the celebrities in the flesh, so to speak.

Lee stepped into the corridor's shadows, then entered the now deserted room. With the empty boxes haphazardly arranged alongside oblong piles of books, the scene looked like something out of a *Twilight Zone* episode on TV.

Da-da, da-da; da-da, da-da.

So this is why George instructed me to shoot from the sixth floor. Somehow, some way, he—the puppet-master as well as chess champ—arranged for such work to be done at this juncture in time so there would be no one around but me.

Fine. I'm here. If only to turn the tables on him.

Swiftly Lee reassembled his rifle and headed for the open window. Hundreds, perhaps thousands of people were lining the streets below. All joyously awaiting their brief glimpse of greatness. Also, as Lee alone grasped, out there somewhere were a pair of deadly assassins, possibly together, more likely in separate enclaves, planning to shoot the president, assuming Lee would fire the third shot from here.

He had to out-fox them, get one, then the other in his sights; knock 'em out before they had a chance to fire.

It wouldn't be easy.

He could achieve victory if not a single split second were wasted as Lee raised the rifle to his chin.

Lee couldn't imagine anything that might cause him to hesitate, as he had with that fascistic general back in Dallas.

He had missed then. There was no margin for error now.

Too much depended on his being prepared ...

Lee ran through a litany of things in his mind that might give him pause, and could imagine none of them interfering here.

George, Rosselli, any of them ... To save the president?

I'll put a bullet right between each man's eyes. Yes, I'm human. There are those things that could cost me a moment, destroy my plan.

But I can't imagine anything that could interfere today.

The motorcade moved at what now seemed a snail's pace in the direction of Dealey Plaza. Lee scanned the entire area with eyes that had once observed the skies through radar devices and thanks to hours of such study had become keen as an eagle's.

So many nice folks, waving and cheering. Eyewitnesses to history. Yet somewhere, out there, in the midst of them ...

Then, déjà vu set in. Even as the Lincoln limo slowed to a near halt at an intersection directly across the way, where Elm, Main, and Commerce converged ...

That rings a bell! Where ... I know! Seventh grade English class. With the best teacher I ever had. She taught us Greek tragedy and the kids all laughed, breaking her heart. Because she had hoped we might be moved by anything so old.

I'm moved by it! I will never forget what you told us. About fate overwhelming free-will. Me, the pathetic little guy sitting here in the back of the room. The boy no one notices.

A face in the crowd ...

Oedipus on his way from Corinth to Thebes, got into an argument during the journey ... History's first example of road rage, you called it, hoping that would make this more relevant to the arrogant kids seated before you ...

Young Oedipus killed old King Laius, the man he had been journeying here in hopes of saving ... Oh, the irony of it all! ... His own father ... And he did so ... I recall what you said now ... At a place where three roads meet ...

"A magic meeting place, students. The harbinger of true tragedy. Which is not drama in an ordinary sense, even those with sad endings."

"So what is it, teacher? What then *is* a tragedy?"

"'Tragedy' implies a special kind of tale. One that allows the individual to comprehend his place in the universe."

"Give me *Wagon Train* any day."

"Say what you will. Someday you'll understand. Only tragedy can help us understand ourselves as unique human beings."

The Connollys in the convertible's front seat, the Kennedys in the rear, Secret Service men surrounding them on all sides, and police riding motorcycles on the flanks...

Lee spotted something in Dealey that caught his attention. It was ... how to describe it? ...

... a grassy knoll ...

Of course. Just like the one in Suddenly. *Where Sinatra as 'Johnny Barrows' had been planning to shoot the president!*

Sensing the moment had arrived, Lee brusquely brought his weapon up under his chin. Through the sights, he could clearly see that grassy knoll.

And, off a ways from the gleeful crowd, several tramps, lumbering around, grouped together.

That's George on the right. Johnny Rosselli beside him. Despite their hobo costumes both are wearing cowboy boots. As, for that matter, am I. And the time is ... high noon. So what is this: the final wild west shootout, right here in Dallas?

Still, Lee held his fire as neither seemed armed. Then, from behind a small bush, a third man appeared, bringing a rifle that looked identical to Lee's up and ready to fire.

He's the one. I'll take him out before he has a chance—

For a split-second, though, Lee found himself unable to squeeze the trigger. Peering through a telescopic site from the grassy knoll crouched ... Lee Harvey Oswald!

I'm about to shoot myself!

Then the twin shifted positions, bringing the motorcade into his sights. Less than a split-second later, Lee regained his composure and fired. But before he heard the roar of his rifle, another shot went off, this one from his double up on the knoll. That caused Lee to jerk ever so slightly.

Lee's own shot passed over the shoulder of his twin. The double glanced up, winked at Lee, and ran away, accompanied by George and Johnny, even as everyone in the area gasped.

Another shot exploded, Lee knowing it came from the same building he occupied, either the third or second floors below. Twisting around to see the results, Lee watched as JFK's head flew backward, blood bursting upward and outward.

Secret servicemen swarmed over the area, throwing their own bodies over Mrs. Kennedy and the Connollys to protect them from more potential firings. Cops rushed into the crowd, hoping to locate the culprits.

Do whatever you want. It's too late. Can't you see?

Hungry for vengeance, Lee, not realizing that he'd dropped the rifle, rushed down the stairs to the third floor, hoping he could find the shooter there. And, if the man didn't plug him first, kill the son of a bitch with his bare hands.

Who could it be? Perhaps Buesa! Leader of the anti-Castro Cubans. That would make the triad complete along with the Mob and the CIA.

No one was there. Lee hurried out and down to the second, that area likewise deserted. If someone had been here, and Lee guessed there had, that person had already slipped away.

Like a ghost in broad daylight, this a nightmare at noon.

George said the shooters would be rescued at once. But no one is here for me. It can only be this: George figured out my plan to try and stop him.

And—checkmate!—left me to hold the bag.

I've got to get out of here ... Got to get back to Marina and the kids ... Got to ...

If I don't make it? Please, God: Have Sinatra play me in the movie. No, no. Way too old now. What was the name of the kid who played Frankie's younger brother in Come Blow Your Horn?

Can't recall ... but he'd do ...

*

Lee, now possessed by an eerie sense of calm, realized that he'd left the rifle with its fingerprints up on the sixth. Not willing to go back up to retrieve it, he proceeded to the stairs as if to exit the building. He collided with a policeman, gun drawn, dashing up, truly behind and to the side of him.

"Does this man work for you?"

"Oh, yes. That's Lee, one of our most dependable—"

The policeman, Marrion L. Baker, rushed past Lee and on up to the next floor, Truly dutifully following behind.

Got to appear steady. Calm. That's important. What did FDR say? Nothing to fear but fear itself ...

So Lee, controlling his desire to cut and run, stepped over to the soda machine, popped some coins in, then descended to the first floor swigging his Coke.

As he left the building, Lee noticed some two-dozen boys in blue readying to seal off the area he had just left.

In the nick of time ... Got to get away.

Let's see, how best to proceed? First, head back to the apartment, which is what any innocent man would do ...

Lee jogged seven blocks up from Elm Street. He hailed a bus proceeding in the opposite direction and rode on it for two blocks.

Most passengers looked drawn, bloodless, as if they still could not comprehend what they'd been told.

At the next stop Lee disembarked, standing on the street corner until a taxi came by. He raised a hand, requesting to be driven over to Neeley Street.

Before they reached it, Lee told the driver to stop and let him off. After paying, he rushed the remaining block to the house on North Beckley in which he had rented a room for the past month.

As he entered, the hall clock struck one.

"Mr. Oswald, did you hear what—"

Lee did not pause to speak with the landlady, frozen in shock. Rudely sweeping by, he hurried into his room.

Again relying on his marine's carefully acquired instincts, Lee grasped at once that someone had been there.

George! Of course. Aware that I might not be playing ball with him anymore, he would have created a dual scenario. In case I betrayed his trust, have 'evidence' ready to plant so that I'd become the fall guy here ...

Immediately Lee realized his snub-nosed Smith & Wesson revolver was missing. At first, nothing else seemed gone. Then he noticed one of his favorite light jackets, the gray one he wore most often on cool nights, was not in the closet.

Wait a minute! My double, the twin on the grassy knoll ... he was wearing it!

"Mr. Oswald, where are you going now?" the landlady asked as Lee tore past her, out onto the street. Again, Lee did not answer Mrs. Roberts. As he hurried down the street, Lee saw a police car approaching from the other end, its siren wailing. The vehicle stopped directly in front of the house he'd just left. Two boys in blue stepped out, greeted by a concerned Mrs. Roberts.

This is all like a bad movie ... with me as both the star and the main character, rolled up in one.

That's not the problem. George is the writer, director and producer. I'm lost in the maze of his movie, not my own.

Keeping his head down, not sure precisely where he was going but knowing he had to get away, back to Irving, Lee heard three shots just around the next corner. Momentarily he froze.

Then, drawn as if by a magnet, he found himself moving in that direction, where people were all at once wailing.

"The poor cop!" someone yelled. "Some man just shot him!"

More sirens, whirring in this direction. As Lee approached the corner, ready to turn, around it flew a man on the run. A man in a gray jacket, carrying a smoking gun in his right hand. A man

333

wearing cowboy boots much like Lee's own. A man identical in appearance to Lee Harvey Oswald.

"Hey, guy!" Lee's twin, almost bumping into him, laughed. "What d' ya know?"

With that, the double tossed the pistol to Lee, swiftly wriggling out of the jacket, allowing it to fall to the side-walk. Like a wisp of smoke, the twin vanished into the crowd.

"That's him!" someone screamed, rounding the corner at the head of an angry mob, pointing at Lee. "I saw that man shoot officer Tippet."

You see me? You actually see me? I'm not an invisible man today? Everyone's looking at me! If for all the wrong reasons.

"I bet he killed Kennedy, too! Get him!"

Someone in some old movie once said: This is like a bad joke without a punch line. *Only I don't want to be in a movie. Not anymore. Home with my family, watching this on TV ... Just like everyone else ... All those Normals.*

I mean, That was then, this now. Things change.

"Kill him! Kill him! Kill him!"

I've got to get rid of this evidence. That's the first thing I must do. Then I'll make my way to Marina ... Did I once actually associate with Sean Connery in a James Bond movie? The undefeatable, irresistible spy? Not anymore. Now? At this very moment? Boris Karloff as the Frankenstein monster ... anguished, confused, terrified ... pursued through a fairytale woodland by angry villagers ... the Normals ... why, God, wasn't I allowed to ever be one among them? Would that somehow have messed up your master plan? If there even is such a thing ... or a God behind it ... life actually adding up to something meaingful rather than simply survival or the failure to do achieve that in the here and now ...

Scooping up the gray jacket, still holding the pistol, Lee turned and ran. Moments later he ducked into an enclave by a shoe-store as police cars roared down the street, searching for him. The fall-guy. The ... What's the word? Oh, of course—

What did Warhol say? In our time, every man will be famous for fifteen minutes. How I once longingly awaited my turn.

Now? Please, God. Let it be over!

Then, there it was. Directly before him. A movie theatre!

The Texas, in appearance, with its old neon lights offering visual echoes of faded grandeur from the golden days of screen palaces, not very different from the one in New Orleans.

There, long ago, Lee had seen *Suddenly,* and his adventure began. More recently, *The Manchurian Candidate,* when such dreams died. And Lee resolved to at long last reclaim his life.

That's it. I'll go to the movies. That'll make everything better, just like always. I'll watch what's up there on the screen and figure out from what I see where to dump the jacket and the gun before heading to Irving.

What's playing? Cry of Battle *with Van Heflin.*

Great. I missed that on its first-run. Here's my chance to catch up on a WWII flick. I'll go to the movies.

And even if should they pick me up today, I have nothing to worry about. Because I'm 'covered.' I dropped off the portfolio, telling everything, naming names, for Hosty at FBI headquarters.

Wow! I'm actually depending on the FBI to save me from the CIA. But that's how it goes, I guess.

Any enemy of your enemy is your friend ...

... though I can only hope they remain enemies today.

*

At the home of Ruth Paine, Marina sat glued to the TV. Beside her, Marguerite wept openly. Mrs. Oswald, the older of Lee's two 'Mamas,' had been watching the presidential motorcade when all hell broke loose.

She, like millions of other Americans, had been held spellbound by the obscene spectacle that followed. Only for her, as for Marina, the terror felt specific when it was announced that a suspect in the killing of police officer J.D. Tippet, who was trying to arrest a guilty looking fellow, a few minutes earlier had been taken into custody. A few minutes earlier taken into custody.

He might also be the man who earlier shot the president, though that was not yet confirmed.

The man's name was Lee Harvey Oswald.

Marguerite wailed at the top of her lungs, threw herself down on the floor, kicking her legs, waving her arms.

When, after a half an hour she finally calmed down, as much as Marguerite ever did calm down, she couldn't be alone.

Robert? I could go to him ... Though, no, that doesn't seem exactly right. I know! Marina. I should be with her at this moment of crisis. Mama will go to 'Mama.'

So she had come by, greeted at the door by an ashen Ruth Paine, who ushered Marguerite in. Neither she nor Marina were able to say anything to each other. They exchanged glances and sat still before the TV set, watching the world go by ...

And, on this dark day, understanding that they, two women together in a Texas suburb, were connected to the heart of the matter as no one, save only perhaps Mrs. Kennedy, could be.

"Is that a way of praying?" Marina asked, dumbfounded, when Ruth Paine and her little daughter stepped into the room. Each carried a candle they'd lit in the kitchen.

"Yes," Ruth replied. "It's just my own way."

She set the candles down carefully on a table and was about to ask the two Oswald women, Mar the younger and Mar the elder, as she had always thought of them, if Ruth could be of any help. Anything, however small or big, to relieve their shared horror.

Before Ruth could speak, Walter Cronkite on CBS announced that the president had officially been pronounced 'dead.'

"Now the two children will have to grow up without a father," Marina mumbled.

"I don't understand, dear," Marguerite asked, speaking for the first time since her arrival. "Do you mean Mr. Kennedy's children or your own?"

Marina uttered a strange sort of noise but did not speak. At that moment there came a knocking at the door. Ruth rose and crossed the room to answer it, returning momentarily with six members of the Dallas police force.

They circled Marina and Marguerite. "Mrs. Oswald," one policeman ventured.

"Yes?"

"Yes?

That took him off guard, for Marina and Marguerite had answered simultaneously, two voices merging into one. Like a chorus in some musical play. Or, for that matter, in a Greek tragedy.

"I would imagine you understand why we're here."

"Whatever Lee did, he did for his country," Marguerite announced in her best faux Southern-belle accent.

"Marguerite, for once in your life, shut up."

"Why, what a terrible way to talk to your mother-in-law. And after all I've done for—"

"Just please shut the fuck up."

"If Lee were here, he would never allow you to speak to me in such a manner."

"Lee's not here, Marguerite. And, more likely than not, he never will be again."

"By that, Ma'am, are you suggesting that your husband may indeed be the person who killed Tippet and Kennedy?"

"My boy? No such thing—"

"I said *shut up*! No, officer, I can assure you that Lee most certainly did not harm either of those gentlemen."

"If you'll forgive me, all the evidence points his way."

"Well, the cards will fall as they will fall. But I know in my heart Lee is innocent of both these crimes."

"Why can you say that with such authority?"

"Officer, I hate to agree with Marguerite on anything. But it's as she put it: Lee Harvey Oswald loved his country."

"More than anything else?"

"Yes, officer. Even more than me and our babies."

"Perhaps. But right at this moment, the entire country perceives him as an enemy of the people."

"Is that so? Well, here's one thing I learned from Lee. Perception and reality are usually two different things."

"Is there anything else that you learned from him?"

"Yes," Marina concluded after a long pause. "Just because you love something, doesn't mean it has to love you back."

*

"There's nothing we can do now, nurse, to help him." The doctor took a step back from Lee Harvey Oswald as life left the ruined frame on a table before him.

"He seems such a little man, doesn't he?"

"Short, certainly. Then again, so was Napoleon. If he truly is what they said on TV, even as the ambulance was delivering him to us, here, then I can assure you: Lee Harvey Oswald will figure greatly in American history from this day on."

"Is he what people claim he is? The killer of Kennedy?"

They walked out of the sterile white room together as aids covered up Oswald's body. "All that's known for certain is that he was arrested for shooting a police officer who was trying to arrest him on the possibility that he might be JFK's assassin."

"You said, doctor, that you were watching the TV in the lounge when somebody shot Oswald?"

"Yes. And a minute later I saw it again on instant replay."

"Who possibly would have done such a thing?"

"Some local club owner named Jack Ruby. He stepped out of the shadows as Oswald was being brought to a car for transfer to the city jail. Ruby fired a gun and then they arrested him. As the authorities took Ruby away, he wept and said he did it for Mrs. Kennedy, and the children, and how terribly he felt for them."

They proceeded down the long corridor, removing their cotton surgical masks and thin rubber gloves as, like zombies, the two trudged along. "That all sounds ..."

"Unbelievable?"

"Yes. That's the word I was searching for."

"Well, I concur with you. It's all a bit ... much."

"Almost as if ... Oh, I don't know, I'm just a nurse ... but ... as if this Jack Ruby wanted to silence Oswald."

"That occurred to me, too. I imagine it will to many others as well. Today, and for a long time to come."

"With Oswald dead, that will cloud things terribly. Make a full and thorough investigation nearly impossible."

"It certainly will that."

The nurse stopped in her tracks. "Will we ever find out the truth, doctor? If Lee Harvey Oswald really did kill Kennedy?"

The doctor halted, too. He thought her question over in his mind before answering. "That, nurse, may well turn out to be one of those things in life we never do know. Not for certain."

"Good lord! And what were Oswald's final words?"

"Before Ruby shot him? He didn't have a chance to say much. He had a weird smile ... more a sneer ... on his face. I'll never forget this! He stared into the TV camera as if he were the star of his own show. Then, like on, oh, I don't know, *The Untouchables* maybe, that big Ruby guy came up and just shot him. Right after Oswald spoke his last words."

"Which were?"

"'I'm a patsy.'"

POSTSCRIPTS

AADLAND, BEVERLY ELAINE had appeared in the classic musical film *South Pacific* at age fourteen, playing one of the pretty nurses. Though she never did make another movie after *Cuban Rebel Girls*, Bev briefly toured as a singer. In 1960 she ran afoul of the police when her then-current boyfriend was found shot dead in his apartment, Bev unable to fully explain her own involvement. She was never arrested for a crime, though, and after two ugly divorces had a baby girl with her third husband. As to Errol Flynn's death, Bev always insisted that she could not reveal the actual circumstances out of fear for her own life. Once, though, while in Florida, she did tell all to a young man she met at a night club where she performed and, while under the influence of alcohol, spilled everything. Bev would not, when pressed, reveal that man's identity. Bev took all such secrets to the grave with her in 2010.

BISSELL, RICHARD M., JR. necessarily stepped down as director of the CIA following the Bay of Pigs disaster. He was asked to head up a new Pentagon planning committee that would develop a replacement for the U2, rendered obsolete after Gary Powers was shot down over Soviet territory. He turned this offer down in order to join United Technologies, an independent company where he would prove instrumental in developing state-of-the-art weapons systems. Two years following Bissell's death in 1998, *Reflections of a Cold Warrior*, his autobiography, was published.

BUESA, MANUEL F. ARTIME was captured shortly after the Bay of Pigs fiasco and imprisoned, then returned with other Brigade members on Dec. 24, 1962. He stood beside Pres. and Mrs. Kennedy when the First Couple welcomed survivors home five days later at Florida's Orange Bowl. Working on his own, Buesa attempted to assassinate Fidel Castro in 1965. Following the Watergate break-in, Buesa became a key fund raiser for the defense of the "plumbers," most of whom he had earlier known and worked with. Though his death in 1977 was ruled as "natural," there are many who consider it highly suspicious in nature.

CAMPBELL, JUDITH INMOOR (EXNER) called a press conference in 1975 when a senate committee, headed by Frank Church, set out to explore the Mob-CIA connections that may have led to the death of Pres. Kennedy. She announced to the press that she had never been Kennedy's mistress and, though she did know Sam Giancana and Johnny Rosselli, they were platonic friends. When Rosselli broke the Mafia "code of silence" by speaking out and was soon thereafter whacked, then Giancana killed before he could "sing," Judy apparently wanted to say whatever might save her life. In 1977, she reversed her position in an "autobiography" claiming that while she had been JFK's mistress, never did she work with the Mafia, despite her close relationships with many Made Men. When Judy and her second husband, the famed golfer Dan Exner, separated in 1988, she hinted to friends that she was guilty of most of the accusations against her. She lived out her final years in Newport Beach and died of breast cancer in 1999.

GIANCANA, SAM during the late 1960s pioneered Iran and Central America as possible places to build new casinos. However, his stinginess with the profits caused him to fall out of favor with the Mob and in time be replaced by Joey "Doves" Aiuppa. Exiled to Mexico, Giancana lived in luxury there for many years until the authorities chose to arrest him, sending Sam "Gold" back where he came from. Returning to America, Giancana announced his plans to tell all to the FBI during their long-overdue probe of organized crime in America. He was shot in the back of the head in his home in Oak Park, IL shortly thereafter. Between his coming home and passing on, Giancana confided to several close friends that his long-time mistress, Phyllis McGuire, knew all that was taking place between the racketeers and the CIA and that she too had been one of his "plants" in Pres. Kennedy's bed. However, those claims have never been substantiated.

JOHNSON, PRISCILLA (MacMILLAN) reached out to Marina Oswald shortly after the assassination about collaborating on a book that would relate the entire story from the widow's point of view. Called *Marina and Lee,* it was first published in 1977. There are those who consider it the most honest and revealing book ever written about these historical figures. Others though claim that owing to Ms. Johnson's loyalty to JFK, her status as a CIA operative, and her personal knowledge of Lee Harvey Oswald while both were in Russia, her tome should be considered highly suspect, one more attempt to put the official spin on the tale.

KENNEDY, ROBERT joined the race for the Democratic presidential nomination when Pres. Lyndon Johnson announced early in 1968 that he would not run for re-election. Initially, Kennedy lost primaries to another contender, Eugene J. McCarthy from MN. In the wee small hours of the morning on June 5, 1968, Kennedy, at Los Angeles' Ambassador Hotel, learned that he had just won the all-important California primary, pretty much cinching his grip on the ticket's top-spot. Moments later RFK was shot to death. The young Palestinian immigrant Sirhan Sirhan was arrested, charged with the crime, found guilty, and imprisoned.

LORENZ, MORITA is the name of the actual woman on whom 'Lorita Morenz,' a fictional character in this book, is based. Lorenz attempted to assassinate Castro with botulin pills for the CIA and Mob connection after her relationship with The Beard soured. Following that, Morita shifted back to dictators and began an affair with Marcos Pérez Jiménez, former Venezuelan strong-arm, with whom she had one child. Later she worked as a spy for the FBI, informing on Eastern block diplomats who lived in the New York apartment building she and her then-husband owned. In 2000 she attempted to reconnect with Fidel but he would have none of it.

MAHEU, ROBERT served for several more years as Howard Hughes' "bagman," a courier trusted to deliver large sums of cash from that billionaire businessman to his shadowy contacts. Among them was Bebe Rebozo, one of Richard Nixon's closest friends. This led to Maheu becoming involved in the Watergate conspiracy. Surviving that fiasco, he returned to Vegas where Maheu opened his own company, having been given the heave-ho by Hughes, who publicly announced Maheu had been robbing him blind all those years. Maheu sued over that; Hughes settled out of court.

OSWALD, MARINA (PORTER) appeared four times before the Warren Commission, incriminating her husband for the assassination of Kennedy as well as his attempt on the life of Gen. Walker. She also announced that Oswald hoped to assassinate Richard Nixon. However, some Washington insiders insist that she bore witness against her husband only to avoid deportation to

Russia for herself and her children. Two years later, she married a man named Jess Porter and had a child by him. They were divorced in 1974. Since then, as a naturalized citizen of the U.S., she has on many occasions proclaimed, and explained in detail, her full belief in the absolute innocence of Lee Harvey Oswald. At the time of this writing she continues to live in the Dallas area.

OSWALD, MARGUERITE passed away in 1981 at age 73. For more than fifteen years she had relentlessly crusaded to clear the name of her son, who had been declared by the Warren Commission as the sole killer of John Kennedy. Marguerite insisted that, owing to certain intimations from Lee over the years and things that she learned from Lee's wife Marina on the day of the assassination, if only someone would listen she could verify that JFK had been assassinated by a conspiracy and her son, though he previously had met with members of that group, did not in any way partake of their decision to assassinate the president.

ROSEELLI, JOHNNY, aka JOHNNY HANDSOME, was on April 9, 1976 found floating in a 55 gallon steel fuel drum located in Dumfounding Bay, not far from Miami, FL. An autopsy revealed he had been shot and strangled, and that both his legs were sawed off, likely while the man was still alive. Probably a hit was carried out by his onetime compatriot Santo Trafficante, Jr. (after being ordered from above, likely by Sam Giancanna) as retribution for Rosselli's "singing like a bird" when he was called before a Senate Committee to testify on joint attempts by the Mob and CIA to kill Castro and assassinate Pres. Kennedy.

SINATRA, FRANK, continued to reign as the world's greatest singer of ballads and pop-standards until his passing in 1998. When distribution rights to the film *The Manchurian Candidate* eventually fell into Sinatra's hands, the movie disappeared from re-release in theatres or on TV for many years. Though it has been claimed that the aging film was "played out," that makes no sense since other classics from that era continued to regularly be broadcast. Even before *The Manchurian Candidate* slipped out of the public's view, *Suddenly* had long since ceased to show up on TV.

STURGIS, FRANK, aka 'George,' was along with four other men arrested on June 19, 1972 for breaking into and attempting to set up a wire-tap in the Democrat party's headquarters in the

Watergate Hotel, Washington. One possible reason was to learn if that party's presidential candidate, George McGovern, was in contact with Fidel Castro in hopes of normalizing relations between the two countries should McGovern win the upcoming election against former vice-president Richard Nixon. While serving his prison term, Sturgis insisted "I will never leave this jail alive" if the full truth came to be known. Before his death in 1993 Sturgis confessed to Cardinal Cook of New York City's Catholic church that he had arranged the assassination of John Fitzgerald Kennedy and framed Lee Harvey Oswald for that crime.

WALKER, MAJOR GENERAL EDWIN, continued to live in Dallas until his death from natural causes in 1993, at age 83. His political ambitions were based on his continuing insistence that for America to flourish as it, in his mind, once had, segregation must be re-established between the races so that a "pure" white ruling class could control what he believed to be the mongrel ethnic minorities. Always, he insisted that the unknown person who had attempted to assassinate him in his home on April 19, 1963, had to be the same shooter who killed President Kennedy.

SELECTED BIBLIOGRAPHY

Bissell, Richard, Jr. *Reflections of a Cold Warrior: From Yalta to the Bay of Pigs*. Yale University Press, 1996.

Bugliosi, Vincent. *Four Days in November: The Assassination of John Fitzgerald Kennedy*. W.W. Norton, 2008.

Castro, Fidel. *The Prison Letters of Fidel Castro*. Nation Books, 2007.

Douglass, James W. *JFK and the Unspeakable: Why He Died and Why It Matters*. Touchstone, 2010.

Dulles, Allen W. *The Craft of Intelligence: America's Legendary Spy Maser on the Fundamentals of Intelligence Gathering in a Free World*. Lyons Press, 2006.

English, T.J. *Havana Nocturne: How the Mob Owned Cuba and Then Lost It to the Revolution*. William Morris Paperbacks, 2009.

Ernest, Barry. *The Girl on the Stairs: My Search For a Missing Witness To the Assassination of John F. Kennedy*. CreateSpace, 2011.

Escalante, Fabian. *Executive Action: 634 Ways to Kill Fidel Castro*. Ocean Press, 2006.

Evan, Thomas. *The Very Best Men: The Daring Early Years of the CIA*. Simon & Schuster, 2006.

Exner, Judith Campbell & Sloan, Sam. *Mafia Moll: The Judith Exner Story*. Ishi Press, 2008.

Fischer, Steve. *When the Mob Ran Vegas: Stories of Money, Mayhem and Murder*. Berkline Press, 2005.

Garrison, Jim. *On the Trail of the Assassins: My Investigation and Prosecution of the Murder of President Kennedy*. Sheridan Square Pub., 1988.

Giglio, James N. *The Presidency of John F. Kennedy*. University Press of Kansas, 1991.

Hancock, Larry. Nexus: *The CIA and Political Assassination*. Lancer, 2011.

Hunt, Jim & Risch, Bob. *Warrior: Frank Sturgis—The CIA's # 1 Assassin Spy*. Forge Books, 2011.

Janney, Peter. *Mary's Mosaic: The CIA Conspiracy to Murder John F. Kennedy, Mary Pinchot Meger, and Their Vision For World Peace*. Skyhorse Pub., 2012.

Kelley, Kitty. His Way: *The Unauthorized Biography of Frank Sinatra*. Bantam, 1986.

Lane, Mark. *Last Word: My Indictment of the CIA in the Murder of JFK.* Skyhorse Pub., 2011.

Latell, Brian. *Castro's Secrets: The CIA and Cuba's Intelligence Machine.* Palgrave, MacMillan, 2012.

Maheu, Robert and Hack, Richard. *Next to Hughes: Behind the Power and Tragic Downfall of Howard Hughes by His Closest Advisor.* Harpercollins, 1992.

Mailer, Norman. *Oswald's Tale: An American Mystery.* Randhom House, 1995.

Mallon, Thomas. *Mrs. Paine's Garage: And the Murder of John Fitzgerald Kennedy.* Mariner Books, 2003.

Marrs, Jim. *Crossfire: The Plot That Killed Kennedy.* Basic Books, 1989.

McMillan, Priscilla Johnson. *Marina and Lee.* Random House, 1980.

Munton, Don & Welch, David A. *The Cuban Missile Crisis: A Concise History.* Oxford University Press, 2011.

O'Brien, Michael. *John F. Kennedy's Women: The Story of a Sexual Obsession.* Now and Then Reader, 2011.

Posner, Gerald. *Case Closed.* Anchor, 1994.

Rappleye, Charles and Becker, Ed. *All American Mafioso: The Johnny Rosselli Story.* Barricade Books, 1995.

Rasenberger, Jim. *The Brilliant Disaster: JFK, Castro, and America's Doomed Invasion of Cuba's Bay of Pigs.* Scribner, 2011.

Reeves, Richard. *Kennedy: Profile of Power.* Simon & Schuster, 1994.

Russo, Gus. *The Outfit.* Bloomsbury, 2003.

_____ & Molton, Stephen. *Brothers in Arms: The Kennedys, the Castros, and the Politics of Murder.* Bloomsbury, 2009.

Schwartz, Ted. *Hollywood Confidential: How the Studios Beat the Mob at their Own Game.* Taylor Trade Pub., 2007.

ABOUT THE AUTHOR

Douglas Brode is a novelist, graphic novelist, produced playwright, Hollywood screenwriter, film and TV historian, and multi-award-winning journalist.

His more than thirty-five published books include the novel *Sweet Prince*, a retelling of the Hamlet legend, and *Shakespeare in the Movies* for Oxford University Press. He and Carol Kramer Serling collaborated on *Rod Serling and the Twilight Zone,* the only official analysis of that late author's work and vision. Among Brode's best known books are studies of the careers of directors Steven Spielberg and Woody Allen, such genres as the gangster film and the Western, and the relationship of popular culture to contemporary politics. Brode's op-ed pieces are regularly syndicated to newspapers across the country.

During the course of his lifetime, Brode has been employed as a TV talk show host, radio commentator, drama and film critic, regional theatre actor, and magazine editor. As an educator, Brode teaches at the Newhouse School of Public Communications, Syracuse University, during the fall semester, and for the department of Philosophy and Classics, University of Texas at San Antonio, each spring.

22807024R00188

Made in the USA
Charleston, SC
02 October 2013